The Queen Of Thorns And Gold

E.R.Browning

Thank you to my friends and
family who believed I could.

A Note of Story

The characters in this book all have their own personal story. Some stories may span weeks or months, while some may happen simultaneously.

The darkness has now grown, spreading upon the world, and casting it in flame, for only the light of Velara shall save us from our sins. For from Her womb, the prince shall rise, and cast light unto shadow...

Enchanter Ernis
The Spoken Word of Velara

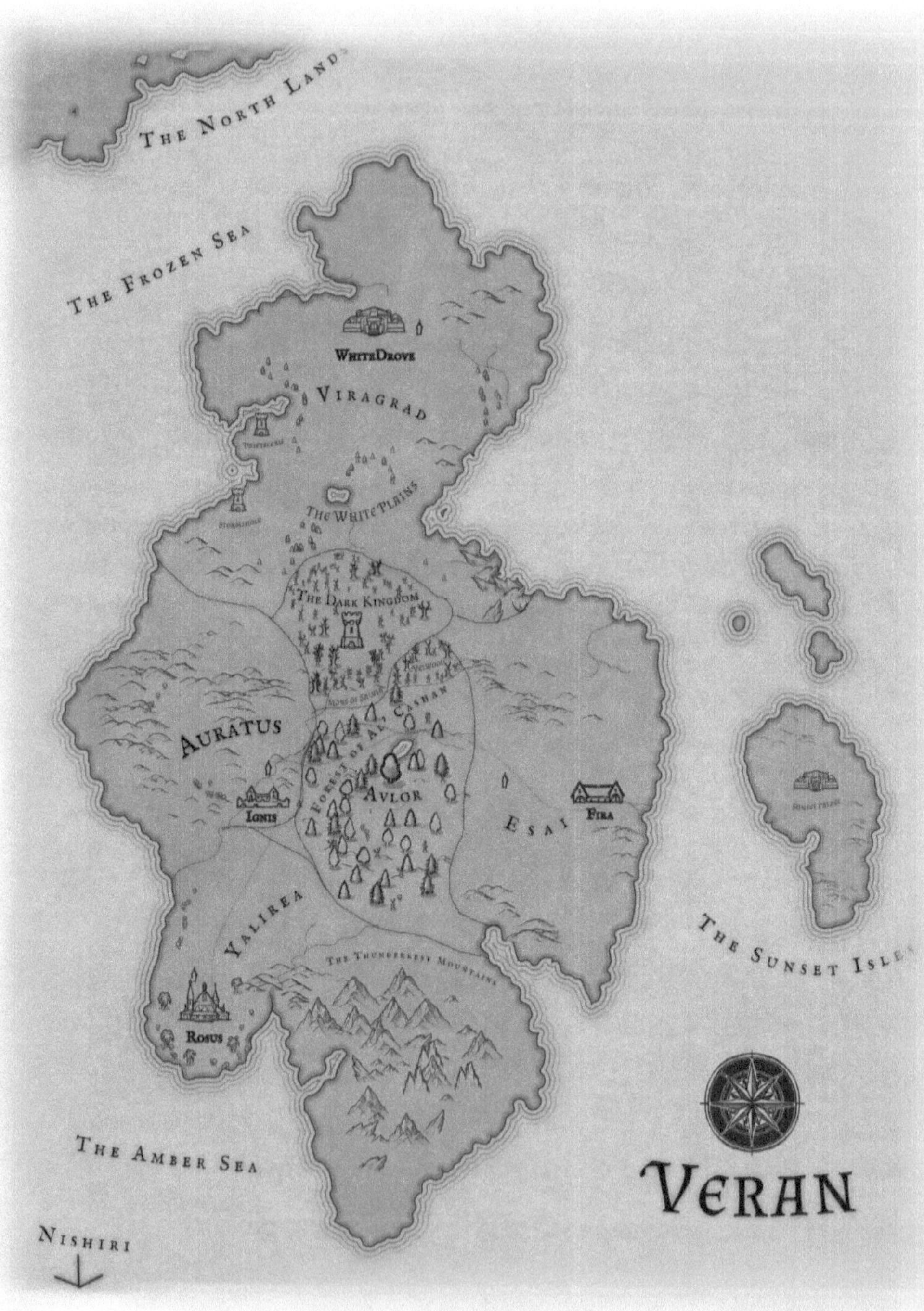

THE NORTH LANDS
THE FROZEN SEA
WHITEDROVE
VIRAGRAD
THE WHITE PLAINS
THE DARK KINGDOM
AURATUS
Ignis
Forest of Al' Cashan
AVLOR
ESAI
Fira
YALIREA
THE THUNDERKEST MOUNTAINS
Rosus
THE AMBER SEA
THE SUNSET ISLES
NISHIRI
VERAN

PROLOGUE

Within the kingdom of Auratus stood a forest teeming with birdsong and the chittering of squirrels. The lights of fae faded in and out of sight as they danced in jubilation around the honey blossom trees.

Giant oaks soared to the sky, hundreds of feet tall, to kiss the heavens. As the leaves left splotchy patches of golden light on the forest floor, two young girls bounded after a wisp, almost touching it yet failing to truly grasp hold. It twirled and sped further up the dirt pathway.

"Come back!" Rose yelled, jumping up, only to have the light slip out of her fingers again.

"I'm getting that wish before you!" her sister, Enara, interjected. Their petite feet padded over the leaves and flowers as they trampled through the immense forested hills.

Their mother had once told them the stories of the wisps, tiny creatures that roamed the forests, and plains of magic—vexatious creatures of wonder and mystery. Noble warriors would hunt them down and catch them in jars to gift their wives and children, believing that if you snatched one, they would grant you one wish or lead you to your destiny.

Rose romped into the water of a small creek after the blue light and jumped once more, her fingers scantily grazing the soft glow of the wisp. It flickered, then zipped away from her touch. Rose squealed as she landed hard in the riverbed, her red dress staining brown with mud. Icy streams of water rushed into her skirt and petticoat, soaking her shoes and clothing as gooseflesh popped on her pale arms.

"Are you alright?" Enara asked, coming up to her sister's side. She held her violet dress up to avoid getting it ruined and bent down to take her sister's hand.

Rose smiled brightly, wiping golden ringlets of hair from her face, then stood up. "I almost had it, didn't I!? I was this close!" she said and held up an inch between her fingers.

Enara waded back to shore and crossed her arms. She had kept her dark hair tied up and out of the way, unlike Rose, who looked more beast than a princess with mud-covered arms.

"I told you I wanted the wish," Enara pouted, puffing out her chest as Rose smoothed down her ruined dress.

"Well, you were too slow," she teased. "But I didn't get it either, so it doesn't matter."

Enara looked away from her sister's gaze and down at the stained dress with a frown. "Your surcoat is ruined now, let alone your dress. What will Mother say?"

Rose climbed out of the water and pulled off her shoes, ringing them out before putting them back on.Enara grabbed hold of the red trim of the dress and wiped away a soggy leaf.

"Well, y—your shoes are muddy," Rose argued, seeing the slightly scuffed brown leather of her flats.

Enara sighed and adjusted the bow on her sister's back. "Yes, but they are town shoes. You're still wearing your heels," she teased, tapping the soft edge of the shoe.

Rose looked away and blushed lightly. "I didn't have time to change!"

"If you had been wearing the appropriate outfit in the first place, we wouldn't be having this conversation," Enara sighed and grabbed her sister's hand. "Well, let's get back home. Trissa will hopefully clean you up before Mother gets back."

The two girls made their way back down the winding dirt path to the capital city of Ignis. Auratus was the third most illustrious kingdom on the continent of Veran, specializing in mining and trade. It sat in the Golden Hills, resting snugly on the continent's western side; the perfect place for wary merchants and itinerant traders to rest on their journey to the other kingdoms. Most days, the streets filled with tanners, tailors, fishmongers, and jewelers before the morn, all trying to exchange their goods. Farmers would set up markets to sell their hoof stock and milk for a pretty *sephim*.

Smoothing out her own dress, Enara took a breath, still reeling at her sister's appearance. She was failing to present herself as graceful with the mud now coating her skirt. *Nothing like a princess*, she thought.

The forest was waking up from its winter slumber as the redbud trees bloomed against the backdrop of brown and gray. The evergreen trees sprinkled their needles along the ground and coated the fallen leaves in their pungent scents. Rose took a newly grown leaf off a tree and smoothed it out in her palm, tracing the veins of green that ran down the face into the stem. She giggled at her squishing shoes, and Enara made a disgruntled noise. Rose pulled apart the leaf at the veins and watched as the pieces fell to the ground.

"It's a vile omen to tear apart leaves like that," Enara said, her face darkening.

Rose shook her head. "No, it isn't."

Enara took the leaf from her, earning a shout of protest. "By tearing this leaf apart, you have taken away a caterpillar's dinner; taking away a bird's dinner. So, when you upset the balance of nature, it will come back to haunt you two-fold," she said and let the leaf fall from her hand onto the ground.

"You have been investing too much time with the tutors. You're not pleasant to be around anymore," Rose answered dejectedly. "'You mustn't go out. You mustn't dirty your dress. You mustn't put your elbows on the table!'"

"And you are a child. When I am declared queen, I will force you into lessons on manners and discipline," she said.

Rose gave her a blank stare before declaring, "When you are queen, I'll run away. You can't make me do what you want."

Enara sighed. "And this is why you would never make a good queen."

"Momma thinks I'm doing fine!"

Enara rolled her eyes. "That's because it's *Mother*. You should hear what the tutors say."

"Maybe she will pick me as queen just to spite you."

"That's not how that works."

The girls were silent for a time, only listening to the sounds of the surrounding woods. Rose kept herself occupied by counting aloud how many kinds of flowers were peeping from their leaves as Enara's thoughts trailed back to her duties. She had already skipped an economics lesson to go on this excursion with her younger sister. One she deeply regretted.

She was only thirteen, but she was ready. She had prepared her whole life to be queen; sat through hours of tortuous lessons on etiquette, diplomacy, and mathematics. At the same time, her sister played dress-up with the ladies-in-waiting. But she was the baby. After all, Rose didn't have nearly as much weight on her shoulders as she did.

"What was that?"

Enara looked up, watching leaves twirl to the ground. "It's just a leaf," she said.

Rose tugged on Enara's dress. "Not the leaf. The noise," she pushed.

They both stopped walking and listened. The usual chatter of the sparrows and robins had subsided, the wind dying out. Enara could taste metal on her tongue as the air grew stifling. She took a breath, then the snap of a tree cut through the silence. It slammed against the ground with a force of thunder as animals darted from their hiding places.

"Run!" Enara yelled. She dashed off into the thicket with her sister in tow behind her.

"What is it!?" Rose asked.

"I don't know!" Enara answered back.

The girls tore through the foliage, through thorns and bushes. They jumped over logs and tripped over rocks. Enara wished she had heeded Trissa's words of caution to not go into the forest without a guard.

Rose's dress caught on a thorn bush, tripping her to the ground. Enara could feel the vibration of something giant pounding against the forest floor as she looked back and grabbed onto Rose's dress, trying to tear it from the thorns.

Then another tree split and crashed onto the ground beside them. Enara screamed as dirt and wood blew into her face, and she furiously yanked on the fabric. It soon gave way, tearing a piece off. Enara pulled Rose up, and they ran for cover.

They jumped over the felled tree and hid in a hollow carved from it. The tapping of horseshoes neared, the metallic *ping* ringing through their ears. Enara clasped her sister, shrinking back further into the hole, feeling her shiver from fright. The horse whinnied, and the clang of rusted metal plates rang through the air as the rider dismounted. A pair of boots thumped hard against the ground—a loud popping noise followed—and suddenly, the plants seemed to die around them, wilting, and turning from green to burnt brown. A dark fog rose from around the tree and caused it to mold and flake, and Rose choked on the putrid stench. She pulled her feet up as the ground cracked beneath them. Enara turned her head, her breath raspy, and looked in the rider's direction.

His person wore scarred and cracked black plate armor that gave off an unearthly green glow. Between his rerebrace, she could see rotting flesh. His bones cracked and shifted with each step he took away from the horse. His sword hung low on his belt, serrated, with dried blood staining the rusted silver. The red cape he donned was torn and charred, and his sunken eyes scanned the surrounding area. He was unusually tall, standing what seemed to be three meters high. The black horse he rode looked to be torn in half at the stomach. Its ribs protruded from its side, and maggots clung to its decaying wounds. Congealed blood fell to the ground from its ripped abdomen with a wet *thump*. Its legs were nothing but bone and blackened muscles. It whinnied and shook its head, showing the missing half of its jaw.

Rose whined, and Enara grabbed her hand and shushed her. They both looked as the rider bent down and picked up the torn fabric of Rose's dress. It brought the material up to its helmet and sniffed. Enara's entire body tensed when a long ghostly moan came from the helmet. She could feel her heart constricting in her chest, and she took short breaths, squeezing her sister. They jumped when he stood up suddenly and wrapped the fabric around his hand. Then, he mounted his horse and, with a guttural command, took off into the forest.

The girls waited with bated breath to hear the hoofbeats fade, and after standing up shaken and wet, Rose said, "We need to go home."

Enara agreed, and they followed the trail towards the city with dire urgency. The forest no longer held its usual liveliness. Instead, it felt decayed and withered, like someone had sucked all the life from it. They stepped over dead birds and wilted plants, covering their ears to the strangled cries of deer.

Within half an hour, they arrived at the city walls. The guards had the gates already opened for them, and Trissa came running up to them with the captain of the guard in tow. Trissa's brown hair was frizzy and sticking out from her bonnet and her stockings were covered in dirt. She latched onto the girls' shoulders.

"We've been searching for hours trying to find you! Where have you two been!?" she breathed. "Your clothes are in tatters!"

"There was a wisp, and we tried to catch it, but it got away. And then there was this knight! It had on black armor. It tried to find us, and it was like it was dying, and we were both scared, so we hid from it before running back here," Rose said quickly, not taking a breath until she had finished.

"There... was a bit more to it than that," Enara added softly.

Trissa's face paled. She turned to the captain of the guard, who had a grim expression on his aged face.

"Shut the gate. No one goes in or out until I give my say," he ordered. "All trade is hereby ceased until the morrow." The guards obeyed and scurried to the lever, slamming the gate shut and stationing themselves atop the wall with shields and spears.

Enara watched as the metal bars slammed into the ground and the wooden doors creaked shut. Trissa, their nanny, pushed them into a carriage and motioned for it to start forward. Enara looked out the window, watching as the captain barked orders and hurried people into their homes. Guards placed themselves at street corners while others climbed the ten-meter-high stone walls of the city. The traders in the town square quickly fled from their stalls, and children ran for their mothers.

The gates to the castle courtyard opened, and Enara watched as more men positioned themselves atop the enceinte. When the carriage stopped, they escorted the girls towards the castle doors as they passed yelling men and wagons of weapons. Enara sidestepped a squire with an armful of arrows. Trissa pushed the girls inside the castle, slamming the doors shut behind them.

"Get dressed and meet your mother in the throne room," she said, her blue eyes scanning every dark corner of the vestibule. Then, when the girls did not move, she pushed them towards their rooms. "Hurry!"

"Come," Enara said and grabbed Rose's hand. They made their way towards their room, where an elven servant passed by, saying a prayer to the goddess. Another one held a basket of linens that had been cut into strips to use as bandages. Soldiers monitored the girls as they navigated the expanse of hallways. Enara peeked out a window to see the setting sun and the torch lights upon the walls. They had never glowed so brightly.

Enara pulled Rose down another hallway, walking past the potted plants their mother had taken a liking to. When they reached their room, the maids stripped them from their clothing.

Their comments of disappointment at the ruined dresses flitted about the room as they placed Enara in a simple purple dress and apron. Their hands were shaking as they brushed out her hair and she could hear them whispering to one another.

After they dressed, they took the main stairway towards the throne room, passing more frantic servants. Enara held steady at her pace, but Rose was falling behind. The energy in the air was draining and overwrought to her, but Enara could not let that phase her. Every darkened expression they passed made her feel more wary, though. The girls finally made their way into the throne room with little energy to spare.

Towering marble pillars held up the rounded ceiling in the throne room. Their shoes clicked against the polished ground as sprinkles of light danced along the walls from the windows gracing the far-right side of the room. The throne sat along the far wall, simple yet elegant—a throne carved from the thousand-year trees of the elven kingdoms. A gift, so it was told. A blanket of fur rested around the rounded edges. And in the middle of the room stood their mother.

Their mother was Queen Elena, the loveliest lady in the Six Kingdoms. Nearly every noble of Veran admired her for her eloquent and calming voice. Her whole head of golden curls and emerald eyes caught the gaze of many a man, her youngest daughter being nearly the twin of her. She wore an exquisite white and brown fox pelt around her shoulders, and a flowing samite gown adorned with silver diamonds. The red ruby around her neck pulsed slightly as she stepped over to her daughters. She bent down and ran a manicured finger down Enara's face.

"Come, it's time for a story," she said, her lips pulled tighter than normal.

She sat down on her throne and brought Rose onto her lap, Enara sitting down at her side. "There is a story of the Dark Knights. One I haven't told you before. Not because you were not old enough, but because I was frightened that it may come true." Her voice paused. Enara felt her fingers graze over her hand. "The Dark Knights were the first group of warriors made to protect the starting kingdom of Esai. Fira, the capital city of Esai, is said to have been built on the ruins of the ancient elven temple of Kildan. The first children of magic were born there, the enchanters."

"I thought they were born from flowers," Rose said.

Enara rolled her eyes. "That's not how babies are born, dummy."

"Girls!" Elena scolded. The two quieted down as their mother shifted on the throne.

"The enchanters were born of magic and able to heal the wounded, cure ailments, and light torches aflame. But every few generations came a child more powerful than that of an enchanter. They called them mages. Beings of pure energy that could control the skies and seas, see into futures and call to the surrounding spirits. The Dark Knights protected the first mages from the vicious rule of man. Man wanted to use them as weapons, forcing them to do their bidding, locking them in towers, and burning them if they did not obey.

"In appreciation of the Knight's protection, the mages granted them power that no other man could have. They could wipe out entire armies by themselves, conquer nations, and live for eternity. But soon, the power they wielded had twisted them, turning them mad. They became bloodthirsty, cruel, and abominable. They started slaughtering everyone in their thirst for more, including their wards. The mages worried for the safety of the people and had them cast from the kingdom, but that did not stop them. They eventually rallied together with their leader, stormed the city, and hunted down each mage for their magic until only a few remained. In a last attempt to protect the world, the last mages banded together to banish the remaining four Dark Knights to the Otherworld forever." She adjusted Rose on her lap.

"But the mages knew they would someday return. The Dark Knights would rise from the Otherworld and hunt the last mages down. That's why they built the five kingdoms of Veran. Each kingdom would be prepared to defend itself against the threat of the Dark Knights when the time came. Unfortunately, the corruption of the Dark Knights had spread into the people of Fira. They became twisted and vengeful. They fled Fira, and together, they created the sixth kingdom of Veran. The Dark Kingdom. Cultists roam the streets now, forever bowing to their lost gods."

"But Mother, why are they here now?" Rose asked.

Her mother smiled down at her. "They want to claim something long forgotten to them. But don't worry, no harm will come to either of you while you are within these walls." She paused for a second, listening to the torches puff along the walls. "You two are my stars in the darkest of nights. And I will always love you. Now, off to bed with you," she said and kissed each girl on the head. A guard came and Enara and Rose were escorted from the room. With one last look back, her mother's face turned from joy to abject sorrow.

Enara woke up to the sound of screaming from outside her room. She sat up in bed and looked over at her equally confused sister. When a thunderous *boom* rang through the room, she climbed down from her bed, grasping onto Rose's hand.

"We have to go!" she ordered quietly.

Together, the girls quickly fled the room and pushed outside the door. Rose looked out the window to see the trees beginning to wilt and collapse in the courtyard. Fire exploded outside the castle and shook the walls, rattling the windows.

"The Dark Knights," Rose whispered.

"This way," Enara said and turned, leading Rose through the hallway towards the staircase. The girls skidded to a stop when a guard stumbled into their line of sight, holding his bloody abdomen as he clashed swords with a being in black armor. The Dark Knight towered over the man, but its person was contorted and elongated, twisting like a mangled tree. Its arms were too long for its body and as thin as bones. The bulky armor it wore clanked against its sunken rib cage.

The guard cried out as he swung his sword up, but the Knight evaded the attack, pushing forward inhumanly fast, its sword cutting clean through the guard's stomach. Clutching his torso, the guard spat blood and fell to his knees. The Knight's sword swung down and the guard's head fell to the ground, his eyes rolling up towards his forehead. The body fell after, still convulsing as the Knight turned towards the girls. Rose screamed when its hollowed eyes trained on them.

"Run!"

They broke off down the hallway, and the Knight sheathed its sword.

The sisters ran past body after body, tripping over fingers and boots. Their feet squished against the red-stained carpet. They knew most of the servants that lay dead. Enara pushed the body of one of the handmaids away from the stairs and pulled Rose down the narrow passageway. The torches had all been snuffed, so they felt their way down the stairs, tripping over fallen buckets and shoes. Enara stumbled into the main hallway as Rose trailed behind her. The bodies of cultists and guards surrounded the throne room as the girls darted for its doors.

Enara crashed through the doors to the throne room and stopped, Rose right behind her. Another one of the Knights stood in the middle of the blood-coated room. His sword was lodged in the throat of the captain of the guard, a sneer drawn on his face. He pulled the sword from the captain, who fell to the floor with one last gurgling breath. The mandibles on the Knight's dark pauldrons clanged at his movement. His icy eyes trained on the other person in the room—the queen.

"Malum, you fool," Queen Elena hissed.

Enara took a breath at the green ball of flame flickering in her palm.

"Mother's... an enchanter?" Rose asked.

"No." Enara shook her head.

Malum wiped his sword on the captain's coat with a small laugh. His armor shone in the dim torchlight of the room; his deathly pale skin glimmered slightly.

"I expected better from you." His deep and guttural voice chilled the air around him.

"You know nothing about me," Elena replied. The air began to vibrate, and the girls took a step back.

"She... She's a mage," Enara breathed.

"Where is she?" the Knight asked.

The queen raised her chin. "You will never have her," she hissed. "You will fall just like the rest of them."

"You are weak, mage. Even I can sense your power is waning. How much blood magic did it take to stay alive this long?" he mocked. "How many sacrificed for your rituals? And they call you *just*."

He raised his sword at her.

"Mother!" Rose screamed. Malum stopped and turned. The queen's eyes widened as her head snapped to her children. The Knight took a step towards them.

"There you are," he hissed. Enara cried out, and their mother raised her hand.

"No!" she yelled. An explosion of magic burst from their mother, and the sisters were thrown onto their backs. The walls and columns shook and cracked as the air vibrated with dense magic, nearly crushing them. Malum was tossed into a pillar with a roar. Rose watched as it split, breaking apart from the ceiling, and came crashing down towards them. Enara screamed, and their mother lifted her hand, covering the girls with a barrier of magic. The pillar slammed into the barrier and shattered around them. Dust and debris filled the air as Elena took a breath.

Enara stood up, coughing, wiping the dust from her face. She saw a dash of black shoot past them, and before she could react, Malum lodged his sword through the queen's chest.

"Mother, no!" she cried. Elena gasped and grabbed onto his arm.

"Foolish mage. Now you will watch as your kingdom falls," he spat.

She sneered back at him, blood trailing down her chin. "Burn in the fires of the Otherworld," she hissed. She put her hand on his chest and the ruby around her neck lit with the intensity of the sun.

"*Ave atras Ignis Vene'alas!*" Green tendrils wrapped themselves around Malum, and he pulled the sword from her chest. The tendrils coiled around him, burning his armor and skin. He screamed as his body went up in a blazing inferno that coated the room. The girls covered their eyes as a pillar of fire shot into the air and vanished.

With a shaky breath, the queen fell to the floor, holding her chest.

"Mother!" Enara cried as they ran over to her side.

Tears streamed down Rose's face, and her mother carefully wiped them away. "Do not cry, child," she cooed. She reached up and took the ruby from around her neck. "Take this."

Rose clasped the ruby in her hand, and their mother smiled. "You are a mage Rosellena," she whispered. Enara's eyes widened.

Rose gripped her mother's dress. "Momma, please!" she cried.

"Never lose this… Rose. Keep it with you… and you will never be alone."

"Mother…" Enara whispered.

"Malum will return. You must be crowned queen, Rosellena," she said softly. "Only you have the power… to stop him. It has been foretold… I know you are ready."

Rose shook her head. "I don't want to be a queen! I want you to be it. Please don't leave, Momma!" she cried as Enara looked down at the ground, a growing void in her stomach.

"I... love both of you so much," she intoned with a smile. "Your father would be so proud of you." Her eyes shut, and her hand went limp.

"Momma? Momma!" Rose cried. Enara gripped her skirt and wept, for the future she had wished was ruined.

The night was long and arduous. The council members who had survived the battle hid in the council chambers in the northmost tower. Their coats had barely dried of blood, and the fires still raged along the city's streets. The howling wind outside rattled the windows, along with the inhabitants of the room. The sisters stood to the side of the large table as it broke into yelling and cursing.

Enara could hear the servants outside the room dragging the bodies of the fallen to the courtyard. Their sniffles and wails of anguish made her body rigid. Rose stood beside her, still crying, clutching the ruby pendant in her hand, her other clinging to her sister. Their mother's words rang through their heads.

Mage…queen…

"Stop crying," Enara reprimanded Rose, who only sucked her bottom lip into her mouth. Her attention was once again drawn to the bickering council.

"We have no ruler! Queen Elena died at the hands of these beasts, and who was there to protect her?" Sir Alran asked, his pale face still covered in soot. He had been the trusted advisor of the late queen.

"The captain of the guard died defending her. As did hundreds of good soldiers," another lord, Calis, argued.

"And yet they were all slaughtered and now the continent is burning. We must send word to Fira immediately!" a lady demanded, hitting her hand on the table.

"The portal was destroyed, Vivianna. It will take weeks to reach Fira. And by that time, it may be too late," Sir Alran retorted, wiping his brow.

"We thought Velwood was the end of it. We were wrong. And we paid the price. We should thank the goddess that we are still alive, and the cultists have retreated," Calis said with a sigh.

"At the loss of a beloved queen. Now we must hand the crown to her daughter." All eyes turned to the sisters. Enara stood still, gazing at each of their darkened expressions. Rose had finally stopped crying, now resorting to whimpering, her hand squeezing Enara's.

"The queen's last wishes were to bestow the rank to her youngest, Rosellena," Sir Alran said, shifting his coat.

"She is a child. Barely old enough to dress herself," Vivianna argued. "Enara is the eldest and must take the crown."

Enara sighed as she spoke, a feeling of hope rising within her. Rose shifted uncomfortably beside her.

"We cannot go against the late Elena's wishes," Calis argued. "If she wishes for Princess Rose to become queen, then that is what we shall do. We will wait until she is of age."

"Ridiculous! This has been the law of the land since the Great Merging of the continent. The *eldest child* shall take the crown. Queen Elena had no son and heir, only daughters, so the crown must be given to Enara."

"Elena was a mage Vivianna, the most powerful one on this continent. Her word is the law," Sir Alran asserted.

"And what will become of the princess' magic if she becomes queen? We have no mages—"

"I can train her." All eyes turned as an elderly man walked through the door, escorted by a wary guard. His beard hung low against his stomach, and his grey tunic was muddy and scorched. He shuffled into the room and sat at the table with a groan.

"And who may you be?" Lady Vivianna asked, looking at his bedraggled appearance.

"I am—was the magic advisor to Queen Elena. I kept her appraised of matters of the arcane and helped prepare her..." He trailed off, and his eyes turned toward Enara, who looked away.

"And we are supposed to simply take your word for it, Sir..."

"Enchanter Dravis. And you can trust me or not. But if you wish to put that girl on the throne, you will allow me to train her," he said and sat back in his chair, his ample stomach sliding against the table. The council members all looked at one another and started whispering. Enara could not make out what they were saying, and she dropped her sister's hand, who whimpered in protest. She knew what they were going to say. All her training for nothing. Everything she had prepared for. All for the fact that her sister held magic. She looked down at the darkened ruby pressed to her sister's chest.

"All right. It is settled. Rose shall take the crown once she is ready." They agreed. Cold resentment filled Enara's body, and she fled from the room, ignoring the cries of protest. The bitter taste of ash in the air only fueled her anger. Her spite. Her hand burned as she strode down the hallway towards her room. The fires outside could not burn hotter than the heat in her eyes.

2 ENARA

Enara took a sip of her wine as the council continued to bicker back and forth. Her head was pulsing from the ignorance tossed around the room like children playing with balls.

"If the farmers do not have enough room to grow their crops, Auratus is useless!" Duke Floric exclaimed, one of the new advisors to the Regent Council. They were learned but blunt. Enara enjoyed him for the sole purpose of his argumentative disposition.

"We cannot give up any more land to the farmers without running into the Exalted Forest! The elves will skin us alive if we try to take their land," Sir Alran retorted. The once very poised man had become half the man he was in the ten years since the battle. The lines on his face grew more prominent, as did the dark blemishes. It still pained her to see his grayed hair and shaking hands. Was it so long ago that she would beg him for a piggyback ride?

"Those elves do nothing for us! I say we take it from them and deal with the consequences later—"

Enara put up a hand, and the table quieted. She placed her wineglass on the table.

"There is no need to make an enemy of the elves. Instead, we can send a messenger to WhiteDrove to discuss more trading options with their livestock and land claims. We can build several farms on the plains with a mutual tax agreement if they allow it," she said calmly. "For the meantime, look for flatter land north of the Hills that can be used as farmland, I am sure we can find land suitable enough for logging."

Sir Alran nodded and gave a side-eye towards the duke. "Excellent choice, Your Grace. I will send a scout after the coronation tomorrow evening," he said.

"If I may ask," Duke Floric interrupted, shifting his coat. "Where is the princess? Rosellena should be here when the elven emissary arrives as well, should she not?"

Enara scoffed and took another drink of her wine, glancing out the window. "My dear sister has decided she has more urgent matters to attend. As per usual, you may speak to me about any urgencies that arise in the kingdom."

Rose had been to as many council meetings as Enara had toes. The girl barely knew the names of her advisors, let alone how to rule the people. Her mother was playing a dangerous game with her.

"Of course, Your Grace."

Once her advisors had left the room, Enara stood up and walked over to the window, swirling the red liquid in her hand. She watched the city around her bustle with life. She could see the maids hanging laundry in the yard, guards trailing along the walls and the hints of the garden where her sister sat with her frivolous texts.

Suddenly, Enara felt the hairs on the back of her neck stand on end as the window frosted in front of her. She watched a sheet of ice climb towards her face as her breath became chilled. She heard his voice in the air around her, nagging her, laughing at her. Enara gripped her glass and felt her hand go numb.

"Your destiny awaits," he called. *"All you need to do is ask."*

"What are you?" she whispered. She remembered the voice. The same voice that came to her in dreams since that night a decade ago. That clouded her mind and twisted them into nightmares.

"I am your legacy. Take what is yours."

"Leave me!" she yelled.

"Milady?" a voice called. Enara turned to see a kitchen maid standing in the doorway, a tray of fresh pastries in her hands. Enara laughed nervously and ran a hand through her hair.

"My apologies, it's nothing," she said quickly, sitting back down at the table. The lady brought the tray over and set it down in the middle of the table, cleaning off the empty dishes. She hummed to herself, and Enara held her right hand that began to pulse, looking back at the transparent window—not frosted at all.

"Is there anything else I can get for you, milady?" she asked.

Enara turned back to her and shook her head. "No, you may leave." The maid bowed and took the dishes from the room. Enara took a pastry from the platter and bit into it, attempting to silence her nerves.

Her teeth met something hard, and she quickly spit out the pastry, grimacing. A golden coin fell onto the table with a *ting*. She felt her chest tighten as it stared at her. She picked it up with a shaking hand and turned it around to show her an engraved image of a dagger on the other side. Enara took a shaky breath as dark laughter filled the room once more.

3 ROSE

"Try again, Rose. But only the middle candle this time." Within the green walls of the castle garden, three candles sat on the ground, all flickering slightly with an orange glow. Two extinguished, and the first grew steadily before flickering out as well.

Rose flushed, looking out at the greying clouds traveling closer to the castle. She smoothed her dress down where she sat, then sighed.

"I cannot; it is too difficult. I would light the forest afire before lighting the damned candle," she groaned.

"You will need to learn to control your magic, Your Grace," her tutor, Enchanter Dravis, instructed, visibly annoyed. "You will be seven and ten here soon. Your coronation is but a day away." Rose wanted little to do with the stuffy old man who smelled of candle wax and parchment.

"I doubt you will have the will to study after that," Trissa, her old nanny, added.

"I'm well aware of my predicament, Trissa."

"Then you should try again and light only the middle candle." Trissa pointed towards the white candlestick. Nodding in agreement, Enchanter Dravis pushed it in her direction. The grass under them was charred black from numerous failed attempts at lighting the garden on fire, to her displeasure.

"Only concentration can lead to success. You must will the magic to life, or else it cannot grow."

"Not this again," Rose groaned. "We've been at it for hours."

"The sun is barely in the sky. Try again. You've barely learned to summon your magic in these ten years."

Rose gave him a sideways glare and huffed, standing up. "I'm done, for now. I want no more part in this. I'll return later," she said and turned away.

"If you continue to run from your problems Rose, you will run out of ground to tread upon," Trissa commented with a soft grin.

Rose turned back towards her. "I am not running from my problems. I'm just... delaying them," she countered and smirked. Trissa rolled her eyes and picked up a candle sitting on the ground. She fingered the black wick, and it broke apart, falling to the ground in black puffs of ash.

"We will start again the day after tomorrow. But beware, Your Grace, you will be very busy once you are crowned queen."

"Once I am crowned queen, I will order you two to quit pestering me," she huffed, earning a pinch to the ear. Rose squeaked.

"You may be a queen, but you are still my little girl. Remember that *milady*," Trissa tittered with a devious grin.

Rose looked away and swatted the hand from her ear. "We will see," she said and started down the path out of the garden.

"And where are you going?" Trissa called out.

"To town! I'll be back for supper," she called back. She ran into the thick brush of the garden, avoiding the guards that tried to follow, a troublesome grin on her face.

Rose navigated the city, ducking behind boxes and carts to avoid the guards as they searched for her. She took a rugged cloak she had hidden inside a box and wrapped it around herself, pulling the hood up over her head as a soft sprinkle of rain pattered against the rooftops.

The city itself was expansive, with three main sections. Goldtown was where the nobility made their homes and rarely ventured out except to travel out of the city. Many held stocks and trade in large companies across the continent, making coin from mining and farming for the magical arts. The estates were large and gaudy for her liking, but very pleasing to the eye from the castle balconies. The castle was located in Goldtown, so there was little need to venture any further for their diplomatic needs.

Most of the commerce was in the Traders' Den, which had countless shops and taverns to explore. It was the busiest part of the city throughout the day, and sometimes into the night. People from all kingdoms came to trade there, and some from overseas as well, from the Sunset Isles or past the Amber Sea. Though she was never allowed, she desperately wanted to explore the Traders' Den during the evening hours, basking in the soft illuminance of the street torches and dancing with the drunken travelers.

Lowtown was on the very outskirts of the city, next to the walls. It was not an unfriendly place, but only the wariest of travelers ventured there for cheap supper and a warm bed. The people were affable—if not a bit stiff—and kept to themselves. Most gossip that traveled to Lowtown from the other sections was snuffed out as they kept their secrets and watched over their own. She enjoyed it for the fact that there wasn't a single noble to gawk at her or a knight to hoist her up on his shoulder and carry her back to the castle.

Most of the houses she passed in the Traders' Den were new or rebuilt from the battle; barely any had survived the fires that night. The new houses were built of stone, and several new aqueducts had been dug outside the city to allow more water to flow into the city reservoirs in case of another attack. Rose sidestepped a group of playing children and entered the main square. Where once numerous carts filled the area in a massive cluster of bodies, now they congregated around the edges of the square, allowing people to navigate the streets easier and allowing them to view the statue of the late queen that had been erected in her honor. The statue's face held a soft grace that Rose had yet to master. One arm was adorned with a swath of fabric and the other with a sword, a symbol for their kingdom. *Commerce and vigilance.* Something her mother was always proud to achieve.

At the bottom of the statue was a plaque with the names of the fallen soldiers in the battle and an engraved phrase.

Here the fallen lie, but the kingdom survives.

Rose looked into her mother's face and took a breath before turning around and fleeing to the outskirts of the city.

"Olivia!" Rose called out excitedly. She held her dress up to avoid the puddles of mud and ran up to her dearest friend, who turned around and smiled.

"There you are, my dear!" she gushed.

Olivia was the daughter of the local tavern keeper. Her father owned the most prominent tavern in Ignis, called the Golden Doe. Olivia was a bard by day, entertaining the local guests in her cute skirts and ruffled blouses, playing the violin, and dancing around the wooden stage. But she also took up a few jobs a month for 'trading', whether that be for pleasure or joining mercenary guilds in the fields. Sometimes she would come back to the tavern covered in blood and sweat, the stench of death wafting off her like a spirit. She would wash off in the creek outside before going into the tavern to greet her father. Rose would often stitch up bleeding wounds and put makeup over bruises.

Rose constantly told her to stop her night work. Still, all Olivia would respond with is, "Money is money, anything to keep my pa's tavern up and running." Only a few, including Rose, knew of her night jobs.

Rose grabbed Olivia up in a hug. "It's been ages, my friend," she sighed.

Olivia pulled away and raised an eyebrow. "It's been a day, Rose. You might wish to check your ability at telling time."

Rose swatted her shoulder playfully and earned a hiss of pain from the bard.

"Oh! Sorry!" she apologized.

Olivia waved her off and pulled her black curls up into a ponytail, showing off a nasty purple and blue circle on her neck. Luckily, her tanned skin helped hide her softer bruises.

"Just a flesh wound. Nothing I can't handle. I got forty *sephim* from this last job, enough to buy another keg of Old Man's Ale for the tavern," she said and fiddled with her purple skirt.

"Come in, the tavern just opened, and Jared has already downed half the bar." The girls entered the building, and Rose scrunched up her nose at the smell of rum and smoke. The tavern was well kept but still had sticky puddles of alcohol gracing the aged and creaky floor.

Beautiful women danced and sang on the wooden stages as Rose followed Olivia to the back of the building. They passed drunken men and gambling nobles. Several new patrons dotted the tavern as well, hoods pulled up and hands twisting around their drinks. The noise of laughing and coins dropping paired with the licking of flames in the hearth created a warm and comforting atmosphere.

A woman stepped past Rose and over to a nobleman. Her bare breasts bounced slightly as she sat down next to him. Her long legs crossed over his lap and made her slim figure even more alluring to her.

"You coming?" Olivia asked. Rose nodded and continued behind her friend. "It gets rowdy in here sometimes. I'm surprised the guards allowed you in here by yourself."

"What's the harm if they don't know?" she answered with a shrug.

"Don't get my pa in trouble for your sneaking, princess."

The girls walked to the back of the tavern and up to the table currently occupied by a man in an ale-induced stupor. Several plates and tankards occupied the table as the man's head rested on his arm, the other holding the sword laid on the bench. Olivia pushed his shoulder as if to wake him, but to no avail.

"Get up!" Oliva ordered. When he still did not respond, she grabbed a flagon of water off the table and poured it over his head.

Rose stepped back as the man jumped up and started swinging his sword, crying curses and slurs.

Jumping in front of the queen-to-be, Olivia stopped the swinging blade with the flagon. "Jared, it's us. If you want to be hung, please continue to swing your sword wildly," she hissed.

The man stopped and blinked several times before sitting back down and grabbing a drink. "Velara's ass, why'd you do that for?"

Olivia set the cup down and crossed her arms. "You're a drunkard; you know that?"

"And it's not even midday," Rose added, peeking out from behind Olivia.

Jared took a drink and wiped his mouth, ignoring his tangled beard. "It's nighttime somewhere."

Jared was Rose's other friend. She and Olivia had stumbled across him lying face down in a ditch some three years ago. He used to be the apprentice of the city's most well-accomplished blacksmith until he was killed, and the forge burned to the ground by bandits. Now he stayed in the tavern with Olivia and her father and worked as the "ale taste tester." Rose figured Olivia simply felt sorry for Jared. The blacksmith had been the only family he had.

Olivia shoved him over and sat down beside him. Rose sat opposite them and watched happily as Olivia attempted to fix up Jared's ruffled brown hair. Jared also helped carry the barrels and food for the tavern, occasionally throwing out men who got rowdy or too handsy with the girls. He was but twenty and seven, older than Olivia by three years, but still had a child's temper. He also had a bad habit of getting into brawls around town, earning him the title of City Troublemaker. Jared had a great sword hand, though, if nothing else.

"Quit messing me up, Liv," he cried and swatted her hand away.

"I'm trying to help, you arse!" she replied and wiped his face. "You act like you're a pirate by the amount of liquor you drink."

"I'm no damned pirate!" he retorted.

Rose put her chin in her hand as Olivia dried out his hair with a rag. "When will you two finally get married?" she asked teasingly.

Both stopped and looked with wide eyes at their friend.

"Ma-marriage?" Olivia asked, her cheeks flushing.

"I'd rather fight a dragon than deal with her for the rest of my life!" Jared wailed; his face also reddened. Olivia scoffed, driving the butt of her knife into his stomach.

"You lazy sack of pig shit," she growled, stabbing the knife into the table.

"Perhaps not," Rose chuckled.

"Speaking of which," Jared said and climbed back into a sitting position after regaining his breath. "I heard yer becoming queen tomorrow. How is your sister taking that?"

"Well, to my understanding, she has accepted it. Since our mother's death, we've known who was to be crowned queen. She hasn't talked to me much about it, though."

"Yeah, 'cause she is a stuck-up priss."

"Jared," Olivia scolded. Jared shrugged, taking a flagon from the table, and pouring himself another ale.

"She isn't a priss. She is just… a bit disagreeable sometimes."

"She kicked Olivia out of the castle and called her a whore's daughter when you tried to sneak 'er in," Jared snorted, taking a long drink of his ale. Rose watched as the liquid ran down his beard and dotted his shirt.

"To be fair to her, we did have diplomats from the Sunset Isles in attendance."

"Yes, but you aren't exactly—"

"Stop," Olivia said suddenly, bringing her hand up and searching the room with her eyes. "Someone is watching us."

"I don't see anythin'," Jared replied, shrugging his shoulders and taking another swig of his drink.

"Olivia?" Rose asked, looking around the room.

Olivia stood up. "We need to leave, now." She pulled Rose up, and Jared followed with a curse. She pushed patrons out of the way, and right when they were about to reach the door, a figure stepped in front of it.

"Hello, Princess," he said. He moved his hand to his scabbard, allowing them to see the black leather under his cloak. He pulled his sword, and Olivia pushed Rose out of the way.

"No!" she yelled as the sword swung down, nearly grazing her arm.

Chaos rang through the tavern as girls fled into the back, and men pushed back their chairs and grabbed swords and daggers. More cloaked figures stood and started towards them in a rhythmic pattern.

"Princess, run!" Jared yelled. Rose darted past the assassins, ducking out of the way of a sword, but a hand grabbed her by the hair, and she cried out. He flipped her onto the ground and raised his sword. Rose crossed her arms over her face.

"Stop!" she yelled. Bright flame exploded at her scream and encased the man. He cried out, arms wildly swinging, dropping his sword. She bolted up and out the door into the street. Another assassin followed close to her, and she sprinted down the dirt pathway and rounded the corner of a house. She felt a sharp pain in her right arm and looked down at a thin trail of scarlet streaming down to her hand.

Another dagger whizzed past her, and she flinched, holding her wounded arm.

She knocked over a stack of hay bales and turned again to flee. The assassin jumped over the hay and grabbed hold of her cloak, jerking her backward.

She slammed into the assassin and screamed when they wrapped an arm around her chest and brought a dagger to her throat; the cold of the metal stung against her hot flesh.

"Any last words?" They asked.

"Hey, fucker!" Jared yelled, and a dagger lodged in their back. With a cry, they released hold of Rose, and Jared lunged and swung his sword up, decapitating the assassin. Their head fell to the ground, the body following shortly after. Jared wiped the blood from his face and sheathed his sword with a sigh. He bent down and touched her arm.

"Are you alright?" he asked. Rose nodded, feeling her heart hammering in her chest. He took a handkerchief from his pocket and wrapped the cut, careful not to hurt her further.

"There you are!" Olivia called, running up towards them.

Jared turned to look at her. "Took you long enough."

Olivia gave him a look of disdain before bending down to examine the corpse. She pulled a letter from their pocket and skimmed the wording.

"The Dark Guild of Zelonoth..." she muttered.

"A dark guild? What does the Dark Kingdom want with Rose?" Jared asked.

Olivia gave the letter to Rose, and she scanned it over.

Death Wish,
Rosellena Victoria GoldThorn
To be eliminated for 50,000 sephim

She set the letter on her lap and took a breath.
"More importantly, *who* wants to kill me?"

4 ENARA

Within the stone walls of the castle, a young woman looked out the window of the library towards her rainy kingdom. The library was dimly lit, and the only noise came from the soft pattering of the rain against the castle windows. A door opened behind her, and her gaze slid left to the reflection in the glass.

"Princess GoldThorn, Princess Rose has been targeted. We must ensure your safety," a guard called out.

Enara continued to stare out the window, her pale eyes sweeping the landscape. "I am fine. That's what I have you here for, is it not?"

The guard paused, then nodded. "Yes, of course, Your Grace. I was only concerned for your wellbeing."

Enara sighed softly and finally turned towards the guard. "I am well aware, and I am thankful for your loyalty. But I assure you I am fine; you need not worry about me. Nevertheless, it is crucial that our elven diplomat is escorted to the castle and into the council chambers safely," she said with a grin. The guard saluted and then left the room.

Once Enara heard the clicking of the guard's armor retreat down the hall, she turned back towards the window. The books that littered the room sat in disarray, opened and thrown with little heed. Pages were torn and scattered; some singed from coming too close to the torches. Nothing held the information she needed. She figured no place she could look *would* have the information she so desperately wanted.

She twisted the coin in her palm and heard the flap of a bird's wings outside the window. *So, someone wants to assassinate my sister the day before the coronation*, she thought. A bit tactless, she would say. *At least have it on the day of the coronation to bring some liveliness to the ball.* The bird—or raven, as it would seem—perched on the windowsill and pecked at the glass. Its beady eyes watched her flip the coin and then pecked the glass again. She flipped again. It pecked again.

It cawed, and she looked down at the coin, at the dagger engraved on it. It pecked again.

"Princess Enara?" a voice called, causing her to jump and the raven to fly away in a fit.

Enara turned to a servant with a huff and put the coin in her pocket. "What—Yes, what is it?"

"The elven emissary is awaiting you in the council chambers."

"Yes, of course. Thank you." Enara started from the window and passed the servant towards the council chambers. She noted the guards that followed, hands on the pommels of their swords. She also noticed the lack of her sister. Turning towards them and stopping, she folded her hands together. "Where is my sister now?"

"We believe she is with her… friends," one said, a twitch to his lips.

Enara raised a brow. "You *believe* so? Wasn't she just attacked?"

"We lost her, Your Grace. She ran off again as soon as we saw to her."

Enara took a long breath and pinched the bridge of her nose. "We are paying you to guard us, and you lost the princess a day before her coronation. Goddess bless us." She took another breath as the guards shifted uncomfortably. "Well, find her!"

The guards quickly bowed and fled her sight as she turned back around and continued down the hallway. *Of course. She is almost assassinated, then runs off again without her guards. At this point, it will be a miracle if she survives past a week of sitting on that throne*, she thought.

She knew her younger sister had a habit of finding trouble, fleeing from the castle whenever she could, and fraternizing with miscreants. How many times had it been that she had seen the guards carrying her back to her room, covered in mud and smelling of ale? She was to be the queen of a country, not a vagabond wandering from city to city with little thought as to which way was up.

Enara stepped in front of the chamber doors and composed herself. With a quick comb of her hair and a puff of her skirt, she nodded to the guards to open the door.

Inside the chamber, sitting in one of the many chairs at the table, was an elf. He wore modest brown robes that nearly matched his chestnut hair, a green sash, and a pendant necklace of a leaf. A basket of fruit waited on the table beside him, where he sat with his hands folded over his lap. Enara gave a polite nod when he turned at her entrance, his honeydew eyes creasing slightly.

"I do not believe we have met before. I am Princess Enara, a member of the Regent Council," she began.

He bowed his head. "I am Amdelas." He had a heavy accent.

"Well, Amdelas, I trust you made it to Ignis with little difficulty? It can be easy to get lost within the Hills," she asked, sitting down at the head of the table.

"Thank you, *Aretove*. But the forests of this continent are not lost to me," he responded.

Enara laughed, crossing her ankles primly beneath the table. "Nevertheless, it is always a pleasure to keep in contact with Avlor."

The elf slid the basket her way, and she picked through it, trying to identify the fruit. "These are fruits from our Gleaming Orchards within the forest. They are the sweetest fruit you will eat, and their juices make splendid wine," he said. Enara picked up a purple lobed fruit and slightly squeezed it in her hand. It was fuzzy and soft, and she could hear the liquid inside it move. She placed the fruit back in the basket with a pleased expression.

"Please give my thanks to Queen Areválla," she said. "I will have the winemakers come to pick these up tonight. I am sure it will be a welcome change from the regular variety I am served."

He bowed his head and Enara looked toward one of the several soldiers at attention in the room. "Bring the gifts to the table, please," she ordered. The guard bowed and left the room, returning shortly with a bundle of pelts and a small wooden box. He set it on the table in front of them and Enara slid the items toward the elf.

"These are white lion pelts from the desert of Nishiri. They have been blessed by their shamans and told to bring good fortune to those who wear them. In the box are pearls from the shimmering clams in the Amber Sea. I am sure they will look lovely crafted into a necklace for the queen."

Amdelas ran his fingers through the white fur of the pelts and inspected the quality of the small shimmering pearls before giving a satisfactory hum.

"Thank you, princess. Queen Areválla will surely enjoy these gifts.

We hope that this is one of many warm gestures we can make towards our sister kingdoms," he started. "And we acknowledge your openness to trading with our kind. We do not see many hold such affection since before the Crusade."

A cupbearer brought over two metal goblets and filled them with wine. Enara took a sip before continuing the conversation.

"Our kingdom's border one another and Auratus strives itself on the commerce that flows into its cities. To ignore possibilities of alliances and growth based on transgressions that occurred millennia ago is an affront to the goddess."

She watched a hint of a frown grace the elf's face as he adjusted his robe and crossed one leg over the other. "Yes. I suppose we can agree on that."

"Now what brings you to Ignis? The letter did not state intentions—not that I mind the blessed elves visiting."

Amdelas looked at the pelts on the table and then at her. "We have come to ask—"

The door suddenly opened, and Rose entered. Enara looked up and saw her sister's dress worn at the hem and covered in dirt. Her muddy shoes left prints as she curtsied and stepped toward her sister. Her hair was in disarray and windswept, cascading around her right shoulder, and she smelled of ale and cheap perfume.

"Please forgive me. I was running about town. I am Princess Rose," she greeted. The elven ambassador looked to Enara, who held her temper as Rose impatiently tapped her toes against the floor.

"Excuse us," Enara said sharply with an unsteady smile. She gracefully stood from her chair and stepped past her sister. "A word?" She motioned towards the door, and Rose followed her out. She closed the door behind her.

"What in the maker's name are you wearing?" she hissed. Rose looked down at her dress.

"I did not have time to change. I was told the elven ambassador arrived and wanted to greet him. I've never seen one of the forest elves before—"

Enara pointed a finger at her, closing her eyes with a prolonged intake of breath. "You came into the chamber room that you have been in four times in your life to visit an ambassador you haven't even met, wearing muddy shoes and a torn dress. Am I correct?"

"Well, when you put it like that...."

Enara opened her eyes and glared at her sister. She had been running this kingdom with the Regent Council for nearly a decade and Rose had the audacity to show up like she walked out of a pigsty. "You are going to be crowned queen in less than a day. And this... go get dressed. I will handle this. Just—let me handle this." She waved Rose away and reentered the room, closing the door behind her.

With a soft sigh, she knitted her fingers together and gave a warm smile to the elf still sitting at the table.

"Excuse my manners for leaving you unattended. Shall we continue?"

5 RYE

"Commander, the front lines are holding steady, but they will need more reinforcements to sustain hold of the plains," a knight said as he approached. Commander Rye stood along the edge of the encampment, his golden hair sitting upon his gleaming pauldrons. He had a strong visage, deep brown eyes that scanned the horizon, his body rigid and unyielding.

Their small encampment sat in between the Black Mors of Salvia and the kingdom of Viragrad. The emperor had tasked them with defending the ever-growing demonic presence along the borders of the kingdoms; a task that felt farther and farther from completion with every long passing day. The energy in the camp was dim; many of the soldiers sat huddled together over the fires or inside their hastily built tents. The stiff wind that rang in their ears smelled of moss and rotten meat. The scouts paced back and forth along the outskirts of the camp, watching for signs of undead or demons. Their fingers gripped their bows too tightly, so their knuckles cracked and bled.

"And here I thought they could hold their ground. Those damned cultists are stronger than I thought," he muttered, taking the letters the knight was holding. He headed towards the main tent, reading through the reports and hastily written letters. As he passed, the soldiers acknowledged and saluted him with great respect, but he could see the fatigue in their eyes. A guard opened the curtain for him, and he stepped into the warm tent.

"How goes the battle, Lion?" Lieutenant Garding asked, his feet propped negligently on a chair. Rye threw the reports onto the table and bent down, looking at the map of the Winter Plains.

"The Dark Kingdom's forces have breached past the Mors of Salvia. There are at least four hundred of them, possibly more. If we don't stop them soon, they could hit WhiteDrove within the month, Ignis within weeks."

Garding pulled his feet back and stood up, scanning the map. "How did they get past the Mors? That place is deadly. The fact that a full army could traverse the region does not bode well for us."

"Nor for the few men who stand between them and us."

"Aren't there a few villages just to the west of us toward Black Shore? Maybe some of the men could be conscripted to defend the territory till our reinforcements come." Garding grabbed one of the letters and skimmed through it. "Do these sods even know how to write?"

"That one," Rye started, taking the letter from the lieutenant, "Was written by a farmer in the Golden Hills south of here. He was heading to Viragrad to trade when he spotted them."

"Well, that makes more sense now," Garding shrugged. "Can we take a farmer at his word? What did the front lines say?"

"The farmer said a couple hundred. The front lines say less."

"Then the farmer can't count," Garding laughed, taking an apple from a bowl on the table and shining it with his shirt. "If our men saw no more than a few cultists, then I say we stay here and let 'em deal with them."

"And if the farmer is right?" The other person in the room stepped out of the shadows, her cloak pulled up over her pointed ears. "WhiteDrove is no fortress. It will be taken over within hours if we do not lessen the numbers they believed to have seen."

Rye looked at her, his gaze falling over her gray skin and white hair.

"You believe this farmer?" Garding scoffed, taking a bite of the apple. "Shouldn't your birds have picked up an army that large?"

"The Mors are vast and dense. It can readily conceal an army within it," she retorted.

Garding sat back down in his chair and crossed his ankles, leaning back and examining the apple. "An army of hundreds that somehow made it through the Mors in such numbers and somehow have gone unnoticed by our men?"

"If they have maleficarum with them, they could pass the Mors with ease, and undetected. We should either pull our men back or send them the reinforcements they require until I can gather more information."

"The spymaster is correct," Rye agreed, earning a groan of protest from the lieutenant.

"You always take her side."

"Because she is right," Rye argued. "They must have maleficarum with them. We should send a group of scouts out to find and eliminate them. We don't need the dead rising and turning against us. Let alone demons." He pointed to a large field just north of the Mors. "If we cut them off here using blocking wards, we can force them to camp. Then we can send Via's agents around the back to scout the area."

Via turned to him, hands behind her back. Her obsidian eyes gazed meticulously at him. "The maleficarum are known for their foul uses of magic. They have eyes in places I myself do not. My agents will be killed if they travel into their ranks without proper wards."

"We don't have enchanters in our command, and it will take time to send word to the College to receive any. Do you have an idea?" Rye asked, resting his hands on the pommel of his sword.

She gave a nod and glanced outside the flaps of the tent. "We should call upon Nexis. He can give us the runes necessary to slip past the scouts."

Garding looked at her and shook out his shoulders. "You think the elves will help us? They've made it clear they want nothing to do with Esai."

Via glanced at him and back down at the map. She picked up a wooden marker and ran her thumb down the lion carved into it.

"The elves have the wards that we do not, and they better understand magic than we do. Without the wards, your plan is doomed to fail. The cultists will detect us coming from miles away. But, if you have another option, I am all ears," she said smugly. Rye knew that she had their hands tied.

Garding sighed and ran a hand through his messy hair. "Fine, let the Raven send her letter. But I expect nothing to come of this. Elves are selfish creatures."

"Being selfish has kept their lands from being assaulted by the Dark Kingdom, Garding. I will leave as soon as possible."

"Leave? Why not send a letter?" Garding asked, finishing his apple and throwing the core into a bin across the room.

"I know Nexis, he will not send ward stones with some common scout. I will go retrieve them." She left no room for debate as she fled the tent, pulling the hood further down her face.

"You actually trust that cursed elf?" Garding asked, looking after her.

Rye crossed his arms, watching the tent flaps rustle in the humid breeze. "More than I trust my brother on the throne."

"I would say that's blasphemous, but you've been in higher spirits ever since she arrived," Garding quipped, taking a marker from the table and twirling it in his hands. "How do you know her?"

"We fought together in the Battle of Velwood ten years ago. She was the one who put the sword through the Damned King's chest," Rye said.

Garding raised an eyebrow. "She's the one who did that?" he asked, leaning back in his chair. "Velwood was a shit fest, I heard. Demons, undead, crazy-ass elves. Glad I was stationed at Sullenport for that."

"*Everyone* was stationed at Sullenport. My ass was handed to the emperor on a silver platter for disobeying orders."

"Eh, what was he going to do to his son? Give you a slap on the wrist and go cry to Mommy?" he snickered. "That's why I like you more than the nobles up in their high towers. You may have been born one of them but you don't act like one of them. Bet they haven't seen a battle that isn't depicted on a stage."

Rye looked over at Garding, who was flipping the marker in the air and catching it. "And our duty is to make sure they never *have* to see war, Garding."

"Yeah, yeah, I know. That's why I signed up for the army, isn't it?" he paused, setting the marker back down on the table and looking outside the tent. "The last royal elven bloodline was killed at Velwood, wasn't it?"

Rye nodded. "All for one." He thought back to that night, the screaming, the terror, the burning trees, and the sobbing elves. The little girl clinging to her dead father as Via tore her from his chest. *Not just a shit fest... a nightmare,* he thought. And people still wondered why the Dark Kingdom was so feared when its magics can corrupt even the most sanctified.

"Cursed elves, blessed elves, all elves are the same. Some just look greyer than others," Garding muttered. "Think the elven queen will ever allow access through the portal into the cursed city? I'd like to see it."

Rye gave a disheartened chuckle and placed his hands on the table, his eyes locking onto Avlor, the home of the elves.

"Somehow, I doubt that. Via did us all a favor that night; I don't wish to see the day the portal must be opened again."

6 ROSE

"Ouch!" Rose cried as a maid forced a pin through her hair to hold it in place atop her head.

"Please stay still, Your Grace," the handmaid said and put another pin through her hair.

Rose glanced in the mirror to see her full head of curls swirled up in an intricate bun, except for the loose curls framing her face that the handmaids brushed away.

Rose had woken up at the crack of dawn to get ready for the coronation. The castle was a blur, with servants cooking food, maids cleaning and setting up chairs, and clerics casting blessings in the throne room. She had yet to see her sister, and that made her slightly nervous.

Rose could only guess how many people were in attendance from the long line of chariots and wagons that reached well past the gates to the city. She had wracked her mind trying to think of every house that would be in attendance and dreaded having to remember them when they came up to congratulate her. She would much rather be out and about town with her friends, drinking and feasting on the imports from overseas.

"Your dress, Your Grace," a servant said as they entered the dressing room with a brilliant red velvet dress with golden embroidery. The servant set it on the plush bed before her maid led her to the center of the room. They stripped her down, and Rose grimaced as they stuffed her into a corset.

"This... is quite tight," she added. She held a viselike grip on the maid in front of her. Without her, Rose surely would have fallen off balance.

"Your mother's waist was the size of an apple at your age," the maid tutted.

"Quite an accomplishment, I'm sure."

With one more heavy tug, the maid tied the corset, and Rose let out a shy breath.

Meanwhile, Trissa sat on the couch with her hands folded over her lap, a nearly perfect smile on her lips. "Remember, shallow breaths," she laughed. Rose adjusted the corset around her breasts as the maids brought the dress for her to step into. Prompt alterations were made, and a sash of gold was draped around her shoulders. She situated the sash comfortably around herself and stepped into her shoes.

"You look tall," Trissa smiled and earned a glare from the to-be queen.

"I'm a perfect height, mind you," she snapped.

Trissa nodded. "But of course. And you would be even taller if you took the time to manage your posture."

"So, what if I am not of perfect stature!" she pouted. "I am still a queen. My posture has nothing to do with my station."

"Of course, *Your Grace*, but do well to remember that power is often corrupted by ignorance and a lack of will," Trissa added. The maids flattened the dress—not making eye contact—and finished the rest of the alterations while Trissa tapped Rose's chin to get her to straighten up.

"Why aren't they done with the dress yet? It is ungodly stuffy in here. Can I at least get a fan?" she protested.

"They would have had the alternations already done before you entered had you the mind to actually come to the fittings," Trissa pointed out. Rose scrunched her nose at her, and Trissa gave her a disapproving eye.

Rose heard the door open behind her before Trissa curtsied slightly.

"Princess Enara, it is good to see you," she greeted.

Enara gave Trissa a warm smile as she walked towards them. "You may leave now. I must speak with my sister in private," she ordered. The maids bowed and fled the room. Trissa put a hand on Rose's shoulder and nodded before exiting the room as well.

The door shut behind her with a click, and Enara composed herself before running a hand through her sister's silky golden sash. "Cloth made for queens," she purred and let the sash fall from her hand.

"It's good to see you again, Enara. I hope the rest of the meeting with the elf went well?" Rose asked.

Enara's smile faded, and she sighed, fixing a stray hair from her eyes. "About as well as expected. You can never trust them at their word. They wanted over four million *sephim* simply to build a new wall around their city. As if their precious trees weren't enough to protect their kingdom from invaders," she said begrudgingly. Rose watched as her sister walked over to a dresser and smiled slightly.

"Well, Mother made several treaties with them in the past. They bring quite an abundance of herbs and elixirs for us to use. Winter is not kind here towards the north. And maybe we could explore their cursed city," Rose pointed out.

Enara pulled a box from the dresser and turned back around. "I've never seen the city. For all we know, it is but a myth."

Rose glanced at the box and back at her sister. "I heard the Imperial army has a spy from their kingdom. It's hard not to believe," Rose countered.

Enara rolled her eyes. "Enough talking of elves, Rose. I have this for you," she said and walked over in front of her sister. "Open it."

Rose looked down at the small wooden box elegantly carved by hand. She carefully opened the lid and inside sat a small silver brooch. The brooch was a sword and a diamond, the family crest.

"Where did you get this?" she asked, carefully lifting it.

"It was fathers. Mother said that he bequeathed it to me before he died. So now I am gifting it to you," she said. She took the brooch and carefully pinned it to the dress.

"Now, you will always have a piece of him with you," she said and touched it softly.

Rose smiled brightly. "Thank you, Enara." She pulled her into a hug and felt a moment of hesitation before Enara squeezed back.

Enara kissed her cheek softly. "You're welcome, little sister." She pulled away and assessed her once more.

"I thought I was supposed to be queen. But fate chose you. I hope you are prepared," she said softly.

Rose touched her hand and squeezed it softly. "Don't worry; I will be."

The sisters turned when a knock came at the door. "Enter," Enara called.

A servant opened the door and bowed. "Princess Enara, the maids have prepared your gown for this afternoon," he said. Enara gave a soft sigh and put her hands on Rose's shoulders.

"Remember to breathe and don't mess up the ceremony," she warned.

Rose laughed and placed a hand on her sister's. "As if *I* could ever mess anything up."

Enara gave her a stern look and Rose pulled away from her. "Oh, go on now, I'll be fine! I promise everything will go smoothly today."

"As you say, *my queen*," Enara teased and shook her head. "I'll see you at the cathedral."

She left the room with the servant in tow and Rose glanced at herself in the mirror and took a long intake of breath. *You can do this; you are a queen now. There will only be hundreds of people in attendance. Don't trip over your dress, say nothing stupid, and you'll be fine.*

With one last breath, she composed herself and headed out the door, ready to face the day.

7 VIA

Within the Exalted Forests of *Al' Cashan*, a giant kingdom sat in the canopies of the Thousand Year trees. From the ground, one could barely see the wisps and nymphs that floated gleefully through the trees, hundreds of feet above. As one of the last kingdoms of elves that had refused to kneel to man, it held the glory of the ancients.

Elves roamed the canopies of the trees within the winding carved trails, trading woven cloth for furs and pelts. They were courteous to one another as children scampered by, careful not to disturb the animals that slept in baskets and branches.

So far up in the trees, it was nearly impossible to see the forest floor or the dangers that lingered there. Only the scouts traveled to the ground, watching for signs of cultists or anything that could harm their kingdom. Via noticed the wilting flowers that had barely begun to bloom among the dewy spring morning. She had seen none of the scouts as she walked, but she could feel their gazes on her, the traitorous cursed elf. The one who killed their beloved king. Not that she had any choice. Just like the city and village elves, she would not be welcome in their home. She was hardly welcome back in Nevrak either. She had no home. Except for the camp that rested barely out of harm's way. It was no home in a material sense. It was home because the only people she cared about were there. And she worried about what her absence may cause.

In the far reaches of the forest, away from the kingdom itself, a lone hut stood made from two trees twisted together like the Gemini twins.

A robust magical aura flowed around it, the tinkling of bells ringing throughout the area. The smell of herbs and smoke wafted from the hut as the Raven ascended the wooden stairs.

As soon as Via opened the door to the hut, a powerful wave of bubbling energy swirled through her nose and spread about her body, sending little shocks down her spine. She would never grow used to the tingling of her toes around magic. She looked around at the books scattered along the floor and tonics boiling in beakers. Entering the hut, she picked up a forgotten scroll and set it on the stand beside her. A smile crossed her dark lips as she heard a crash and a curse coming from downstairs.

An elven man came up, rubbing his head and whispering elven curses under his breath. Like most blessed elves, his skin was pale ivory—nearly translucent in the light—and ears as long as knives. While he was quite aged, he showed little signs of it. The only way a regular mortal could tell the difference between him and a newly trained hunter was the wise look in his eyes, like an owl who has explored the world too many times over. He stopped when he caught the eye of the woman.

"*Ar'eálla!* Raven, you scared the gods from me. Why do you always insist on coming in without knocking?" the man asked, pulling his singed vanilla-colored hair from his face.

Via picked a book off the ground, turning it in her hand. "Trying to blow the hut apart again, I see."

The elf carefully snatched the book from her and set it down on a desk. "Of course not. I was trying to make a new tonic for the scouts to sense undead," he said with a grumble, wiping his hands on his soot-covered tunic.

"And that is obviously going well for you. Is it necessary now?" she asked.

"Actually, yes, mind you," he huffed. "The undead are rising more and more frequently in the forest nowadays." He gave a glare, then smiled. "My Via, it has been too long. But I can't say I missed your attitude," he said and turned towards her. He took her hand and kissed it gently.

"I have missed your presence as well, Nexis."

Nexis was a hedge wizard for the queen of Avlor, tasked with keeping the kingdom's guards fit with magical potions and healing ointments. He was also the brother of the late king of Avlor, though he rarely spoke of it. He was cast out of the main kingdom years ago for his... explosive tendencies with tonics.

"Regarding that, I need your assistance with wards. You know the most about them," Via said.

Nexis scoffed and sorted through old scrolls lying around a table. "I am no mage, *Are've*, and know only so much of how to cast wards. I would think *your* kind would be the more practiced on that magic," he said.

Via pushed a strand of hair behind her ear. "You know I am not very welcome into Nevrak. I might be a cursed elf, but that doesn't mean I follow their doctrine."

Nexis nodded. "I could have told you that. What type of rune do you need?"

"A shadow ward. I must be able to sneak into the dark cults camp and find a maleficarum."

Nexis raised an eyebrow. He set the scrolls away and rubbed his chin, pondering.

"A shadow ward, you say. With that, I am afraid I cannot help you. That is a powerful spell, one that only a mage can cast. Lady Ravana may be your only hope," he said with a hint of repugnance.

Via sighed, then nodded. "*Vir'achel*, Nexis. I shall head out." She turned to leave, but his voice stopped her.

"Wait. I'll come with you. The guards aren't kind to strangers. I'll be of assistance to get the key to Nevrak," he said, and patted down his robe.

Via smiled slightly. "Of course. Who wouldn't want the company of the Mad Hedgewitch."

As the two elves made their way through the city's winding pathways, they earned many glares and gasps. Via ignored them as she passed, but she could feel Nexis' unease. Mothers brought their children into their huts, and animals hissed at their approach. An older elf sat on a stool, and when she passed him, spat at her feet, cursing her in the elvish tongue.

In the middle of the blessed city, the throne of Queen Arevälla rested atop the largest and oldest tree in the forest. Ancient branches were interwoven together to form the throne, magic pulsing through them, giving the throne a golden glow.

On the golden throne sat Arev*á*lla, older than Avlor and wiser than all. She kept her amber waves away from her porcelain face with a crown of woven thorns. Her emerald eyes watched carefully as the two elves made their way up the steps toward her.

"Halt, go no further," a guard said, stepping slightly in front of the queen. He raised his sword at them, and Via critiqued his stance in her head.

"*Aretove*, Your Excellence. I wish no harm upon you, only to speak," Nexis said and carefully bowed his head.

The guard looked at the spymaster distrustfully. "Why have you brought a cursed elf here, witch? You know the cursed ones are not to step foot within Avlor. Let alone the one who slaughtered our king."

Via ignored the guard and looked toward the queen. "I am only here to ask for entry to Nevrak. That is all," she said calmly.

The guard stepped closer to the outsiders. "Why should we allow that—"

"Let her speak," a soothing voice spoke above the guard. The guard turned and sheathed his sword. He bowed before stepping out of the way. Via's eyes caught the queen, and she bowed slightly.

"My queen. I need entrance to Nevrak in order to obtain a rune. It will aid us in the war against the Dark Kingdom," she said.

The queen folded her hands across her lap, the key around her neck gleaming in the setting sun. "You wish to help the humans?" she asked lightly.

Via nodded. "Yes, *Aretove*. Without them, there may be no stopping the Dark Kingdom. They would be powerful allies yet."

"The humans are the reason for the destruction of *Elu'lathan*, and you expect us to ally with them?" a voice asked. A woman stepped from the shadows, swords sheathed in scabbards on her hips. Her light auburn hair was tied into a messy bun, and her leather vest was torn and scraped. She favored her right leg and smelled of soot and dirt. Via could only assume she had a run-in with the undead.

Nexis smiled and gave a light bow to the young elf. "Caeda. It is good to see you again," he greeted.

She did not return the bow, instead sneered and walked up toward the queen. "*Aretove*, a situation within the forest demands your attention," she whispered.

Queen Arev*á*lla nodded and stood up. The huntress watched with careful eyes as the queen took off the necklace and walked down the steps toward the two elves. She handed Nexis the key and looked towards Via.

"You always had a devotion to the humans. Give this to Myrrah. He shall open the gate for you. Return the key to me once you have returned," she said politely.

Nexis bowed low."*Vir'achel*, my lady."

The queen stepped away, and they watched as she followed the Elven huntress down the winding stairs toward the forest floor. With a look back, Caeda gave a glare to the Hedgewitch, who only waved in return.

"One day, justice shall be served," she hissed.

"Perhaps next time I shall let the queen be slayed by her own husband," Via shrugged and Caeda flushed and turned away.

"Let us be off," Nexis said, gently nudging her. Via watched as the queen's silhouette faded into the distance, then turned to follow.

8 ENARA

The cathedral was bustling with nobility, ranging from the southernmost kingdoms to the Sunset Isles. They stood in anticipation of the soon-to-be queen, their flowing gowns and cotton capes sliding against one another as they shifted in the day's growing heat. The songs of the choir echoed along the shining marble walls, and soft whispers from the audience carried their way to Enara's ears. She stood poised at the altar of the goddess, her eyes scanning the nobility, placing names to faces. Her dress was a darkened violet with a diamond trim that she picked at. Her hair was curled and pinned, flowing down her shoulders, and her necklace was cold against her throat. She tried to ignore the pulsing in her hand.

The head cleric made his way to the altar, giving a small prayer and setting the golden crown down on a blessed piece of cloth. Enara studied the crown, how it glimmered in the light, the engraved prayer on the inside, the spotting of diamonds in the band. It was small, light upon the head, but still held enough weight to crush one not prepared. *The crown which should be placed upon my head*, she thought. She looked up to spot the Duke and Sir Alran standing close to the altar, and they gave her a small smile. She gave a strained smile in return as the doors to the cathedral opened.

"Guide your hand, Velara," the head cleric said. The cathedral was silenced as Rose appeared in the doorway and walked toward the cleric. Her velvet dress trailed behind her, the jewels gleaming in the candlelight. Her hands were folded in front of her; her head held high. All eyes locked onto her as Enara caught whispers of conversation.

"By the goddess, she looks just like her."

"If you'd say that was Elena walking down that aisle. I'd believe you."

Enara had to admit that their frivolous whispering was right. Rose did look like her mother, from her golden hair to her emerald eyes. She carried herself with dignity, though a bit stiffly, and her eyes met Enara's. She gave a small nod and Rose's lips turned up slightly.

Rose stopped at the altar of the goddess and knelt. The statue of the goddess stared back down at them with a loving smile, one hand held over her heart, the other reaching out to Rose. The cleric walked up in front of her and held the crown above her head.

"Velara, the Goddess of light and magic, created this crown from Her soul, crafting it into the perfect symbol of purity and justice. Each head that it has sat upon has brought everlasting prosperity through all kingdoms of Veran. Now the crown is once again placed upon a child of light. Princess Rosellena, do you swear to protect your kingdom and lead it to peace within the waking world?" the cleric asked.

"Yes, cleric," she answered.

"Do you swear to uphold the law of Auratus and the law of the Emperor of Esai?"

"Yes."

"And do you swear to stand with your people in both war and peace, ensuring that the legacy of the Empire remains seen and never forgotten?"

"Yes."

He set the crown upon the gold locks of Rose's hair and raised his hands.

"Now, we raise our heads to the new queen of Ignis. Queen Rosellena Victoria GoldThorn, ruler of the kingdom of Auratus!" Rose stood straight and turned as each noble bowed low to their new ruler. Her crown gleamed gleefully as the diamonds twinkled within the metallic weaves. Enara spotted Trissa in the back with the servants, wiping a tear from her eye.

"Long live the Queen of Light!" They said in unison.

Beside her, Enara curtsied and held her sister's hand as they walked down the aisle towards the wooden doors to the ballroom.

"Thank you, sister," Rose gleamed.

Enara's smile faded. "What wouldn't I do without you?"

Music filled the ballroom as men and women alike danced elegantly to the tune of the singing choir and thrumming orchestra. Sparkling from above, the chandeliers lit up the dance floor; the diamonds buried in the ceiling reflecting the light down and showering the guests in a myriad of flickering flames.

Enara stood away from the dance floor, watching her sister being paraded around the room with nobility squawking at her every which way. It was amusing, she would admit, watching Rose fail to posture and act the part of the queen. *If she had simply attended her lessons, this would be so much simpler,* she thought. She plotted ways to turn the ball around if things went south for the new queen. Maybe everyone would be too drunk to notice any errors she made. For once, Enara was perfectly fine not being in the spotlight.

She took a sip of her wine and her eyes flitted about the room, locking onto a man who had made quite the scandal with his arrival. Supposedly he was from a town south of Fira in Esai, with little to his name. How he received an invitation was beyond her.

He was well dressed for such a lowborn lord; he was quite handsome as well. His dark hair, carefully kept beard, and honey-colored eyes had caused many of the women in the room to be taken with him. They turned to bragging and displaying their wealth in not-so-subtle whispers around him, trying for a dance with him, no doubt. Enara tried not to be as ostentatious.

She watched as he easily conversed with the people around him as if he were a king himself. He laughed and gossiped and danced his way through the room before finally setting his eyes on her. She felt her fingers tighten around the glass when he started towards her.

"I am surprised you are not dancing, Your Grace," he said, coming up to her with a bow. Enara took a sip of her wine, sparing a glance at her sister taking a tiny cake from the buffet and shoving it into her mouth.

"Yes, well, it is my sister's night to shine. I would not wish to out stage her," she quipped. "What is your name?"

"I am Lord Aldrian, princess. I am from Southmire, a day's ride from Fira," he said with a small smile.

Enara tapped her finger on her glass, trying to visualize the map of the continent. "I apologize. I do not believe I am familiar with that town," she admitted after a moment.

He gave a chuckle. "Few are. We are not known for our mining or cathedrals."

"Though you seem to be well established," she noted, looking towards his jerkin and fur-trimmed coat.

He looked down bashfully and put a lip between his teeth. "I am embarrassed to say that my father spent a small fortune to bring me here."

"And your House?" she asked.

He hesitated for a moment, his eyes staring into her own. "Silvand," he stated. She did not recognize his House, but she knew little of the nobility in Esai, so she took him at his word.

"I am surprised you have not asked the queen for a dance," she said.

He shifted his gaze to Rose, who was encompassed by a throng of women expressing their admiration for her. "I came here for the coronation, but it was not the queen who caught my eye…" he trailed off and returned his gaze to her. She felt heat rise to her cheeks, but quickly blamed it on the wine.

"I am not looking to court, my lord," she blurted.

"I did not mean to come across that way, princess. I only wanted to ask for a dance," he corrected, holding his hand out to her. She took another glance at her sister and back at Lord Aldrian.

"I'm sorry, but no," she said sternly, setting her glass down on the table with more force than she intended.

The lord seemed unfazed by her actions. "As you wish, but I assure you would have been the talk of the night."

"I do not wish to be the talk of the night, surrounded by harpies."

Lord Aldrian chuckled. "I can concur. I have not had the pleasure of spending much time among the higher court, but I can feel their piercing gazes upon me even now."

"Then a word of advice, my lord? Do not wish to ever have to reside among them for long. They sap the strength from you and feast upon your corpse," she told.

"Does that come from personal experience?" he asked.

She nodded, crossing her arms over her chest, glancing around at the partygoers whose eyes locked onto her own. "I have been surrounded by those who would call themselves allies and yet plot to take the throne from my hands since I was a little girl. I have grown to recognize the face of betrayal and call it a friend."

"That seems like a dispiriting life to live, princess. I hope you may find some comfort among peers," he said sadly.

Enara bit her lip from saying more. *Foolish girl, moaning to a lowborn lord about how terrible life is in a giant castle,* she thought. She didn't even know this man, and yet he seemed to reach into her chest and pull every emotion she kept locked away to the surface. She hated it.

She took a soft breath and plastered a smile onto her face. "I'm sorry, my lord. I am sure you did not wish to hear my woes this evening. This is a ball for the new queen. I should be in higher spirits."

"And yet the crown was not placed upon the right head," he remarked. Enara's eyes widened, and she gazed into the swirling honey of his iris.

"I—"

"Princess!"

A knight rushed over to her and quickly bowed. She turned from the lord to the knight, who quickly brought his lip to her ear. "There has been an incident at the gates."

Enara kept herself calm and glanced at Lord Aldrian, who tilted his head slightly and took a drink of his wine, a smile brightening up his face.

"An *incident,* ser? What kind of incident?" she asked.

"Two of the townsfolk tried sneaking into the castle. We caught them on the second-floor balcony of the queen's room. They said they knew her, and the queen went out to investigate."

Enara internally groaned. She knew exactly the idiots who would risk breaking into the castle to see Rose. "Where are they now?"

"Queen Rose just allowed them inside the ballroom."

Enara felt the veins in her hand burn and quickly clenched her fist. *By the goddess, tell me she didn't.* But she could already hear the gasps and whispers across the ballroom as a crowd formed near the doors. She waved the knight away and composed herself.

"My sincere apologies, Lord Aldrian, but there are matters I must attend to," she said with a curtsy.

The lord bowed low to her. "Of course, princess."

Enara quickly moved through the ever-growing crowd toward her sister and found her with a glass of champagne in the air, the two miscreants behind her with uncertainty written across their faces. She grabbed hold of Rose's shoulder, her nails digging into the fabric of her shawl.

Rose turned around to see Enara's eyes alight with flame.

"What in the goddess do you think you are doing?" she hissed. "Why are they here?"

Rose pulled her hand from her shoulder and tapped her fingers on her glass. "They snuck into the castle and wanted to see the ball. I don't see any harm in it."

Enara looked around the room and at the nobles, who were whispering in abhorrence. "Rose. You are the queen of Auratus. There are princes here, lords here. From every kingdom in Veran. And yet you are conversing with commoners instead of them."

"I've talked to them all evening—"

"You are slighting them is what you are doing. Inviting your…*friends*. It not only makes them look like vermin, but you a fool," she scolded. "You are a queen. *Act like one.*"

Rose glanced from Enara to the rest of the ballroom as they watched in sickened amusement. She glanced at her friends, who held their eyes down. "I—"

"You will go back. You will dance and play the role of a naive, untried ruler who is fond of her people. You will apologize to those you snubbed and befriend those you haven't. Go. Now."

Rose put her head down and stepped away from her sister.

Enara took a breath and composed herself. Then she turned around, clapped her hands together, and smiled.

"Forgive that scene. Queen Rose is adored by her subjects, and sometimes they can get overzealous in wanting to be in her presence. But they will be dealt with. Now, let's toast to Auratus and our newest queen!" she cheered. The crowd raised their glasses and drank gleefully as the music picked up again, nearly disregarding the two people behind her.

She turned to them and shook her head. "Throw them out."

The guards grabbed onto Olivia and Jared, and Olivia backhanded a guard across the face. He stumbled back before another grabbed onto her wrist and twisted it behind her back. She hissed in pain.

"You aren't the queen. Rose is you bitch," Olivia barked.

Enara tilted her head at her and snorted. "We shall see for how long. One more word and I will cut your tongue out." She motioned for the guards to take them, and they were pulled from the room.

"See? Hate noble pricks," Jared muttered. The doors closed behind them, and Enara felt her pocket grow hot. She watched as Rose bowed and apologized and kissed the asses of the lords and ladies around her. It was shameful. *They should be bowing to me*, she thought.

Her pocket burned hotter, and she took the coin from it as it seared her hand. She gripped the coin in her palm and fled from the room towards the library. When she entered it, she closed the door behind her and put her head on the warm wood.

She took a long breath, feeling her heart pump quickly in her chest. She just needed a moment. That was all.

Tap. Tap.

Enara snapped her head up and turned to the window. A raven rested on the sill, tapping its beak against the glass. Her breath became cold as a chill came through the room. It crawled up her spine and arms, resting on her pulsing hand. She stepped towards the window, and the raven pecked again. She gazed at her reflection, watching it sway with the torches that littered the city. Fireworks shot into the sky and exploded above the castle as the courtyard was alight with dancing people.

Another tap. The coin burned through her flesh. She opened her palm to see the dagger that rested on the gold.

Tap.

Rose would never survive the court. They would eat her alive and spit her out on the tomb of their mother's legacy. She would bring nothing but despair and ruin and mockery to her kingdom.

"I will be queen," Enara breathed. "I will lead this kingdom to greatness before it all collapses. It's for the best, for the fate of Auratus," she told herself. Her eyes flickered red, and she held up the gold coin. A burst of light enveloped the room as the gold disintegrated and a black portal opened. She stepped back as the wind blew books and scrolls around the room, and in the vortex emerged a shadow.

Her mother's portrait smiled on the wall next to her. Beside her, two girls stood happily next to one another, one with gold hair and one with black. Green eyes gleamed brightly in the light, but blue eyes stayed shadowed. A haunting stream of laughter echoed off the stone walls.

9 ROSE

Rose sighed tiredly, finally able to sneak away from the gazes of the court. With the amount of profuse apologizing she had to express, her throat felt like needles. She walked to the dessert table stacked with cakes and pies at the end of the room, only deciding on a small pastry before being disrupted by a soothing voice.

"The sugar and cinnamon drop cakes are the better of the choices."

Rose turned and found a young gentleman bowing to her. She set the sweet down and turned to face him fully. "I'm sorry, I don't believe we've met," she said curiously.

The man smiled and ran a hand through his dark brown hair, just darker than his skin. "Excuse my manners, my queen. I am Prince Valek Farvell of Rosus," he greeted.

Rose's eyes widened slightly before curtsying. "Oh! Beg your pardon, Your Grace. I did not realize it was you."

Valek shrugged. "Do not worry about it. We were mere children when we first met. I do believe you were no older than a toddler."

Rose pursed her lips, attempting to remember her mother bringing her to the shining blue waters of the South. She could remember it nearly as well as her father's face, which was to say, only vaguely.

"If I'm not mistaken, you've yet to meet my sister, either," he noted.

Rose shook her head. "No, I'm sure she is beautiful, though," she admitted.

He chuckled and held out his hand. "May I have this dance, my queen?"

Rose smiled and took his hand. "Of course."

They walked out onto the ballroom floor, taking her place beside the other noble ladies as the prince stood at the other end of the dance floor with the men. When the music started again, she curtsied and stepped over to him, her hand grasping his. Their feet followed the others as they spun in the dance.

"You should visit Rosus soon, Your Grace. It is beautiful this time of year. The golden roses have just started blooming," he said as she spun around, taking hold of his other hand.

"Really? I thought it was summer all year long down there," she pondered.

He squeezed her hand with a gentle smile and she felt her face grow hot. "It is, but the roses only bloom once a year on the blood moon. My sister was born that day nearly two decades ago. The clerics say it's a gift from the goddess. I say she's just a spoiled brat," he teased, earning a giggle from the queen.

"Little sisters can be quite the handful."

He raised an eyebrow and spun her in a circle. "You admit to being a spoiled brat?"

Rose laughed as they parted, bowed, and began again. "Trissa doesn't keep silent about my manners. Neither does Enara," Rose said. "I won't disagree with the fact that being royalty is not a specialty of mine."

"And yet you are queen. So, you must have some talent to obtain the title out from under your sister," he added.

Rose nodded sadly. "Yes, I'm afraid you're right. I never wanted the title of queen. But my mother insisted that I rule over Auratus, and I won't fail her," she said and put a hand on the ruby around her neck. They spun and stepped apart again. With one last bow, they grasped both their hands together in a waltz.

"It is quite a beautiful gem. Matches both your beauty and spirit," he said, and Rose looked up. His eyes held a steady kindness, and Rose blushed slightly.

"You are quite the charmer, aren't you?" she breathed.

He shrugged and twirled her around once more. "Despite my family's saying, I do have certain redeeming qualities," he laughed, and Rose stumbled, tripping over her dress. Before she could fall, Valek graciously hooked an arm around her waist and grabbed her hand. The music stopped, and all eyes fell upon the couple in the center. Rose stared shyly at the face mere inches from her own.

"I am also proficient at catching queens," he laughed and pulled her onto her feet. Clapping began filling the ballroom, and Rose quietly stepped away and curtsied.

"Umm, thank you for the dance, Your Grace," she said and turned away quickly. Valek moved towards her and took her hand.

"You're quite flushed, my queen. Are you all right?" he asked.

Rose collected herself and fluffed out her dress. "No, I was just a bit warm from the dance," she diverted and pushed a curl behind her ear. Valek touched her necklace, and his eyes slid downwards.

"It is quite warm in here, I agree. Shall we go to the garden for fresh air?"

Rose blushed deeper and looked toward her sister. Enara caught her gaze and made a shooing motion with her hand. Rose smiled and hooked her arm through his.

"I would love to," she answered.

The garden was drowned in shades of orange and red as the torches puffed and waved in the gentle breeze of the evening. The moons basked in their full glory in the sky, observing the twinkling stars around them. The city was jovial and glimmered against the silver light of the sky—the sound of cheering and drums could be heard from the courtyard beyond. A melodic tune carried through the air as the water from a fountain rippled and bubbled as it fell from marble tiers.

Two figures walked through the garden, arms linked, and voices raised in joyful tête-à-tête. Rose ran her fingers along the cashmere of the prince's coat and hummed happily as a laugh escaped his lips.

"I find it increasingly hard to imagine you sneaking a pig into the court with no one noticing," he laughed, covering his mouth with his gloved hand.

"It's true! My sister and I were always getting up to no good when we were children. She was aghast at my suggestion, but I still did it. Snuck him right into the throne room while my mother held court. No one batted an eye until it started oinking."

The prince laughed again. "And you... dressed it up?"

"Yes! In the stable boys' clothes. I had to cut the pants to get them to fit, but it worked well enough. When everyone turned to me, the pig escaped my grasp and ran right through the doors. It took a quartet of guards, accompanied by a frightened maidservant, to finally find him and lead him out of the castle."

"And what was the name again?"

"Mr. Toofles the stableboy pig. I still miss him."

"Oh, I can imagine," he chuckled, wiping a tear from his eye. "What happened to him?"

"I am unsure," she said, shrugging. "But the ham served to break our fast that next morn was quite delightful."

The two burst into a rapturous laughter, clinging to one another for support. She looked up to see his broad smile and eyes wet with unshed tears. She hated to admit how handsome he truly was. He could have any woman he wanted if he wished—he was a prince. And yet his gaze lingered on her own and his hand was warm against hers as he squeezed it gently.

"I cannot say I've had adventures such as yours before. You must be a delight to the kingdom."

Rose scoffed, and they made their way to the fountain, her heels clicking against the stone walkway. "Oh, I don't know about that. Enara seems to have a knack for making me seem a fool. Or perhaps I am one; I was never good at being royalty."

"Is anyone truly? Even being born into it, I cannot say I am perfect. My sister, on the other hand, oh they cheer her name in the streets. The Princess of Roses."

"So, you are saying we both have perfect sisters and are stuck being the unruly ones?" she asked, nudging him with her elbow.

"Such a terrible thought, that is. Though I've heard that like minds attract." They stopped at the fountain and Rose laid her eyes upon the rippling of the water. Their reflections twirled and twisted, and she noticed the prince turn to face her. She glanced toward him, and he brought her hands up in his own and squeezed slightly. She felt her face grow hot as his eyes bore into her own.

"I must say, Your Grace, that your beauty outmatches even the brightest of stars in the sky. I came here simply to offer my congratulations on your ascent to the throne but found myself bewitched from the first moment I gazed upon your face.

"I..." Rose could feel the words failing her as he pulled her closer to him.

"Our sister kingdoms have been at peace for generations. They have held together a steady bond through trade and commerce. And I would be honored to continue that bond, together.”

Is he proposing what I think he is? Rose asked herself. *He couldn't possibly be.* It felt like the world was spinning around her as this handsome prince confessed his love for her in front of the glimmering pool of water.

“Would you do me the great honor of merging our Houses, Queen GoldThorn?”

By the goddess, he did just propose to her. Merging their Houses? It would suit both kingdoms well, even elevate them to higher standing within the continent. But what would her sister think? Marrying a man she just met. No matter how charming he was, or how well-mannered he was. *Oh, hells,* she thought.

“Yes. I will marry you, Prince Valek,” she breathed. He brought her into him with a long and breathless kiss. Her body melted into his own as his hands slid down her back to firmly grasp her waist, his other hand pushing up her chin.

For the moment, she was content, for nothing could ruin such a magnificent moment.

Rose opened her eyes sleepily and sat up. Her hand rested lightly on the prince's chest, softly rising and falling with his breaths. They had fallen asleep together in the garden, watching the twinkling stars brighten the night. She looked around as a muffled boom echoed through the garden. She glanced toward the sound but saw nothing but the night sky. It was quiet; the ball guests had left or slept in the guest wing. It was a relief to be removed from the scrutiny of the court.

A sudden burst of light shot across the sky and exploded above them. She thought it was a firework until it rushed closer to where she lay. Frantically, she shook the prince awake as a massive blue ball of flame descended toward them. Valek jumped up, pushing her out of the way. The fireball exploded when it hit the ground, sending embers scattering across the yard. Valek shielded Rose from the fire and looked up after the ash stopped falling.

“An attack!?” he questioned.

“That can't be,” Rose said, memories flickering back to the night she held her mother's limp hand in her own.

"We need to move!" He pushed her up.

Rose turned towards her crown, still lying on the ground. "But the crown!" she yelled.

"Forget the bloody crown!" he retorted. He led her through the garden as shouts and screams began emitting from throughout the castle. Rose saw several more bursts of fire hit buildings, causing them to explode in a fury of fire and wood as townspeople ran for cover.

"We must help them," she pleaded. Valek kept an iron grip on her as they exited the gardens and went into the castle. A dagger went flying past them, and Rose cried out as it lodged into the wall, inches from her head. Valek turned and parried a sword. A cultist cloaked in black swung his sword down, and Valek dodged the attack, shouldering the cultist into the wall. He slashed his sword across the cultist's chest, and they fell to the floor.

"The Dark Kingdom," he huffed.

"No, not again," Rose whimpered, her fingers trembling. Blue fire exploded outside, and the windows shattered around them. Rose screamed as glass went flying, and Valek started down the hallway.

Outside the windows, Rose caught glimpses of guards firing arrows down at the cultists. She watched as black creatures scaled the walls and knocked the guards off, screaming as they fell. Another blast of fire rocked the castle as it slammed into the gates, sending wooden boards flying across the courtyard. The mass of bodies that moved inside the walls reminded her of maggots.

Valek dodged another sword and put it through the throat of the cultist before jumping out of the way of an arrow.

"Stay behind me!" he yelled to Rose before clashing blades with another cultist. He swung down, cutting off an arm, then swung up, slashing them across the chest.

Rose heard a scream come down the corridor, and she watched as a cultist dragged a noble lady to the ground as she kicked and screamed. He laughed as he put a knife through her eye, and Rose grabbed onto the prince.

"Where is Enara!?" she asked, scanning the bodies of the nobles before a chill ran down her spine. Both turned to see a Dark Knight coming towards them from the garden. The Knight's armor was made of thick metal plates, weathered but still solid. It seemed like it had seen a thousand battles, and broken swords hung on its belt.

Rose froze in fear as two monstrous wolf-like creatures walked behind it. Standing over four feet tall, their human-like faces were horrendously mutilated. Their wolf paws thumped against the ground behind the Knight. The heavy, dented armor they wore clanked against their bodies.

"Those can't be demons," Rose said in terror.

Clutching his sword, Valek wiped the blood from his face. "You should have stayed in your little kingdom," he spat.

The Knight unsheathed its broadsword from its back holster, and the demons growled and lunged for the couple. Valek shoved one away before the other bit into his shoulder, ripping away pieces of muscle and flesh.

"Valek!" Rose cried. Her ruby flashed red, and fire erupted from the ground. Howling, the demons jumped back from the burning flames. The Dark Knight turned its head towards her as she caught Valek in her arms. He groaned and held his bleeding shoulder.

"Run, Rose," he groaned.

She shook her head. "I'm not leaving you!"

"*Viras kata verel'nan*," the Knight chanted as it stepped through the wall of flame. Valek shakily stood up and pointed his sword at the Knight.

"Valek, don't!" Rose cried.

Valek stumbled but caught his footing, his shirt drenched in blood. "You and your damned kingdom will fall. On the Kingdom of Yalirea, I swear it!" he yelled.

The Dark Knight stopped and waited, his sword at his side. Rose watched as Valek let out a war cry and darted toward the Knight. He swung his sword down, and the Knight parried it with ease. Taking the advantage, it brought its leg up, kneeing the prince in the stomach. Crying out, the prince fell to his knees.

"No!" Rose yelled.

"See you in the Otherworld, demon," Valek growled.

The Knight raised its sword and brought it down, slicing clean through the prince's neck. Rose screamed as his head fell to the ground, his body thumping against the tile beside it. The wall of fire dissipated as Rose fell to her knees, sobbing.

When the Knight looked toward her, she stumbled to her feet, running back through the hallway. She could hear the demons on her heels as she tripped over bodies at a frantic pace to avoid them. Feeling them closing in, she toppled a table over, but the demons easily leaped over it. She screamed as she was thrown to the ground, a hound ripping into her side.

Thrashing and fighting back, she grabbed the demon by the face, and her ruby lit again. A bolt of lightning exploded into its body, and it was thrown from her.

Quickly, Rose leaped back to her own feet and rushed through the nearest door, holding her bleeding and ravaged side. *Goddess save me*, she prayed, feeling the warm liquid soak through her skirt.

Before she could close the door, both demons slammed into it, momentarily knocking her onto her back. With a painful cry, she got back up and shouldered the door, leaning all her weight against it. On the other side, the demons clawed and howled in anger before one broke its head through the ornate door. Grabbing its head, Rose sent another bolt of magical lightning through it. With a pained screech, the demon was thrown back. Using the momentary lapse, Rose shoved the door closed and managed to lock it before the demons could rebound. Panting heavily and wiping the tears and sweat from her eyes, Rose backed away from the door as the demons once more slammed against the weakened wood.

"Rose?"

Rose twirled around and was greeted by her sister's face. Rose was overwhelmed with a sense of relief upon realizing she was well.

"Valek... everyone... they're dead," she cried, running to her sister and throwing her arms around her.

All too soon, Enara was pushing Rose away.

"I never wanted this to happen," she said sadly, an odd glint in her eye as she twisted one of Rose's curls around her finger. "The people were not supposed to be part of this. But it's too late."

Rose's brow creased slightly. "Enara? What's wrong?" she asked.

"You were never prepared to be the queen, Rose. You could never properly rule Auratus," she started, meeting her eyes.

Rose backed away slightly. "Enara, why do you speak such ways?" she asked.

Enara stretched her arm behind her, and Rose spotted a glint of metal. "You have forgotten who the true queen is," she growled, raising her hand and revealing a carved dagger. "*I* was meant to rule, not you. Just because you are a mage gives you no right to take what is mine!"

"Enara, how could you do this? I thought we were sisters!" Rose cried.

"We are Rose and will always be. But I cannot let you ruin our kingdom."

Abruptly, Enara lunged for her, and Rose jerked back. Hitting the ground, she continued to scramble away on her hands. "Enara! Please don't do this!"

"Shut your whore mouth! You took what was meant to be mine. You always acted like a child. While you played in the fields, I was trapped in this damned room. I spent *years* of my childhood locked in this castle learning to be queen just to have some brat with magic take it from me. It's your fault!" The dagger in her hand shook with seen anger.

With shock and fear pumping through her, Rose scrambled to her feet and bolted out onto the balcony, ignoring the continuous throbbing in her side. "Enara, I'm so sorry. I never wanted this!"

Enara shook her head. "You took everything from me. You took my legacy, my throne, and my mother! Now the city burns because you couldn't give up your title. My mother would still be alive if you hadn't been born."

At the balcony's balustrade, Rose could see the ground below, nearly fifty feet down. She would never survive a fall that far. She turned back in time to see her sister following her out onto the balcony.

"Mother gave her life for both of us. She would never want this Enara," she pleaded. *This isn't Enara. She wouldn't hurt me.* She took a step toward her. "Our people are dying, Enara. Can't you hear them?"

Enara paused, seeming to listen to the screams surrounding them. Rose could smell burning flesh and feel the fires in the city below. The people were dying.

"Let's end this," Rose pleaded. "Then we can rule together."

The dagger lowered as Enara's face twisted with emotion, blue eyes brimming with tears as she bit her lip.

"I—"

Suddenly Enara gripped her hand, and she dropped the knife, screaming. Rose quickly reached for her, but Enara jerked away.

"Fuck!" she cursed. "It's your fault. It's all your fault!" Enara's hands came out and pushed Rose. She stumbled, and her eyes widened before falling from the balcony. She felt the wind rush past her, felt herself become weightless as her sister disappeared and all she felt was intense pain. Then a bright flash of light invaded her sight.

Then nothing.

10 OLIVIA

"Hurry!" Olivia yelled, running past screaming townsfolk and howling demons. The city was aflame. Cultists had ransacked every noble house in Ignis, forcing any men out onto the streets to kill them, leaving wives and children behind. Screams of terror rang through the city as blood flowed through the cracks of the cobblestone. Those who did not submit or hide were killed ruthlessly by the hungry beasts and knights clad in black that roamed the alleyways.

Children screamed into their dead mother's clothing, and men took up arms just to be slaughtered seconds later. The smell of burning flesh and corpses was familiar to Olivia. Still, it did not lessen the gut-wrenching feeling crawling through her stomach.

Jared ran in front of Olivia, swinging his sword in an arc to cut the arm off a demon, spinning back around in time to dodge an incoming arrow.

"Where is Rose!?" he asked as they turned into a back alley and jumped over a barricade of carts. Both were covered in muck, wounded, and bleeding. Olivia held her pulsing arm and looked around. Smoke had filled the night sky, hiding the moons and stars. The only lights that illuminated the city were the burning buildings and torches.

"I don't know. The castle is completely overrun," she breathed and turned at a deafening explosion as a building erupted into flames, screams muted by the sounds of the crackling fire.

"This is madness. We have to escape the city," Jared said.

"Not until I find my father," Olivia retorted before abruptly scaling a wall and jumping down onto another street.

With little choice, Jared followed suit, and she turned at a loud cry. Before she could realize what was happening, a demon slammed into her and she flew onto her back as it latched onto her arm with its human-like teeth. Crying out, Olivia yanked a knife from her belt and stabbed it through the eye. With a yelp, it jumped off her.

These demons were nothing but tortured souls, bodies twisted and morphed into beasts. This one had the face of a man but the body of a skinned wolf. Its fur had fallen off of it, leaving charred bits of flesh and blood to rot on the coated ground—

"Olivia!" Jared yelled. He crashed into her as a pillar of fire erupted feet from where she once stood. They landed on the stone street, and Jared covered her with his body. The explosion rang in her ears as the fire faded, and she looked up. A Dark Knight walked towards them from the fire, sword in one hand and a woman's decomposing head in the other.

At Olivia's panicked shove, Jared moved off of her so they could both scramble to their feet and face the Knight. The flesh from the head fell onto the cobblestone, maggots crawling from the eyes as it walked. He dropped it to the ground for the demon to eat as its rusted armor clanked against its body.

"Why are you here?" Jared hissed. The Knight stopped. It said nothing as it took a piece of fabric from his pocket and held it up.

"That's Rose's," Olivia gasped. "I'd know that heraldry anywhere."

Jared stepped forward. "You bastards! You'll pay for this!" he yelled. He rushed the Knight and swung his sword down. The Knight dodged it and slashed up, skimming his chest. Olivia ran towards the Knight, slashing with her knife, but the Knight turned and caught her by the shirt, lifting her off her feet. Sunken black eyes returned her glare when she looked into its helmet before she was abruptly thrown back down to the street, landing hard against the stone.

"Jared!" Olivia called, as she heard her friend stumble back up.

"Get out of here!" he yelled back. "Get out of the city and warn the others!" Olivia shook her head as the Knight turned his attention to the swordsman. "Now!"

Olivia got up shakily as Jared swung again, clashing blades with the Knight. A laugh erupted from it as Jared's sword shattered. The Knight quickly brought its knee up, slamming it into Jared's stomach, who cried out as he fell to his knees. The Knight brought its sword up once more, but Jared was fast enough to evade the attack as it came down on the stone, a sharp clang ringing through the street, before smoothly stabbing his broken blade into its calf. With a guttural screech, the Knight grabbed Jared by the throat, flinging him into a burning cart.

"Jared!" she cried.

Glancing down at the knife in her hand, then back up at Jared's limp form, Olivia bit back tears and turned, running down the street. Her boots thumped against the stone even as she heard a cry erupt from her friend as the Knight pounced upon him once more.

She turned down an alleyway and jumped over carts and bodies. She sprinted past demons and dying children, avoiding more knights and cultists. Her mind raced as she set for the tavern. She didn't know if Jared would survive. Rose was dead, and Enara could be as well. She had to find her father and get out of the city. Maybe not all of the kingdom was taken. She could find a town and demand their aid.

Olivia turned down a road and onto a dirt path that led towards the tavern, immediately spotting a large black cloud billowing down the pathway. Sprinting harder, her heart pounded in her chest.

She skidded to a halt as flames burned through the tavern doors and windows. She stepped back as the heat singed her arms.

"Father!" she cried. She got no response besides the crackling of the flames. She ran around back and through the door. Flames rose as she attempted to reach the inner part of the tavern. She could see burning corpses littering the floor, and she screamed for her father as it forced her back. More dead patrons scattered the ground near the tavern, eyes wide in terror. All of her belongings, violin, clothing, and her father were destroyed. Burnt pieces of fabric fell from the sky, and she fell to her knees.

She heard the whinny of horses, and she looked up to see a black one coming down the path towards her. Dark mist fell from its snout and Olivia gasped before staggering up onto her feet and sprinting away from the burning buildings toward the city gates. She ran towards an old well near the tavern, remembering that it led to a cavern that went out of the city. She had fallen down it once when she was a girl and found her way outside the gates back home and had used it often afterward. One more way to sneak out of the city for her jobs.

Water crashed around her as she landed, coating her head and body. Water streamed into her nose, and she blew out, resurfacing. She gasped for breath and winced at the cuts wracking her body. She looked up as the horse whinnied again. Quickly swimming out of sight and behind a large rock formation in the wall, she closed her eyes as metal gloves hit the side of the well, peering down. It seemed hours that she held her breath, waiting for the rider to lose interest. The stench of decay filled her nose, and she covered her mouth. She reopened her eyes as she heard the rider leave and the horse's gallop fade away. Looking around the well, she swam to the side, pulling herself onto the hard surface. She laid on her back, panting and soaked. Blood streamed down her arm and vest, trailing down her legs. She rested her head on the cool stone and thought to herself.

They're all dead. Everyone she loved was killed. They took everything from her. But she was still alive. That was all that mattered now.

She shakily got up and started forward into the darkness. A burning sensation filled her chest as one goal crossed her mind.

To kill the bastards who murdered my family.

11 RAVANA

The cursed city; The city of black. Most dared not even speak its name for fear of the dead coming to haunt them. It was nearly impossible to enter the cursed city without the key the elven queen held around her neck. The key was the only thing that could open the portal to Nevrak.

The city was lost to the Otherworld, seeming to be an entirely different plain of reality. The skies were never bright, just swirls of purple and gray. The city itself was carved from magic and stone, holding more than a million inhabitants, with shrouded forests surrounding it on all sides—if you could even call them forests. The trees and flora glowed blue and purple, wisps and fae floating around in the air. The ground they walked on lit up their footsteps, and haunting echoes of spirits drove men to their deaths.

Some called Nevrak the Wellspring of Mana. It needed nothing from the outside world, relying purely on the actions of the queen for survival. The vortex of the sky and abundance of black magics had turned the skin of the elves to deep grays, purples, and blues, as well as darkened the souls of their eyes.

Knights roamed the city from the palace to the outskirts of the forest on top of their spirit hounds, eyes watching for prey like hawks on a mountain. The lower class were mere peasants, cleaning, cooking, and crafting for the city's nobility. They barely scraped by with what they had—stealing when need be. And then faced punishments worse than death to both them and their family.

There was no such thing as politeness within the cursed city. You either killed or were killed. You stole or killed those who stole. It was unwise to bring any valuables along with you outside your home for fear of being mugged or worse. Blood often ran through the streets, staining the stones a bleak red.

The only ones who had nothing to fear were those of high birth within the confinements of the Bone Castle. Those who had enough wealth or earned the queen's favor lived richly. They took what they wanted, slept with who they wanted, and killed who they wanted. Slaves were not an uncommon sight to see behind a noble, along with the bruises on their faces. Only that of royal blood had the right to wield magical weapons and runes, or to even read spell books. If a commoner were found practicing the craft, they were cast into the forest to be devoured by the demons that roamed it.

The queen sat upon the throne, the beauty of the cursed elves. With hair the color of the moons and skin the color of sapphires, Queen Ravana was one of the last true mages in the kingdoms of Veran, cast from the world due to her betrayal so many ages ago. Now, none could leave, and she was forced to rule her little kingdom alone for eternity.

None could leave… but one. She paid no mind, though; she pleased herself with watching the world above slaughter each other while she ruled from her cursed throne. She thought them all foolish creatures, including her sister Queen Arevälla, the very one who cast her into this world. The woman had the kingdom wrapped around her little finger. She never aged like Ravana, but she had no such curse placed upon her. She just refused to age. Ravana knew better to believe such stories of her being a goddess. She was using blood magic. The enchanters she had in her staff could rival the Dark Kingdom itself. The very thing the blessed elves condemned. It put a smile on the queen's face. She was not one to fall for the little queen's tricks and knew her sister too well to fall to her charms.

The queen tapped a clawed fingernail on her chair, dark blue eyes scanning the room. Black silks adorned her body, gold embroidery swirling around the edges of her skirt. A gold chest piece fit snugly against her breasts, and her diamond necklace pulsed slightly as two figures entered the throne room.

The two figures crossed into the blue torchlight and the guards stood on all sides of the throne room, fingers itching for a fight. Nexis stood slightly behind Via, who stood tall and proud, a foreboding look flashing across her face. The queen leaned on her hand and motioned for them to come forward. Via inclined, and Nexis shuffled behind her.

"I forgot how much I did not miss this place," he whispered and squealed as a guard stepped closer to him. Via sighed, and the queen cleared her throat.

"It looks as if the raven has returned from breaking free of her cage," she purred.

Via bowed slightly. "But of course. You should know as well as any other that a raven will always find her way back home... Lady Ravana."

The queen's eyes slit, and her smirk dropped. She sat up straight and flicked her hand. The guards walked toward the two. "Take the blessed elf to the hallway. I wish to speak with her in private."

Via grabbed Nexis' arm and gave a challenging glare to the guards, her other hand gripping the dagger on her belt. "He stays, or we leave, and I cut you all down along the way," she threatened.

The queen laughed coldly, her voice bouncing off the stone pillars of the room. "You're the one who has come into my kingdom, little bird. I do not need your assistance as you do mine. He may stay, but his mouth will be kept shut. Or I shall find a better purpose for it," she purred, earning a blush from the elf. The guards bowed and left the room, leaving only the three of them. Via's hand dropped from his arm, and she took a step forward.

"It has been many years, *Aretove*. How does your son fare?" she asked. The queen's lip turned up as she adjusted herself on the throne, pulling part of her skirt away from her leg, and watched as the blessed elf's eyes roamed her body.

"As well as any boy trapped within the cursed city for eternity could be. But that blessed elf keeps him occupied most nights," she said, tapping her finger on her bottom lip.

Nexis' eyes widened slightly. "Lady Laerdya! She lives?" he asked. The queen sent a feral look toward the elf, and he sunk further behind the spymaster.

"Yes. I see that your raven has not been so... forthcoming," she clucked.

Via shifted on her feet. "Her survival has nothing to do with why we are here," she retorted.

The queen shrugged and looked past the two elves towards the door. "I must admit I missed having you by my side, Raven," she said with a hint of disappointment before returning to her usual stoic posture. "You should have stayed."

Via put her hands behind her back and tilted her head up. "I do not follow the Dark Kingdom, and if I remember correctly, you betrayed your kin to them," she argued, her eyes flickering in the torchlight.

The queen chuckled and licked her lips. "I do not choose sides, little bird. I chose what was best for our people. Areválla was the one that led to the downfall of our kind. Now we are reduced to ash and bone while the mundane slaughter themselves over our land. Or had you forgotten such things in your absence?" she asked slowly, reading the way the spymaster picked at her nails. *She is nervous*, she thought.

"I am quite aware of the downfall of the elven kingdoms. But you, Ravana, played your part in killing them as well."

The queen knitted her fingers together on her lap, a fire dancing within her eyes. "I am not the only one playing games here, am I?" she smiled. Ravana stood up off her throne and stepped down from her perch.

"What is it you really want, hmm? Not to come visit your *dear* queen, I know that. Have you come to collect the child? Bring her back to the waking world? You wound me greatly." She ran a finger down Via's stomach, to the scar that rested above her pelvis.

Via quickly grabbed her hand, her eyes piercing through her. "I have not come for Laerdya. We have come to speak of more pressing issues," she said. The queen pulled her hand back and turned away, walking about the room while listening to the Raven.

"We need a shadow ward in order to assassinate a maleficarum within the Dark Kingdom," Via said.

The queen rubbed her hands together. "Why should I help you?"

Via crossed her arms. "Because with enough power from these maleficarum, they may have the ability to destroy the portal without the queen's key. Then you will be face to face with the army of dead and corrupted," she said.

The queen's lip turned up, her eyes scanning the carvings engraved on the walls of the room. "You seem to believe that they would reach the city without being killed first."

"I'm not as foolish as you think I am. And you are not as clever as you think you are," Via started, "We both know that you do not have the numbers to defend against the Dark Kingdom alone."

Ravana clicked her tongue and tapped her heel on the floor. "And if I give you this rune, what will you give me in exchange?" she asked, turning back to the visitors.

"What is it you want?"

Ravana's gaze fell upon the man with pale skin and sun-kissed hair.

How long it had been since she had seen such a man? A clawed finger came up to point to the hedgewitch. "I want him."

"No."

Nexis took hold of Via's shoulder, and her hands twitched.

"Then you shall have no ward. Go ask the golden queen for one, oh wait..." she laughed and put her hand down.

"Via," Nexis warned.

She shook her head. "Why do you want him? You hate the blessed elves," she hissed.

The queen climbed the steps towards her throne and turned, looking down at her guests. "He has knowledge that I do not. If I tire of him, I shall return him. He will not be harmed in my care. You have my word. Do you accept?" she asked.

Via opened her mouth, but Nexis beat her to it. "I accept," he said. Ravana watched as Via's face twisted into fury as the blessed elf stepped away from her.

The queen hummed in anticipation. "Very well," she nodded.

Via turned towards Nexis. "Do not do this, Nexis!" she hissed.

He gave her a disheartened smile. "Take this. I will gladly stay here to ensure the life of my people," he said and handed her the key to the portal. The queen walked towards the two of them and ran a hand down the blessed elves' chest, then raised her hand towards Via.

"*Nocturnium.*" A pulse of power rang through the room as the blue flame rose from her palm, and with a burst of light, four runestones appeared.

"Here are four. If you need more, only ask, and you shall receive. I believe this meeting is concluded," she sang and dragged Nexis along with her out of the throne room. With one more glance back, she watched as the Raven fell to her knees.

12 THYMAS

Within the thawing plains of Viragrad, Prince Thymas followed a trail of muddy snowprints past the city walls of WhiteDrove and beyond the eyes of the keep. It was not difficult to find the young girl of ten who sat alone, perched on top of a large boulder, fur wrapped heavily around her petite frame, shielding her from the still bitter morning air. Papers were scattered across the base of the rock with quick sketches of flowers and deer. Small ink-stained fingers slid across a page with angelic fluidity. Swirls of black and gray flowed along the paper, forming clouds and mountains. The girl hummed a soft tune to herself as she drew, casually wiping her face and smudging black ink across a cheek.

When the wolves howl to the sky
A new song is born, through snow and ice
a child of frost awakens in the night
bringing peace and prosperity
along with threads of silk and gold
The child of frost will lead the lone wolf home

"Now, where did you learn such a song?" Thymas asked, coming up beside the child. His dark, curly hair blew in front of his eyes as the wind swept across the thawing sea. She looked up and took off her fur hood. A smile lit her face as her brother sat down beside her, picking up a sketch of a wolf.

"I learned it from the wolves," she mumbled, still humming to herself.

Thymas glanced down at his sister's face and wiped the ink from her cheek. "Is that so? Which wolves taught you that?"

She looked back down at her paper and folded a piece of sun-kissed hair behind a pointed ear. "Fang and Shade," she sang.

Thymas raised an eyebrow and smiled slightly, tapping her ear. "The wolf gods? You must be truly blessed to have those tricksters talk to you," he said teasingly, taking one of her sketches.

She set her painting down and huffed slightly. "They are not tricksters. They are just... misunderstood," she retorted and took the wolf sketch from his hands.

"Of course. They only shape-shift into men to lure unsuspecting girls to their deaths," he said, earning a glare from the princess.

She hugged the paper to her chest. "Fang is a girl— "Anya snapped, "—and they are more than that... I trust them."

Thymas jumped from the rock and held his hands up. "Trusting them will get you killed," he scoffed. "Alright, come along. Let's get you home. It's still frigid outside, and I don't need Mother scolding me for letting you fall ill again."

She let him take her from the rock and collected the papers. Flipping through the tanned sheets of parchment, he was slightly amazed at her artistic ability. *Perhaps I should get her a tutor*, he thought.

As they walked home, he kept a steady grip on the young girl so she didn't slip and fall in the mud. He wished she would stay closer to the city than she tended to.

WhiteDrove itself was confined within white plains of ice and snow, just above the reaches of the Dark Kingdom. It was not a place for one used to temperatures above freezing and could reach a warming temperature on a good day in the summer, but stay well below freezing at night. The kingdom was known for its beautiful landscapes and views of the Frozen Sea. Summer allowed many things to thaw, and one could see the true beauty of the Winter Plains and droplets of water that clung to the blades of grass. But winter was harsh and brutal. Most wouldn't dare leave the main city without fear of being lost in a snowstorm. A fear Anya did not seem to have.

The Plains were not welcoming, from wild boar to bears to wolves that hunted sheep. Not including the forests that spanned the northern part of the country. It seemed that every time he sent guards out with her, they lost sight of her within the hour.

As they approached the city, Thymas pulled Anya's hood back over her head, and she squeaked in protest. Anya was a half-elf. Not having every quality of the blessed elves, but still having a slight point to her ear and bright, wide eyes. Few knew of the princess's lineage; she was not truly blooded to the crown. It was rumored the queen had found her outside the walls of the city when she was just a babe. Lady Kesanda says that she can still hear the howl of the wind that night.

Thymas had fallen in love at first sight of her. Her light hair, blue eyes, and soft, snowy skin. She had taken his heart the moment she came into their life. He had lost a brother and a sister to the chill when they were just children, and after his father had died, all hope for another heir had vanished. His mother had refused to remarry, claiming that she was too old for such trivialities. Now he had something to look after. Anya was a sweet child—he would do anything to keep her safe.

It didn't mean there still weren't troubles around the keep. Half-elves were looked down upon with disdain across the continent. Creatures of mixed blood were often mistreated. Cast out by both humans and elves; they were left to fend for themselves in the cities or wilderness. It had taken many years to get the people of WhiteDrove to accept the young half-elf as part of the royal line.

They entered the gates to the farms as chickens passed by, clucking as dogs herded them toward their pens. Farmers began pulling their stores of seeds from sheds and charting their crops. Their boots squished against the muddy ground, and Thymas pondered how long it would be till the next hunting season could be called. The last winter was not long, but it was cold. They had more trouble finding game this year than any previous he could remember. The wind that came from the Frozen Sea carried a baleful tune.

The city itself was small, no larger than a village, with wooden houses and hoof stock running about. The walls around the city were rotting and breaking, standing no taller than the houses themselves. Only the keep was made of stone that stayed colder than it should. And fires were roaring through the summer seasons and on. The people here were used to such things; they held pride in their kingdom—and their future king.

Anya leaned against her brother's arm, and he bumped her away, earning a laugh. He bolted away before she could respond with her own bump, and the two sprinted down the farms and towards the city gates. They jumped past puddles and baskets of vegetables. He apologized as a farmer dropped his eggs as Anya barreled into him.

She almost had a hold of his coat before he darted away again and through a river. She paused, not wanting to get her feet wet, and went towards the main bridge instead. She crossed the wooden structure and jumped, colliding with her brother. Both went down to the ground in a fit of laughter, and papers scattered everywhere, dancing to the ground around the pair. Anya grabbed a paper from the air, turning it to face him.

"Oh, look, it's you!" she laughed. The wolf's face was smeared and contorted, showing that of a monster face with fur.

"I do not look that bad, Anya," he laughed. He pulled himself up and lifted her onto her feet. They collected the scattered papers and made their way toward the keep. The guards opened the large doors for them, and he shuffled her inside. He handed her the papers and pulled off her heavy cloak, giving it to a servant. Her boots were covered in mud and her cheeks were rosy and bright.

"Now, let's get you warm," he said, rubbing her arms. She smiled up at him, and he ruffled her hair before sending her toward her room.

"You'll be at supper tonight, right?" she asked.

"Yes, Anya. I will be there," he told. She twirled back around and hopped to her room. He watched her leave with a warm chest and heard heavy boots come up to him.

"Lord Dicesare. There is something you need to see," the voice said. He turned to his side to see Captain Mulliner coming up to him, the leader of WhiteDrove's small defense force. He had a strained look on his lined face.

"What is it?" Thymas asked. The captain bowed and looked towards the doorway. He looked at the servants, passing them with a wary eye.

"You should see for yourself."

The two made their way out of the keep and towards the back of the city. They passed several other guards, who kept curious villagers out of the way. By the looks on their faces, what awaited them was unpleasant. They let the two pass as they grabbed a child and picked him up.

"I wanna see!" he complained.

"Go back to your mother," the guard warned. He set the boy down and pushed him back towards the houses. They stopped in the shadow of a grain storage shed, and he looked down to see the mangled corpse of a dog. Its entire stomach was ripped open, and the protruding intestines were charred black. The claw marks on its skin were still oozing black blood, and the snout of the body was covered in writhing maggots.

"What killed it?" Thymas asked. The captain bent down and touched a piece of the scorched intestine. It nearly collapsed under the pressure of his finger.

"Nothing that we have ever seen," he said. "It could be a demon."

"A demon this far north?" Thymas asked. He prodded the dog with his foot, and its eye fell from its socket, dropping to the ground in a tuff of dirt.

"We haven't seen one this far north in ages. But nothing else could make these marks. It has to be." The captain stood up and turned to his lord. "What do you command?"

Thymas looked at the dog, then at the captain, contemplating. "Burn it. Make sure it does not rise from the dead. And speak nothing to anyone but the soldiers under your command. We don't need to cause a panic. And find the beast that did this."

"As you say, prince," the captain bowed. He stepped away, and Thymas stared at the decaying dog. This did not bode well for WhiteDrove. If demons had made it this far north, that meant their masters were not far behind.

13 TALIA

Down on the southern coast of the continent, surrounded by a peninsula of water, the princess of Yalirea looked out over her balcony, watching the waves crash against the stone. Her thoughts were flowing through her mind like the wind through her veil. Her brother had not returned her letter. He was supposed to write as soon as he was in Ignis. She had pestered the messengers several times over the day to see if any word had come from Valek. But yet, nothing had come from either her brother nor the city itself. A ball of worry and stress filled her chest. No messenger that went to Ignis before or after her brother had returned. It had been days since the last letter came through. Her father, King Farvell, seemed not to care, but his eyes showed tension, as well as the lines that marked his face.

"Milady, you have been out here for hours. Perhaps you wish to eat something?" a court maiden named Lia said, coming up to the lone princess, an expression of concern flashing across her face. Talia did not waver from her gaze. She listened to the soothing crashes of the waves and the sweet scent of saltwater. Part of her wondered what would happen if she jumped. Would the ocean consume her like the salt from the mountain, dissolve her into its own being? Or would she simply hit the rocks, impaling herself on a dark spear?

These thoughts were for later. She finally acknowledged the court maiden beside her. Then with a slight glance and a wave of her hand, she dismissed her worries. "I will eat once I have word from my brother. Not until then," she said.

The court maiden calmly grasped her lady's fingers. "It takes time for couriers to come. I'm sure they are only delayed. When you get the letter, you shall want enough strength to read it, will you not? At least have some tea and grapes, princess," she insisted. Talia sighed and complied with her servant's commands. She turned and went inside, sitting down at her glass table. She still held a steady gaze towards the ocean as the maiden brought in the tea and grapes.

"I'm sure your brother will arrive shortly," she said with a courteous curtsy. Talia nodded and motioned for her to leave. As the door closed, Talia picked up a grape and squeezed it till the juices flowed down her hand. She liked Lia. She was the closest thing she had to a friend in Rosus. There was always something she liked about her, whether that be her personality, charm, or charisma. The only thing she didn't like about her was one simple fact.

She was a terrible liar.

That evening, a merchant ship from Nishiri arrived, and it was Talia's duty to greet them. In normal circumstances, an ambassador or the prince would be the one to greet them, but her father had holed up in his study and refused to send an ambassador at all.

Rosus, the capital of Yalirea, was home to the largest port on the continent and imported many goods from across the seas. Fruit and grain were its chief export, along with exotic wines and cheeses; the best Veran had to taste. Foreign dignitaries often spent their days enjoying the ocean breeze and festivals of wine and music before traveling to Fira to speak with the emperor. The trading tunnels that ran below the city were used so as to not disturb the streets above with carts and wagons. Though, some tunnels could lead to unpleasant circumstances. Talia knew it would not end well if there was no one of higher rank to greet their most generous trading partners, so she poised herself, took a long breath, and pushed away any thought of her brother.

She waited by the port, barely able to make out the massive ship in the setting sunlight. The veil over her eyes made it easy to hide the puffy redness of them, and she knitted her fingers together, her dark curls kissing her cheeks. Soon the ship arrived in port and began making its preparations for docking. Two guards walked beside Talia as she made her way down the wooden dock and stopped at the gangway. Several large crates were being hauled from the ship by the stevedores, the insignia of a lion's head adorning each one. Each container was marked and counted before being transported into the tunnels below the city.

The chilly wind blew through Talia's dress, and she carefully pulled the shawl she was wearing further up her shoulders. Two figures soon emerged from the ship and stepped down the gangway: a man and a woman. The woman was tall and slender with deep dark skin and dreads that were braided down her back. The man was heavyset and with a shaved head and a menacing look in his dark eyes. They both wore white lion pelts draped around their shoulders and spears sheathed upon their backs.

They stopped in front of her and gave a polite bow.

"I was expecting the prince, not the princess," the woman said, looking Talia up and down.

The man beside her cocked his head. "I don't mind, Talahe. As long as it is not that stuffy old man 'ambassador' again."

"Ha! Yes, he was a scared puppy, whimpering and shivering from fright."

Talia forced a smile. "We welcome you to our shores. The Nishiri Empire has long been a trading partner and friend to the Veranese people. There have been some… troubling developments in the other kingdoms as of late, but fear not, the road to Fira will be well guarded for your supplies," Talia said. She glanced over at the abundant number of crates sitting on the dock. If the Nishiri Empire were ever to stop trading with Yalirea, it would mean economic disaster. She had never had the opportunity to greet the merchants before now, and she feared one wrong word could send them back on their way out of their ports.

"If we were so worried about such a thing as bandits and monsters, we would have made port on the Silver Coast. We fear no man who may try to take our things, princess. Though your concern is cute."

Cute? That is one way of putting it. "We can send the shipments through the portals instead of the roads, just to make sure. If any cargo is displaced, the crown will reimburse the Empire. Does that sound suitable?"

The two glanced at each other, and Talia hoped they could not see the sweat gathered on her face. The portal could be the best way to ensure the shipment made its way to its intended location. Though if any were destined for Ignis, that would be a problem. A problem she could solve.

"As you say, princess. We brought a gift for the king as well, but it may be better suited for you." He motioned for the man to come and handed her a small wooden box. She carefully opened it to see an exquisite amber necklace resting on a purple silk cloth. "These were harvested straight from the Amber Sea, and worth quite a fortune. You can wear it or sell it, I do not care, as long as the commerce is flowing."

Talia touched the delicate stones on the necklace and closed the lid, handing it over to a guard. "Thank you. I will take great care in wearing it. Now I assume you must be weary from your long voyage. Perhaps you two would like to stay in the palace for refreshments?"

The man and woman spoke to themselves quickly in a foreign tongue before the man looked over to the stevedores and snapped at them. He then turned to her.

"I could take some of your wine, princess," he agreed. With a small breath, Talia led them toward the palace. All was right at the moment. Now she just needed to make sure her father did not fumble next.

14 ROSE

The crunching of snow beneath her feet left her frozen and grimacing in pain. Holding her chest with her hand, she could feel the blood pulsing through it. She took a ragged breath and pushed herself forward.

Rose could barely remember how she had come into the snowy wilderness. She only remembered the agony of having a demon rip into her abdomen. Red coated the white ground as Rose lost her footing. She caught herself with her free hand and watched as blood poured from her mouth.

She would die here.

Why had her sister betrayed her so? She let the very things that murdered their mother into the castle. She couldn't fathom why.

Had her sister hated her? Had the crown upon her head caused such madness within her sister to lead to the death of her kingdom? She didn't believe it. Enara would never do such a thing. At least, that's what she told herself.

Suddenly, the ground beneath her shook. She felt the tremble of the earth and heard the neighing of horses. She felt panic overcome her as she looked for a place to hide, but the white landscape left nothing for her to cower behind. At least now, maybe her death would come sooner. She forced herself up on two feet and wobbled as the horses drew near. Her vision could barely make out the figures riding the beasts. She blinked and forced her vision to focus.

Six riders circled her, trapping her in a ring of their horses. They wore thick fur and leathers, covered head to toe in studded armor. Their war cries carried to her ears, and she could see the shields strapped to their backs. The horses backed up slightly, and the riders stopped, facing her. Rose watched as a woman in front of her dismounted and walked up to her.

She was tall, two feet above Rose, at least. The male riders were taller. Her cloak was covered in painted runes and lettering in a language foreign to her. Her dark hair was braided down her back, and her blue eyes locked onto her green ones. The midnight paint across her face made the pale of her skin pop.

"*Feh, ophae tei?*" she spoke. Rose looked at her quizzingly. She was not familiar with the spoken language. She had not heard it in any of her studies—at least the ones she attended.

Rose tried to stand as tall as she could. "I am Rosellena Victoria GoldThorn, Queen of Auratus," she said in a demanding tone. She grimaced at her chest, and the woman looked down at the blood pooling around her feet.

She laughed and motioned as a man came forward, the same blue paint across his face. His hair was braided in several sections down his back, along with his beard. His eyes scanned her trembling form.

"*Fo cel waz rah,*" the man said with a small smile. The woman nodded and turned back to Rose.

"What are you doing in our territory, lowlander?" she asked, her accent heavy.

"So, you do speak Common," Rose said.

The woman scowled. "I will not ask again."

Rose felt a lump form in her throat. "I... am uncertain," she answered truthfully. "I ended up here after my kingdom was sacked."

The man beside her chortled. "You, from the lowlands, made it across the Frozen Sea with that wound?" he asked.

Rose nodded.

"You take us for fools then," the woman said. She turned away and mounted her horse.

"*Rofeh tei,*" she said. Two men grabbed onto Rose's arms, and she fought against them.

"What are you doing!?" she cried.

"You are coming with us to *Rolheim*. We shall see if you are a spy," she said and turned. Rose was forced onto a saddle in front of the man who had eyed her before. He covered her shaking form with bear skin and started forward with the rest of the group. Tears crystallized in Rose's eyes as she knew she could never see her homeland again.

"I am no spy," Rose pleaded to the man behind her. "You must believe me."

The man stayed silent; his eyes trained ahead.

"Stay quiet, child, or you will be thrown to the wolves," the woman said in front of her.

Rose glared at her. "I am not a child."

"Then why do you look like one?"

"You are massive. How do I *not* look like one?" she argued and bent over in pain with a hiss. The man gripped hold of her and pushed her back upright. "Who are you?"

The woman strode back beside the horse. "My name is Nadahi of the Tribe of the Wolf," she announced.

"Tribe of the Wolf?" Rose asked.

The woman snorted. "For a spy, you know little."

"Because I am not a spy!" Rose countered. The woman ignored her and rode to the front of the party as they continued across the frozen land. She could barely make out shrubbery within the white blankets of snow; the trees curved under the weight. Tracks of horses and small animals littered the area, and Rose covered her reddened nose to keep warm.

As the party made its way through the snowy terrain, Rose turned her face up to the sky. The clouds that blocked the sun wavered in shades of black and gray—an unease set in the wind as it howled against her ears. The frigid cold was more than just a casualty of winter; it echoed something far forgotten. It whispered in her ears and crawled through her skin. There was something there. And it called to her like a siren in the sea.

Rose spotted a wolf casually following the party, occasionally stopping to look at her, then disappearing into the frozen waste. Nadahi spoke something in her language towards the wolf and it seemed to understand her. *This place feels wrong. These people feel wrong,* she thought.

The party eventually came to a halt in front of large wooden doors to a gated fence. The doors were covered in runes and carvings of wolves and hunters. She could not guess what they meant.

Nadahi whistled, and the doors opened, allowing them access through the large fence. The party entered the settlement, and Rose's eyes wandered around the village. Men and women who all bore face paint and leather traded furs, secured horses, and mended swords. The houses were carved from trees and grass, and the children there were nearly her height. They bore no markings, though, as they ran around the village with toy horses and wooden swords. The guards held hatches and shields as they walked the village and atop the walls; they seemed unfazed by the brutal cold.

The townspeople looked at Rose with bewildered eyes. She folded into herself as she held her chest. The cold helped numb the pain somewhat, and she chose to be thankful instead of worried.

The party stopped in front of the steps of a massive wooden building. Carved statues of a woman stood protection in front of the building. The statue wore no clothes and held a pot in one hand, the other reaching out to where a large fire was burning. Rose almost seemed to recognize the woman. She could not place her face, but something in the back of her mind tingled as she looked at it.

The man hopped from the horse and pulled Rose down with ease. The woman dismounted and walked over to her, taking her arm.

"What is it now?" Rose asked.

Nadahi looked at her amusedly. "I am taking you to the mother healer. You are no good to us dead little spy."

Rose groaned as she led her away from the party and down a dirt pathway further into the village.

"Where are we?" Rose asked, looking at several children painting their faces with berries and chasing each other around.

"*Rolheim*, home to the Tribe of the Wolf," she answered.

They passed women hanging laundry on poles and men sharpening blades. A group of young girls was amassed around a loom; all taking turns weaving the threads through. They glanced at her as they passed and whispered to themselves.

"They wonder why you are not with them," Nadahi said, amusement clear in her voice.

"Why?"

"Because you look like them."

"Are you having fun taunting me?" she asked angrily. The woman did not respond, but the smirk on her lips gave her the answer she needed. If her head wasn't so foggy from her wounds, she would wipe that smirk from her face.

She led Rose further down the street to a small shack. Nadahi knocked twice and spoke in their native tongue. A woman soon answered the door. The woman looked at Rose with an indescribable gaze. She eyed her up and down before finally resting on her ruby. She took Rose's hand and shooed the other woman away with a word.

"But mother—"

The woman shushed her. "I will have no one in here while I heal the lass. I will send her your way once she is healthy," she said. Nadahi made a face but left, leaving the two of them alone.

Rose was forced onto a cot as the mother ran around the hut, grabbing various jars and bandages. The woman wore a beautifully crafted raven feather headdress that blended with her dark brown hair. The many hides that covered her were dyed purple and blue. The hut smelled of herbal remedies. There was a small cooking pot in the center of the room on a large fire, and various jars and bowl stacked on shelves and tables. Dried herbs and animal pelts hung from around the windows. Rose could only assume the mother was an enchanter. As the woman neared Rose, she shifted back. The woman sat the jars and bandages on the counter beside them and grabbed Rose's dress.

"Hey! What are you—"

The mother shushed her and took a knife, gently cutting through the fabric and peeling it from her wound. Rose hissed and dug her hands into the cot.

"I'm no spy. I don't know how many times I must tell them," she pouted. The woman smiled and set the knife down, helping Rose from the garment.

"I know you are no spy," the woman said with a heavy accent.

Rose perked up and resisted the urge to cover herself up with her hands. "Then you believe me?" she asked.

The woman pointed to the ruby around her neck. "That is how I know," she said. Rose looked down at the jewel sitting in the valley of her breasts. A slight red glow faded in and out through the stone, and the woman exclaimed, "You are a *Runa*." She scooped her hand into a yellow jar and spread the cool ointment over the wound. "You would not have survived your wounds if not."

"*Runa*? I'm not familiar with the term," Rose said.

"A *Runa* is a child of the Mother Goddess. Born of magic and light. She birthed them from Her womb to cleanse the world of darkness."

Rose scoffed and grimaced at her wound. "You're mad."

The woman gave Rose a curious glance before starting to bandage her chest. "Her own child does not believe in Her?"

"I knew my mother. She was no goddess," Rose refuted.

"We all have a mother, *Runa*, but we all have a beginning mother as well. She gave our ancestors life so they could birth us."

"Then you're saying the mages, *Runa*, came from this goddess? There is only one goddess," Rose argued.

"The Mother Goddess takes all forms within the land and sky. She takes many names around Her heavenly sphere. The goddess you worship is no different from ours. You may be wary of Her now, but you cannot deny the fate She has given to you."

"And what is this fate? You've kidnapped me, thinking I'm a spy. If my fate is to rot in a dungeon, then I wish to refute said fate," Rose groaned angrily.

The woman tied the bandage and stood up, walking to the fire. "Your fate does not lie in a dungeon. It is to defeat the Forsaken and destroy the False God."

"No. No more tales! I must return home!" Rose argued. "I cannot stay here! Find someone else."

The woman pulled a stack of sheepskin from a wardrobe and set them next to Rose. "We cannot decide the will of the gods, only to travel down the path they have chosen for us." She turned away from Rose and went towards the door. "Dress. I shall speak with the Chieftain about your arrival. Meet me in the Great Hall when you are able."

With that, she left the hut, and Rose took the skin from beside her, running her hands through the thick hide.

"Oh, Velara, what path have you put me on."

Rose exited the hut; the furs wrapped tightly around her person. The bandages were tight against her skin, but the salve had lessened the pain considerably. Even with the extra layers, she was shaking from the cold. She hated it here. It was windy and wet and terrible.

She started down the dirt path, watching the people come and go, some turning to look at her with oddity, others moving out of her way. Dogs barked at her as she walked by, and she hurried on her way.

She reached what she could only assume was the Great Hall, with the statue looking down at her. It towered over the other buildings and hung dyed drapery along the walls. Rose took a breath and climbed the stairs towards the heavy oak doors. Two men bearing axes and shields allowed her inside, and when she entered the hall, she noticed a man sitting on a carved wooden throne.

The hall was long and held up by knotted wooden pillars. A large fire crackled in the center of the room, and deer pelts littered the floor. She noticed a white wolf laying in front of the fire, and it lifted its head at her as she neared. The woman who had taken her here, Nadahi, was standing in front of the throne with the elder mother. They were jabbering quickly in their native tongue, but Rose could make out the word *"Runa"* within the conversation. The man on the throne laughed heartily. He wore snowy white pelts with a wolf's head strung over his shoulder. He was laid back on his throne, tapping his hand against the armrest. His beard was long and braided, the same color as the huntress. A sword was laid against the throne, its engravings shining in the firelight. Rose could only assume this was the chieftain. All eyes turned to her as she mounted the steps carefully.

"Who are you, girl?" the chieftain asked in her language.

Rose stood up straight. "I am Rosellena GoldThorn, heir to Ignis and the Kingdom of Auratus," she said.

The man rested his chin on his hand, a smirk rising. "A lowlander? And a royal one at that. This must be a trick from the Goddess," he snorted.

"I am not to be laughed at. I will return home!" Rose yelled.

The chief abruptly stood up, walking toward Rose, who moved away.

"Father," Nadahi called, trying to grab his arm. She was thrown from his way and stood face-to-face with the young queen. Rose had to look straight up to see his eyes and his smirk.

"You are either mad or courageous for raising your voice to me, young spy," he said.

"I am not a spy! How many times must I tell you for you to get that through your thick skull!" she retorted. All eyes widened and turned to the chieftain, who only laughed.

"Yes, good," he said and turned away. Nadahi looked at Rose and shook her head.

"Take her to the square. We shall execute her and send her head back to the Forsaken," he ordered.

Rose screamed and backed up. "No! you can't do this!"

Two guards grabbed her arms and dragged her through the room. The mother healer pleaded with the chieftain as he grabbed the sword from his throne. Nadahi spoke quickly with her father in her tongue, seeming to plead as well.

"Please do not do this! I must return home! My kingdom is in danger!" Rose cried. The guards pulled her further from the throne and opened the door to the outside. Tears streamed down her face as the ruby began to burn against her skin.

"I said, *release me!*" she screamed. A sudden wave of red exploded through the room. The pillars beside Rose ruptured on impact and sent splinters flying. The ceiling shattered above her and fell to the floor around them. The guards were thrown from Rose and splattered across the walls with heavy wet *thunks.*

Rose fell to her knees as red waves flickered across her hands. Murmurs turned to gasps as everyone fled from the rubble. The elder mother seemed smug as the chief's face grew pale. Rose looked up at the chieftain, eyes alight with flame. He sheathed his sword with a heavy sigh.

"Then the battle of winter shall finally come to an end."

15 JARED

Blood trailed casually down Jared's scarred arm as his hand went up to press down on the wound. His muddy boots slugged through the rough forest terrain and stumbled as they hit roots.

Jared tripped and crashed against the ground, pebbles and twigs jamming into his sides. He muttered a curse and forced himself onto his knees. He moved his foot under him with a weak breath and pushed himself up. His shirt was torn, the worst being on the front, where large slashes had split the thin fabric. His chest was painted in dried blood, crusted, and pulsing with every breath he took. He had no potions nor any wraps to cover his wounds. His best guess was that death waited for him within hours. He had escaped the clutches of a Dark Knight by a scant few seconds. He had evaded several killing blows but took a harsh slash to the chest and arm. If the Knight wanted, they could easily follow the blood trail to him.

He didn't mind death. He wasn't scared of it. But he was scared for *her*. Had she survived? Or had she fallen victim to the claws of a demon?

Olivia.

He fell to his knees once again and rested on the trunk of a tree, laying his head back with another raspy breath. He had welcomed death the day she had found him in the street, soaked to the bone and starving. She had given him shelter in her own home, fed him, and clothed him. He would never forget that day in the rain.

How her locks stuck to her face and shoulders, her white blouse soaked and see-through. Her ruffled purple skirt was pulled up just enough to show the bare hint of her tan legs. She was the most beautiful thing he had seen. But his torment of bandits and thugs had jaded his mind. He had to find her. He never was good at having a family or friends. His only family had been killed in front of him—no. Olivia was his family, and he'd be damned if he let anything happen to her. By the goddess, if they had hurt her, he would hunt them down one by one.

And then Rose. He knew she was dead, yet another failure on his part to protect his friends.

Jared rolled out his shoulder and stopped when he heard the snap of a bow. He darted to the side, and the arrow lodged into the tree not a foot from his head. He fell back onto his backside and cursed.

"Oh, for fuck's sake." He turned his head and came face to face with an arrowhead.

"Identify yourself," a voice said. Jared went cross-eyed, looking at the arrow, and opened his mouth.

"You know it's not polite to point sharp objects at strangers," he said. The arrow drew down, and he looked up at the owner.

A woman stood before him, quiver strung over her back, dagger hanging from a worn leather belt. Her clothing was threadbare and tarnished from the weather, and a dark green cloak was cast around her back, her hood hiding most of her face. Amber eyes met honey ones as she shifted her gaze to his arm.

"You reek of death and blood. Did you run into a boar?" she asked. Jared scoffed and attempted to stand before being pushed back down by the woman. "I sense fire in the distance. Did you cause it?" she questioned again, and he groaned.

"No, I didn't. It was the Dark Knights, you know, black armor, magical mist shit coming off them?" he said.

The woman's lip curled downwards. "The city, that is what's burning?" she asked and shook her head when he nodded in reply. "Curse the fools who play a part in this war." She slung the bow over her shoulder. She bent down and grabbed his arm, looking at the wound. Her braided copper hair fell in front of her round eyes. "Tell me your name?"

She gently touched the pulsing slash on his arm. Jared grimaced and tore his sleeve open to get a better view.

"It's Jared. Yours?"

She paused and looked at him, curiously examining his face.

"Nava," she said, her accent showing through. Jared raised an eyebrow as she pushed a brown strand from her face.

"You're a half-elf," he acknowledged.

She glanced at him, then took a bandage from her pouch and dressed his wound. She tied it forcefully, earning a hiss from the man. "You know this how?" she questioned.

"Your accent. When you speak in the Common Tongue, it's hard to tell, but when you said your name, you gave away the elvish accent. I'm guessing you were raised by elves then?" he asked. She shot him a glare and stood up, forcing him up with her.

"You are very perceptive, swordsman," she said.

It was his turn to give her a look. "How'd you know I was a swordsman?"

She sighed, and Jared glanced at her pointed ears within the hood.

"Your right hand is calloused where your left is not, and your arms hold more strength than your legs," she said, and he smirked.

"It seems I'm not the only perceptive one here."

She huffed out a laugh and started walking.

"Hey, wait. Where are you going?" he asked. She turned to him, eyes slightly glowing in the dimming light of the sky.

"I wrapped your wound and told you my name. You are of no use to me. I am continuing my journey to Fira."

"Why Fira?"

She sighed and pulled down her hood. "I am searching for a personal piece and wish to reclaim it. Now leave me alone."

"I'll come with you. I'm looking for a woman. Dark, curly hair, tanned skin, looks like a bard. She may have gone to Fira as well," he said and stepped closer to the half-elf. She eyed him warily.

"Go yourself. I'm sure you can find a caravan to take you there."

"Go on the road? Did you not listen when I told you of the Dark Knights? They'll head to WhiteDrove next, if not the elven kingdoms. Taking the road is not an option for me. I'm coming along."

"And I want nothing to do with it. They may fight against each other all they like," she retorted.

Jared took another step. "Look, I don't even have a weapon. I-I'll tell you what, you get me to the next town, and I'll be off your back," he pleaded. Nava groaned and shifted her belt.

"The next town is days away. Fira is more than a month by foot. What more do you expect from me?" she asked harshly.

"Well, food for one. I'm not a hunter like you. I'm a blacksmith's son. Just help me reach the next town, and I will give you all the *sephim*

I have."

He watched as her eyes trailed down his body, then she bit her lip, seeming to contemplate. Finally, she released a wary sigh.

"Come, it will be dark soon, and these woods are dangerous at night."

A small smile spread across his lips, and Jared slouched. "Thank the goddess," he whispered and ran to catch up with the young archer.

16 LAERDYA

A girl of fifteen sat alone within the safe confinements of the library within the Bone Castle of Nevrak, books stacked high around her as she flipped through the page of a tome on spirits and demons. Silver eyes scanned the course pages as a wisp of a smile graced her lips. Her complexion was soft and light, and her eyes were bright and wide, making her a fascinating sight to other elves around her. Her snowy hair fell down her shoulders, graced to her by her mother, and her hands were delicate and smooth as they ran down the carefully inked pages.

"Once, long ago, there was a demon so powerful, he conquered the Otherworld. Born of hate and greed, his wrath spread across the world, tainting it in darkened light. His jaws reached up from the ground and consumed the moon, spitting it back out in two broken pieces to litter the star-struck sky. Only those of benevolent hearts could escape his bloody clutches, banishing him back to the Otherworld. But one day this beast shall return to claim the world above, and the light shall cast its shadow upon man."

"Laerdya!" a voice called, and the hairs on the back of her neck stood on end. She closed the book and looked up as the prince strode into her sight. His smile was feral as he walked up to her and grabbed her by the arm, hoisting her up onto her feet.

"M-my lord. What may I help you with?" she asked nervously. He pushed her against the bookshelf, so her back was pressed against the binding of the tomes.

"I have a surprise for you," he said. Laerdya bit her lip. His white hair invaded her gaze as his dark indigo fingers wrapped around her neck.

"And... what would that be, my lord?" she asked.

Elmaer tugged forcefully on her hair as he kissed her, pulling up her dress and groping her thigh. She flinched in pain as his teeth grazed her lips. "You want me, don't you? A sweet surprise to greet you in the middle of your frivolous studies. You enjoy my company, right?" He pulled her hair back, and she cried out.

"Wha-whatever pleases you, my lord," she cried.

He licked her ear and wiped a tear away with his free hand. "Your father would have kept you away from the world, from me. This is his punishment," he grabbed her face, and she bit her tongue to keep from crying out. "You are mine forever," he growled.

"Of course, my lord. I beg your forgiveness," she gasped. He tore her top and released her. She fell to the ground and covered her breasts with her hands. Elmaer fixed himself and turned away.

"Make sure to come to bed early tonight. I need to be up by brightening tomorrow," he said and walked from the library. Laerdya pulled her dress down and fixed her hair. She stood up and picked up the books scattered on the floor, placing them back on the shelf. Her head pulsed in pain, and she rubbed her jaw. Luckily, she didn't think it would leave a bruise.

She had been trapped here for years, barely old enough to remember when the cursed elf woman had taken her through the portal nearly a decade ago. She couldn't even remember what the sun looked like. Every time she looked at the sky and tried to imagine, the black void stole any memory she had.

She knew she would never leave here. She would grow old and die before Elmaer even aged a day; one of the curses placed upon the queen and her son. One that would taint her. Once she had a child, she would be useless to him. He could easily find a concubine to please himself with. Part of her wanted to die, to finally be released from this dark prison of fate. But the other part of her wanted to see the sun once more—to feel the grass beneath her feet and the cool wind of a summer morning.

She sighed and placed the last book on the shelf before padding over to her room. She passed several guards as they watched her walk down the hallway, their faces blank. They had been witness to the prince's harsh behavior before, only lifting a finger to help her back on her feet afterward. She hated this place. The only one who seemed to care for her well-being was the queen.

Queen Ravana, the woman who sealed her fate by stealing her away from her mother, her kingdom. She could barely remember her father's face, but she remembered the first sight of the Cursed City. The darkness that spread through the stone and the swirling vortex in the sky. She had screamed and cried when the cursed elf woman set her down, never to return and leaving her with the queen.

She saw the way Elmaer looked at her, having never aged a day, as she grew into a young woman. She had been betrothed to him the moment she stepped through that portal at only five years. When she had reached her twelfth name day and bled for the first time, was the first night he had come into her quarters. He had forced her to take off her clothing, showing her growing body. He had touched her that night and from every night, then on.

At the very least, the queen had given her a room to herself that she could retire to when she did not wish to see Elmaer. She would send maids to clean her wounds and make sure she ate enough to stay healthy. The elven princess knew that the queen only did it out of pity, though. Pity for the young girl sent to her son as a peace offering between the elves.

She had grown used to the dim halls of the castle; she even managed to say that she enjoyed seeing the ceiling dance with enchanted paintings. But she could never shake the tingling of magic against her skin. As if icy fingers ran down her arms and neck. The queen had expressed interest in teaching her magic, but Laerdya did not want to try. It scared her as much as the beasts that roamed the courtyard below.

Even now, she could still get lost within the castle. She felt like some hallways never ceased to expand around her. There were some she dared not go down. The dungeon scared her the most. Some nights, she could hear screams echo from the chained metal door to the darkness beyond. Not even her insatiable curiosity could make her step foot near those guards at that door.

She made her way to her room and donned a new dress, throwing the torn one out, and sat on her bed, opening a drawer beside it. She pulled an ointment from the drawer and rubbed it onto her cheek and neck. The cool mixture gave a heavenly relief of pain from her stiff muscles. She had grown addicted to the stuff, the only thing that could truly ease her pain.

She heard a knock on the door, and she set the container back in the drawer.

"You may enter," she mumbled. The door opened, and a man came in. She did not recognize him at first, but as soon as her eyes glimpsed his fair skin and soft smile, she jumped from the bed into his arms.

"By *Ethena'ethal*, Nexis," she cried.

The hedge witch held back a sob of relief and cradled the girl in his arms. "My dear Laerdya. You were so young the last time I saw you," he said and patted her hair. Her hands dug into his tunic as soft sobs wracked her body. "Hush, love. I'm here now."

"Why are you here, Nexis? Your kind are not welcome here."

He pulled away and wiped a tear from her cheek. "It seems that the queen took a liking to me as well. But no worries, my dear. I shall have you to keep me company," he said with a light smile.

Her eyes darkened slightly. "My fiancé will not appreciate another man in my presence," she said lowly.

Nexis stopped petting her head and placed a hand on her shoulder. "Your fiancé?" he questioned.

She nodded sadly and walked over to a table, pouring a glass of wine. "Yes, Lord Elmaer. Lady Ravana's son," she stated.

Nexis's smile faded from his lips as he noticed the various bruises and cuts along her arms and back. "He is not kind, is he?" he asked.

"He is not unkind. He just does not know affection as we do, I suppose. But I am still alive, and Lady Ravana is nice enough to me," she said. "She granted me permission to stroll the gardens and library whenever I so choose. It could be worse." Flashes of the slaves within the castle went through her mind. She had been locked in her room for trying to dress one's wounds. Elmaer had insisted she never even look in their direction. They were not worthy of a queen's gaze.

Sometimes she still snuck pastries from the kitchens into the slaves' quarters and conversed with the young children there. The slaves were the nicest people there; they treated her as if she was a friend, but she knew they would not come to her aid if she had fallen. They were the same as her, trapped in a life of slavery and obedience. How many times had she thought of flinging herself off the balcony of her room after a night of torture? She had come close to slitting her own throat once or twice before a guard stopped her and locked her in her room for weeks at a time.

The only time she would be occupied with something other than her escape was when Elmaer brought her jewels and dresses for her to wear. He was a strange man, possessive and ruthless one minute, then generous the next. He was just another thing that scared her about this world.

"I am glad you are here, Nexis. I don't think I could have survived much longer here without a familiar face to gaze upon," she said sadly. Nexis walked over to her and kissed her forehead.

"Your father would be proud of the woman you have become, my dear. I promise you that," he said. She looked up at him and saw the soft reflection of her father within his features. If she squinted, perhaps she could mistake him for her father.

"Father never shared stories about you and him, Nexis. You must tell me about them someday... or of my mother," she added. Nexis smiled and nodded slightly.

"Of course, my lady. It seems we shall have all the time in the world to discuss it."

Laerdya gave a heavy-hearted laugh. She felt at odds with herself about feeling happy that Nexis was trapped here with her. Why should he be subjected to the pain she endured as well? But that was not her choice to make.

They heard a knock at the door, and Laerdya pulled away from him as a slave stuck her head through.

"M'lady, the queen requests your presence in her quarters," she said. Laerdya nodded solemnly and started towards the door.

"We shall speak another time. Perhaps the library?" she asked.

Nexis bowed slightly. "Whatever you wish, princess."

17 ROSE

Rose sat outside of the Great Hall, the doors to it still hanging from their handles. She watched as men around her picked up wood and clay pieces, throwing them into piles next to the building. The ceiling had caved entirely from the explosion, and snow had suffocated the fire pit in the center. She couldn't help but feel sorrowful for what she did. She had no choice. They were going to kill her.

And for all that, she still didn't know where she was in the world. She had heard stories from her mother about thundering giants across the Frozen Sea, but even as a child, she never believed the tales. The closest to the cold she had ever gotten was WhiteDrove, and she had been there only once. But sitting there now made her rethink everything her mother had told her.

She rubbed the ruby on her neck that was still warm with magic and sighed. *I do not belong here*, she thought. *I must return home. I must save my kingdom and save Enara.* She didn't know how to sail, though, or how she would ever retake Ignis. She didn't even know if Veran still held strong or if the Dark Kingdom had slaughtered their way to Fira. She feared for them all. And mourned her sister.

And here she sat with people cleaning up her mess—and calling her *Runa.* Whatever that meant. She was not their savior. She just wanted to go home.

The snow fell in soft, fluffy pieces, attaching to her nose and cheeks. Her eyelashes felt heavy, and she pulled the fur closer to her person. These people were strange. Large and unyielding even in the bitterest of climates. She no longer wanted to see the sand dunes beyond the Amber Sea if they were the opposite of this.

Rose looked up as Nadahi came over to her and sat beside her, looking at the still-standing statue of the goddess. Her hair was pulled into one long braid down her back and the wolf skin pelt she wore around her shoulders made her appear as large as a wolf herself.

"I apologize for mistaking you for a spy, *Runa*," she said with a bow of her head.

Rose groaned and rubbed her forehead. "Please don't call me that. I'm just as confused as you are."

Nadahi smiled slightly. "The elder mother says that you are not in control of your magic."

"Was it that obvious?" Rose asked, earning a small laugh from the huntress. "My Arcane Advisor tried to teach me, but he was no mage." Rose heard a crack and a thump as wet snow fell from the broken rafters behind them onto the floor below.

"Do not worry, *Runa*. We have come to an agreement to take you to the Ruins of Astira. The Mother Goddess will teach you magic, and then we shall be able to defeat the False God," she said.

Rose rubbed her hands together as they went numb from the cold. "Ruins of Astira? What is that?"

"The Ruins are a sacred temple of the Mother Goddess deep within the Frost Mountains. We have not traveled there in many spans since the Forsaken gained strength." Her face grew dark and she glanced at the walls of the city. "Once, we would make pilgrimages there every year to give sacrifice to the Mother. She would reward us with bountiful game and years of warmer winter. She will speak with a child of Her own flesh. I know this for certain."

"So, I'm not returning home then," Rose sighed. Nadahi put a hand on her shoulder, watching the way the light reflected off her hair.

"I promise you that when we defeat the False God, we will fight with you to destroy the ones who took your land."

Rose's eyes widened as she turned to the huntress. "Certainly?" she asked. The woman nodded, and Rose smiled. She sat up and stared at the goddess statue. "Who is this False God?"

"The False God is the one who controls the tribe of the Forsaken. By breaking away from the Mother, they caused Her deep anguish. It is Her tears that fall never-ending upon these lands. They have caused a winter that has lasted for a thousand spans. The other tribes cannot see reason and have been so divided that we cannot defeat them until you came. With your magic, we have the power to unify the tribes once again and finally end this winter," she said excitedly.

Rose watched the snowflakes coat the statue and cocked her head. "You have never experienced the other seasons? Never felt the sun on your face?" she asked.

The huntress shook her head. "No. I have never been kissed by the sun before as you have," she laughed and tugged lightly on Rose's golden curls.

Rose felt heat rise to her cheeks. "I cannot imagine what that must be like. No grass. No flowering spring. I don't think I could live that way."

"It has been hard." Nadahi nodded. "But you have given us faith." She took a sword from its scabbard and laid it on her lap, trailing the inscription carved into the metal with her finger.

"What do they mean?" Rose asked.

"With each swing brings me closer to the Mother. With my death, I shall protect Her once more," she read.

Rose eyed the inscription. "Quite the oath. I can't say if many of our people have such devotion."

Nadahi huffed out a laugh. "You are small. The Goddess' blessing runs through our veins. She gives us strength and life. When my time comes, I will gladly go to Her side."

Rose shifted and watched as another plank was thrown onto a pile.

"You all seem to have much faith in me. If I told you I could barely remember the names of my own court advisors, you would not think so highly of me."

Nadahi shifted the sword on her lap so she could rest her elbows on her knees.

"You have survived a fatal wound, blown apart a building, and made my father cower in fear. I have faith in you because you do not. And seeing my father's stupefied face is worth frostbite."

Rose snorted and blew into her gloves to warm her nose. "I'll try not to disappoint everyone, then."

Nadahi stood and sheathed her sword. "Tonight, we shall feast and celebrate the new hunting season and return of the *Runa*. Try to stay close to the fires; it will get even colder at night."

"Feast?" Rose asked.

Nadahi gave a mysterious smile. "You will see."

The drums were heavy on her chest and thundered against the air. The people of the tribe stood around a blazing fire. It burned hotter and higher than any she had seen before. The smoke filled the night sky, and she could hear the howls of wolves around her.

She had been dressed in the finest of cloth, adorned with carved bones and metal talismans. The women who dressed her did not meet her eye and whispered words of reverence each time they touched her skin. She was swathed in white wolf pelts and dotted with winter rose perfume on her neck and chest. She felt queenlier here than she did at her own coronation. Instead of adoring nobles gawking at her, it was men and women with pensive expressions and bowed heads that kept their distance and kneeled before her as if she were a goddess.

Now, she stood off to the side of the sizeable crowd and crackling fire, watching as the people gathered and the mother healer walked through them up to the flames.

"Tonight, we give a blessing to the Mother for sending Her child to aid us! Tonight, we give sacrifice to Her and the warriors who protect Her. Tonight, we raise our axes to *Shor'vaker* and ready for the hunt!" she called. Rose watched as the people cheered and howled. She looked over the sea of faces but could not find any she knew.

The drums grew louder as the mother flung herbs onto the fire, and it burst with blue and purple flames. A vision of something appeared in the haze. *A face*, she thought. Chanting rose through the crowd, a woman's voice calling above them all. Even though she could not understand the language, still it spoke to her, echoing through her ears.

Several men brought over an elk by the lead. Its long antlers were woven together on its head and carved with symbols she could not read. They brought it over to the mother, and the men handed her the reins. She took the reins, and the men backed away into the crowd. The mother pointed to Rose.

"Come, child, bear witness to your mother." She spoke in Rose's tongue, and she hesitantly walked through the group of people up to the mother. As she neared the fire, she could feel the heat swell within her and sweat beaded around her forehead. All eyes were on her as she stopped beside the elk. The drums stopped, and the mother pulled a knife from her robe.

"The *Runa* gives us blessing this night. Her fire shall cleanse the souls of the damned and banish the False God to the Otherworld forever!" she shouted. A wooden bowl was brought over and placed under the elk by a young girl wearing a white robe. Rose barely had time to process what was happening before the neck of the elk was slit, and it cried out in pain. Rose watched as it fell to the ground and its blood pooled in the bowl. More herbs were thrown onto the fire, and blue smoke filled her vision. She heard something whisper to her.

Child.

The mother healer bent down and picked up the bowl, holding it out to Rose.

She looked down into the dark red liquid, and her stomach churned. She wanted to run away, to flee, but she had nowhere to go. And the venerational looks they gave her—she didn't know what they would do to her if she tried. Rose took the bowl of blood, watching the glimmer of her reflection shift in the liquid, and the mother spoke again in their tongue.

"Let the goddess see her child mark those of the Tribe of Wolf and grant her blessings upon us!" The drums picked back up, and she could feel the ground shake underneath her. The wolves howled again to the sky above, and she turned to see the chieftain walk up to her.

"*Runa,*" he said. He knelt before her and turned his face up to the sky. Rose glanced at the mother, who motioned with her hands dipping into the bowl. Rose took a breath and tried not to make a face as she put her fingers into the warm fluid.

She took her fingers out and watched as the firelight reflected off the dripping blood back into the bowl. She hesitantly brought her fingers down the Chieftain's forehead and eyes, stopping at his cheeks. He opened his eyes, lowered his head, and stood up. Rose gave an unsure glance to the mother healer, who nodded in satisfaction.

The line continued, and Rose only grew more uncomfortable as she marked each adult with the elk's blood. She could feel it pool around her feet and soak into her shoes as the night wore on. The looks they gave to her, the thanks she received. It felt like she was something more than a girl. More than a lost queen. Something she did not want to be revered as.

The ones who were marked danced and chanted around the colored flames. Their loud cries reverberated through the air as the snow began to come down in heavy white blankets.

At the end of the line stood Nadahi. Rose could not explain why her chest tightened when she stepped near and bent down, staring into her eyes. Rose shyly looked away and swirled her fingers in the now chilled blood. Nadahi closed her eyes, and Rose ran her fingers down her face. Her skin was softer than she imagined; the blood stood out against the blue running across her nose. She felt the heat come off her cheeks as she stopped and pulled her hand away. Nadahi bowed her head and whispered something Rose could not make out. She quickly stood and gave a faint smile before stepping away and back into the crowd. Rose turned to the dimming fire, and a young girl took the bowl from her hands.

"Today, we give thanks and blessings. Soon may we all feast in *Shor'vaker!*" the mother called. Howls and whoops erupted, and Rose pulled her wolf skin closer to her body. Her blood-stained hands shook against the cold. The mother threw more herbs onto the fire, and Rose watched as it turned bright green, the same as her eyes. The green flames filled her vision, streaming into her mouth and nose. She heard a voice call out to her in the haze, beckoning her forward. She saw the shadow of a woman flickering on the ground. She felt flaming hands wrap around her shoulders and touch her skin. It did not hurt her, instead feeling like being enveloped by welcoming warmth.

Find me.

The voice was distant, like an old echo.

Four there are. Four shall remain.

The woman vanished, and the hands released her. As the fire faded and her vision cleared, the drums reached a crescendo into the night sky.

18 TRISSA

Trissa held the open wound of a young girl. The gash was long and deep, black puss dripping from the injury on her stomach. Trissa knew she would not survive the day. She, like so many other children, would be buried with no headstone and forgotten by all who knew their names. She had resided in a tavern with the wounded and scared, trying her best to help the injured, and saying prayers to those who were beyond hope.

It had been only a day since the attack, and now cultists roamed the streets. The few remaining soldiers were forced to swear fealty to the new queen and the Dark Knights. The bodies of the dead were taken and burned outside the city, but she could smell the burning flesh from there. She feared for Rose. She had not seen or heard from her since and hadn't the heart to ask Enara what happened. Part of her didn't want to know.

Enara… She had run from the demons that stalked the halls and found the young woman on the balcony of one of the guest rooms, sobbing and clutching her pulsing hand. The blood that soaked the carpet had seeped into her shoes and left a trail to the balustrade. She hadn't said a word to her, only held the girl in her arms and shushed her agonizing cries.

"I did this, Trissa," she had said. "My kingdom in ruins."

And now that young woman stayed in the castle with the Dark Knights and ordered the cultists around like she was born their ruler. A thought that left a hole in the old nanny's heart.

The howls of the demons outside the tavern made her want to cry in fear. But the little girl in her arms kept her trembling silent. Trissa looked down at the dark girl's dirty face. Her soft brown eyes held terror and pain within them. Her body shook, and her small, calloused hands cradled a woven doll. Trissa held her hand with her free one and hummed softly to her.

Go to sleep, my little blossom
May your dreams be filled with light
May the goddess protect you
From the terrors of the night
Dream of hope and honey
Play with the singing trees
Follow the wisp back home
So you will come back to me
I will hold you in my arms
And sing of a place of light
For the next time you open your eyes
You will find the goddess bright
Sleep my little darling
Close your eyes and drift away
Remember that I will always be here
Keeping the terrors at bay
Sleep my little blossom
Nothing can hurt you now
Velara will come to guide you
To a place that's safe and sound

Trissa watched as the girl looked up at her, tears making clean streaks down her face.

"Momma is waitin' for me?" she asked softly.

"Yes, my darling child, now sleep," Trissa cooed. The girl smiled softly before her chest stilled moments later. Trissa closed the girl's eyes and gently laid her down. She pulled the blanket over her head with a stifled sob. She kissed the blanket and rested her forehead atop it, saying a prayer to the goddess.

The agonizing groans of those around her were too much to bear, and she lifted her head from the blanket, wiping her nose with a blood-stained hand. She picked up the small woven doll the girl had held. Her black yarn of hair was tangled and frayed. The little dress it wore was stained red, and initials were sewn into the foot. LV. Trissa held the doll as she stood up.

"Her name was Lily. She had just turned six," a healer said, walking up to her.

Trissa ran a thumb across the doll's face. "How many were lost?"

The healer wiped her hands with a cloth, not meeting her eyes. "You don't want to know—"

"How many?"

"The children had gathered around the square, lighting fireworks when the attack came. Forty and two were gone last I counted."

Forty-two children, she thought. Murdered and cast aside by cultists. Trissa clenched the doll in her hand, feeling a numbing pain spread through her chest. She quickly turned away and started for the door, stepping over the girl's body.

"Miss Trissa. Where are you going?" the healer asked.

"To teach a young lady some manners," she replied. She left the tavern, and the doll's button eyes faded into the blackness of the early morning.

19 VAREN

The Imperial Kingdom of Esai stood proud amongst the other kingdoms. Their capital city, Fira, was the heart of the continent. It was something to behold with thick stone walls that reached the heavens and towering spires of libraries. Built on the ancient ruins of the once elven temple Kildan, it still held some of the magic within its foundations.

Many were born of magic here—though few ever mastered it. The College of Enchanters rested in the middle of the city, where the magical advisors to the kings and queens studied and learned their craft.

The city itself held over a million inhabitants, with many more flowing to and from. Four quarters sectioned off the city: The Grand Quarter, the Low Quarter, the Beggars Quarter, and the Elven Quarter. Each of these quarters tended to govern themselves and wanted little to do with the other quarters. Only the writs and demands of the emperor were followed to the word, and many could not even reach the other quarters without express permission from the city guard.

The Grand Quarter held most of the city's nobility and estates of lords and ladies from the other kingdoms. Diplomats traveled to and from the different houses and to the grand palace as well as courtiers. Carriages and guards littered the streets, and shops stayed open into the late hours of the night. Those there dressed in extravagant and gaudy outfits meant to show their wealth and status. The size of their estate was often spoken of during their soirees and the latest gossip from outside the capital. Most of the nobility thought the other kings and queens of Veran to be subservient to them and their emperor.

When one of them did visit, it was quite the show to earn favor, though, because becoming a council member to any king was the most prestige one could acquire. That and marriage.

The Lower Quarter held the lesser nobility and common class of the city. The main trading hub centered here with livestock, milk, and cloth. While not nearly as large as Ignis, the trade still held well enough to keep many families fed through the winter. The main city gates opened into the Lower Quarter, so it was often congested with people and carriages. Most days, one could barely pass from one side of the cobblestone to the other without being trampled. From the singing of street bards to the yelling of merchants, there was never a quiet moment there.

The Beggars' Quarter rarely had guard patrols in it, as only the lowest of the low traveled there. It was not uncommon for sickness to spread like the plague across the quarter with little medicine to go around. The College of Enchanters made frequent trips there to heal the ailed and wounded. The houses were decrepit, and rumors of guilds ruling the streets at night kept many from wandering too far into passageways. While the emperor knew of the quarter's state, there was little he could do to help without the council's support or the lords he relied upon to keep his throne.

The Elven Quarter held the most significant elven population in all of Veran aside from Avlor itself. Here the elves mainly kept to themselves, trading, mending, and working for themselves. They only made rare ventures out of the city to farm and trade with the other kingdoms. The elves here lived as any human did and spoke as any human could. Apart from the ears and shining skin, it was hard to tell they once came from the Exalted Forest. The quarter was well kept and held festivals several times a year that garnered a large crowd from all around Veran. The lords of the city did not look kindly upon the elves, though, and the ones in their employment were often mistreated. Those that rose higher in repute with the emperor were often shunned from assemblies and earned more disfavor than allies. The highest an elf had ever risen in the court was the Spymaster of the emperor. And no one dared speak ill of her.

Within the Grand Quarter sat the Imperial Palace, home of Emperor Varen De'shelven. The Imperial Palace gleamed against the rest of the city, covered in gold from the throne to the windowsills. Stained glass covered every window, and paintings of the late emperors and empresses decorated the halls. Those of high station wandered the castle in their bliss of pontifical elegancy, vying for a chance to meet the emperor himself.

The emperor was cloaked in gold and white, his long coat trailing behind him. Immaculate fox fur ran down the trim, and the rings on his fingers glimmered with each step. A silver crown sat on his head, and his dirty blonde hair, spotted with white, was short and groomed. He paced the gardens, waiting for a sign from the kingdom that had yet to return any letters of concern.

His uncertainty was justified when one of his council came up to him at a hurried pace.

"Your Imperial Excellence, you must see this," Duke Percival said, catching up to the emperor. Yellow roses had begun to bloom as the emperor picked one to inspect.

"What is it? Have you brought news?" he asked. Duke Percival handed him a folded letter, blood staining its edges.

"A raven came to the gates and gave this to the guards before dying. We assumed it was of utmost importance," he said. The emperor set the flower on a bench and sat down himself. He opened the letter and examined the contents inside. The letter was hastily written and coated in dried blood, but he could make out the more essential pieces of information. His eyes narrowed as he slowly reread the letter.

"This... is this true?" he asked.

Percival crossed his hands behind his back and nodded solemnly. "We believe it to be true. The Dark Kingdom has taken Ignis. We have no confirmation whether the royal family is alive or dead. None of our messengers have returned."

The emperor's lips turned downwards. "We must deal with this immediately." He stood up, forgetting the flower on the bench, and started towards the antechamber, handing the letter back to the duke.

"Call the council. We must plan for an attack as soon as possible. Tell the other kingdoms to prepare their troops. If they have taken Ignis, they will spread their forces across Auratus, and WhiteDrove will be next." He entered the antechamber and started towards his mahogany desk. He sat down and scattered the parchments littering it away, quickly making space for a new sheet.

"Isn't it wise to send troops to Ignis? We must quash this force before they can do more harm," Percival advised.

Varen dipped a quill in ink and began scribbling. "Commander Rye and his forces are the closest to Ignis. They are holding their position near the Mors, but they do not have the numbers to take back the kingdom. Their position between the Mors and WhiteDrove is the best way to defend the remaining kingdoms. If they are to hold their position, they will have to know what they are facing," he responded.

"What of the portal? Could they enter through one and reach Ignis?"

"No," Varen said, "The portal to Ignis was destroyed during the last siege a decade ago. We cannot enter the city without alerting the troops."

The duke seemed to deflate at his answer, and he ran a hand through his balding hair. "There are few remaining council members here in the city; I will send word to them with haste. The rest are in their estates just west; I will send word to them as well."

"I will need to speak with the captain of the guard as well. If Auratus has been taken, then there will be those fleeing from the kingdom. They will come here for protection."

"I'm afraid we do not have room to accommodate refugees here within the city. Perhaps we can set up small encampments on the outskirts instead," Percival suggested.

"And do we have the men to protect each camp?" Varen asked, not looking up from his letter. He noted the duke's long pause.

"I see your point. I will send for the captain as well." He bowed and left the room, leaving the emperor to his thoughts. Ignis fell in a single night. There had been no warning. Nothing more than skirmishes outside the Mors. He didn't even know how they entered the kingdom without alerting the commander. Something didn't add up, and it was driving him mad. He sighed and set the quill down.

"Father?" a voice called. The emperor looked up to find his son leaning against the door.

"Oh, Marrin, I did not hear you enter," he said. His son walked over to the desk and peeked at his letter.

"Is something wrong?" he asked.

Varen shook his head. "No, everything is fine," he lied. He did not need his son worrying about the Dark Kingdom when his own grandparents were slaughtered by them. He was merely twelve, a child. Varen was crowned emperor when his parents were killed, though it should not have gone to him. It should have gone to the first-born son, Rye, but he had refused to take claim. They were the last of the main royal line. His council helped him through the darkest of days after the Battle of Velwood, but even now, he felt a deep weight on his shoulders.

His son placed a gentle hand on his shoulder. "You're tense. Something is wrong."

Varen smiled slightly. "Go back to your studies, Marrin; this is a matter for adults."

The boy puffed his cheeks out but obeyed, leaving him alone in the room. *If word spreads through the city, it will cause mass panic*, he thought. *But not telling them could cause even more issues in the future.* He ran a hand through his hair with a sigh. One thing at a time. For this moment, he needed to send letters to the other kingdoms. That would have to do for now.

The candlelight seemed dimmer than before, and the shadows sketched and waved. He took a breath and continued writing.

20 RYE

Rye stood in the haphazardly constructed wooden cell within the camp. His arms were crossed over his breastplate, and the small bit of light that streamed in from the cutout windows reflected off his golden armor and hair.

Two men sat on the dirt ground in front of him, tied up with rope. The dark leathers they wore outed them as cultists. They had tangled hair and attenuated arms and boots that were so worn he could nearly see their toes. Their heads were downcast, but they had said nothing since their capture. They were found a mere mile from their camp, walking and taking notes. The notes were indecipherable, though. Rye had spent a good day attempting to read them, with little luck.

Garding leaned on the side of the narrow cell, tapping his foot against the ground. He had a piece of grass in his mouth that he blew on occasionally.

"How many are in your encampment?" Rye asked sternly. The two did not respond. "They are fools to send only two of you. And during the day. What did they think to achieve?"

They gave no answer, and Garding stepped from the wall and up to them. He hit one hard across the face. The man's head snapped to the side and nearly hit the other cultists beside him.

"Answer the commander when he talks to you, arseholes," he barked.

"Garding," Rye snapped.

The lieutenant turned to him and shrugged his shoulders. "Words don't work. Maybe violence will."

Rye ignored the lieutenant and stepped past him. He bent down to the cultist's height. Seeing the man Garding punched in the face, he could tell he was young. Maybe sixteen years. He looked down at his bulky leather that was too wide for his malnourished body.

"If you tell us what we need to know, you will be fed and clothed. You have my word. What were you scouting? How many of you are there?"

The boy finally looked up at the commander, blood trailing down his cut lip. He smiled. "The gods will judge ye souls. And we will watch yer cities burn."

"You won't get anything out of these bastards," Garding said, shaking his head. "All of them are fucked in the head."

"You think yerself high and mighty. Livin' in yer castles of gold," the other cultists said. "Ye feast on the swine that live below. But both squeal the same when ye die."

"Is that what you will do when I stick my sword through your chest? Squeal like a pig?" Garding asked.

The cultist laughed a bloody, gurgling laugh. "The gods guide us through the Otherworld. I 'ave no fear of death."

Rye stood up, and the cultist nudged the boy. They looked at each other, and Garding stepped in front of the commander.

The boy broke free of his restraints and lunged at the lieutenant in the blink of an eye. Garding quickly shoved him away, and he stumbled back into the other cultist who managed to cut his bonds. Rye pulled his sword with Garding, and they stood ready. The two cultists did not make another move toward them. Instead, they took their knives from their holders and slit their throats down the middle. Rye watched in sickening dread as their bodies fell to the ground. The smile never left the boy's face.

"What in the fuck?" Garding cursed. He sheathed his sword and bent down, picking up a dagger.

"I thought you checked them for weapons," Rye said.

"I did." Garding dropped the knife, and it vanished into the ground in a puff of smoke. He stood up and turned to the commander. "Looks like there are more maleficarum than we thought."

Rye looked down at the cultists and shook his head. "What a waste." He stepped from the cell and took a long breath of fresh air. Garding came beside him and looked around the camp.

"Maybe we will get lucky, and they will all kill themselves. Make our lives easier."

"I have doubts that will happen." Rye walked over to the command tent and entered it, setting his sword down on the table. He sighed and looked at the notes the cultists had written.

"Now this is all we have to go on, nonsense scribbled on parchment."

"I told you they were fucked in the head," Garding said, taking a letter and sitting down. "Maybe it was a letter to his mum. I've been a good cultist today, Mum. Youde be proud of how many cats I drowned in the stream."

"You find levity in any situation, don't you?" Rye noted, laughing out a sigh. "We will just have to wait—"

"The Raven has arrived, ser," a recruit said, walking into the tent. Rye glanced at him and then at Garding, who sat back in his chair with a nonchalant shoulder roll.

"It's been a week. What happened?"

The recruit could not answer as the spymaster entered the tent. She was quiet as she always was, but Rye could tell from the look in her obsidian eyes that something was amiss. She said nothing as she threw the runes onto the table.

Garding picked one up, examining the black stone. "This is what's going to save us?"

"It damned better be," he heard Via mumble under her breath. Rye looked up at her, and her face returned to its stoic nature.

"We caught two spies this morning. We will need to scout the area as soon as possible," he told her. He saw her ears perk up, and she glanced around the tent.

"Where are they? I will interrogate them."

"Dead," Garding said, tossing the rune back on the table.

"What happened?"

"A knife."

"Garding—"

"They killed themselves," Rye said, ceasing the bickering. Via raised an eyebrow but stayed quiet. She looked down at the runes on the table and he saw her mouth twitch. "We have these notes, though, that were on their bodies. We can't decipher them."

Via took the notes and scanned through them, seeming to understand what they said. "It is old Elvish."

"Old Elvish? They can't even speak properly, but can write in a dead language?" Garding asked with a bewildered look.

"Apparently so."

"What do they say?" Rye asked.

"Scouted from Riverbend to Northshire. No sign of the girl."

"Girl? What girl?" Garding asked, sitting up in his chair.

Via shrugged her shoulders. "I cannot say for certain. These are all locations around Auratus, mainly the villages and towns neighboring Ignis."

"Ignis? They have barely made it out of the Mors and they are speaking of a capital city. What are they planning?"

"Nothing at the moment," Via said. "There are no plans for invasion or anything that would state otherwise."

"But they've already had men in the area. Which means we've overlooked something," Rye pondered, looking at the map on the table. "Could they have come out of the Mors in another location? Somewhere to the south?"

"Unlikely. There are very few trails that lead to and from the kingdom. I would have seen something traveling to Avlor. It must just be a few spies," she said.

"You're quite sure of yourself. But if she says we're fine, I suppose there is nothing to worry about."

Rye watched as Via threw the papers onto the table. "I will send out my scouts tonight to make sure," she said and rubbed her hands together and put them behind her back. *She's worried*, he thought. *Or there is something she isn't telling me.*

Garding gave Rye a look before standing up and taking the recruit with him out of the tent. Via turned to leave as well, but Rye caught her arm.

"Via, talk to me," he pleaded. Via's head turned slightly, her white hair falling out of her braid.

"I got what you needed, Commander. What more is there to say?" she asked.

Rye let go of her arm, and his lips turned down. "What happened in Avlor, Via?"

Via made a *tisk* noise and crossed her arms. "Ravana took something from me, that is all," she said curtly. She left the tent, and Rye put a hand on the table. It took much to make the spymaster visibly upset, and he hated to see his friend like that.

In the ten years he knew her, she barely spoke her feelings at all, much less showed them. The most he had ever seen from her was when she pushed her sword into the elven king's heart. That night still haunted his memories. The cries of the elves around them. The screeching of demons below. The wailing of the little girl who held her father's hand as he bled from his chest.

And without a word, she lifted the girl into her arms and never spoke of that night again. Sometimes he wondered what her life was like. She never spoke of anything before that night, either. He barely knew what a cursed elf was until they were near the portal to Nevrak, and she stepped out of it. The gray of her skin, the white of her hair, and darkened eyes. He would have mistaken her for a demon.

And yet they had become good friends in the time after. She actually gave rise to a smile every once in a great while. She was bestowed the bow which she had on her back from the cursed queen, said to have magical properties that could vanquish a demon with one arrow. The enchanted runes carved into the wood proved that to be true. And he feared they might have need of it.

Rye patrolled the camp as his soldiers prepared for the long night. His fingers rubbed the stones in his hands, and he watched as light flickered inside them. At night, he could hear the clicking of undead and the yowls of demons. None had strolled close to the camp, but he positioned more guards towards the Mors, nevertheless.

Since he took the position as Imperial Commander, he had seen more death and darkness than he thought possible. Even after Velwood, the curse placed upon the land never ceased to writhe and grow. The Dark Kingdom was growing bolder. And the look in those cultists' eyes as they died, the smile on their dying faces. It worried him. They were sure of themselves. He half-minded the thought of sending a letter to Fira to see of any news, but he had heard nothing. And from the look on his friend's face, things were becoming more and more strained. His only hope was that these runes could give them the information they needed. And if not, then there was something far greater they must heed.

A star shot across the sky, and the commander followed it with his eyes. It danced off into the sunset sky, and he took a breath. Tomorrow would come. And they would get their answer.

21 ENARA

"Lord Cassus. Duke Prevel. Knight Captain Legus. Lord Calis. Lady Vivianna. And Enchanter Dravis is gravely injured." The squire continued to rattle off the names of the dead as Enara stared out the window of her burning city. The library was quiet except for them; not a book had been moved. She once found solace in this place. Now it lay as barren as her castle. The rain had begun to fall and quench the flames, but the charred stone and smell of rot continued to remind her of what she had done. The crown on her head was heavy and dull and the diamonds in it no longer gleamed. The gold had rusted to brown. She had no coronation. No adoring nobles. No handsome prince. For once in her life, she felt completely, utterly alone.

She rubbed her fingers across the brooch in her hand. The one she had given her sister before she killed her. It, too, was dull and rusted. The blood coating the diamond wept in her hands.

When the squire finally finished naming the dead, she had forgotten what number they had reached. Four hundred? More?

"Y-Your Grace?" the squire asked, gripping the parchment tightly in his hands.

Enara turned to him, a frown on her lips. "If that is all, you may leave."

The squire bowed before fleeing the room, and Enara turned back to the window. She could still feel cold fingertips grip her neck, and she rubbed her hand. No matter how close she got to the fire, she could never shake off the darkened chill that hung around her. She wanted nothing more than to be warm. To be happy. And hearing the weeping of her servants in the hall did little to help.

Oh, how the night had passed. She had stood in the throne room, looking up at the darkened throne, every thought crossing her mind, yet none fully formed. She had felt the crown being placed upon her head and the chilling laughter of the Dark King in her ear.

"The queen of ash," he whispered to her. *"The queen of ruin."*

And how he had been right. Still, her people suffered and there was nothing she could do to stop it. She pocketed the brooch and walked over to a table and poured herself a glass of wine. The red liquid churned against the glass walls, and Enara set the pitcher down with a force she did not intend. She took a long drink and focused on the tingling in her mouth. Her hand throbbed painfully in tune with her heart, heat rising toward her elbow. It seemed almost mocking to her, a pulse for each innocent she murdered.

She caught the sound of footsteps coming near the library doors and she turned away, looking back out the window. The door opened, and she heard a huff.

"What do you want?" Enara asked.

Trissa closed the door behind her and walked over to the new queen. "Are you proud of yourself, Enara?"

Enara's jaw set, and she turned around. "You speak ill of your new queen?" she hissed.

Trissa scoffed. "You are no queen. I raised you like my own flesh and blood, but here you are. You have killed your sister along with your kingdom. If your mother were here, what would she say?"

"She would know that what I did was justified."

"Justified?" You call *this* justified?" Trissa argued. "The murder of children? Or innocent people?"

Enara set her wineglass down, anger burning its way through her chest. She stared at her old nanny, who had her arms crossed defiantly. "What would you know, Trissa? We both realize that Rose would have dragged our kingdom to filth."

"We both know this was never about Rose, Enara," Trissa countered, shaking her head. "You think your sister a nuisance for being naïve, but look at the city around us, Enara. Can you not hear their cries from your actions? Your people are suffering."

"I hear them. I can do nothing about it. Do you think I wanted this? That I wanted my people to die?" Enara argued.

Trissa stepped up to Enara, forcefully grabbing her hands. "Then what did you want, Enara? Power? Wealth? You had all of that already. You simply refused to see it."

Enara could feel tears well up in her eyes, and she forced them down, glaring at her nanny. "You know nothing of what I wanted. No one ever did. While I was alone, trapped in this damned castle, you stayed with her. Singing her lullabies and doting on her like some treasured pet, filling her head with nonsensical stories of kings and queens. She lived her life thinking not about the world around her but of her own self-importance. I was the one who ruled this country alone. I stayed in council meetings for hours on end, and I listened and learned from the tutors. I mourned my own mother with no one there at my side. None of the council cared about me. They only saw a lone princess with nothing to gain except being used as a bargaining chip. Once Rose was named queen, I would have been sold off to some noble lord like some breeding stock. I had *nothing*." The words that came from her mouth felt like venom on her tongue and she could no longer stop the angry tears that fell down her face. "Don't you understand? What I did was the only way to save myself."

Trissa kept a grip on her hands, pulling them closer, and she noticed her eyes wavering. "You were never alone, Enara. You had a sister who loved you. A kingdom that adored you. And a nanny who wanted nothing more than to see her girls thrive."

Enara sniffed, and Trissa finally let go of her hands to wipe a tear from her cheek.

"What you have done can never be mended. The people are fearful. They need food and herbs. The cultists are still killing many who do not concede. What are you planning?"

Enara stepped away from Trissa, pouring another glass of wine and downing it. "I will have a word with them, Trissa. Malum said they would stop."

"And you believe them? That the demons roaming the streets will not hunt for sport? There will be no one to save and serve if they are all killed. I do not trust this Malum."

Enara bit her tongue as a pulse of fire shot through her veins. The glass shattered in her hand, causing blood to seep through her fingers. Trissa huffed and walked over to her. She took a cloth from the table and gently wrapped Enara's hand.

"Never betray me, Trissa, please," she pleaded softly.

Trissa looked up into the blue eyes of the queen and, with a slight frown, wiped the rest of the blood away. "It is not me who will betray you. I know the little girl I raised is still there. You can still make the right decision, child. Remember that. And remember the little girl you just murdered." She let go of her hand and turned away. Enara watched as she left the room without another word. When the door closed, she looked down at the blood-covered doll that lay lifeless in her wrapped hand. She watched as its eyes seemed to stare straight through her. Enara's lip quivered before she threw it into a bookcase. It flopped onto the ground, eyes still staring at her own. Enara shook her head, and with a mournful cry, fled the room.

22 JARED

Jared leaned against the wooden wall outside the tavern. He watched as torch lights flickered in the setting sun of the evening, a soft hue of orange against the purple and pink sky. He closed his eyes and took a breath of chilly air. They had just reached the first town of Northshire, a few days' hike outside the city. His wounds were still sore, but the town seemed unaffected by the takeover. Miners still carried their gear to work, traders still took goods to and from, and children still played in the pigpens. He could hear whispers inside the tavern, though, of traders coming back empty-handed, of smoke in the air. The cultists would reach the town eventually, and Jared did not wish to be there when they did. He had scraped together the last of his *sephim* to get them a room for the night at the inn, even as the half-elf insisted upon sleeping in the field. He didn't want to tell her he did not feel safe out there. He was not used to forests or roads. The smithy was outside the city walls but still close enough to never need to travel elsewhere. The Golden Hills were something to admire, he would admit. But it wasn't his home. And he wasn't with his friends.

He knew he had no right to be upset, as the half-elf had taken him in with little argument. She had rarely spoken to him in the few days of their companionship, and he doubted she would ever open up. She kept to herself during the day, always staying a few steps ahead of him during their journey and staying on the other side of the fire at night. She would disappear for a couple of hours in the morning and then return at luncheon with a rabbit strung on her belt. She didn't speak then, either.

He didn't flinch when he heard soft footsteps approaching him. He did, however, flinch when a pile of clothes landed on his lap.

"What is this?" he asked, slightly agitated, opening one eye to peek at the girl. Nava put her hands on her hips.

"It's a new pair of clothes. Yours are in disrepair," she said.

Jared set a hand on the pile and laid his head back on the wall. "Thanks, and don't worry, I'll be out of your hair by the morning," he said.

"What do you speak of?"

Jared scoffed. "Well, you seemed very adamant about me leaving your presence a few days ago. I asked you to take me to the next town, then I would leave. A deal's a deal," he said calmly.

Nava sighed and turned away. "Get dressed and come inside." After looking up at the sky and sniffing, she added, "It's going to rain soon."

Jared huffed and stood up, following Nava inside. He took the clothes and stepped into their room on the upper floor of the tavern, setting them down on the bed. He pulled off his dirty ones and threw them in the corner to deal with later. Pouring water into the basin on the far wall, he washed his hands and face, looking at himself in the cracked mirror. He was much worse for wear than he thought. A new scar ran down his chest and arm, mingling with the many other scars running from his cheek to his groin. His bandages were crusty, and his beard was matted and bedraggled. He laughed to himself and grabbed a blade, shaving it off, and attempted to fix his hair. He did his best to re-bandage the wounds and, with a groan, pulled his fresh shirt over his head. He could be appreciative of not smelling like he walked out of a sewer.

When he returned from dressing, he strolled down to the tavern and found the half-elf sitting in a far corner; hood pulled up over her head. He passed several drunken men playing a round of cards and dodged a splatter of mead as he sat down beside her. She was looking down at her tankard, seeming lost within her own thoughts.

"Are you thinking about how stunning I look?" Jared asked with a slight grin. He earned a glare from the girl in return.

"How anyone could find a man covered in dirt and reeking of week-old ale appealing is beyond my comprehension," she replied.

Jared's smile widened. "Speaking of which," he stated and grabbed the tankard from her grasp.

"That was mine, you know," she sighed.

Jared quirked an eyebrow at her and wiped his mouth. "I haven't had alcohol in a week. This is my present."

He noticed her study his for a moment and contemplated saying something about it before she got a word in.

"What happened to you in Ignis?" she asked.

He set his ale down, a twisted expression on his face. "I told you already. The Dark Knights attacked the city."

"I don't mean that. How did you find yourself there in the first place? The forges are outside the city," she stated. Jared looked over her shoulder at the various people drinking and fraternizing. They seemed a lively bunch, with little cares in the world but who to bed and when to be back home by to rest before returning to the mines. A wench brought over another flagon for them, and he gleefully poured himself more ale.

"A blacksmith found me alone and freezing one rainy day in the city and raised me as his son, taught me to use a hammer and anvil as well as how to swing a sword. No one was missing a son around those parts, so he kept me for himself. A bastard boy that no one would remember." He laughed at himself and took a long drink of the ale, feeling some of it drip down his chin onto his shirt.

"The place was burnt to the ground years ago and my pa was killed. I just happened to stumble into the right alleyway one night and found myself face to face with a bard."

Nava raised an eyebrow. "You don't know your actual parents?"

leaned back in his seat. "No. He said I was covered in blood, stumbling around Lowtown crying. He had just come back from delivery to the armory. Never knew what happened. I barely remember myself."

"And this bard. Is she the one you're looking for?"

Jared sighed. "Yes. She is the only family I have left."

"I doubt she would make it much farther than us. No one has seen her around here?"

So many questions. She's never been this talkative, he thought. "No one that I've talked to has seen her. There are many roads through the hills, though, and she knows them well. I'll find her in Fira."

"Is she your lover?"

Jared cocked an eyebrow at her, and Nava pushed a stray hair behind her ear. "I was only curious. You seem keen on finding her."

A cocky smile lit up the swordsman's face. "She never thought of me like that. It's hard to lose the only family you've got."

Nava's face darkened for a moment, a flicker of emotion he

recognized too well. "What are you looking for in Fira?" he asked, shifting in the wooden chair.

"I told you that it's something I lost," she answered, shrugging her shoulders, and looking away from him.

"Yeah, I got that. But what is it?" he pushed.

Nava slammed a knife into the table, making him jump. She abruptly stood up and threw a few *sephim* onto the table.

"It's none of your business. I'm going to bed," she said. She disappeared up the stairs, and Jared leaned back in his chair, running a thumb along the hilt of her blade.

She was a curious one, he would give her that. Also irritating. She had asked about his life, then closed herself off to any questions he might have had. *Maybe it's an elf thing*, he pondered. The only elves he ever saw were the ones employed by Rose, and they never spoke to him.

"Nava…" he said, rolling her name across his tongue. Raised by elves and thrown into the world to fend for herself.

Heh, maybe we aren't so different after all, he thought.

Jared woke up the following day, greeted by the warmth of sunshine on his face. He rolled over groggily in his bed and opened his eyes. His blurred vision soon focused, and he noticed the lack of a woman in the bed next to him. He sighed and rubbed his eyes with his hand.

He sat up in the bed and stretched. He heard the cooing of mourning doves outside the window. He raked his fingers through his hair and stood up off the bed. The bed the elven woman slept in was made and tidy, with almost no indication that she had been in there at all the night before. He wondered if she even slept.

After washing up and dressing, he headed down the stairs and gave the keeper a quick goodbye. As he moseyed his way outside, he noticed Nava prepping a horse for her departure. Jared leaned against the wall of the tavern.

"Leaving?" he asked. Nava pulled on the girth and patted the horse with a stubborn look adorning her face.

"Of course we are. We cannot stay here longer if we wish to get to Fira," she replied.

Jared stood up off the wall. "We?" he asked.

Nava sighed and turned around. "Yes, are you coming?"

A quirky smile appeared on his face, and he picked a bag off the ground, attaching it to the side of the saddle.

"Of course. I thought you were done with me?" he asked. He caught a faint red tinge to her cheeks as she put her foot through the stirrup.

"It would be needless to go in the same direction alone. That is all," she said. She brought a leg over the horse and situated herself into the seat.

"Where's my horse?" he asked.

The half-elf bit her lip. "I could not find another one suitable," she murmured.

"Wait, you stole it?" he asked.

"I commandeered it," she implied. Jared shook his head and jumped onto the horse behind where she sat. He grabbed hold of the bridle and, with a cocky voice, said, "Onward, my lovely steed."

He firmly received an elbow to the stomach.

23 TALIA

Talia sat on the white sand of the beach. She held an unfolded letter in her lap, her fingers grasping the faded paper. A messenger had finally come, but it was not from Ignis. It was from Fira. And as soon as she was given the letter, she knew what it contained. Her mind wrapped around the cursive flow of the words.

King Baren,
I have learned of an assault on the kingdom of Auratus. There have been no reports on the casualties, but it is presumed that the new queen is dead. Therefore, I am informing you of the urgent necessity to send your herald to the council for an assembly. The darkness is upon us, my friend, and we must ready ourselves.
Emperor Varen De'shelven

Talia knew within her chest that her brother was dead. It had been over a week, and she had heard nothing. At this point, all she could hope for was for his body to be returned for a proper burial.

She folded the note and set it on the sand beside her. She had seen her father's face when he read the letter. The anger and anguish washed together as he slumped back against his throne. He had sent the herald to the capital not a moment after. Talia had grasped her father's hand and reassured him that everything would be fine. His son would return. They both knew that was a fallacious sentiment. She had never thought the day would come when she would bury her brother. He was supposed to be king; he would have married the queen of Auratus if given a chance and possibly handed the throne of Yalirea to her. And now he was dead. Murdered by the Dark Kingdom and its cultists. She knew they had to do something. They had to avenge his death.

"Milady, are you well?" Lia asked, stepping over to her lady. Talia stood up off the sand and looked toward her servant.

"Yes, I am fine," she assured. Lia went up beside her on the beach, watching the waves pull back and forth along the shore.

"I heard what happened in Ignis. The entire kingdom is speaking of it. They think we will be next," she said. Talia scoffed and pulled the shawl she was wearing further up her shoulders.

"That will not happen. We have the Golden Hills and many lands between the Dark Kingdom and us. It is WhiteDrove and Avlor we must worry about."

"Milady, is Prince Valek going to return?" she asked carefully.

The princess looked back out at sea, forcing the words she had refused to say out load. "No, Lia. He is not."

The two stood there for a time in silence. Talia raked her fingers through her sandy hair and fixed her dress. She wanted to laugh at herself for appearing in such a state, even to a handmaid. Just a day ago she had wished the traders from Nishiri farewell with gifts and a promise of lower trade taxes on the Amber Sea, and now she sat there like a small child, crying over her brother instead of acting.

"Perhaps I will prepare a bath for you, milady?" Lia asked.

Talia turned away from the beach. "I will speak to my father," she said, ignoring her maid's concern. "We shall not allow another kingdom to fall."

She started up the pathway to the castle, and Lia watched her go with a frown.

Talia entered her father's study, ignoring the guards outside of it. A mess of treaties was on his oak desk and the floor. Books were piled high atop it, and crumpled pieces of parchment were thrown thoughtlessly around the room. Her father sat in his chair, rubbing his balding head. His crown was tossed haphazardly onto the leaning stack of papers at the end of the desk.

"Talia? What is it?" he asked, sitting up in his chair.

Talia walked over and set the letter on the desk. "The people of Auratus have suffered enough. We must help the other kingdoms now," she said. "Food, supplies, trading routes, anything to help the war."

"War? What makes you think a war would be on the horizon?" Her father asked, ignoring the letter.

"Because an entire kingdom was just taken by the Dark Kingdom. Why would there not be war or the horizon?"

"Because, Talia, you fail to realize that it was a sister country that was attacked, not ours," he retorted, taking a stack of paper and organizing it.

"Sister country? What makes you think that they will stop with Auratus? They will go north and conquer the other kingdoms given enough power, and we will only sit here idly, waiting for our turn to kneel. That is not a solution."

"I already sent a herald to the capital, you know this. We can do nothing more for the moment."

Talia felt like she was talking to a wall. The way her father would not meet her eye, the way he kept reorganizing the papers. *Nothing like a king*, she thought. "We *can* do more. Avlor and WhiteDrove will be the next to be sacked without our aid. We have the largest port on the continent, we can send ships—"

"I am not putting more of our people in danger, Talia," he argued. "This is not our war to fight."

Talia placed a hand on her hip, pointing to the map of Veran that hung on the wall. "Look at this. These are your people, too—your allies. If you do not help, Ignis will not be the last to fall," she pleaded. Her father stood up from his chair and poured a glass of wine, drinking it down with one long gulp. "You cannot abandon your people," Talia said, walking over to her father. She placed a hand on his arm, feeling him tense.

"And what do you suppose I do? Curb the trading lanes? March my men hundreds of miles north to fight in a war they will not win?"

"Yes! Deploy your army. Or at least send a few of the kingdom guards to assist the front lines. If we keep them from taking WhiteDrove, we can ensure the safety of the others. We have more than a hundred infantrymen armed for combat at this moment."

Her father shook his head and escaped from her grasp. "Pirates, Talia. We deal with pirates and belligerent traders. We do not have men who have seen a land war in a decade."

"Velwood was costly to everyone. I know this. But doing nothing is equal to bending the knee. The emperor will send men as well; the Dark Kingdom can be crushed in a fortnight."

The king turned toward her, and she stepped back slightly, wary of his venomous gaze. "And if we stop them? They will turn their gaze south and we will be attacked next. Keeping them north is our best option. We take care of our own people before the care of others."

"That is no option, Father! Valek is dead. We must avenge his name," she cried.

"You are a little girl, not a soldier!" he yelled. "Do not speak as if you know bloodshed."

She flinched and backed away. He took a breath and set the glass down on the desk. "You have your mother's spirit," he sighed. "But this is not a war we can win."

"You don't know that if we don't try," Talia said softer this time.

He rubbed his forehead with a pained expression on his face. "The Dark Kingdom has been around for millennia, Talia. They are not some pirates looking to loot a few trading ships. They are coordinated and deadly. I know you mean well, but a princess can do little to sway the course of a battle."

Talia clenched her fists and took a long, deep breath. "Shouldn't that be why we must meet them on the field? If they gain strength—"

"Let the Empire handle it. You are just a girl. They are legion. We shall discuss this no more. Leave me to rest," he said.

Talia shook her head and left the room, slamming the door behind her.

24 OLIVIA

The soles of her boots were worn and thin. She felt every uneven stone and pebble she stepped on. Her toes were numb from the cold water and stung with every step she took. The damp, muddy walls made grip nearly impossible, as she could barely see what was in front of her. Normally, she would have carried a torch with her, but she had nothing but a knife in her haste to escape the Knight. What would have taken her a few hours to navigate now took her days. She drank from the water that streamed by her feet and forced herself to choke down the buzzing insects that scaled the walls. Her stomach churned with every squishy bite, but it was better than starving.

She kept her hands to the walls as she went on, turning when she reached free space. The rushing of the water made hearing impractical, and the darkness surrounding her tricked her mind from night and day. The only thing that kept her moving was the hatred that boiled in her veins for the ones who took her home from her. *I will avenge them*, she told herself. *If I ever make it out.* She did not want to think of herself rotting in the waters of the well where no one who would ever find her. No, she would survive.

She felt a slight breeze ruffle through her matted hair, and she quickly picked up her pace. She stumbled and fell many times as she grabbed at the walls, pleading to feel the wind on her face. Soon enough, she could see a fraction of light ahead of her, beckoning her towards it. An exhausted smile graced her lips as she ran for the light. When she bounded past the entrance to the cavern, she fell to her knees in the grass.

She laughed out a sob and ran her hands through the slick wet plants, digging her nails into the mud. *I am free!* She thought. She navigated the cavern in the dark; she had done it enough to know where to go. She had trusted her instincts and took a few long breaths and sat up, wiping the mud and sweat from her face.

Olivia looked back into the cavern as the black bid her farewell but felt something call out to her from the dark. A voice that was barely a whisper in the wind. She shook her head and ignored it, shakily standing up and walked for several minutes through the thick brush of the forest before finding a creek to reside by.

She took off her boots and rung out her socks, rubbing her pruned toes. Her clothes were shredded, her skirt was torn and muddy, and her shirt was barely better off. She pulled off her skirt and rinsed it out in the river, attempting to salvage what was left of it and cleaned her face and hair, rubbing her swollen knuckles. She bore not nearly enough scars from the battle she had survived. Jared had sustained much worse than her—if he was alive. She shouldn't have run away; she should have stayed to fight. She would not make that mistake again.

When she was done washing herself, she pulled her clothes up to dry on the branches of a tree. The forest was too wet for her to attempt to start a fire, so she would have to hope on the sun for her warmth. She was simply happy to be out of the cavern and clean. She sat on the riverbank and let the warm rays of the sun dry her tanned skin. She ran her fingers through her hair to pull out any knots when her stomach growled loudly. She resisted the urge to retch when she thought about eating more of those damned bugs and decided on the possibility of hunting. She only had a knife and knew little of snares, but she could work something out. Squirrel or rabbit sounded much more appetizing than anything back in that cave. After a few more minutes of sunbathing, she pulled herself up and folded down her shirt that barely covered her smalls. Her skirt and boots were still too wet to wear again, so she left them behind.

She traversed through the forest, careful not to step on pointed thorns and venomous snakes. She knew a bit about the forests within the kingdom—she had set up camp more than once for her jobs. But now that the Dark Kingdom had control of Ignis, who knew what may lie in wait?

She paused when laughter waded through the forest and into her ears. She held her breath and listened as patches of conversation swirled around her.

"Ye can't be serious."

"It's true! I saw one with me own eyes. Armor black as night, tall as the King's Tower."

"Aint no way you saw one of the gods."

Cultists. She knew it. She started toward the sound of the voices, letting her feet fall softly on the grass. Up ahead, she saw three men around a campfire. They wore black leather armor and red capes. They laughed merrily while drinking whiskey and roasting a deer over the fire. One held a guitar in his hands, strumming lightly.

The scent of the deer wafted through her nose, and her stomach growled loudly. She scanned the group for weapons. They all had swords that were placed together near the end of the fire. She may catch them by surprise, but three to one did not favor her odds. She decided to go with a different approach instead.

She straightened her shirt, fluffed her hair, and sauntered over to the group. All the cultists quieted and Olivia leaned against a tree with a small smile.

"You look like shit," one said and made the others laugh.

Olivia smiled slightly. "Yes, I just came back from a swim in the river after visiting a local tavern. I was quite busy," she said and ran a finger up her thigh. All eyebrows went up, and one nudged the other. The smallest one, with brown hair and wide eyes, quickly made space for her on the log.

"Wanna drink?" one of them asked. Olivia nodded and tipped over to the group, catching pieces of their whispers.

"Is she a siren? Comin' out of the river like that?" The younger one asked.

"If she is, I ain't gonna complain. Never had sex with a siren before."

The boys started laughing again, and the young one handed her his deerskin pouch. She sat down next to him and took a long drink, wiping her lips with a finger. She caught the boy looking at her lips with a small blush and handed the skin back, gliding her hand over his own. He blushed deeper, and the other two laughed.

"You ever been with a woman before, boy?" one asked. The boy made a face and shook his head.

Olivia giggled and ran her fingers through his hair. "So, what brings you, handsome men, to this part of the continent?"

One put his elbows on his knees, and a bestial smile crossed his face. "You heard we took over Ignis, right?" he asked. Olivia nodded, and the boy pulled the deer from the rack, cutting off a piece for her.

She thanked him and bit into it, nearly moaning from the tender meat.

"Of course. It has spread across half of Veran," she answered after chewing. "But that doesn't explain what you are doing out here instead of in a nice tavern."

"The same could be said for ye, love," he responded.

"We're making our way to Stormshold. They've got a fresh new shipment of slaves," the other answered.

Olivia raised a brow. "What do you need more slaves for?"

"The king wants a statue erected for his new queen. Need more fresh bodies to carve th' stone."

Olivia nodded in mock understanding. "Well, I'm sure the statue will be nearly as beautiful as the kingdom itself."

"Ye got that right, sunshine. Soon Reverand will be the new capital of Veran," he boasted. Olivia finished eating, pleased to finally be free from her hunger. She looked over at the man with the guitar.

"May I?"

"A bard are ya?" he asked. She gave a smile, and he handed her the instrument. She tuned it and opened her legs slightly, watching the men's eyes trail down her body.

The emperor of fire
With a throne made of gold
What secrets do you hide
In the hearts that you hold
The emperor of fire
The king of the free
The one who will stop
The darkness that be
The emperor of fire
The King of the Thorns
The blood that runs from his hands
Belong to his foes
The emperor of fire
Veiled by the sun
The golden light
Will bear the new dawn

Her voice echoed through the forest, earning the attention of every creature. The wind seemed to quiet as the birds silenced to hear. All gazes were set on her as she finished the song, and they didn't even realize when she had stopped.

Olivia put the instrument down, stood up, and walked over to the other men. She sat down on one's lap and leaned into his ear. "I could show you more of my talent if you want, milord," she whispered. She felt his hands slide up her bare legs and caress her ass.

"If you insist," he said. She giggled and ran her hands up his chest, kissing his neck and ear.

"Same some for the rest of us," the other said. She grasped his shirt and pulled him over, kissing him hard, her tongue sweeping over his. She heard him groan and moved her hand down the other man's chest. Her gaze wandered over to the other youngest boy. His eyes were wide as he watched.

Her eyes darkened, and before the boy could react, a knife had lodged into the throat of the man she sat upon. Blood spurted from his mouth and throat, covering her face. She pulled the knife out and stood. He fell to the ground, gagging and clawing at his neck, and the other man lunged for his sword. She kicked him, and he stumbled onto his stomach. She pounced on his back and lifted his head. He fought against her, screaming as she slid the knife across his throat. She dropped his head and stood up, wiping the blood from her face.

She turned to the young boy, and he fell from the log, backing up on his hands and knees.

"Gods protect me," he prayed, crying. She stepped over the bodies and up to him. She bent down and took his chin in her hand. Sweat beaded around his head, eyes wide in fear and shock. She pointed the dagger at his throat, speaking softly.

"Take me to the Dark Kingdom."

25 THYMAS

Thymas bounded through the quiet village. Lanterns swung in the chilling breeze of nightfall as dogs howled to the moons. Farmers ushered their chickens inside their coops and locked their goats in their pens. Only the sound of slogging boots and whistling wind could be heard around the village.

He could feel the darkness that lingered in the air. The guards were tense atop the walls, and the keep glowed dimly in the candlelight. The halls were no different as he entered. He ignored the servant's request for his coat and started for the main hall.

He knew about Ignis; the letter had reached his hands not a few days ago. Now lords from all over the kingdom had come to WhiteDrove to discuss the matter. They all congregated around tables and sat on benches. Spilled drinks and left-over venison were flung on the tables and floor. Their shouts of anger could be heard before Thymas even entered the hall, but they quieted when the doors opened to allow him inside. Thymas walked to the long table set up in the back of the room, and the people positioned themselves to be able to see him. He turned when he reached the table and looked at their worn and hardened expressions. Most had traveled days to get here and were weary, leaning on their knees and staring at the ground. Others were standing tall and proud, their swords hung on their belts.

"First, I would like to thank all of you who traveled far for this meeting. Your loyalty has been gracious. Now, I have called you all here today to speak of the Dark Kingdoms advances on Auratus," Thymas started. The rest of the voices ceased as he spoke, eyes trained on him. "We need not panic yet, as all the facts have still yet to reach our ears… but Ignis has been sacked."

A chorus of angry and fearful voices rose in the room. Some lords quickly stood up out of their seats.

"What does this mean for us? That is our sister kingdom!" one shouted.

"Who cares about Ignis? We must close the border!" another said.

Thymas put his hand up, and the room quieted again. "I know you are all frightened by this attack. But the Imperial army is currently positioned between the Golden Hills and the borders of Viragrad. They will hold off the Dark Kingdom if they make an advance here."

"You trust those noble pricks?" a lord asked near the front. Thymas recognized him as Lord Downor; his town was just south of WhiteDrove, mostly farmers. "They play in their palaces and take our cattle for their fancy feasts. Their men can't tell their arse from their heads."

The room erupted into agreements and boos, and their hands slammed on the tables.

"The emperor has sent word of this attack and called for a herald to go to the capital for a council," Thymas said, attempting to quiet down the crowd.

"Shit on what the emperor thinks. You are our king, and we need nothing from him. We will protect our own lands, not kiss the ground that Imperials tread upon." More cheers of agreement filled the room, and Thymas took a breath.

"They will push the Dark Kingdoms forces back. Commander Rye is a trusted man—"

"Then what do you say about this." Someone threw open the door—another lord, Lyall, with three guards behind him—holding something black in their arms and threw it to the stone floor of the room. A wolf-like being was bound in chains and frantically throwing its arms and legs about.

A demon. The rest of the room quickly burst into yelling and cursing as the demon thrashed on the ground.

Captain Mulliner quickly came through the doors and up to the prince. "I'm sorry, Your Grace. A group of villagers found it west of here." Thymas looked about the room as lords pulled their swords and neared the beast.

"They have it under control?" Lord Downor asked, pointing the blade at the demon. "Damned that be."

He put his sword through its neck and loped its head off. It rolled from the body, and its red eyes landed on Thymas. As the body faded into black mist, the rest of the lords turned to the prince.

"I say fuck the emperor. This is our kingdom. His men will do nothing but feed the demons who prowl our lands." He sheathed his sword, and Thymas watched the room unfold into chaos around him. The people hit their cups on the tables and argued amongst themselves, and Thymas raised his voice.

"We will not let another kingdom fall!" he yelled. "We will send our herald and ask for men to help fight. He has already promised more men to us, and we do not have enough fighters ourselves. You know this. If the Imperial army does fail, we will need every man to defend WhiteDrove and the surrounding towns. I know you put your trust in me. Now let me help this kingdom. Go back to your villages and your homes. Prepare them for the worst and pray for the best."

The room turned to silence, and Thymas took that as acceptance. "Go home. All of you."

He fled the room with his guards in tow, stepping past the dark spot on the floor where the demon had been. He turned to his captain once he was outside the doors.

"Make sure the lords return safely to their homes. I want patrols out nightly in search of more demons in each town and village south of here to the border."

"I am not sure we have the men for every settlement," Mulliner told.

"Make it work." Thymas turned away and went down the hall toward his mother's room. His feet had become heavy and weighted, and he finally pulled his cloak off and handed it to a servant.

When he entered his mother's room, she was conversing with her advisor, though knowing her, their words meant nothing. WhiteDrove was no fortress. If they took Ignis, his kingdom would surely fall. Something he would not tell his people. The queen rested the letter from the emperor on her lap, holding her chin in her hand.

"We should tighten the defenses, reinforce the walls—"

"And what would that do?" Kesanda asked with a wave of her hand. "This place is hardly defensible as is. The guards we have here are nothing but farmers. Unless pitchforks and decrypted cattle scare the cultists."

The advisor's brow creased. "But, Your Grace, the emperor has warned us about the Dark Kingdom. If we do nothing about it, WhiteDrove will be taken."

The elder woman set the letter on the desk beside her with a sigh. She situated herself, so she sat more comfortably by the fire.

"Yes, and the emperor said that he would send soldiers to deal with it. The best we can do is wait. It would be a waste to die of worry rather than a blade, Naldi," she said and waved him away. He bowed and scurried from the room. Thymas watched him close the door before stepping up to his mother.

"You would think they would send more soldiers to help the kingdom, which gives them their livestock," she huffed, pinching her nose.

"I thought the emperor was sending troops?" he asked.

His mother gave him a cold grin. "I lied. It's better to keep the people thinking they are safe than having mass panic run through the streets," she said and took a drink.

"So, we are getting no help?" Thymas asked, a hint of anger rising in his voice. He thought back to the men in the hall downstairs, thinking they were getting reinforcements to protect their people.

His mother looked over at the letter on the desk. "I need to send a herald to the council, as you know."

"Who?"

"You."

"What?" he fumed. "I must stay here and protect you and Anya!"

The queen knitted her fingers together, a disapproving gleam in her eye. "And I need you away to speak with the emperor. I trust you more than any of these fools who claim to advise me. And if the Dark Kingdom does attack, I will need an heir to keep the place up and running," she finished.

"Then send Anya—"

"She is but a girl. And a naïve one at that. No one will take the word of a half-elf child. You are my only option. This is not a choice."

Thymas bit his tongue from saying more, instead resorting to sitting in the chair opposite of her. He ran his hands through his hair with a vexed huff.

"WhiteDrove has little defenses. If we pull our people back from the villages, maybe we will have enough men to man the walls..."

The queen leaned back in her chair, seeming to contemplate their situation. They both sat silently for a time, watching the licking flames crackle in the fireplace.

"I remember the night you were born," she started, "There was a terrible storm that night; the windows had shattered under the ice. You could hear the waves crash against the cliffs miles away. All the fires had died out in the keep. The wind simply snuffed them out the moment they were lit. The snow was so high the doors to the keep could not be opened. Your father was caught in that storm, coming back from Ignis. I thought he would die out there in that cold; Goddess knows it was just as cold in here as it was out there.

"I was in labor for two days. The maids resorted to using the melted snow for drinking and kept adding more wood to the fire to try and keep it burning. When you came into this world, you never even cried; I had thought you dead when they put you in my arms. Cold as the winter outside, you were. But you breathed."

Thymas looked at his mother, who had a forlorn look in her eye. "And then years later, when I lost two of my children from the frost, I found a little girl outside the gates of the city, screaming like a banshee had hold of her. I never understood how my children came to be in this world, but all I can hope is that winter shall be kind to us a bit longer."

She finally looked at him with an indistinguishable gaze, and she picked up the letter from the table. "If we are to die at the hands of a demon, at least it will be in my warm room and not out in the blasted cold shitting myself."

Thymas choked out a laugh and stood up. "I will post more guards around the keep tonight," he said and turned. "I will leave through the portal in the morn."

Before he could leave, his mother's voice rang out. "Thymas. When are you going to marry?" she asked.

Thymas turned back to her. "What does this have to do with anything?" he asked.

The queen gave him a long stare. "I am as old as the woodland forest boy. You are nearly thirty and have yet to marry. I bless the day you were born, but when I die, you will become king of WhiteDrove, and without a proper marriage, it will be all the more reason for Viragrad to be cast from the map."

Thymas creased his eyebrows. "Marriage has nothing to do with war—"

"Marriage has everything to do with war, you stupid boy. Without the alliance of the other Houses, we are doomed to fall. We have no gold to buy our men weapons or mercenaries, no bonds with the other kingdoms. While you are in the capital, I expect a courtship. Now go, you have lots to do before the morn."

Thymas gave a small bow as he left the room.

Thymas opened the door to his sister's room. He paused for a moment, just watching her breathe. She was curled up in her bed, furs wrapped tightly around her petite frame. Her fingers grasped her drawing pad, still stained black from the ink. The hearth was still warm as the fire crackled and waved. He could feel the heat on his cheek as he walked over to her bedside and sat down carefully beside her. He pushed a stray hair from her face with a soft smile.

He watched her eyelashes flutter as she breathed, and wished he could stay for just a bit longer. The thought of leaving her with the Dark Kingdom so close made his stomach churn. She was only a child; she knew nothing of war or suffering. She didn't remember the skirmishes in the plains or the sickness that spread through the north years ago. He didn't want her to. He knew he couldn't protect her from everything, but he would have to try. He also knew that going to this council was the one way to ensure her safety.

"I'll return soon, Anya, I promise," he whispered. He kissed her forehead and stayed beside her for a while longer, listening to her snoring. It reminded him of the night when the winds rocked the keep and tore down houses in the villages. The snowfall was so thick he could not see past his feet. The cold gripped his nose and cheeks and turned them red as a cherry. The guards stationed outside glowed like lanterns with the ice that hung on their armor.

He had held Anya in his arms as the sounds of howling filled the halls. They had taken shelter in her room, sitting by the hearth. He rocked her while telling stories of the tribes of the sea that taught them to sail and hunt. She had never cried that night, only snuggled into her blanket with a melodic cooing. At points, he didn't think she was even breathing, but then she would wake and give a small smile. That smile that she would continue to give to those around her no matter the tension in the air.

She was too good for this world.

Thymas stood up from the bed and carefully made his way to the door. With one more glance at her sleeping figure, he shut it and made his way to the portal.

26 JARED

Jared knelt down in the newly blooming flowers of the forest as he attempted to knot an animal snare. He had been at it for what felt like hours at that point, and his frustration did little to help. His shaking fingers clumsily fidgeted with the knot, and he cursed and threw the rope to the round. He sat back on his heels with a sigh and listened to the wind ruffle the leaves above. Birds chirped happily in the canopies, and the fresh air of the flowers brought a calm sense of repose. His stomach growled, and he snorted at himself before standing up and grabbing the rope.

"You've been at it for nearly an hour," the half-elf said, coming up beside him.

He held the rope out to her. "Then please, indulge me with your infinite wisdom."

She rolled her eyes at him and took the rope. She knelt down and drove a stick into the ground. She wrapped the rope around it and motioned for him. He reluctantly kneeled again, and she took his hands, guiding him through the knot. He noticed how small and delicate her hands were around his calloused and cracked ones. The only noticeable blemish he could see was her fingertips which were worn from her use with a bow. She hummed softly as she guided him, prudently pulling the rope taut against the stick. When he managed to tie the knot, she gave a pleased smile.

"There, maybe we will catch something."

"You do this often?" he asked.

"I've lived on my own for years. Of course, I do."

Stupid question, he thought. She stood back up and pulled her bow from her shoulders, running her finger along the string.

"I need to go hunting for tonight's supper. Go back to the fire."

"Why... don't I come with you?" he asked.

She gave him a blank look. "Do you know how to hold a bow?"

"No."

"Do you know how to track?"

"No..."

"Do you know how to move silently through the forest?"

"Not particularly."

"Then go back to the camp."

Jared sighed and resigned himself to flee. She turned away from him, and he clomped his way through the brush back towards the horse and soft fire he had managed to make. The one thing he *could* do. He hated to admit that she was the reason he was alive. The wounds still stretched and burned uncomfortably along his torso, but she had made ointments from the herbs she found around the forest and used the last of her bandages to patch him up. He had no knowledge of how to hunt or fish or trap. He would have died of starvation if his wounds hadn't killed him first. Once again, he found himself in the debt of someone he could never repay.

A headache had already begun to wrap itself around his head, and he took a long drink of water. It wasn't ale, but he told himself not to complain. The nausea that crept its way into his stomach made him drop the drink and sit down with a sigh. The horse was tied to the tree beside him, and it gnawed on the thawed grass with happy enthusiasm. He watched the sun begin to set through the canopy of trees and stretched his back with a groan. He pulled his shirt off with a grimace and unwrapped his wounds. The blood had clotted a couple of days prior, but with some rigorous movements, small droplets would still ooze out. He pulled Nava's pack up to him and scrounged around for more bandages, grabbing hold of the puny amount left and taking a vial of ointment she had made, and spreading it over his chest. He hissed in pain at the stinging of the mixture. *Damn knight.* He still didn't understand how he had escaped its clutches. He barely remembered fighting it. He remembered crawling on the ground, dodging demons and cultists, praying to the goddess to help him. He remembered the knight hissing at him. *"Boy."* It called him—damned thing.

He barely knew about the Dark Kingdom before they came that night. He heard the stories Rose spouted out that her mother told and the things Olivia had seen on the roads, but that was it. He was outside the city the night they first came.

He was barely seventeen and was helping his father pull water from the well. It had been a dark night. They had closed off the entrance into the city and told the surrounding villages to stay in their homes, but they hadn't said why. His father ignored the orders; he had steel to carve and mouths to feed. But Jared had felt something that night, like a shadow had run past him. The chill he felt crawled all the way up his spine. He had dropped the bucket and ran straight home. His father beat him for that, but he was too scared to go back out. It wasn't until the next day that word spread about Queen Elena's death and Rose's rise to power.

He wanted to believe it all myths and legends. But he would never forget the heat of the houses burning or the screams of the people around him. Every time he closed his eyes, he could see the face of the Knight, his rotting teeth, and sunken eyes. If he could go back, he would have grabbed Olivia and run as fast as he could. But it was too late for that. And the scars he bore were a heavy reminder.

He heard soft footsteps approach and looked to see Nava with a rabbit and a few apples. He finished smoothing the ointment across his wounds and took hold of the bandages, attempting to wrap his chest and pull the small cloth around his back. The half-elf watched him as he clumsily tied the bandage and shifted it. *I am as dimwitted as a horse*, he sighed. He quickly looked up as Nava set the rabbit and apples down in front of him. She kneeled down and grasped the bandage, and he jerked away from her.

She flinched back, holding part of the bandage. "You are doing a terrible job. You need my help," she said. Jared let out a vexed sigh and sat up stiffly. He said nothing as she gently pulled the bandages off and retied them. He felt the soft skin of her fingers run down his chest as she pressed the cloth to his wounds, her mouth moving silently.

"What are you saying?" he asked.

She ran her hands down his chest, securing the bandage. "*Ave etha' valans.* It is a healing hymn... the old healer would sing it to the ailing patient in her care."

Jared stared at the woman mere inches from his face, watching her eyes focus on her work. She spoke softly under her breath so he could hear, and her voice was soft. He couldn't understand her, but he could feel the power in her words, like a blanket wrapping around him. It was enchanting.

She suddenly wrapped her hands around his chest, leaning into him. He held his breath as her hair tickled his neck. He felt her pull the bandage around his back and over his shoulder, ignoring the feeling of her chest on his skin. She smelled of lavender and cloves. He closed his eyes and focused on the feeling of her touch, trying to focus on a picture. She reminded him of *her*. Her touch, her smell, her voice.

Too soon she moved away and tied the bandage and Jared opened his eyes. Nava gave a soft sigh of approval and a nod of her head. "Hopefully that will last. I have no more for you."

"Thank you…" he muttered, eyes still locked onto her. She glanced up, catching his gaze, and quickly looked back down. She pulled a knife from her belt and flipped it over and held it out to him.

"What?" he asked.

"You're going to skin these," she said, grabbing the rabbit and squirrel.

"Me? I don't exactly know how—"

"Then learn," she interrupted. She sat down next to him and slowly showed him how she moved the knife into the rabbit. She would stop and show him how to not cut too deep and how to preserve the meat. He half-listened as he studied how easy she made everything seem. From skinning to hunting to healing, she was better than him. Once she skinned it and threw the intestines into the fire, she stuck a stick through its body and placed it near the flames.

"It isn't much. But it will feed us tonight. Hopefully, the snare will provide us for the coming days," she told.

"Who taught you to hunt?" he asked. She looked at him warily before responding.

"I learned on my own."

"Sounds lonely."

"It was not." Her voice grew harsher, and he stopped prying. The horse gave a knicker, and Jared threw it an apple. It neighed happily, and he gave a half-smile.

As the sun began to set, he pulled his shirt back on with a groan, and she cut off a leg of the rabbit for him. She handed it to him, and with a small thanks, they began to eat. He sat back against the tree and picked through the bones of the leg, his gaze wandering back to the half-elf. She sat quietly; her legs folded under her. Her cloak was pulled tighter around her body as the night grew chillier. Her hair was unbound and fell around her shoulders in soft waves. Her eyes were large—larger than any normal human—and gleamed dimly in the dying light. When she moved her hands around the rabbit, he could barely see a shimmer to her skin. The elven blood in her was undeniable, but he didn't think her queer. If he didn't chain his thoughts, he could almost think of her as strangely beautiful.

He pulled his eyes away from her and towards the fire. She gave no indication that she wanted more conversation. He shrugged out his shoulders and continued eating, content with the silence for now.

27 ENARA

Cloaked in black and shrouded by night, Enara made her way down the streets of her city. They were dark and barren; the rain had quenched the remaining fires, and now the city looked like a crypt. From Goldtown to Lowtown, the remnants of the city seemed like long-forgotten tombs. The noble houses were ransacked and pillaged, and furniture was thrown to the streets and discarded. Torn clothes and rotting food littered the yards.

The once lively main square was now quiet; the carts turned over and broken. She watched as a group of cultists tore through boxes and pouches, searching for jewels and gold. They ignored her as she passed and stopped at the statue of her mother.

She looked up at the now-defaced statue. Mud and blood were smeared along the base, and rope hung from her outstretched hand. Her head was cut from her body—now resting at the foot of her—covered in bile. *My mother's legacy*, she thought.

The smell of rotting flesh churned her stomach as she slid by a group of people lighting candles in their loved one's honor. Her eyes caught the gaze of a young girl. Her tear-filled blue eyes tore through her own as she held a flickering candle in her grasp. The wails of her mother filled her ears as she begged for the Goddess to bring back her son, her husband. Enara looked away and started further down the street. She could feel her chest tighten painfully as she gasped for breath.

She could feel the girl's gaze on her. She could see the blood running from her hands, the aura of death that emitted from her. The dogs howled at the cloud-covered moons, low or sorrowful. Enara leaned against a stone wall of the alleyway, clutching her chest. Flashes of her sister's eyes went across her mind—the look of betrayal, the screams of her people still rang in her ears—the wails of children, the howls of demons.

She heard a low moan, and she turned to her side. A young soldier sat leaning against the wall, holding his stomach beside her. His cheeks were sunken with hallowed eyes, blood caked his pale lips. Enara bent down, touching his shoulder. He jerked slightly and looked over at her. He didn't seem to recognize her.

"How long have you been here?" she asked.

He took a shaky breath and flinched, fresh blood seeping down his chest. "A few hours... milady. A cultist was harassing a young girl... pulled her skirt down... I took a knife to the gut," he answered slowly.

Enara bit her lip and hooked her hands under his arm. "Come, I will get you to the apothecary," she said. She pulled him up, and he cried out. She snapped her head to the side when two cultists looked their way. With a glare and a defensive hiss, the cultists seemed to recognize her and backed away. She brought the soldier's arm over her shoulder, and they began their long limp to the apothecary.

She hadn't the heart to tell her people she was the cause of their suffering. She was the reason that children went motherless, and boys died fighting a pointless battle. But it would be better. She would make sure of it. She would be a good queen. She would fix this. Rose would not have done well for Ignis.

The couple slowly made their way toward the apothecary. With each wet step through mud and puddles, Enara could hear the gurgling of blood coming from the soldier. If he had a puncture wound within his lungs, he wouldn't last the night. She felt a sharp pain run down her chest.

"Keep your strength with you," she told the soldier, who only mustered a small nod in response.

Fear crept into her chest when she realized there may be *no* apothecary left living. She only knew of a few in the city; they mainly came to the castle when she or Rose had fallen ill. And now...she didn't want to think about it.

They passed through several rubble-ridden streets and corridors and the soldier tripped several times. She managed to hold on to him and boost him back up and walking.

She sighed in relief when she spotted the mortar and pestle carved into a sign nearby. She slowly guided him to the door, and Enara knocked. An older man opened the door and looked towards the soldier's wound. With a sigh, he opened the door the rest of the way to allow them access inside. Enara guided the soldier over to the table and helped him up onto it.

"This is the twelfth one this evening," the apothecary said with a shake of his head.

"The twelfth?" Enara gasped. The man stripped the soldier's chest bare, throwing the torn garments to the floor, and examined the wound. It was small but deep. There was dark blood smeared and crusted around his stomach, and with each breath he took, she could see blood bubble up from the wound.

The apothecary tapped his fingers down the soldier's chest and brought his head to his mouth. After a moment, he shook his head with a *tisk*, and he patted him on the chest.

"The wound has pierced a lung. I cannot help you, boy, but give you herbs to dull the pain," he said.

Enara stepped over to the apothecary. "What do you mean, there is nothing you can do?" she asked, her voice shaking. The man looked over at her and paused, scanning her face. A look of recognition passed over him, but he said nothing.

"I am no enchanter, *milady*. I have nothing to cure him, only help him to the Eternal Plains where the Goddess Velara awaits."

Enara looked back over at the man on the table. Blood had begun to pour out of his mouth as his eyes locked onto hers. Enara went to leave, but a hand grasped her wrist.

"Please, milady. It would... do me great honor to have a pretty lass by my side when I pass," he mumbled. Enara bit her lip, her face reflecting off his marbled green eyes. Enara sighed and nodded. She pulled up a stool and sat down, her hand on his.

His eyes ignited when she pulled her hood down to show her face, and he coughed, and the apothecary put a blanket under his head. He started mixing herbs, and Enara could smell the strange minty scent of the concoction.

Enara pulled a damp cloth from a bucket and wiped the soldier's dirty face, just beginning to see the pale flesh underneath.

"What is your name?" Enara asked while gently running the cloth over his eyes.

"Elden... milady," he croaked.

Enara smiled lightly, then a sudden stabbing pain shot through her as black lightning filled her arm. She took a shaky breath and pushed the pain aside. "Elden, where is your family?"

A glaze went over his eyes as he stared at the ceiling. "I don't have one... they were killed... in the battle by demons," he said.

Enara's heart dropped in her chest. Of course, another family had been destroyed. This man had given his life, and the life of his family, to protect her from the Dark Knights that she had summoned. And she reaped what she sowed.

"You shall see them again. I promise on the goddess," she swore.

The boy smiled and turned his gaze toward her. A look of infatuation crossed his features. "I have... never received a kiss from a lady before," he muttered quietly. Enara laughed slightly, rubbing his hand with her thumb. The apothecary came over, and Enara stopped him from giving the soldier the medicine. Instead, Enara took the bowl from him and took a sip, then she bent down and kissed the soldier. She could feel the calloused wear of the boy's lips on hers. She tasted the metallic tinge of blood and the minty solution in her mouth. The boy's hand squeezed hers, and she pulled away. She wiped the trace of the mixture from his lips and ran her fingers through his damp hair.

"Go to sleep. The goddess will greet you when you wake," she whispered.

The soldier smiled and coughed violently. "I can't feel much anymore, thank you, milady," he said. Enara ignored the tingling of her lips and ran a finger down his cheek. She watched as he slowly passed, not leaving his side until the sun was well into the sky.

Enara held her still blood-covered hand. Her thumb slid over the crusted flakes of red as her glazed eyes scanned the dulled city of light from her balcony. She felt her breath grow cold as goosebumps formed along her skin. She heard the clang of metal on the stone and a clawed iron hand placed on her shoulder and she closed her eyes, a shudder running down her spine.

"You are frightened. Why?" Malum asked, his cold voice breathing against her cheek. He had taken off his helmet, so now she could clearly see his ashen skin and icy blue eyes. His gaze held a frigidness that frightened her more.

"You told me my people would not come to harm any longer," she answered.

She heard a chuckle from the man, and his hand trailed through her hair. "I told you no harm would come to those who submit. Those who would still fight are a threat to your reign," he replied.

Enara bit her lip as the face of the soldier ran through her mind. "No more. I will not have my people's blood run through the streets," she said sharply.

"What if I could give you more? This entire continent could be yours to rule. The mage is dead. You have nothing stopping you," he purred. Black lightning shot through her hand, and she hissed. Her mind darkened, churning like a pig's stomach.

"I... this is my kingdom. I need no more!" she cried.

Malum ran a finger down her cheek. "You will change your mind," he said and left the balcony. She heard a second pair of footsteps enter the room.

Trissa moved out of the way as the Black King left. He gave her a sneer, and she gave a mock bow in return. He laughed—seeming amused by her insult—and with a disgusted look, she turned to the queen. Her form was visibly shaken, and her breath rattled.

"Enara, you are pale," she said. The wind had grown considerably colder, so she grabbed a blanket and draped it over the queen's shoulders. Enara looked down at the black marks that now grew to her forearm.

"Am I dying?" she asked shakily.

Trissa frowned and took her hand. "I don't know," she answered.

A tear ran down her cheek as she looked back out at her kingdom. "What have I done, Trissa?"

28 ROSE

Rose's feet padded down the pathways of the village. As she passed the villagers and their livestock, she took in every sight, every sound. The birds that cawed above her were puffed and hopping from house to house to keep their feet from freezing to the snow. Several women were hunched over buckets of water by a fire, dipping clothes and scrubbing them with red hands. They set the clothes on the line next to the fire and began again. Rose wondered how much more difficult it was for the maids back home to wash her own clothes. No wonder they grumbled when she ruined a new dress.

The women paid her little mind as she passed, intent on finishing before their hands grew frostbitten. The children, however, noticed her. A group of them came up to her, young but nearly to her shoulders. They all squealed at her, quickly dropping into messy bows.

They spoke quickly to her in their native tongue, and she tried her best to understand them, but they seemed content on simply showing her around the village. They took her to the armory, where the blacksmith greeted her with frightened reverence. He insisted on her taking any weapon she wished, waving his hands around the forge and showing her his newest creations, swords and axes and engraved necklaces. She did not take anything from him as the children pulled her away soon after. Then they guided her to the stables, where they insisted she touch every single one of the horses. She could only assume they thought she could bless them. She did not believe she could do so. It still made the children happy, though, so she tried her best.

The last stop was near their homes, where she was greeted by toys and carvings the children had made. They held them out to her with joyous enthusiasm. She couldn't say no, so she scooped them all up and placed them in her satchel. They finally released her when their mothers called for them hours later. She admitted that she was grateful for the quiet.

She started back down the pathway and towards the entrance to the village when she noticed the guards stationed along the high wooden walls and climbed the stairs to reach the top. She looked out over the frozen landscape and saw nothing but white in a mix of snow and ice. How they navigated it all was a surprise to her. They had no stars in the sky or landmarks to guide them. The wolf fur cloak she bore kept her warm, but she could still feel the unnatural chill around her. She began to wonder how true the stories of the Forsaken were. Had they truly caused an eternal winter?

Her mind trailed back to her sister and her friends. She would be lost if she could never see Olivia or Jared again or ended up facing their corpses on the battlefield. And Enara, every time she thought of her she could feel the wound on her stomach burn.

She turned when the sound of a horn rang through the village, and the gates were opened to a small war party. Rose watched as seven men returned from the bitter plains. All were wounded and bloody. One was limping, and another was on horseback, unmoving. The rest looked crippled and weary, their armor torn, and blood matted their hair and beards. The guards greeted them and ushered them to the healer's huts.

"What happened to them?" Rose asked a guard.

He turned to her with a tired and despondent face. "They were hunting. Party of Forsaken ambushed them," he said, pulling together a proper sentence in her language. Rose frowned as a pair of guards pulled the limp man from the horse and set him gently on the ground, covering him with a blanket.

"Six survive," the guard started. "Twenty men who left last week."

Rose grimaced. "I'm sorry. That must hurt dearly to lose those close to the village."

"We lose more and more men. But they are now protecting the Mother. You are here now. You can help us, *Runa*," he smiled.

Rose did not return the smile. "Yes, I suppose I will." She left the man alone and walked past the remaining group of hunters. They had set about collecting wood and placing it together in a stack. Even though they still bled, they did not complain, did not rest or drink.

Their focus was determined, and she didn't dare interrupt them.

She noticed the mother healer walking towards them, an armful of herbs and tokens in her hands.

"They are preparing his funeral," Nadahi started, strolling up to the golden-haired queen. "He died a warrior. He shall be accepted to *Shor'vaker* with open arms."

Rose turned to look as the men set the hunter onto the wooden pyre, and the mother placed the herbs and tokens around him. "What is *Shor'vaker?*" she asked.

Nadahi pointed to the top of the Great Hall, where the wooden carvings depicted a woman being shielded by men and women. She held her arms to her sides as if she welcomed her fate, but the warriors stood strong with swords and shields raised. "It is the Afterland, where the hunters go to protect the Mother Goddess from the demons of the afterlife. It is their sole duty in death to keep Her safe. It is the greatest honor to have," she said.

Rose scanned the carvings, thinking to herself. "Sounds... quaint," she paused.

Nadahi laughed. "It is full of drinking and fighting. No Lowlander would make it into *Shor'vaker*. Not without the Goddess's permission."

Rose and Nadahi watched as the mother dipped her hand into a bowl she was holding and wrote a rune on the man's forehead. She whispered prayers in her language as a family stepped up to the pyre. She recognized one of the children from that morning standing next to her mother. The mother did not cry, but she placed a hand on the warrior's still chest, closing her eyes. The little girl held a wooden carving of a wolf in her hands, and she reached up to place it onto the pyre. The other warriors stood around the pyre and the chieftain, Alrik Wolf-Caller, thumped down the steps of the Great Hall and over to the group. He gave Rose a nod before taking a torch from one of the warriors and stepping over to the pyre.

"Here we witness the ascension of our brother to the great halls of *Shor'vaker*. The spirits of the frost will fight over the right to guide him to the Mother Goddess, and forever shall he be by Her side. We feast tonight alongside the fallen, for tomorrow may be our hour to die." He held the torch to the pyre, and it lit in a bright haze of red and orange. The herbs crackled and popped and colored the smoke a hazy blue, and Rose swore she saw a body in it. It reached down to the man and jumped high into the sky. It rippled and faded from sight, and soon, the entire pyre was lit up in flames.

No one spoke a word as the mother and daughter mourned the loss of the warrior, and Rose felt Nadahi give her a small pat on the shoulder. She saw in their eyes the same thing as her own when she looked in the mirror. Her unshed tears had crystallized in her eyes, forbidden from falling.

The last funeral she had attended was her mother's, and she still vividly remembered that day. The chapel windows had been broken and barren, and she could still smell the smoke in the air. The remaining nobility bore bruises and cuts, and the common folk were worse for wear.

Her mother had laid on a blanket of woven gold and silver. Her dress was a shining shade of white and blue. Her hair was pooled around her, and her hands rested gently on her chest. If Rose hadn't known better, she would have thought she was sleeping. Enara had gone up to her mother's side and stood there, still as stone, for what felt like hours. She did not shed a tear, only gave a look of resentment towards their mother's closed eyes.

"Does your goddess choose everyone who gets into *Shor'vaker*?" Rose asked, pulling herself from her thoughts.

Nadahi nodded. "Yes. She chooses those who have fought valiantly and died in battle."

"Then..." Rose started, "Do these Forsaken I've heard of get chosen, as well?"

A clouded look crossed the huntress's face. "No. The Forsaken are no longer the warriors and protectors of the Goddess. They have forsaken Her and the tribes. They belong nowhere but left in the snow. Their bodies shall not be burned," she said.

Rose touched the paint on her arms. "Do your markings have meaning? Everyone I have come across except for the children has them," she asked curiously.

Nadahi nodded her head. "Yes, we wear these markings as proof that we belong to the tribe. The blue marks us as the Tribe of the Wolf. Green as the Tribe of Bear. Red as the Tribe of Stag, and purple as the Tribe of Fox."

"Why do the children not have them?"

"You must undergo a rite of passage to earn your markings. When the children become of age, they will claim their markings, and we shall feast to their many battles to come."

"Does the Forsaken have markings?"

"Yes. Black. As the Forsaken crawl to darkness," she answered, waving her away and starting through the village.

"Come, you should not be out in this cold for long." She brought her back to the hut they had given her and ushered her inside. Rose sighed happily at the warmth of the hearth and shed her pelts.

The hut was small but cozy, with heavy drapes covering the windows and soft candlelight decorating the walls. There was a desk sitting in the corner of the room next to the bed, and a large hearth and fireplace along the front wall. Small vials of ointments and bags of herbs sat on the wooden desk that the mother had given her to help her wounds.

Rose set the satchel down on a chair and went through the little gifts the children had given her.

"They like you," Nadahi said, coming up to her. She pulled a carved bird from the satchel with a small chuckle.

"I don't know what to do with all of them," Rose said, piling them all onto the desk.

"Keep the ones you think will bring you favor from the Goddess. You may leave the rest here to protect this hut."

"You believe tiny carvings will protect me?" she laughed. "I may need more than that."

"These are more than just carvings. They were offerings to the goddess that they gave to you instead. It is a great honor, if not slightly unwanted." She handed Rose the small bird, and she turned it over in her hand.

"I suppose I can keep one if it will make them happy, at least." She placed it into the pocket of her undercoat and patted it affectionately.

Nadahi walked about the room, feeling the wool of the curtains and putting her hands to the fire. Rose fingered the jewel around her neck and felt it pulse lightly. She had never felt it so active before. The thrumming reminded her of the hum her mother used to sing when putting her to bed. She could barely remember it now. Nadahi walked over to the windowsill and took a pitcher from it. She came back with a cup of water for Rose, who gladly took it. The huntress sat down on the bed as Rose took a sip of the drink.

"What is on your mind?" she asked.

Rose laughed to herself. "Is it that obvious that I'm thinking?"

"The crease between your eyes. My father gets it when he is deep in thought."

"Then I suppose you caught me... your father is the chieftain, right?"

The huntress nodded. "Yes, he is. Just as his father and his mother before him."

"Will you claim the throne next?"

Nadahi gave her a curious look. "Yes, but that will hopefully not be for a while yet."

"I wish I still had my mother. I didn't know my father," Rose said, sitting beside her on the bed.

"Both are dead?" Nadahi asked.

"Yes, my father died on a hunting trip gone wrong when I was just a babe, and my mother died at the hands of the Dark Kingdom."

Nadahi suddenly clasped Rose's small hand in her own, looking into her eyes. "Your parents are with the goddess now. I promise you, *Runa*, the False God, and the Dark Kingdom will crumble beneath your feet."

Rose blushed slightly and pulled her hand away. "I—thank you, Nadahi. I've been meaning to ask, what is this False God? Just a man who controls the Forsaken?"

Nadahi shook her head. "The False God was once the lover of the Mother Goddess before even the sun had lit the world. They together created the children, *Runa*. The *Runa* were tasked with creating life in the world they had built for them. And so, they did. They created the trees that towered above the clouds. Deer as large as the huts they lived in. Flowers that held their bloom through every season. They created new life through one another and led villages, built cities, and ruled empires. Their children had become so powerful they could rival the goddess herself. The goddess wept in her happiness, bringing the rains and oceans down onto the land. But the False God grew resentful of His children and the power they carried. In his rage, He began killing his own children and taking their power for himself. As the Mother did not have the strength to turn against her lover, the *Runa* had to banish and chain the False God within the Afterland to stop His corruption. Now the Forsaken wish to awaken the god and use His power to take over the lands," Nadahi said.

Rose looked down at the water in her tankard. "So, if they manage to awaken the god, will it be stoppable?"

Nadahi frowned. "Possibly, with the help of the other gods. But they have distanced themselves from our Mother for thousands of years."

Rose sighed. More talk of gods and goddesses. She was barely worshipping her own, let alone the many that supposedly existed now. How was she supposed to believe this?

"If you kill the god in its sleep, though, the winter will end, and you may return to your home," Nadahi assured.

Rose ran a hand through her hair with a pout. "I'm well aware of what I must do to return home," she groaned.

Nadahi chuckled to herself, earning a glare from the girl. "What's so funny?"

"You are like a newborn pup, mewling for her mother's milk. I mean no disrespect, *Runa*, but you are young and naïve. You may doubt now, but soon you shall see." Rose glared at her, and the woman gave a hearty laugh. "Do not worry, *Runa*. We shall leave for the ruins in the morning with the hunters. This shall not be easy, but you will be back home sooner than you know."

"I hope you are right, Nadahi," Rose frowned.

"And perhaps I may teach you our language along the way? It would make things much easier."

"I have a hard enough time learning Elvish. Now I must add this on top," she sighed.

Nadahi moved the hair from her face. "Do not worry, I shall keep you safe from the Forsaken," she said.

Rose blushed deeper and straightened her posture. "I—thank you," she stuttered.

With a nod, Nadahi stood and pulled her pelts close. "Rest well. Tomorrow, we journey."

29 VIA

Via paced back and forth in the encampment while her mind wandered to her agents and to the letter that had arrived not an hour ago. She had reread it four times over before finally handing it to the commander. She still couldn't wrap her head around it. Ignis had been taken by the Dark Kingdom. There was no army, no preemptive battles, nothing. It was as if they appeared from the Otherworld. She cursed herself for not sensing it—for not seeing the signs.

The dread that crept into her mind at the thought of them taking the princess…. no. She wouldn't think of it. She either escaped or was killed. Any way was better than captured. If they took her, then the gods would be their only savior. All she had sacrificed would be for naught.

She heard a *caw* above her and looked up to see a raven circling her head. She brought her arm out and he landed on her forearm, chirping happily. She rubbed him under the chin and hummed softly. His beady eyes closed, and he purred, leaning into her touch.

"Veleros, where have you been?" she asked. The raven snapped his beak and ruffled his feathers. "I see. You could have warned me."

He chirped and flew off into the sky above. Via put her arm down and frowned, watching him disappear into the sunset beyond. She hardly noticed when she began pacing again, back and forth with her thoughts swirling in her mind.

If Ignis had been captured, that meant that the scouts with the notes were searching for the other villages, possibly for an attack. The farms would be the most valuable asset to the Dark Kingdom, along with the several coal and ore mines in the hills. With trading being the main support system of the kingdom, they will be reliant on other means of obtaining *sephim*. Perhaps if they cut off supply lines to the mines, burned farms, and cut off trading routes it would force them to abandon the city at the very least—

"Via, you're wearing a hole in the ground." Rye interrupted, coming up to her, his hands resting gingerly on the hilt of his sword. "What is worrying you?"

Via stopped pacing, putting her hands on her hips. With a shake of her head, she sighed and replied to Rye's comment. "My agents, they have yet to return," she answered, looking past the camp into the swampy marshes.

"I'm sure they are only delayed, Via. Your agents are some of the best I know," he said and walked over to her, placing a hand on her shoulder.

"I know, but things seem to not want to favor me this week. First Ignis, now this," she sighed.

"I'm sure everything will be fine, Raven; your men are safe," he assured. "I already sent a messenger to the capital. We will hold our position here until we know more from Ignis. Our duty now is to protect WhiteDrove."

She nodded in agreement, but she feared the pit in her stomach was more than just a hunch. Something was wrong. She knew it.

"I'm going to go and scout the camp," she said, earning a retort from the commander.

"Via, I cannot allow you to do this. Wait for your scouts to return with a report," he pleaded.

Via turned to him. "They will not return. I will only be gone a few hours. I will be back by daylight," she assured.

With a sigh, he motioned over a soldier. "Then I shall come as well."

Via's eyebrows creased. "No. I will not allow it."

"So, I cannot have a say in matters, but you can? As your commanding officer, I believe that is a bit offensive," he smiled.

Via sighed. "I cannot lose another—" She cut herself off before saying more. "Fine. But you will not leave my side."

Via waited for Rye at the edge of the camp. He had left to give orders to Garding and the rest of his commanding officers while she readied the mounts. She thought him ridiculous for coming with her; he was the commander—she a spy. The army would survive without her, but they would lose everything if he were to fall in battle, no less doing something stupid as scouting a camp. She knew it was because he worried about her—which he shouldn't. She could take care of herself. But he always seemed to be pressed about her well-being. One of the righteous qualities that would get him killed. Now he gave his power away to Garding in hopes that he would not die and leave the army without its head.

Via rubbed the snout of the horse as it nickered and pressed against her. *I must do better,* she thought. She sacrificed someone important to her just to obtain runes that might not have worked at all. Perhaps Ravana gave her faulty runes or cast a curse on them. She wouldn't be surprised. She had done worse. And now her agents were dead or captured, and Ravana was standing there laughing as she always did.

Her hands tightened on the reins, and she felt a presence come up to her.

"Are you ready?" Rye asked. Instead of his armor, he wore worn leather bracers and a vest. She noted his appearance.

"You want to die, don't you?"

He laughed. "If we are to sneak into a camp, I doubt being in full armor clanging around is the best idea."

She took a long breath and shook her head, mounting her horse. He did the same, and they started away from the camp.

They did not speak for a time, simply taking in the sunlight that played along the dirt pathway they traveled. Via kept her eyes on the Mors ahead. She noticed every shift of movement, every creak of the trees. She could feel her back muscles tighten as she thought of something jumping from the shadows. Things that shouldn't startle her. How old was she? And yet she acted as if she were a child still, terrified of the things that waited in the corner of her room. Her mother would have scolded her for such trivialities. And now, she would welcome those shadows again if it meant never facing what lay beyond the Mors.

"Via."

She pulled herself from her thoughts and looked over to the commander. He had a small smile on his face.

"What?" she asked, a hint of disdain in her voice.

"The one thing I know for certain about you is that you always get that look in your eye when you worry."

Via kept her face a mask. "I do not give a look."

"You do. You may be stoic when others are around, but you will always get that dark shadow in your eyes. Like you're lost in the Otherworld."

"You presume to know me so well," she huffed.

"If you let me know you better, perhaps that would not be the only thing I see."

Via sighed and shifted in her saddle. "You already know much about me. We've been together for a decade."

"And yet you still have yet to speak of Nevrak. Or Ravana. As the commander, you would think I should know more about the other kingdom. Allies, or enemies."

"They are behind a portal. They are no threat."

"And if that portal is destroyed?"

"Then we will deal with it then."

Rye gave a forced laugh and shook his head. "The ever-elusive spymaster…" he trailed off as the Mors grew closer. She could feel the heavy emotion that burdened the area. It weighed on her like a weeping mother mourning the loss of her child. She could almost hear the dull thrum of the ground beneath them, still alive yet struggling to breathe.

"How did they make it past us?" she heard Rye say with a sigh. He looked out over the landscape towards the fallen kingdom. "There are several villages between here and the city. None of them carried a warning."

"I can send men out to scout the villages. Perhaps they slaughtered their way through. No survivors mean no preparation."

"Possibly."

She looked back to the Mors as she trailed through possible scenarios in her mind. Ignis fell in a single night. Missing scouts. No reports of fighting in the Golden Hills. It didn't add up except for one possibility. And she pushed it from her mind. It was not possible. They could not return. She had made sure of that. And after the events of Velwood, the scar the earth bears from their curse. If what she knew to be true in her heart was, she would end it forever. Whatever means necessary.

30 OLIVIA

"How much farther?" Olivia asked, staring at the boy across from the fire who was curled in on himself. He had told her his name was Ladrin. His dark hair was matted atop his head, and his forehead was slick with sweat. His eyes had yet to leave her own. His sword was confiscated, now resting on the bard's side.

"A week or so..." he paused, scanning the woods around him. "Are you going to kill me?"

"How old are you?" she asked, ignoring his first question. She turned a bow around in her hands, testing the balance. She had taken it from one of the other men she had killed. The boy looked at the bow, then back up at her.

"I just had my fifteenth name day, milady," he blurted.

Olivia investigated the crackling embers of the fire. "You're young to be fighting in a war like this."

Ladrin twisted and shrugged. "It's not unusual for a commoner to be conscripted at thirteen milady," he answered.

Olivia looked up at him. "Is that so? Here I thought all you lot were just demons."

"Only the gods control their servants. It's a privilege to serve our masters," he argued. He visibly flinched when she gave a haunting laugh.

"You are either foolish or ignorant, kid. They are no gods."

"Our gods have kept us alive!" he retorted, raising his voice. "Without them, we would be dead."

Olivia stopped laughing. This boy truly believed the Dark Knights were doing what was best for them. He probably grew up in a shit hole infested with rats; the best thing that happened to him was conscription. She didn't know whether to feel pity or anger.

"Well, then I hope your gods bleed," she said, running her fingers down the string of the bow.

"Y-you can't kill a god. You wouldn't make it into the kingdom."

"That's what you're here for, isn't it?" she asked, looking up.

The boy paled. "Deserters are killed. We cannot enter the city."

"Then we find a way around," she hissed.

Ladrin slumped down, defeated. He pulled his knees to his chest and stared at the fire. Olivia noted his emaciated body and the leather vest that was too big for his torso. His sunken eyes made him appear much older than he was.

"You have parents?" she asked.

Ladrin nodded. "My father is a baker. My mother died giving birth to me. My siblings were conscripted," he muttered.

Olivia sat back on her heels. "My family was murdered by your gods," she said flatly. The boy glanced up at her and grimaced. "My home was destroyed by your gods. My life was stolen by your gods. And if you think I will spare anyone who follows your gods, you are utterly wrong."

The boy said nothing else as she stood up and threw a bundle into the fire. "I'm going hunting. Stay put," she ordered. He did as she said, and she took off into the forest.

The night was dark and cold. She took the clothing of dead soldiers and used it for herself. The coat was too big and the trousers too wide. They smelled of smoke and soot, and the blood that coated the collar was crusty and nicked her skin. She traversed the moonlit forest with the bow in hand. She honestly wondered if the Dark Kingdoms' forces were that incompetent to rely on a child—who could barely hold a sword—for war.

Then again, those soldiers were the ones that managed to slaughter an entire city and burn her father alive. There were no children in war.

A beam of moonlight slid against the ground in scattered fragments through the leaves of the trees. She noticed an occasional light in the distance that did not come down from the sky. It blinked an orange hue, then disappeared for a moment before popping back up in a different place along her line of vision.

This trail did not seem like the ones she was used to taking in the Golden Hills. This trail seemed... queer. She felt as if something was watching her in the canopies; her hair had begun to stand on her neck. When she walked, she could hear the crunching of something beneath her, like brittle bones. But when she looked down, she could only see moss and patches of dark grass.

She should be used to the semi-darkness of the forest, but tonight it held no warmth or comfort. She used to enjoy staring up at the moons and listening to the croaking of frogs and chirping of crickets on her jobs. It was a pleasant change to the hubbub of the tavern patrons and the songs of the bards.

Olivia stepped over a fallen tree branch and stopped when she heard a bird cawing above her. She looked up through the silver light of the canopy to see a crow perched on a branch above her. Its beady eyes glowed in the light, and it puffed its feathers before cawing again. She carefully took an arrow from her quiver and raised it at the bird. It did not move as she pulled on the string. She set her sight on its chest, and it cocked its head at her. She took a breath and—

"My child, you should not be alone here at night."

Olivia flinched, and the arrow went through the forest. The crow *cawed* and flew from its perch down towards her head. She ducked, and it swooped above her. She turned to see it land on the shoulder of an old woman.

Olivia stood upright, and the woman smiled at her. She was tall and gaunt, cloaked in black, with ragged feathers adorning her shoulders. Her scraggly white hair puffed out around her head, and her nose was long and upturned. The wrinkles on her face creased when she smiled.

"It is not safe in these woods at night. There are terrors that lay in the shadows," she said. Her voice was pitched and nasally.

"I... I was only hunting for supper," Olivia told her. The crow on the old woman's shoulders cawed and flapped its wings.

"*Dinner. Dinner,*" it cried. The woman's shoulder twitched, and her dark eyes turned towards the bird.

"If it is supper you need. You may come with me. We have plenty to spare."

The strange light flickered into view behind the woman, and Olivia could make out the dark shadow of a hut. The windows welcomed her gaze with a glimmer of yellow light. Olivia could feel a pull of her body towards the woman, and she took a breath. The stench of rotting meat filled her nostrils, and she resisted the urge to gag.

"I am with someone. I cannot leave him."

"Another one!" she yelled happily. The sudden outburst made the crow fly in the air and then land back on her shoulder. "All the more! I insist." The woman's smile grew wider. Larger than it should be.

"I can show you where you seek. I can feel your anger. I can help." The moons disappeared behind a cloud, and the forest was entrenched in darkness. She blinked to adjust her eyes, and the crow cawed again.

"Embrace it. Child. I can sense your hunger." The voice became twisted and low, and Olivia started to back away. Even though the dark, she could see the outline of the woman in front of her from the lit windows of the hut. She heard a rat scamper underneath her.

"I—I need to leave," she said hurriedly. The crow suddenly dove for her, and Olivia backed away. It sunk its talons into the rat and flew up into the tree. Blood splashed down on top of her like rain as the bird threw the rat onto a branch above her.

The woman's high-pitched laugh came, and she put a hand to the quiver on her hip, and the crow cawed again.

"*Dinner. Dinner!*" It cried.

"You will embrace me. You will embrace the song," the old woman laughed.

The moon reappeared from hiding behind the clouds, and with a burst of wings and wind, the woman was gone. Olivia fell to her knees and clutched the bow tightly. The blood soaked through her coat and ran down her chest and hair. More blood than a rat should carry in its body. The light of the hut diminished from her sight, and she looked to the green forest floor dotted with red. She was hungry no longer.

31 NAVA

The horse trotted at a steady pace along the worn dirt path. Jared stayed silent; his arms pressed against Nava's thighs while holding the reins of the horse. She seemed to not pay any mind to him. Her eyes glazed over, staring out towards the setting sun.

"Something botherin' you?" Jared asked casually. He watched as his words passed right through her pointed ears. With a sigh, he moved a hand up to her ear and flicked it.

Nava jolted and quickly swatted his hand away. "Do you mind!?" she hissed with a flush.

"You weren't paying attention to me."

Nava gave him a hard glare over her shoulder. "I should kick you off this horse."

"Why?" he teased. "I was only playing with your ear."

"The—" She shook her head and brushed her hair over her ears.

"Are they ticklish?"

"No, so leave them alone," she argued. Jared gave a laugh and held the reins once again.

"Fine, but I like them."

Nava opened her mouth to retort but quickly shut it again, biting her lip.

"What were you thinking about?" he asked.

"Nothing."

"Yes, I think of nothing too. Butterflies and dandelions. Braiding my hair in a field of orchids."

"You're mocking me."

"You're being secretive."

Nava sighed and pushed his hands off her lap, taking the reins herself. "I was thinking about Fira. That is all."

"Have you been there before?" he asked.

"No. I have not."

"Are you expecting to find the thing you are looking for in the largest city in Veran? I do hope you have an idea where it is."

"I have some idea, yes. And I trust you believe you will find the woman there too in such a big city. I hope *you* have an idea where she is."

Jared smirked at her mockery. "I do. She will be in a tavern or off with a thieves' guild, I imagine. I will find her."

Nava sighed softly and flicked the reins. "I wish you luck."

The fire was the only thing illuminating the blackness of the night. Nava had made her bed on the cool ground; her cloak being used as a pillow. She stared up at the sky, attempting to glimpse the stars behind the clouds. She remembered always staring up at the same sky each night as a child. Counting the rows of stars and painting figures with her fingers. Her mother told her each star was a lost soul, guiding the others to *Zeles* in the Otherworld. Their camp was a mere mile from the Exalted Forest, where the blessed elves took refuge. She had never seen a blessed elf, but her mother always said they were no different than them.

Jared flicked the embers into the air with his stick, seemingly lost in his own thoughts. He rested his back on the log he pulled over earlier that night. His shoulders were slouched, and he kept sitting upright and back again like he was keeping himself awake. Nava looked over at him, studying his face. His hair was a mess, tangled, and windblown. The shadows under his eyes helped darken the honey of his iris.

Nava had barely talked to him in the week they had traveled together. She was used to being on her own, and now, with this strange man, she had little privacy.

"Are you mesmerized by my handsome face or just looking at me?" Jared asked, his eyes now resting on hers. Nava snorted and looked away from him.

"I was thinking, I meant nothing by it," she responded.

Jared shook out his shoulders. "Shame, I really am handsome," he said with a grin that didn't quite reach his eyes.

"And very pompous."

"You wound me," he laughed lightly and yawned.

"Sleep; I will keep watch," she said, sitting up. Jared gave her a curious look.

"Why?"

Nava took the stick from his grasp and poked his shoulder. "You look as if you are about to keel over," she replied.

Jared gave a huff and leaned back on the log. "I'll take that as a compliment."

Nava rolled her eyes and turned her gaze to the fire.

Within a few minutes, Nava could see the rhythmic rising and falling of his chest as sleep claimed him. His face softened as he slept. He looked almost peaceful. The years of fighting had shown on his dirty skin. She could now make out the small scar that ran from his left cheek down to his chin. His shoulders were still stiff, even as he slept like he was perpetually in a fight-or-flight mentality.

Nava wondered if he was more than what he appeared. The wear and tear aura that fell from him gave hints of his tribulation. He had brought up his past before, but had yet to fully disclose his childhood. She couldn't complain, though. What had she told him? She had held an arrow to his face when they first met. He had no reason to trust her. And yet there he was, sound asleep next to her.

Nava felt a tightening in her chest. No one had ever really talked to her, given her a chance before. She was always the outcast, the runt of the two species. Run out of every town she came across. And yet, this man had simply treated her as if she was his equal. He pointed out the fact of her nature but never mocked her for it. Not truly. He even said that he liked the point to her ears. Most who had seen her ears had backed away in disdain. *Half-breed,* they called her.

Nava picked at the logs in the fire, watching pieces fall down in a dance of flame. She faced many men—all of whom had abused her for the way she was born. *No more,* she thought. No more would man hold a sword to her.

Her ears perked at a startling sound coming from beside her. Her eyes turned towards Jared. His face was scrunched as if he was in pain. He mumbled incoherently, and snapped his head back. Nava felt the urge to reach out to him, but stopped as he cried out.

"O-oliva. Run," he mumbled. Nava tilted her head as he watched him thrash. Olivia? Was that the woman he sought in Fira?

"Pl-please. Don't leave me here..." he continued. Nava set the stick down and moved over to him. Her fingers carefully touched his shoulder, and he jerked awake. She brought her hand back as Jared threw out his hands in defense.

"It's alright," Nava said.

Jared blinked, seeming to come out of his daze. He brought his hands to his face with a long sigh. "I apologize." He wiped his forehead, and Nava sat back on her heels.

"Nightmare?" she asked.

Jared rubbed the back of his neck with a wince. "Unfortunately. I will be fine."

Nava gave a restless sigh. "Do you have many nightmares?"

"Sometimes. Drinking helps. Get drunk off your ass enough the nightmares turn to fog."

"You can't stay intoxicated all the time."

"I can try."

They were silent for a time, and she watched as his eyes glazed over again as he stared into the fire. He would not be sleeping more tonight. She knew that all-familiar look.

Suddenly, the hairs on the back of her neck stood on end as an icy chill ran down her spine. The horse whinnied and pulled against the reins tied to the tree.

"Do you feel that?" she whispered.

"Yes."

Nava grabbed hold of her bow, notching an arrow. Jared reached for his sword but cursed when he noticed he lost it.

"I think it's—"

Nava was cut off by a decrepit howl splitting the air. A demon hound pounced from the woods, knocking Nava over and sending fire scattering through the camp.

Nava held her bow in front of her, blocking the snapping jaws of the demon. Its sharp rows of teeth clawed its way closer to her neck as she moved her head to the side, drool soaking her face and hair.

"Get off her!" Jared yelled. He slammed his foot into its stomach, and it jumped back with a yelp. He pulled Nava up onto her feet, and she quickly loosed an arrow into its side. The beast howled and fled into the woods, disappearing into the darkness. Their horse bucked and pulled against its rest, squealing loudly.

"A demon hound. They don't hunt alone. Where's its master?"

Jared asked, scanning the forest, his shoulders rigged.

The smoldering embers of the dying fire made it nearly impossible to see beyond a few feet. Jared kept his hand on her shoulder as she raised her bow, listening for the demon.

With a flick of a wrist, a dagger lodged itself into the tree where the horse was tied, cutting the leather and allowing it to escape. It squealed again and kicked, racing into the forest.

"Damn it, no!" Jared yelled, chasing after it.

"Swordsman!" He stopped short as a figure flickered in the firelight. Two sets of eyes locked onto the figure as it walked toward them. A silver mask covered their face, and their body was cloaked in black. Their sword hung loosely in their grip, and they turned towards Jared.

"We have been searching for you for a long time." His voice was unpleasant and scratchy.

Jared creased his eyebrows. "What in the void are you talking about?"

"All the lost will learn their place within the darkness. And welcome it once again," he said and raised his sword.

"Don't even try it. First, you destroy my city, then you come after us. You're not leaving here alive," Jared warned.

"Ignis was only the begging boy," the cultist spat. "Soon, the Black King shall rule all of Veran."

"I can't wait to see you fail," Nava snarled. She set loose an arrow, sending it straight for the cultist. But with a flash of black, the cultist vanished. The arrow went through the vapors and landed outside the camp.

"Damn it, where did he go—"

Nava screamed suddenly, feeling searing pain as a blade sliced through her abdomen, sending a fresh coat of blood to the ground. Nava shrieked, and the blade was ripped from her chest. The cultist threw her away and swung towards Jared.

"Nava!" Jared yelled. He dodged the sword and rolled out of the way of the cultist's foot. He brought himself to his knees and grabbed a log from the dwindling fire. He swung it, clipping the man with the burning wood. The cultists dropped the sword and batted at his flaming clothing. Jared quickly grabbed the sword and swung up, slicing through the face of the cultist, breaking his mask.

"How—"

Jared pushed the sword through his throat with a loud squelch.

With a hard *thunk*, the cultist fell to the ground. Jared dropped the sword and ran over to Nava, pressing his hand against her wound. Nava cried out as he picked her up.

"Nava, Nava, listen to me. Where is the next village!?" he asked frantically. Nava shook her head, biting her lip. She gripped the wound as his hand came to cover her own. She felt the blood pooling around her hand and down her shirt. He gently laid her back down and threw off his own shirt, tying it around her chest. He hoisted her up into his arms despite her screams of protest.

Leaving their supplies behind, he started sprinting towards the road.

32 JARED

The darkness of the night was deepened by the clouds blocking the moonlight. His feet tripped on hidden roots and bushels of plants. He cursed the goddess for not leaving the sun in the sky for longer.

"Talk to me," Jared said. Nava clung to his shoulders; her cries being muffled by his chest. "Nava."

"Damn it! Curse it all, damn cultists," she cried.

Jared's grip on her tightened. "Don't fall asleep," he said. "Keep talking to me."

"Dying is my worry at the moment," she said with a cough. Jared could not take the joke lightly. He refused to lose another one to the Dark Kingdom.

He ignored the burns on his hands from the log and focused on the girl in his arms. His eyes strained against the dark, and he kept looking back to see if the demon had followed. If it did, there was little he could do. If he dropped her, she could bleed out in minutes, if he didn't, they would both die. Both outcomes were not favorable.

As he ran down the dirt path, his legs grew tired and his breath ragged. Nava had stopped crying. She now lay limp in his arms. The warm liquid of her blood now soaked through his pant leg. He refused to stop and see if she was breathing and focused on the path ahead of him. He had to find a town, a healer. He was no soldier or hunter and didn't have the stamina of one. He was only a blacksmith's son.

He noticed the weight of the half-elf in his arms. She was small, more petite than the women he usually encountered. Her scent now reminded him of the honeysuckles he would pick out behind the storefront. She was nearly as pale as the ones that grew there.

He bit his lip at the fact her small frame meant she had less blood to relieve. He had been an idiot and had not paid attention enough to the cultist. Let him get behind her.

Lights of lanterns started to glow in the distance, hastening Jared's pace. Soon a farm appeared, and a farm meant people. He raced up the pasture towards the large wooden house. The bison looked his way as he passed; the chickens clucking at his disturbance. Jared came to the door and pounded on it with the hand holding Nava's legs. He didn't stop until the door opened.

A woman answered the door with nothing but her nightclothes and a candle. Her early graying hair and crow's feet were clear on her illuminated face. Upon seeing the pale elf in his arms, she ushered him inside.

"Save her," Jared said. The woman quickly cleared the table of pots and dishes, and Jared laid Nava atop it.

"I shall ask how this happened later. Help me undress her," she ordered. The woman pulled the blood-coated shirt from the elf and gently peeled away her tunic. Jared's eyes scouted a blemish on one of her breasts.

No, it was no blemish. Jared had received enough burns from his time with a blacksmith to know what a burn from hot iron looked like.

A shooting pain coursed through his chest at the unfamiliar insignia that was burned on her nearly perfect torso. The burn resembled something of a coiled snake. Someone had branded her like cattle. He could only assume for the reason of her being a half-blood.

Red filled his vision, but before he could do something rash, the woman caught his attention.

"In the drawer near the door, there are wrappings. Go get them and then go outside to fetch water from the well," she said calmly.

"Will she survive?" Jared asked, his eyes still trained on the mark.

"Not for long if you do not fetch the bandages," she said. This snapped Jared from his daze, and he turned from the table. He pulled the bandages from the counter and, after handing them to the woman, stepped outside to fetch the water. When the cold air hit him, he nearly gasped. He hadn't paid attention to how much his arms and legs hurt, how the blood on his chest felt. His heart was still pounding against his ribs as he stepped over to the well. As he pulled the pail up from the well. Flashes of memories came across his mind.

The dampness of his shirt as the rain had barreled down on the city. His boots had been soaked through. He had stumbled into an alleyway to try and escape those who hunted him. How many had he run from that day? At least ten. He had merely stolen a bushel of apples from the farm to re-sell for food in the city and had been beaten for it. He managed to keep an apple with a few wounds to spare. It was merely a fortnight since the bandits had killed his only family and robbed him of his home. He remembered the way his long hair had stuck to his forehead and his beard a tangled mess.

Jared lifted the pail from its hook and went back inside the farmhouse. He set it on the ground near the woman's feet. The woman worked quietly with a needle and thread, tending to Nava's wounds with a softness only a mother could have.

"The blade cut straight through. You are lucky it didn't pierce a lung," she hummed. "Velara is on your side today, lad." The woman took the bloodied shirt from the table and threw it into an unused bucket. Jared grabbed the used rages and began washing them in the pail. He watched as the woman worked lightly, cleaning the blood from the young elf's face and chest. Her abdomen was tightly bandaged in tan wraps, darker than her own skin.

"Will she survive?" Jared asked again. The woman placed another rag into the bucket and walked over to the counter.

"I am no healer. She will need medicine that does not grow on my farm. There is a town not a mile up the road. An apothecary lives in the hut just to the north of the town. Speak with him, and he may give you the herbs you need. But the girl is in Lady Velara's hands now," she said and wiped her hands. Jared looked down at Nava. He watched her chest rise and fall; her eyelashes fluttered softly. Her lips were darker than they usually were, blood-caked on the insides of them. She looked years younger than she really was.

"I will watch the girl for you, lad. Now hurry along," she said, shooing him from the room. Jared pulled his hands from the bucket and wiped them on his pants. "I have a shed to the left of the house. My husband's old clothes are on a rack in there. His clothes should fit you," she said. When Jared continued to stare at her, she smiled slightly.

"You'll scare the apothecary half to death if you walk in there like that, looking like a bull stomped on ye. Clean yourself off, then head on into town."

Jared heeded her words and left the house. After washing himself off, the wind picked up. Before he knew it, the rain had begun to come down in blankets. He hurried to the town, clogging through the muddy dirt. The cloak he wore only shielded him from the rain so much, and his mind drifted back to that night.

How long had he laid there in the rain, just wondering when cold or starvation would claim him? He had taken to the streets, even killed a man or two over petty things just to get a cup of ale. His mind had been clouded with thoughts of anger and sorrow. He only knew how to pound out steel, not plow a damned field, or talk up some noble pricks. He had seen the children run past him that night, paying no heed to the man in the alleyway. He had even thought of stealing one of them. Their parents would pay a hefty price for their child back.

That was until he came face to face with a purple skirt.

"What are you doing moping out in the rain for? A lass dump you?" she had asked. Her accent was heavy, less so than the rain. It reminded him of the traders who would come past from the hot sands in other countries. Seeing her was like the veil being lifted from his eyes.

"You gonna keep staring?" she had asked. He had asked her why she was there. She had told him she had been looking for someone strong to help her pa lift the beer kegs in the tavern. He had not paid attention to a word she had said. Only the dark hair that hung around her shoulders. By the heavens, she was beautiful. He would have bent down and prayed to the goddess right there if he wasn't soaked to the bone.

He gazed upon her bronze face, upon the hazel of her eyes. But soon, hazel molded into brown, and dark curls turned to light waves.

Jared shook the image of pointed ears and rosy cheeks from his head and hastened his pace toward the apothecary. The quicker he could heal Nava, the faster he could get to Fira and be rid of his blasted thoughts.

33 NAVA

Sunlight flooded through the open windows of the bedroom. The birds chirped happily outside as the morning dew glimmered on the grass. Oval eyes opened to the wooden ceiling and an arm was brought to her chest, feeling the bandages on top. With a heave and a flash of pain, Nava sat up. She looked around the foreign room that was small but held a soft homeliness to it. The soft cotton blankets on the bed, the wooden dresser with small scratches at the bottom, the jumping candle on the windowsill, and the statue of the goddess that hung on the wall.

Nava jumped when the door opened suddenly, and a young boy appeared holding a tray of biscuits and milk. A black and white cat strolled behind him and jumped up onto the bed, nudging her with its head.

"Nana said to give these to ye once you woke," he said softly, padding over to the bedside. "Don't mind Lula; she likes attention." Nava watched with a cautious eye as the boy set the tray on the bedside table and quietly left the room. The cat continued to prod her while purring, and she reluctantly went to pet it. Several questions ran through her mind.

Where am I? Where is the swordsman? She barely remembered what happened that night. She felt pain and heard herself scream. Then nothing.

Her questions were answered when a woman entered the room next with a small bowl in hand. She came across to her side of the bed and sat down gingerly.

"May I?" she asked. Nava carefully slid over to the older woman and allowed her to unbandage the wound.

"I wasn't sure you would wake. You have been unconscious for four days," she said. The woman placed the bandages beside her and dipped her fingers into the bowl filled with cream. She prudently wiped it over the healing wound, checking the stitches. Nava felt the heat of her mark as the woman continued to pay attention to only the wound.

"You were brought here to my farm by a frantic young man. I never got his name, but he stayed for a good while each day. Wouldn't leave the bedside," the lady said.

"Where is he?" Nava asked. The woman set the bowl aside and took up fresh bandages.

"I believe he is in town. He never specified, but I guessed by the stench of alcohol."

Of course she did. Once the woman clipped the bandages in place and stood up, she said, "I have a fresh pair of clothes for you in the closet. They belonged to my granddaughter, who outgrew them. They might still be a bit big on you, though. My name is Neve, and the boy is Jack. Call on either of us if you need help."

"I owe you my thanks," Nava said. The elder woman glanced at the burn on her chest.

"You have nothing to thank me for, child. I wish you luck on your journey," with that, she left the room to the half-elf.

Nava slid into her clothes and bit into the food given to her. It was buttery and sweet and reminded her of the biscuits her mother would make. The jam was a fresh blend of blueberries and raspberries that tickled her tongue. The milk was fresh and warm, staving off the chill of the morning. Her stomach protested for more, but she ignored it, and wobbly stood up from the bed.

The wound had taken a toll on her body. Her ribs were more prominent than they used to be, and her pants barely stayed up on her hips. The large bruise on her chest from the demon helped accentuate the burn on her breast. She took a coat from the dresser and left the farmhouse with a goodbye. Walking caused sharp pains to go up to her chest, but she knew she had to get on the road to Fira.

She headed towards the town, following the dirt path. She cursed that they had lost all their equipment, which meant no horse and no weapons. Let alone food. She was going to have to figure out something else.

She arrived in the small village and pulled her hood over her head once she saw the quickly darkening sky. Children raced past her without a second glance, and a fishmonger set up his cart with fresh-caught salmon and trout next to the apothecary. She heard the merchant conversing with a young man in a hushed tone.

"They won't allow anyone in the city," he said. "Heard nae a word about as to why. But I swore ye I saw a cultist atop those walls."

"You be serious? You don't think something happened?" the boy asked.

"I don't know. But I nae stay around to argue. Something felt off, boy. Something evil."

She ignored them and continued, passing several houses before arriving at the tavern. She was about to open the door when a voice caught her attention.

"Nevr' seen you around before?" It asked. She turned to face a scraggly man. His clothes hung loosely on his scrawny body, his breath reeked of ale, and she could see traces of food caked on his beard.

"What of it?" she asked. He stepped closer to her, and she flinched away.

"Yer eyes sure are big," he slurred.

Nava pulled her hood further down her face. "Thanks, now I must be going," she said, returning to the door. She quickly opened it and stepped inside before the man could say anything else to her. She shut the door and heaved a sigh, attempting to slow her racing heart.

The tavern was small, mostly filled with farmworkers and maidens. They laughed and played cards while empty bowls of porridge rested on the tables. A lone man played the fiddle atop the wooden stage, and occasionally someone would throw him a *sephim*. She gazed over all the faces, trying to find the familiar one. She spotted the swordsman at a table in the far corner of the tavern and walked over to him, avoiding legs and chairs, and noticed the several empty tankards spread around him.

"Swordsman," she said. He looked up at her with glossy eyes, seeming to try to recognize her.

"What d' you want," he snapped.

Nava raised an eyebrow. "We must be on the road if we are to reach Fira by the end of the month," she said. Jared snorted and took another long drink of his ale.

"Doe' it looks like I care?" he slurred.

Nava frowned. "I'm fine now. We must be on our way. Have you been here all night?"

He smirked and lifted his chin behind her. "Yea' but don't worry. I had company," he said.

Nava turned to see three young mistresses smiling and waving at him from the bar. "I believe you've had enough," she said and went to take the tankard away from him. In a flash, Jared knocked the tankard away, and it flew across the room, splashing against an empty table. Nava jumped back as it nearly hit her, and the music stopped. All eyes turned to them, and she could feel her face heat. Jared forced himself up and looked her in the eye.

"Just leave me be, girl," he said and stormed out of the tavern. The others watched him go, and without a second beat, the music began again. Nava sighed and sat down, rubbing her chest. She could hear the rain beginning to fall on the tavern roof and silently hoped she wouldn't have to buy Jared's new clothes again. Part of her just wanted to continue without him. It would be easier on her. But the other part remembered how he had saved her life. He had carried her *Zeles* knows how far to the farm to save her. She couldn't bring herself to leave the man who treated her as an equal.

She had her doubts, though. Nava took an empty tankard from the table and held it in her hands. That was the first time she had seen him angry. No, not angry. There was something else there in his eyes that she couldn't place. He still wished to find his Olivia in Fira. And the battle had stopped that. Nava sighed and stood up. She put the tankard on the bar counter and headed outside.

The rain came down in fat drops, soaking the already muddy ground. She stepped down off the porch and made her way back to the farm. She watched as children rushed inside their homes to escape the rain, and she smiled slightly to herself. The fishmonger had covered his wares and gone away from the cart; she thought a moment about taking a few of the fish for dinner.

"There she is," someone said behind her. Nava stopped and recognized the voice. It was the man who had stopped her outside the tavern before. She turned to look at him and was met with two other men beside him. They wore the same baggy clothes as well, but she noticed a metal gleam underneath them.

"Can I help you?" she asked cautiously. She reflexively moved her hand to her quiver, then realized she no longer had it.

"We want you," one said. "We hear Half-breeds can sell for a thousand *sephim* in the Dark City."

Nava scowled in their direction. "And what makes you think I'm a half-breed?" she asked, stepping back towards the tavern.

"Those eyes of yours are big, like an elf. And I'm sure you've got pointed ears under that hood," the main one said, pulling a dagger from his belt. The three men started towards her, and Nava felt a rush of adrenalin course through her.

"I'm warning you," she threatened.

"With what? We're just playing with ye until we get to the Dark Kingdom," one said. "Grab her."

Nava darted away from them and down the path of the village. Her feet slipped under the mud and rain, and she could hear the howls of the men after her. Her chest burned as she ran, and she bit her lip from crying out. She could feel her wound tearing up her stomach as she turned down a street.

Something caught her coat and jerked her back. She felt a pair of arms wrap around her, and she cried out. She slammed her foot into his, and he released her. She whipped around and elbowed him hard in the chin. With a curse, he stumbled back, and she turned away to run.

Another man grabbed her arms, and she screamed.

"Don' let her go," the drunken man said. He clamped his hands around her neck, and she gasped for breath. They brought her to the ground, where she fought and kicked. The head man climbed on top of her, and she screamed at his weight on her chest.

"Keep her down so I can tie 'er up," he ordered.

"Get off!" she cried. She swung her arm, but it was easily grabbed and forced to the ground. A gag went into her mouth, and flashes of binding, burning and screaming coursed through her mind. *No, not again.*

She had to fight, to escape. Her gag blocked her airway, causing her to choke. Her nails dug into the arm of the man who had a grip on her torso. His coat protected his skin as she scratched— she was trapped. They brought her hands together and wrapped a rope around her wrists. The burn on her breast caught fire to her blood. She was back there, in that damned cell. She closed her eyes, and she could hear his voice, his laugh.

Suddenly, the man standing over her was thrown away. Nava opened her eyes and watched as the dagger was taken from the man and used against him. His throat was slashed and tossed away, and the savior turned on the others.

Nava's eyes widened as she realized it was the swordsman. With a yell of fury, Jared grabbed another one of the men and punched him hard across the face. He turned and lodged the knife into the other man's abdomen. When the one he punched stood up again, he tore the knife from the man's stomach and stabbed it into his eye.

Nava squeezed her eyes shut as the screams grew louder. *I'm not there anymore*, she told herself. *He can't hurt me.*

She felt arms go around her, and she screamed.

"It's me, Nava," Jared said. He pulled the gag out of her mouth, and she coughed and clung to him. She buried her head in his chest with violent sobs. "It's alright. They're dead. I'm here." All evidence of his drunken state had disappeared, leaving behind a hardened exterior as he ran a hand through her hair.

Once she had calmed down enough, he stood up. "May I lift you?" he asked. Nava nodded, and he gently took her into his arms, careful not to disturb her wound.

"Why did you help me?" she asked softly, ignoring the stinging of her head.

"No one deserves to be treated like that. I would kill them again," he said. Nava looked up at him as he stared ahead. A protective look sat on his face. For once, Nava felt safe within the grasp of a human.

34 LAERDYA

Laerdya strolled the silent garden. Her fingers traced the petals of a rose, feeling the soft, delicate skin. She wondered how such a beautiful thing had yet to wilt in the twisting darkness of the sky. This had been Laerdya's favorite place to sit and relax. Ever since she first arrived here, the garden had been the safest space in the palace. The lady Ravana had taken a liking to the plants in the garden, much to Laerdya's curiosity. According to the garden keepers, the garden was the first addition to the Bone Castle, even before the city was built.

Laerdya could feel the magical energies that surrounded the gardens. It was like the push and pull of tides, a heartbeat in the castle. No plant that she knew of could die here. The same curse was placed upon them as the queen herself. While everyone else withered around her, she would remain beautiful forever. The gardens brought her peace, the only outside place she could stroll.

The purple void of the sky still kept her shielded from the true nature of the heavens. Could she remember running through the lilac fields of the woodland realms? She could barely think of the green of the leaves around her before they began to wilt and die. She could not remember her father's face besides when it was twisted and deformed from the curse that claimed him.

And her people, the ones that waited for her hopeful return, or at least, that's what Nexus had told her. He told her that the elves there mourned her greatly and prayed to the gods to return her home. She didn't remember any of them—how could she? But they remembered her, and they felt the same sorrow as the queen herself.

Part of her wondered what she would even do if she could return home. This city was all she had ever known, and even then, she didn't know the people within it. She had not seen any face but servants and guards. She knew little about ruling, apart from what Ravana had taught her and what she had read in books. She doubted she would make a good princess in Avlor, and she had her worries about being a queen here.

"Blossom, what ails you?" a voice called behind her. Laerdya turned her head to see the queen stride over to her. The chains on her dress jingled lightly against her person as she walked, her heels tapping against the stone.

"Oh, it is nothing, my queen," Laerdya said quickly.

"You only come to these gardens when you are thinking about something," the queen pushed. She touched one of the roses, and it seemed to curl into her hand. Laerdya sighed and strolled beside the queen as they leisurely made their way through the high hedges.

"It is not something that I can ever achieve. I must focus on the present," she finally answered.

The queen pulled a strand from Laerdya's face. "You wish to see the sun once again, blossom," she said.

Laerdya looked up at the queen with a saddened expression painted on her porcelain face. "I—yes," she stumbled.

The queen motioned towards a bench overlooking a fountain in the middle of the garden. They sat down, and the queen knitted her fingers together on her lap.

"I was like you once. I was young—I cannot remember how—many ages have passed since then. But I remember the rage and sorrow I felt when my sister cast me to the Otherworld. I had nothing but my followers and the son I was heavy with. I never thought I would be able to survive here, but I did." The queen paused and looked at the reflection of the sky in the water.

"My people created this city, and within this city, we created life. Though I will not say it has been good for everyone."

Laerdya thought back to the slaves in the city and the guards who always had dried blood on their blades. "What happened to your husband?" she asked.

The queen turned her lips up into a twisted smile. "It was an arranged marriage to my half-brother. Me and him were the only mages left in our family's bloodline, so it was our duty to keep the magic pure. But he was never the agreeable sort. He never loved me, not truly. When the betrayal happened, and the elven cities around us crumbled,

I hadn't realized that I held his heart in my hand." The queen raised her hand and looked at it, running a finger across her nails.

"That was when I knew my fate. And I created a world where I no longer had to pull on the chains he had placed. Here, everyone has the chance to live and die," she trailed off. Laerdya could see the pain reflected in her eyes. "Something we will never know."

Laerdya bit her lip. The queen was a feral woman, but her words stuck with her.

"And here, my city thrived for thousands of years while the elves above were slaughtered in the Imperial Crusades. Pushed from their homes and into villages, forced to live among the people who enslaved them. You will realize if you ever leave that this place is more blessed than Avlor will ever be."

The queen was silent for a time before Laerdya spoke.

"Why did you save Avlor if you hate it so much? You could have watched Velwood burn and still have been safe here."

The queen glanced at the princess and crossed her ankles. "When you are queen, you will have to make decisions that go against your morals and objections for the greater good. I did not want to initially save those above, but even I realized that without Avlor, what is left of the elves?"

"But don't you dislike your sister?"

The queen laughed, and a rose bloomed beside them. "Oh, I despise her. If she keeled over now, I would kiss the ground at her bloated feet. It was not her I wanted to save..." Her gaze fully turned to Laerdya, and she picked at her nails uncomfortably.

"My queen... If I may ask. Why did you choose me to come here? I know you have told me that I was the offering... but I don't understand," she mumbled. A soft look came across the queen's features, one she had only ever given to her child.

"You are a mix of the elves. You hold the blood of both purity and darkness within you. Now I have something my sister cannot. And that is better than her death," she said.

Laerdya's eyebrows knitted. She knew she couldn't expect anything more to come from the queen's mouth. Laerdya was here because she was a trophy. She was the one prize the others could never reclaim.

"Of course, my queen," she said.

The queen's head tilted slightly, seeing the young girl's vibrant eyes tear up.

"Why don't you let me teach you magic? You have the gift, little blossom. You are no mage, but perhaps you can learn enough to keep yourself entertained."

Laerdya shook her head. "I'm sorry. I want nothing to do with it. I have enough magic here." She wiped her eyes with her sleeve and sniffed. The queen sighed softly.

"Go outside. Explore my kingdom. It would do you good," she said.

Laerdya jumped at the proclamation. "But Elmaer would never allow that," she blurted.

The queen scoffed. "He is your intended, *not* your master. You will leave and be escorted by a trusted guard. If my son has anything to say, he will come to me." The queen's gaze slid down to the girl's bruised neck. With a pop of her lips, she stood up.

"You will marry my son soon. Maybe then you will finally bloom, my little blossom," she said. She strolled away from Laerdya, who watched her with silent awe. The queen was allowing her to leave the castle. It had been years since she first tried to escape to the city. She didn't even know what most of it looked like.

A smile rose on the young girl's face, and she stood up and quickly made her way back inside the castle.

35 TALIA

"My lady, a moment?" Sir Lambrin said, coming up beside Talia as she strolled the castle halls. He was an advisor to the king, but also one of the most argumentative of the council.

"What is it?" Talia quipped.

"My lady. I am worried about the state of the kingdom."

"Why is that?" she asked, turning her attention fully towards him.

"The people are beginning to fear. We still have no hearsay from Ignis. Perhaps if the king spoke with the people, it would put their minds at ease," he said.

"Why haven't you spoken to the king on such matters?" she asked, eyeing him.

His brown eyes wandered from her, and he ran a hand through his locks of curly hair. "The king... will not speak to me or any other advisor at the moment. I was hoping you could sway his mind."

"So, you finally object to my father's cowardice?" she asked and crossed her arms.

"Not... without exception. But he has refused to call a council meeting to discuss these matters—or any matters. I fear his mind is waning from the loss of the prince."

Talia set her shoulders back and ignored the squeezing in her stomach at the thought of her brother.

"Yes, I have heard the servants speaking of the loss. My father will have no words to suffice, though. Send out ambassadors to the villages with gifts, and station more patrols around the borders as well. Keep their minds busy," she ordered. Sir Lambrin bowed before taking his leave. Talia watched him pass down the hallway and thought to herself.

Her father was stubborn and would not help WhiteDrove. He

would close the gates to the city before allowing soldiers to march. She had no authority to command the full army, but perhaps if she hired mercenaries, she could send them to help. However, mercenaries were nothing compared to the Dark Kingdom—but it was something. She would have to look into groups scattered across Veran. She knew little of the thugs that were in Rosus itself, but they were there. There were tunnels running below the city for harbor imports. She heard that mercenary guilds would make those tunnels their home and charge obscene prices for safe passage through them. She would enter the tunnels and find the guild that could suffice for her wishes. Though the bloody tunnels were no place for a girl to travel alone.

Talia entered the old archives of the castle. The smell of dust and decaying paper made her sneeze as she shut the door. An exorbitant number of scrolls and books were stacked high along the walls and floors, and she pushed away an old tapestry that lay forgotten. The steady stream of colored light that scattered across the floor illuminated the debris that floated in the air. Her feet tapped against the creaking floorboards as she scanned the shelves of parchment.

She could barely remember the last time she was in this room. She could remember the smell, though, and the guards dragging her and her brother back out. They had created a new archive closer to the kings' chambers years ago and left this room alone and forgotten. Estimates of the population, old land claims, and broken treaties lay lifelessly on the shelves as she scrolled through them. The wind howled outside the windows, and the creaking of the beams above her did little to stave off the claustrophobic feeling that crawled up her body. And now with her brother gone... there was nothing left that gave her joy about this place.

She knew they kept records of the guilds found below the city here. She had peeked through one when she was a child before it was taken away. Now she simply needed to find it again.

Her fingers grazed through the scrolls and threw them away when they proved of no use. She batted cobwebs out of the way and scooted stacks of books. There must have been thousands of records here, and the room seemed to perpetually expand as she looked.

After an hour of searching, she was inclined to give up until she heard the door creak open. She righted herself and patted down her dress as a man came in with a sigh and a jangle of keys. He was an older fellow with a long dark beard and slicked-back graying hair. She did not recognize him as he locked the door and picked up a stack of books from the ground. He wore long blue robes and several colored rings on his bony fingers. She thought the robes looked familiar, from the Imperial College of Enchanters, perhaps.

Talia cleared her throat, and the man dropped the books with a startled gasp.

"P-princess, I did not see you enter," he stumbled.

"It's quite alright. May I ask who you are?" she questioned, eyeing him up and down. He looked older than her father by a few years, at least. The lines on his face were much more prominent. The look in his eyes, though, made him seem decades younger.

"Ah, you probably don't remember me. I am Enchanter Douglend of the College of Enchanters. I was an advisor to the king before he decided to abandon the magical crafts. You were still attached to dear Adeline's tit when we met."

Talia cocked her head to the side, trying to figure out if he was telling the truth or not. She knew her father rarely dabbled in magical knowledge, but she was unaware that he wanted nothing to do with it at all.

"So, he… banished you here, then?" she asked.

He made a grunting noise and picked up the books he dropped, holding his back with one hand as he did so. "In a way. I keep the old archives alive and well for the most part. He wanted all the old treaties and layouts of the city burned, but I talked him out of it."

"Why did he want it all burned?" she asked.

He shuffled over to a bookshelf and carefully stacked them upright. "Some people wish for new beginnings. After your mother's unfortunate death, he wished to start again. But some knowledge should never be forgotten, or we will continue to make the same mistakes again if we never learn."

Talia picked up a dusty scroll and opened it, reading through old alchemy recipes on medicine.

"I remember coming in here once. The guards did not let me get very far."

"I would think not—" he coughed and rubbed his chest, "Some things are far too dangerous for children."

"Now you sound like my old tutors."

"Then your tutors taught you well," he countered. "Now, what did you come here for, princess?"

Talia looked around the room at the hundreds of books and scrolls she had yet to go through. With a sigh, she told the truth.

"I am looking for records of the old guilds within the tunnels below the city. I know that they are there; I wish to hire one."

The old man gave her a cursory glance, his thick eyebrows shifting on his face. "And what might a young lady need mercenaries for?" he asked, moving over to another shelf and sifting through the scrolls.

"My father is not doing what is right to protect our kingdom. I am hoping to remedy his mistakes."

"You are ambitious, princess. Going behind the king's back."

"He will forgive me when I save WhiteDrove."

The man did not respond to her and instead pulled out a long scroll from under a stack of papers. A cloud of dust erupted from the shelf, and Talia waved her hand in front of her face with a cough.

"This is a map of the old tunnel system. However, the captain of the guard had many entrances sealed off a decade ago. It may list a few guilds that are still around," he said and handed her the scroll. She sat down on a creaky armchair and opened it across her lap. The scroll smelled of mildew and had several tears along the parchment, but it showed an intricate map of the tunnel system.

The system spread out over the entire city, with two main entrances at the port and at the city gates. The tunnel split off into chambers for storage and offices. Several rooms had been blacked out along with the adjoining corridors listed as 'guild territory'. She traced the lines back to a key on the right side, listing the guilds that currently inhabited the tunnels. Most names had been crossed out already.

"How old is this map?" Talia asked.

The enchanter shifted his robes and hummed. "At least ten spans. As I said, many guilds have died out or moved elsewhere. The Black City is better suited for such transgressions."

Talia looked at the only name that was not blacked out. The Shrouded Fang. "What do you know of this guild?" she asked, pointing to the name. The enchanter shuffled over and peered over her shoulder.

"The… Shrouded Fang. Hmm," He rubbed his beard and walked back over to a bookcase along the left wall. He moved a few scrolls out of the way before picking up another one. He dusted it off and opened it.

"The Shrouded Fang. A guild so large it can defeat an army of a thousand," he read. Talia's interest was piqued, and she sat up higher in the chair.

"Does it say more?"

"The leader has not been seen in decades. But they supposedly were the most powerful guild in all of Veran."

"If they are so large and so powerful, why have I never heard of them?" she asked.

The man rolled the scroll and put it into a pocket of his robe. "The most powerful beings are the ones who those never knew existed. Or perhaps they simply died out. This place is older than I am."

"Then I have to try. If they can take a thousand men in battle, we are assured of winning against the Dark Kingdom."

The old man raised his eyebrows and walked back over towards the door, fixing a stack of leaning books. "Confidence is a fire that must be tended slowly. If you put too much wood on it quickly, it will quench the flame."

Talia sighed softly and rolled the scroll up. "Well, thank you for your words of wisdom and help, but I must get going if I am to find this guild."

"As you say, princess. Be well."

Talia slid past him and into the hall. He shut the door behind her, and she hugged the map to her chest. This was her moment. To show her father that sitting idly would not bring them peace and that she was fit to rule the kingdom.

36 ENARA

Enara strolled the hallways of the castle as the servants scurried to and from, forlorn expressions weighing heavily on their faces. They carried ripped tapestries and scorched fabrics. She could still smell soot in the air as maids scrubbed the scarred stone till their hands cracked and bled.

As she traversed the buckets and stones, she found herself in the abandoned royal wing where the queen slept. Her feet padded down the carpeted hallway towards her mother's room, and she stopped at the closed door. With slight hesitation, she grasped the golden doorknob and opened it into the dark room. One candle was lit and sat on the bedside table, flickering as she opened the door. She stepped into the room and felt a cold shiver down her spine.

There was no fire lit in the fireplace; the curtains were pulled shut. The servants had cleaned the room the night Elena had died. They cleaned it spotless. Enara could no longer smell the peach perfume her mother wore. She could no longer see the crumpled satin sheets of the bed or the wineglass on the table.

She stepped further into the room and looked up at the painting hanging above the bed. It was a picture of a man standing in a field. He wore not robes nor jewelry, but a simple tunic and pants. His boots were muddy, and his arms were scarred. He held an axe in one hand and a pickaxe in the other. His face was stern but not aggressive, the age showing in his amber eyes and dark graying hair—a picture of the king.

She didn't remember him. Not really. He died quite early into her childhood. But she did remember being held by him. She remembered sitting on his lap on the throne and holding his hand as they walked the ramparts. But every time she looked up, she could not see his face. It was as if a shadow was cast upon it.

She sat on the queen's bed and pulled her legs up to her chest. She still wore her funeral attire—black and shrouded. The dress was as dark as the night sky outside the window. Her eyes were sore from crying, and her lips hurt from the constant smiles she had to give to the attendees of the funeral. They only acknowledged her *as she passed through the cathedral. None stopped to actually speak with her.*

Instead, they showered the youngest daughter with attention and words of condolence. As her sister wept and held the darkened ruby to her chest, they wiped her eyes and told her how good of a queen she would be. No one apologized to Enara.

She easily snuck away from the funeral—no one bothered to look for her. And now she sat alone in a darkened room, mourning her mother and hating everyone else. She watched the candle flicker again as the door closed and the light extinguished—

"Lady Enara?" Sir Alran asked, stepping closer to the bed. Enara looked up from the parchment she held in her hands with a quick intake of breath. She barely remembered walking into the bedroom, let alone sitting on the bed. She looked down at the scribbled names of the townspeople killed in the battle with a look of displeasure. The lord quickly bowed before speaking again.

"My queen, may I speak?" he asked.

"You may speak freely, Sir Alran," she said with a small frown.

Sir Alran cleared his throat. "Yes, well, it has come to my attention that Ignis is running short on grain and meat, Your Grace. The towns around the kingdom cannot support the millions who live in the walls."

Enara stood up and motioned for him to walk with her. They walked from the bedroom, passing cultist guards along the way. They gave a stiff bow as she passed.

"We have not had a food shortage in over thirty years. Why is it happening now?" she asked.

"We are a trading kingdom, my lady, not built for agriculture. We have small farms, but not enough to support the full kingdom. The cultists—we—are turning away merchants and farmers. The other kingdoms cannot trade with us if we do not open our doors, and even then..." he trailed off, his gaze lingering on a guard.

"They are frightened," Enara finished.

Sir Alran nodded. "Yes, Your Grace. Is it not unjust for them to be wary of the Dark Kingdom? They know little of what has happened inside the walls. I suggest we make peace with the other kingdoms—"

"Make peace?" Enara questioned, stopping.

Sir Alran nodded. "That may be the only way to ensure the safety and well-being of our people. Without the support of the other kingdoms, we will not survive into the next winter," he said.

Enara pursed her lips, contemplating. "How long will our grain last?" she asked.

"Perhaps another three months for the city, less if we spare it to the surrounding towns," he answered.

"The other kingdoms will not dare trade with us with the Dark Kingdom allied with us," she confirmed with a sigh. She turned to the window, looking out at the city.

"No, they will not," he stated. "If we end the alliance with the Dark Kingdom, though—"

"How do you intend to break the alliance, Sir Alran?" she asked, setting her icy gaze on him. He adjusted his coat and cleared his throat.

"There are many cultists here in the city… but perhaps a treaty would suffice. Our own guard shall protect Ignis and the towns within the Golden Hills for our word on trading deals."

Enara laughed, watching cultists walk by them. She didn't intend to laugh, but his words were utterly preposterous. They would never leave, this she knew. No matter how much she begged.

"Send a messenger to WhiteDrove. Tell them that they will trade with us, and they have no say in the matter," she said coldly. Sir Alran creased his eyebrows as he was taken aback.

"But, Your Grace, we cannot simply make another kingdom bow to us without going to war. The Empire is already looking our way. They will attack here next if we threaten any other kingdoms!" he exclaimed.

Enara turned to him. "The Empire has tried and failed for thousands of years to defeat the Dark Kingdom. This will be no different, and we have no choice."

"Your Grace, please excuse my manners, but you are no empress. The other kingdoms have no reason to agree to your terms—"

"I will speak to Malum about his, Alran," she snapped. "The only thing that matters now is keeping our people fed. If we must take the grain by force, then that is what we must do," she said, her voice rising.

"And if they do not send us grain. Will you kill innocent people?" he argued.

Enara bit her lip, watching two maids pass them with heavy eyes. The toll was horrendous on her people. Could she subject more to it? She turned from the window with a sigh. "I want four new fields plowed and ready for the next harvest by October. We will ration our remaining stock by each family. Take a count of how many children each have and decide their rations by that number. Set up serving tables around the city for the homeless, and I want a full count of the stock in each village outside the city. And send that letter."

Ser Alran bowed. "Right away, Your Grace." He strode off, and Enara gripped her hand in frustration, rubbing her palm with her thumb. Sir Alran was right. The kingdoms would not trade with them if they were aligned with the Dark Kingdom. The Dark Knights themselves would scare off the men. But she had to do what she could to ensure that her people were fed. She would not allow them to go hungry while others gorged themselves in the capital. She turned towards a guard.

"Send for Malum. I must speak with him," she ordered. The cultist bowed and left. Enara watched his figure retreat and continued to read the list of the dead.

37 OLIVIA

Olivia could feel the damp darkness before they even reached the Mors of Salvia. The whistling of the wind, the stench of decay, the howls of animals she could not name. The Mors spread around the entire kingdom and held spirits of the damned within it. It was a dangerous path, even deadly if you did not know the roads.

"This road will lead straight to Reverand," Ladrin said, following the bard. "It's full of guard towers, though. You'll never make it through."

Olivia turned back to him. "That is why you are here," she said.

When she took her first step into the putrid bog, she felt her heart quicken. The noises of cicadas and bullfrogs began through the expanse of trees and vines. The sunlight was blocked by the immense canopy, and she heard branches rattle above her.

"The first watchtower is only a mile away," Ladrin whispered, pointing down the muddy road.

"Then follow my lead," she answered.

She took off down the path, and the boy pursued. Her feet sunk into the traversed road with thick squelches, and she had to lift her feet higher to keep from getting stuck. The boy had a harder time being shorter than her, and she could hear his panting beside her. The insects started singing once again as they made their way deeper into the bog and the smell of mildew invaded her senses, along with a metallic taste. Sweat ran thick on her arms and face, and she could feel her hair grow heavy on her shoulders.

"You live in this blasted place? No wonder you all have the personality of swine," she said.

"None live in the bog. We all live in the city where the gods protect us," the boy replied.

"A city full of cultists and demons? Must be a wonderful life."

"It is the life I have known. My family was fed, and I helped my pa in the bakery. We are grateful to the king for protecting us from outsiders."

"The king protects you?" Olivia asked, glancing back at the boy struggling to walk. "You look like you haven't eaten in years."

The boy grunted and lifted a muddy shoe. "There are many mouths to feed, and we have little food. That deer was the first piece of meat I've had in two months."

She paused, and the boy did the same, resting his hands on his knees with shallow breaths. "That's ridiculous. No fish? No deer?"

"We… are in the middle of a swamp that wants to kill us. We have no harbor, and little in ways of hunting. The king does what he can to feed us."

Olivia shook her head. "Foolish boy. I bet he sits in his castle and feasts on cherries and boar."

The boy made a face. "Is your kingdom so different? Do you not have kings who dine while the people below suffer?"

Olivia took a breath and grabbed the boy by the arm, hoisting him out of the mud. "My queen was just. And you killed her."

After around half an hour, Olivia could see a small tower built on the road. It was in disrepair and half-fallen over. The outer walls seemed held together by sheer faith alone. The wood roof had large holes, and a group of men stood around it, chatting to themselves. Olivia quickly pulled Ladrin into a thicket of brush and knelt down.

"How do you expect to get past them?" he asked.

Olivia pulled off her jacket and bow, handing it to the boy, who bore a confused look.

"We can't walk around. Who knows what is out there?"

"We aren't going around," she said. She pulled the shoelaces from her boots and held them out to him.

"Tie me up," she told and forced the cord into his hands.

"I-I uh what?" he stuttered.

Olivia rolled her eyes. "I will be your prisoner until we pass the checkpoint. Once we pass, you will untie me."

Ladrin shook his head, rubbing the cord. "I can't do that. They-they'll know if it is just us."

"No, they won't. They're stupider than you think. Just follow my lead. And if you betray me, you will not outrun my knife," she warned, staring darkly into his wavering eyes. He nodded quickly and pulled her hands behind her back. He wrapped the cord around her wrists and held tight to the end.

"I don't know if this will work. We always have a battalion with us," he said.

"Shut up. We're passing. Now."

The boy led her back to the road, and they started towards the tower. She could feel his shaking hands and heavy breaths. She caught the soft speaking of the cultists as they neared. A blockade had been set up along the road, with six to eight men congregating around it. They had swords at their hips and one bowman. Even she knew she would not survive a fight. Her hope was that the boy was too terrified to say anything.

The soldiers looked up as the two came up to the blockade. A man came up to them, putting his hand up.

"Halt. State ye business," he ordered.

The two stopped, and Ladrin tightened his grip on the cord.

"I'm taking this prisoner to Reverand," he said quickly, trying not to falter.

The cultist looked Olivia up and down, placing a hand on the pommel of his sword. "Why are you traveling alone?" he asked. The boy looked at Olivia for help, and she suddenly struggled against the bindings.

"I killed all but him. That's how. This boy thinks that he can hold me hostage, but I will break free and kill all of you," she snarled.

The rest of the men came close, eyeing her up and down, then broke into laughter.

"Sure, you did, girl. I know when a boy is trying to sneak off from the camp with a lass," he laughed, "You can pass. I'll make sure to tell your commander you came through. Give me your name."

Ladrin swallowed and spat out a random name that the cultist wrote down, and stepped aside.

"Alright. But don't get too friendly with those girls. They can be biters," he said and winked at Olivia. She spit in his face, and the others laughed. Ladrin pushed Olivia through the barricade with the whoops and hollers of the men following him. He blushed heavily as Olivia snickered.

Once they were far enough away from the cultists, he unbound her, and she tied the cord back into her boots. "Are you all stupid enough to think that if a woman is pretty, it means that she is getting fucked?" She asked Ladrin.

His face fell. "That's how you killed my friends, isn't it?"

Olivia eyed him and nodded. "Yes, I suppose so. Hopefully, you will not make the same mistake."

38 TALIA

The veil over the young princess' head hid her true identity as she traversed the vast array of underground tunnels. With a map in her right hand, she gripped the far wall with her other. The tunnels were dark and eerie, flickering torchlight being the only source of brightness. Her footsteps echoed off the stone walls, and she looked down at the map to keep her place.

The rats that passed underfoot made Talia hasten her pace. The foul smells of rotting food and mold left her half-choking as she walked. She looked at the map again and entered a small pathway through a broken grate. Her dress tore slightly on the metal bars, and she cursed as she tugged the dress free. The tear spread to her hip, leaving little to the imagination. She pulled the fabric close and continued, soon reaching a small alcove where light streamed in. The only good grace the tunnels had was the cool dampness that helped alleviate her warm skin.

"It should be here somewhere," Talia muttered, squinting at the map. The barely legible writing showed her destination, and she prayed she was going in the right direction.

"Somethin' I can help ya with, miss?" she heard a low voice say. She turned to see a scraggly man standing where she had just come from. His clothes were threadbare, and she could see his protruding ribs through the holes in his shirt. His beard was long and bedraggled, coated with food and snot, and his eyes held a red tinge.

"I am looking for the Shrouded Fang. May you show me the way?" she asked carefully, pulling her veil closer to her face. The man took a step into the sunlight, and she could see the blood and dirt that coated his body, as well as the rusted sword that hung on his waist.

"What would a pretty lass like ye have to do with the bloody guild?"

he asked and smiled. Talia resisted the urge to grimace at the lack of teeth the man had.

"That is my own accord, sir. Do you know the way?" she asked again.

The man cocked his head to the side. "You sound prim and proper. You a noble?" he asked.

Talia quickly shook her head, backing up slightly. His smile grew as he stepped closer to her.

"Yea, I can show ye the way," he said and pointed to an offshoot of the tunnel. "This just that way."

Talia was reluctant to move. She could see it in his eyes. He would kill her, or worse. "I think I will find it on my own," she said, turning towards an adjacent tunnel.

"Hey, wait, lass, but don't ye wanna get to the guild? You won't get there goin' that way. That way leads down further. And there are scary men down there who would take advantage of ye. Come now, ill protect ya," he cooed.

She released a breath and quickly started down the other path. She heard the man call out to her but refused to turn. She bolted down a staircase and through another darker tunnel and could hear his footsteps behind her as she fled, and she stopped at a metal gate. She shook it, but it held firm. Her heart hammered in her chest, and she frantically shook the gate. She could hear him getting closer as he descended the stairs. Talia turned back and looked for another way of escape.

"Come here, little lass. I won't hurt ya."

Talia backed against the gate and tugged on it once more. The jangling of the man's belt rang through the cavity. He turned down her tunnel and pulled his sword. Talia's breath quickened as he pushed his sword along the wall, the metal scraping against the stone, sending pieces of debris falling to the ground.

"I will pay you to take me to the guild unharmed," she bartered. The man stopped in front of her, his foul breath inches from her face. "I could sell you for a pretty *sephim* back to ye family; I do bet." His lecherous eyes ran down her body, and he pushed her dress up with the edge of his sword. "Mighty fine bits you have," he purred.

Talia swatted the sword away. "Unhand me this instant!" she ordered.

The man laughed and pulled the veil from her head, dropping it to the ground.

"I knew it was ye. That little jewel," he chortled. His hand grabbed her chin, forcing her to look up as he sliced through her dress. The bottom fell to the ground, leaving just enough to cover her upper thighs as he licked his lips.

She hit him hard in the jaw, and he stumbled back before putting his fist into her abdomen. She gagged and fell to her knees, clutching her stomach.

"Please don't. I'll pay you whatever you want," she pleaded.

The man laughed again. "Pay me all you like. You be too pretty to pass up—"

The echo of footsteps caught the air, and he was quickly silenced. Talia looked behind the man to see a wolf towering over him. She jumped when the man on top of her was thrown at the wall. She scurried back against the bars as the wolf—or mask as it may be— drew a steel sword with a handle carved from bone. The coat he wore was snug close to his body, and the hood was pulled over his head. In the dark, it looked like there was nothing there at all but the mask he wore. The abuser put his hands up.

"M-m'lord. Please spare me. I was simply showin' her the way to the guild!" he pleaded. The masked man looked down at her. She could barely make out the purple eyes hidden behind the face of the wolf. The man looked back at the abuser.

"I believe you," he said. His voice was deeper than any she had heard, almost having an animalistic growl to it—It was nearly unpleasant to hear. He then sent his sword straight through the neck of the abuser. The man's eyes widened before he slumped against the sword.

Talia stood up as he pulled the sword out, and the body fell to the floor. The rats already started to climb on top of it as the man's bloody gurgles filled the tunnel. Talia looked at the masked man as he sheathed his sword. He took his coat off and threw it at Talia. She caught it and pulled it around herself. Even without the coat, he wore all-black robes. The only color was the gem on his belt that gleamed with a light iridescence.

"You have my gratitude."

The man did not answer, just motioned for her to follow. She did as shown and followed him through another series of twisting tunnels before arriving at a large wooden door. He opened it, and Talia stepped inside to an expansive room that was fully furnished.

The stone walls held velvet curtains, and bookshelves lined the adjacent walls. A plush couch sat in the center of the room, looking at the desk in front of it. Soft carpet lined the floor, and candelabras gave a soft hue to the room. The man motioned for her to sit, then stepped over to a small counter where a kettle was sitting. Talia sat on the couch, and the man brought over a cup that she gratefully took. She didn't notice she was shaking until she could barely hold the cup steady to her lips.

"I can guess who you are," she started. "Are you the leader of the Shadowed Fang?"

The man pulled off his mask, and Talia's eyes widened. Instead of a rugged and belligerent face like she had expected to come from such a voice, a lean and young face looked back at her. With shadowed hair and eyes of amethyst, an elven man took the face of her rescuer.

"You're an elf!?" she exclaimed.

The man leaned against the desk, looking her up and down. "What is the princess doing down here?" he asked, ignoring her question.

Talia ran her thumb down the cup of tea. "I was hoping to hire the guild to fight at WhiteDrove when the time came," she said.

The man gave a fanged smile. "You cannot be serious?"

"You are mercenaries. Why should I not?" Talia frowned.

The man crossed his legs in a lackadaisical pose. "You know nothing of how the world works, princess. You cannot simply hire a mercenary company to fight against the Dark Kingdom. Especially a guild with only one man," he said.

Talia's jaw dropped. "One man? But I had heard stories of the legendary guild who was a thousand men strong?"

The man ran a hand through his hair, seeming almost bored. "I am stronger than a thousand men. But even I cannot face that rage alone."

Talia shook her head. "I don't understand—"

"That rumors are baseless? Especially when it comes to the gentry?"

"I had just thought…" Talia sighed and set the cup down on a side table. "I don't know what I thought."

"Mercenaries fight for gold, my lady. Not for honor. They would leave the second they saw the demons rip apart their brothers."

She looked up into his eyes as he spoke. She couldn't explain it but something twisted in those purple orbs that made her uneasy. If this man was truly a thousand men strong, then he was something to be feared. And he was unwilling to help her.

"Excuse me then," she stood up and wrapped his coat tighter around herself.

"You're leaving? Alone? I thought you had learned your lesson the first time."

Talia turned to him. "Then would you be a gentleman and escort me back to the surface?"

The man stood upright and opened the door for her, putting his mask back on. "I cannot refuse a lady now, can I?" he teased. He followed her out and then cut in front of her to lead the way.

"Why the mask?" she asked.

"Weren't you surprised to see me an elf?" he asked.

"Well, yes," she answered. "But your ears are a given."

"You cannot see my ears with the hood you are currently wearing."

"Then take it back," she argued.

He put up a hand. "No, now it smells like a sewer."

"You live in one," she argued. His bestial laughter echoed through the tunnels once again, and Talia felt the heat rising to her cheeks. *He is taunting me!* She thought.

"Where are the other guilds?"

"Dead or departed. The only things that inhabit these tunnels now are vagrants and rats."

"And you."

"Yes, and me."

"So, you will not help WhiteDrove?" she asked.

"I never stated I was part of the guild."

"You just told me you were a thousand men strong!"

"Oh no, that part is true. I could take on a whole squadron if given a chance. But I won't," he said.

"And why not?"

"Because I simply do not care enough," he put bluntly.

"You won't care if your home is ransacked and destroyed?" she asked. She could not see his expression through the mask, but she could tell he was amused.

They ascended the stairs, and he helped her back through the broken grate.

"I am an elf. Why should I care what happens to you humans?"

"Because all will die without us!" she yelled.

He huffed out laughter. "Yes, but that holds no meaning to me."

Talia fumed, and she grabbed the man by his shoulders. "You are the most hateful man I have ever met!" she declared. He looked down at her with his odd eyes, and she quickly released him.

"You should watch your tone down here, my lady. It is dangerous here alone," he stated, brushing her off. "And remember who it was that saved your most perfect virtue."

He started back down the tunnel, and they rounded the corner to the opening. He stopped short of the entrance and looked at her.

"You may yet uncover the secrets to this world. But not with the mindset you have now. You cannot simply buy your way out of this war, my lady. You must be at the forefront of it." He opened the door for her and bowed half mockingly. "Good day, my lady. And keep the cloak. You're immodest even for Rosus."

She blushed and took hold of the door. "And might I have the name of my savior?" she asked.

The man smiled and pulled up his mask. "You may simply refer to me as the Black Wolf." With the flurry, he closed the door, snapping her hand back. Talia growled and kicked the door.

"Ooh, just you wait, you mangy elf!" she yelled. She turned and blushed when two travelers looked at her.

"Milady... are you alright?" they asked.

Talia composed herself and pulled the coat further inward. "Yes, I'm fine. Now you must excuse me. I have business to attend to," she sniffed and walked down the docks towards the city.

The travelers looked at one another. "And maybe a bath as well."

39 ENARA

Enara paced the throne room, her dress knotting from the sudden shifts of blue silk. She rubbed her aching hand, teeth clenching.

The room felt darker than she remembered. She stood here only a short while ago, and yet it seemed as dull as a millennia-old tomb. There were no flutes or violins playing for the nobility, nor were maids scurrying about with cakes and pastries. The cultists that walked the corridors were in numbers compared to the royal guard still pledged to her.

She could see it in their eyes. Their fear. Their uncertainty. Their resentment. They bowed to her, but she knew they held no love for her. She was not the queen who was crowned by the church; she was the usurper who betrayed her kingdom. Even the crown upon her head could not shine in the desolate space she was in.

She heard the clang of metal and the whisper of frost as the door to the throne room opened. With every thump of his boots on the tile brought a jolt of pain down her spine. When they stopped at her back, the cold brushed past her neck.

"We are low on stocks. We will need to begin re-trading with the other kingdoms," she said. "They have the grain and livestock that we need."

She heard Malum chuckle low in her ear. "So, take it. The other kingdoms are weak," he said.

Enara took a breath to calm herself before facing the Knight. His frosted eyes bore into her own as she spoke.

"I sent a messenger to WhiteDrove. We should hear back within a fortnight. They will agree. I know they will. They are no mighty kingdom."

Malum scanned the throne room with an amused look. "Did I mishear you saying that you would make WhiteDrove bend to your will?" he asked coldly.

Enara rubbed her palm. "I am not here to murder innocent people. It is only idle threats. They have no army. They will trade with us," she paused.

Malum stepped away from her and folded his hands behind his back. His armor clanged against his person as he strolled the room, taking in the stained windows. Enara noticed the new mandible on his pauldron. It was smaller than the rest; a front tooth was missing.

"Do you know how the elven kingdoms fell?" he asked.

"What does that have to do with anything?" she argued. He ignored her and stepped over to a pillar, running a clawed glove down the stone.

"Their arrogance blinded them to the enemies that danced in the streets. They had their balls, and they drank, and they sang. They ignored the threats to their lives. They thought themselves immortal." He turned to her with a sneer spread across his face. "And when we pushed our swords into their backs, did they finally weep and pray. Idle threats do not win wars, girl. We shall put the sword at their throats, and when they plead for their maker, I will show them her head."

"W-what?" Enara shuddered. "You mustn't be serious. That will start a full war. We need only to trade, not to conquer. You have two kingdoms for yourself. Why claim more!?"

Malum turned to her, unfazed by her outburst. "You have already started this war; now you must end it. Who do you think shall win the Imperial throne, child?" he asked.

Enara bit her lip. "I do not want the throne. I only want what is best for my people."

"You should have thought about that before you sent for us. Now your streets run red, and you still think you are a noble queen?"

"It is you who is slaughtering my people. I did not agree to this!" she yelled. Suddenly she was grabbed by the cheeks, Malum's clawed metal fingers digging into her face. She could feel the thrumming of rage under his armor, and she winced in pain.

"I do not obey you. I am a god. You are nothing but a child wearing a false crown. We will lay waste to the capital and rip children from their mother's wombs. We will slice the Empire into fragments of its glory, and when the ash falls around you, you shall wear your crown of thorns," he snarled. He let Enara fall to her knees, blood running down her cheeks. She bit back tears as the knight towered over her.

"You will leave for the Black City in the morning. Greet the king and learn your place in this world," he told, his voice a softer tone.

"I cannot leave my kingdom with no ruler," she pushed out behind a sob.

Malum laughed. "I will be here. Send your servants to do your will. But you will leave here. I will not order you again."

Enara rubbed her face and nodded. Malum turned away from her. "You are a queen now, child, but soon you shall be an *empress*." He left the throne room as tears streamed down Enara's face. *By the Goddess, what have I done?* She had doomed her people only because she wanted to sit on the throne. Her people were being slaughtered because of her. She wiped the blood from her cheeks between sobs and heard the soft patter of footsteps beside her.

Trissa came in and knelt beside the queen and she gently slid Enara into her arms. She raked her hands through her silky black waves and hummed lightly.

"I'm sorry, Trissa. I'm so sorry," Enara cried.

"What's done is done, Enara. You cannot change the past but look toward the future. I have faith that your rule is not a cursed one but one of redemption," she said.

Enara grasped her nanny tight, afraid to let go, fearing she would leave like the others. "Come with me to the Dark Kingdom, please," she whispered.

"I will follow you till my last breath, my child."

40 ROSE

Rose had a bag packed for her, and the party was awaiting her arrival at the front gates. She was dressed head to toe in warm animal hide, and while walking, she could feel herself sweat. She bit her lip as she approached the large men and women waiting. There were six of them in total, including Rose, *too few*, she thought.

Nadahi greeted Rose as she came up. She was dressed in heavy leather and furs—more than normal—and her hood was brought up over her head. "I hope you slept well," she said and smiled softly.

"I did, thank you."

Nadahi turned towards her companions. "These are the men and woman who will accompany us to the ruins." She pointed to each person and gave their name.

The first man she pointed to had short blond hair with a braid that fell down the side of his face. His beard was cleanly shaved, and a scar ran down his right cheek. Two long blue marks came down from his forehead to his chin, and his grey eyes blended into the snow that fell around him.

"That is Torgir. He is the best shield hand we have. And as old as the Mother Goddess herself," she said with a jest. He said something in their own language to her with a grunt, and she laughed.

She pointed to the next person, who was dressed in blue-tanned leather. She had black hair that was pulled back by the braids adorning her head. Colored yarn was woven into her braids and delicately framed her square face. Her markings ran across her face like claw marks of a raptor, and her large green eyes showed affection and warmth. She bowed low to her.

"I am Liv, *Runa*," she said. Her voice was soft and light despite the heavy accent.

"She is our healer in the field," Nadahi said. "She has patched me up more times than I can count."

"I won't let you reach *Shor'vaker* yet, Nadahi."

Nadahi pointed to the next man, who stood a bit taller than the rest. Rose recognized him as the man who had taken her on his horse when she was first found. He had a long brown beard that was braided in several spots and held with metal clasps. His hair was long and fell down his burly back. His dark gaze made Rose slightly uncomfortable.

"That is Hakon. Built like a mountain and strong as a bear."

"Sometimes, I think the goddess has played a trick on me by letting me be in this tribe," he said with a shake of his head. Torgir slapped him on the shoulder, and he looked down at him with an exasperated expression.

"Finally, Erling," Nadahi said and held her hand out towards the shorter man of the group. His belly was large but fit his frame well. His sandy hair was slightly disheveled and stuck out in odd places on his head. His beard was one long braid filled with what Rose could only assume were small trinkets and runes tied in. He gave her a funny look and quickly nodded.

"Short. Shorter than me, and that is saying something. But cute. Like a little fawn."

"He is mad. Don't listen to him," Nadahi whispered in her ear, earning a chuckle.

"You say I'm mad, but the spirits will be the ones fighting over my corpse on the battlefield. You'll just have to wait your turn."

"And I'll enjoy the wait while watching them drag your ass to the Mother. If they can hold your weight," Hakon said with a blank expression. They were silent for a moment before they broke into laughter.

"Enough introductions already. We need to be off," Liv said. Nadahi nodded and motioned for Rose towards her horse. Rose gripped the saddle, and Nadahi lifted her with ease. When she was properly situated, her hand rested lightly on Rose's back as she attached the bags to the saddle.

Rose watched as Liv said something to Nadahi that seemed to fluster her, and she pulled her hand away quickly. Liv laughed and mounted her own horse.

"Nadahi, is something the matter?" Rose asked.

The huntress turned to the girl. "No, *Runa*. We are preparing for departure. The winds are cold, and the nights are harsh. Did you pack enough furs?"

Rose wiggled in her seat, blowing fur from her face. "I believe so. I'm not used to the clothing here. It is less... restricting," she said. Nadahi gave a chuckle and pulled her horse over, mounting it.

"Your old clothing was nothing more than rags. I wonder what you would classify as restrictive."

"I was wearing my coronation dress, thank you very much," Rose tutted. The rest of the group mounted their horses, and the gates opened to them. Nadahi looked back at the Great Hall and saw her father standing in the doorway. He gave a nod to her, and she turned away. Rose kept her eyes on the gates as they exited. The brisk wind seemed to turn even colder once they stepped outside the safety of the village.

"It will take a week to get to the ruins. Possibly longer depending on the weather," Liv said, looking behind her. "I hope you are prepared for the cold, *Runa*."

Rose pulled the coat closer to herself. "And if I am not?" she asked.

Liv glanced at Nadahi. "I'm sure you can find someone to keep you warm," she laughed. Rose felt heat rise to her cheeks as Nadahi grumbled something in their native tongue.

"Come on, you lousy sods! Enough torturing the girl," Torgir said.

"You'll have enough of that tonight," Erling laughed. Rose smiled slightly as the gates faded into the distance. Soon all that could be seen were the white plains of nothingness.

The group had traversed the massive white landscape for hours before finally settling down for the night. She expected to see some kind of landmarks or settlements along the way, but it was just frozen ground and snow-covered trees as far as the eye could see.

Rose sat beside Liv as she hummed to herself while roasting a hare on the fire. The men in the group were all bickering back and forth in their language while drinking happily. Rose assumed it was a game of some sort. And by how much Erling was drinking, she assumed he was losing.

"Are the other tribe settlements close to here?" Rose asked Liv, shifting her coat. Liv nodded.

"Yes, but they are few. Most only stay in the smaller villages in the thawing seasons to hunt and gather, then return to the main tribe in the harsher months."

"Will we run into any?"

"It is doubtful, *Runa*. Where we are headed is a place of corruption. We will skirt some of their territories, but I don't see us running into any of them."

"We will have to be careful, still," Nadahi mumbled. She sat on the other side of Rose, gazing into the flames. She monotonously trailed her fingers down a braid in her hair. Rose glanced at the braid and then at the others who bore them as well.

"If I may ask…" Rose started. "Why do you wear braids?"

Liv smiled slightly and turned the hare. "It is a symbol of our unity. Each strand of hair is weak by itself. It is easily plucked or broken. But when they are interwoven, they are stronger. Some strands may singe or fall away, but there are others that are there to hold it together. Many turn into one, and it is our strength and our passion for each other that has kept us from breaking for all these years," she said.

Rose ran a hand through her own hair and looked down at the many strands that poked out from her ends. "I was never really one for braiding. I enjoyed it being free. It felt less restricting."

"Some enjoy their freedom within their family. Some wish to sail the seas and find what lies beyond, while others stay at home nursing children or helping the injured. It is not a fault to want to be something else as long as you remember where you came from and know those who will carry you when you fall."

They were silent for a time, watching the fire and the men drinking. Rose thought back to her home and her friends. Did she have anyone to fall back on anymore? Or did she stray too far away, like the baby hairs that graced her forehead?

"I could braid your hair if you wished me to, *Runa*," Nadahi said, returning from her daze. Rose bit her lip in contemplation.

"If… if it wouldn't upset anyone," she said. Nadahi smiled at her and motioned for her to sit down in front of her. Rose sat down on the ground and scooted in between the huntresses' legs as they spread out to let her access. Her feet nearly reached her own, and Rose wiggled them in amusement.

"What's so funny?" she asked.

"I never realized how big they are," Rose laughed. "I used to steal my friend's shoes from his room and wear them around the city. I would trip and fall everywhere. I felt like a giant."

"I would not advise wearing mine in this snow. You will slip right out and lose your toes in the frost."

"Maybe. Sounds like fun, though."

Nadahi coughed out a laugh and picked up Rose's mane of golden hair. She ran her fingers through her dense locks and lightly stroked her scalp. Rose closed her eyes and let the warmth of the fire on her face and the gliding of fingers lull her into a state of contentment.

She could feel the soft tugs on her head as the huntress braided her hair down the middle. She worked quickly but steadily, pulling a sewing needle from her bag along with some string and weaving it through her hair like a tapestry.

When she was done, Rose opened her eyes and felt the back of her head where the braid snuggled against her neck. She pulled it over to her right shoulder and looked at the blue weaving through the strands of gold.

"You are unified with us now, *Runa.* And we will be beside you through this trial." Nadahi said. Rose stood up and turned to the huntress. Her face was lit in oranges and reds, the light in her eyes glimmering in the flame. Rose smiled and sat down beside her, pulling her coat closer to her body. For now, she felt at peace.

41 VIA

Via and Rye hid in the outskirts of the cultist's encampment. The camp spread as far as the eye could see, with flickering fires and waving banners, and they had immense numbers compared to their own. From the looks of it, there were thousands of them.

"How did they all make it past the Mors? This should have taken them weeks," Rye whispered to Via. They could see the men preparing weapons and mending armor. Some patrolled the outskirts of the camp, and the couple retreated into the shadows. "We have to warn the emperor. We do not have the men to fight this army."

"They will advance on us too quickly. If we retreat, WhiteDrove is lost," Via argued, her mind reeling. Thousands, there were thousands of cultists. They wouldn't survive a battle. WhiteDrove was bound to fall—*stop it*, she told herself.

"We can station at Stormshold and wait for reinforcements. The fortress walls are more fortified than an open field," Rye suggested.

"The fortress is a day out of the way. There is no guarantee they will attempt to take it before WhiteDrove." Via suddenly took a risk and snuck closer to the camp to the protest of the commander. She snuck around several tents, counting the people, and memorizing their faces. She whistled long and low and heard the flap of Veleros' wings. Soon, she heard a caw above her, and she motioned with her hand toward the middle of the encampment. *Find the scouts*, she thought.

She paused and waited beside a tent, hearing cultists laugh inside. She smelled meat and heard the bubbling of a pot. She put her ear to the fabric, barely being able to hear the vibration of their footsteps. *Three... four... six of them.*

"We hit em hard and fast. Each head takin' is another point," a voice said, a man.

"Think anyone can beat the gods in number?" another asked, a woman.

Gods…? Via narrowed her eyes.

"Ahahaha! If any of you lot do, I'll give ya triple the points."

The group cheered and clanged cups together. She contemplated sneaking in and killing them, but she heard Veleros call above her. She lifted her arm, and he landed on her shoulder and nuzzled her cheek.

"Did you find them?" she whispered. The raven ruffled his feathers and took off to the north. She followed him, darting from tent to tent and across shadows, and she neared another tent, her eyes met with large poles that had been nailed into the ground. Large lumps were skewered onto the poles, and her heart sunk. She realized the lumps were bodies—the bodies of her men.

Their bodies had been skewered with poles, left up to display to the rest of the army. Their mouths hung open and eyes were wide in terror as the wood slid through their necks. She could hear the laughter emitting from the cultists closest to them near the tent. Her blood boiled, hearing them laugh.

"Via!" Rye whispered, grabbing hold of her arm. She jerked her arm free and glared at him.

"Go back, Commander."

"Via, listen to me. This is madness. We must return."

She ignored him, pulling a dagger from her boot and starting forward. Rye cursed and followed her toward the unassuming cultists. There were three of them closest, a small enough number to kill and grab the bodies. The cultists sang and laughed, not noticing the cursed elf sneaking up behind them. Within a second, a throat had been slit, and a dagger had entered the skull of another. Rye grabbed the last scout by the throat and snapped his neck, laying him on the ground.

"We shouldn't be here, Via," Rye said angrily.

"I must know if they still carry the runes," she said flatly. She snuck up to one of her scouts and searched their bloodied pockets. She cursed when she found nothing. They had taken the stones. But it made no sense. They shouldn't have been able to see through the wards. Not even a powerful maleficarum could have the sight to do so. *Unless…*

"Via!" Rye yelled. She turned and was met with an iron fist. She was flung into a tent, the cloth collapsing around her.

The Knight towered over them, rancid black armor adorning his body, a serrated sword in his hand. The smell of rotting flesh filled her nose, and the Knight stepped towards the tent. His bones cracked under his weight, and she could hear the screeching of metal as his armor shifted with his contorted body. The very ground he tread had become wilted and desolate.

"By the goddess," Rye breathed. The Knight turned to him with a snap of his neck. Rye shot up, unsheathing his sword. He swung it at the Knight, who easily parried his blow and backhanded him, sending Rye flying through the air. He hit a nearby tree and crumpled to the ground.

An arrow bounced off the Knight's armor, and his gaze turned back towards the elf. A twisted smile graced his crackled lips. Via growled and loosed another arrow. The Knight grabbed it in mid-air, snapping it in half.

"It's been too long, little elf," he gurgled, spitting up bile as he spoke. He tossed the arrow to the side, and Via switched to her blades, moving around him.

"Gelum," she snarled.

His choking laughter filled the air. "So, you remember me, little elf. I remember you well too. You still have the reminder from our last battle," he told, motioning toward her stomach. Her face contorted in anger, and she sprinted toward him. She jumped high; her blades raised. He dodged her attack and brought his sword down. She rolled out of the way and slashed across his armor, barely scratching the surface. He laughed again and grabbed her hand, twisting her wrist and causing her to drop a blade. She cried out, and Rye barreled towards them. He slashed his sword around, and Gelum parried the blade, pushing Via down and turning his attention toward the commander.

"I shall enjoy killing you," he promised.

"I won't give you the pleasure," he snarled.

They exchanged blows, but the Knight towered over him. Even in his decrepit state, each blow left Rye stumbling further back. The Knight brought his sword down and caught Ryes, tearing it from his hands. He kicked Rye into a tree and turned as Via came down on him. She wrapped her legs around his head and lodged a dagger into his eye. He screeched in pain and flipped her off. When she landed on her knees, he grabbed her by the coat and tossed her away. With a grunt, she landed on her back. With a cry, she forced herself up onto her knees.

Gelum walked over to her and grabbed her by the neck, easily lifting her above his head. She choked and kicked at him.

"You tried once to defeat us—you couldn't, then. What makes you think you can win now, little elf? Your queen is not here to save you this time." He threw her towards the Mors, and she landed next to Rye with a cry.

She pushed herself onto her knees, her skin stinging from cuts and bruises.

"Tell me, how does it feel to lose once again?" Gelum asked.

Via spat in his direction. "*Ave tas al valen*," she growled.

He laughed, and Rye stood up between the two of them.

"Rye don't," she pleaded.

"I'd listen to the elf, human. Is your life worth hers?" Gelum asked.

Rye stood firm. "Your kingdom will fall, Knight. I will make sure of it."

Gelum looked at the elf. "Your kingdoms will lie in ruin while we rise. We have the girl, and soon even your goddess will beg for mercy," he laughed.

Via's eyes widened. "No..." she breathed. *It can't be true.*

Rye looked at her. "What girl? Via?"

Gelum turned his gaze to the commander. "Your trust in her is misplaced. I want you to be there to see it. To watch your cities burn and mothers weep. For once it is finished, you will wish you were dead." Gelum turned away and left the couple bruised and wounded. Rye helped Via to her feet, and they fled the camp.

"What was he talking about?" he asked. Via met his eyes, seeing a look that he had never seen from her before. Terror.

"If what he says is true. Then this war is only the beginning."

42 OLIVIA

The night was dark. The squeals of wild boar and scraping of claws awakened Olivia from her slumber. She sat up on her blanket, looking around the camp they had made. The swamp surrounded them on all sides with dense brush and swaying vines. The damp, dark colors of the trees and foliage made the night sky appear even blacker. Ladrin was still asleep, curled up in himself. Olivia scanned the area, listening to the bubbling of the swamp, the wind howling through the thick moss. The hairs on the back of her neck had never relaxed since they entered the Mors, and she feared they never would. This place was unnatural. The beasts that wandered here were none like she had seen before. The rats had four eyes, the deer dripped in brown ooze, and the insects skewered her neck and arms. The humidity left her nearly always damp, no matter how close to the fire she sat. She wanted nothing more than to leave this place as soon as she could.

She turned her head to the right when she heard a low gurgling moan. She slowly took her knife from its hold and stood up. The darkness of the Mors plagued her senses as she searched for the noise around her. She kicked the boy awake, and he fumbled, sitting up abruptly.

"What—"

"Shh!"

He did not respond as she walked from the fire and towards the noise. The gurgling came again, this time accompanied by a thump.

"Don't... don't go near there," Ladrin whispered. She glared back at him, and he backed up closer to the fire.

The bubbling came once again, and she stepped around a tree and cut through a thick vine. It squirted out black juice as it fell to the ground, and she sidestepped its almost wriggling form. Her boots sloshed into the thick, muddy waters of the swamp, and the squelching did little to stave off her anxiousness.

"It's probably just a hog; please come back," the boy pleaded. Olivia growled and turned back to him.

"Would you shut—" Olivia was cut off as she was suddenly dragged under the water. She screamed and received a lung full of revolting liquid. She slashed her dagger in the water but found resistance against the dense algae growths. She heard a muffled screech as something grabbed hold of her arm and turned her head to the side, caved eyes stared back at her. Its skeletal mouth opened at her, and she thrashed against its grip. Another grabbed her leg, and she kicked at it hard, sending its head snapping back. Her lungs burned as she stabbed her dagger into the face of the thing holding her arm. Its muffled groan bubbled through the water, and it released her. Her other arm was seized and pulled up.

Olivia gasped as Ladrin dragged her back to the shore and collapsed onto the bank. She wiped her face and spit up putrid water with a retch and gasp. She pulled her dagger from the water as a hand shot out. It dug its claws into the wet mud and dragged itself up onto land. Its outer skin peeled back to show the pruned gray flesh underneath its arms.

"Undead!" Ladrin cried.

Olivia kicked it in the face, and it groaned, whipping its head back and forth. "Grab a torch! Now!" she yelled.

The boy ran back to the fire as Olivia watched more undead rise from the water around them. Their mouths hung open, eyes bleeding red. They tripped and crawled their way towards her with anguished screams. She stabbed one in the eye and pushed it back. Another grabbed onto her leg, and she kicked it away.

"Fire now!" she yelled. Ladrin ran over to her, two torches in his hand. She took one and swung it towards the undead. They screeched and backed away.

"Go! Now!" she called. Ladrin took off, and Olivia followed shortly after. The dead continued to rise around them from the mud and leaves, and she jumped from one's grasp before slamming the torch into its face. It caught fire and flailed, falling into others, and catching them on fire as well. Olivia backed away from the burning bodies as memories of Ignis flashed in her eyes.

"Olivia!" Ladrin yelled. Olivia turned back to see an undead pulling him to the ground. He screamed as it wracked its claws down his pant leg. She ran up to him and whacked it on the head with the torch. It cried, and she pulled the shaking boy up to his feet.

"Don't stand still, idiot! Run!"

She shoved him in front of her as the wails continued. She threw her torch to the ground and ran after him, jumping over fallen logs and ducking under vines. He was slow, limping as he tried to navigate the brush. He fell, and she pulled him back onto his feet.

"Do not stop," she said. She could hear the monsters gain ground as she pulled his arm over her shoulder and helped him navigate. She pushed hanging moss and decomposing plants from her way and her trembling slowly began to subside.

When the moans faded and she was sure they were far enough away, she stopped to catch her breath on a dry patch of land. She let him fall to his knees and put her hand on her chest. She hated this place. She hated the undead. She hated the people who forced her into this mess.

"O-Olivia?" Ladrin said, looking up at her.

"What?" she asked with a sigh.

"Are... you alright?"

She looked over at him and then down at her arm that had a burning gash engraved on it.

"I'm fine. What about you?" she asked, nodding towards his leg. It was bleeding severely, and his pant leg was nearly torn completely off.

"I-I don't know," he whispered. Olivia ignored the pain creeping up her arm and knelt down, taking his leg in her hand. He hissed as she touched the uplifted skin. The cuts were not too deep, despite the bleeding.

"It is not as bad as it looks," she said. She took out her water skin and poured it over his wound. He cried in pain and bit his lip until it bled. She wiped the weeping blood away and stood up. She pulled the dryer moss from the trees and wrang them out with a jolt of pain up her arm and carried the moss over to the boy. Gently placing it over the wound, she wrapped what was left of his pant leg over the moss to keep it from slipping.

"Pray this is not tainted," she muttered and set his foot down on the ground.

He took a shaky breath. "Thank you."

"Do not thank me yet. See if you survive the night." She fell back onto her hind and put her head in her hands. It was going to be a long night.

43 ENARA

Enara could feel the darkness seeping into her bones as the carriage carried them closer to the Dark Kingdom. They had been riding in the carriage for days, stopping only for brief breaks. They had even slept in the carriage during the nights. She had heard the noises that came from outside it, seen the way the trees shifted in the wind. It was beginning to feel stifling. Even with the windows open, she still couldn't find a fresh breath to take. The light rain pattered against the top of the carriage, and Enara focused on the rhythmic sound.

Trissa sat opposite her, fingers weaving through a knitted scarf she had started on the way. She hummed softly to herself, seeming not at all concerned with their destination. She looked up at the queen every so often with a small smile. Enara wondered if she was simply putting on a face as a mother would do to calm her frightened children even though she herself was terrified. She didn't want to ask.

Enara heard the soldiers speaking outside the carriage as the horses moved from dirt to stone pathways. Nothing extraordinary, but they mumbled rumors about her. And proudly proclaimed how Auratus was theirs now. It made her contemplate if her kingdom would survive while she was away. She had put Sir Alran in charge of most of the pressing issues. But he was one man, and he did not hold the same loyalty to her as he did to her sister. If he tried to rebel, he would be cut down by Malum, and she would lose one more person who was close to her.

The cobblestone streets they turned onto made the carriage jump, and with each jump, Enara's breath grew shorter. Trissa gently took hold of her hand, and Enara gave her a half-smile in return.

The two could hear the creaking of the doors that opened into the city. Enara recalled the stories she had heard of the Dark Kingdom. That blood ran through the streets. Dead bodies lay piled up, one on top of the other. Murder was favored, and girls were raped in their own beds. She had learned all this from her mother, who died at the hands of the man she now served.

The carriage lurched forward, and Enara closed her eyes and sent a silent prayer to the goddess. After a few more minutes, the carriage stopped, and she heard the driver step close to pull the door open. As the light flooded into the carriage, her stomach twisted painfully. She did not want to know what greeted her beyond the door. She did not want to see blood and misery again. It wasn't until Trissa gave her a light pat on the hand that she finally moved.

She took a breath and stepped out of the carriage. She blinked her eyes at the blinding light, and when they adjusted, she was met with hundreds of faces. Both young and old surrounded her with expressions that turned from blank to outright joyous. She took a step back into the carriage as the people raised their hands toward her.

"Enara! Lady Enara!" they cheered. Their shouts reached the heavens, and her ears stung. They reached for her and were driven back by the guards. Trissa forced Enara to step from the carriage and stood beside her, holding onto her shoulder. Enara scanned the immense crowd. All the faces were alight, some dirty, some clean—no blood on the streets. No bodies. The houses looked like the ones in Ignis, large and built of stone. The streets seemed to stem apart from the main square and went as far as the eye could see. Deep blue banners hung from street corners with an insignia of a four-headed silver dragon sewn onto them. Enara could barely process what she was seeing before a guard took her arm and ushered her forward. They pushed into the crowd as cheering people clambered for a chance to touch the young queen. Trissa stayed close behind her, one hand on her shoulder, the other holding her knitting needle.

The guards pushed those who got too close away from her as they weaved through the various streets. She took notice of people in apartments above her throwing flowers, and she caught a rose in her hand. The guards pushed her forward again, and she turned at the sound of a small child. She saw gold eyes looking toward her, her hand grasping a petite wooden cat. Enara smiled lightly, and the girl shoved the cat into her hand.

"Queen!" she smiled. Enara's heart lifted slightly, and she brushed the girl's cheek. All around her, people lit up in praise and elation at the sight of her as they made their way down the city toward the palace. Children sat on their parents' shoulders, holding lilies and blooming orchids, waving to her. Enara returned the wave and found a genuine smile through the crowd. The darkness lifted from her shoulders as the sights of the citizens around her.

"I don't understand, Trissa," she whispered.

Trissa shook her head. "I haven't a clue either, Your Grace."

They made their way down towards the castle's curtain wall, and she was pulled past the doors, away from the people. Once the doors closed, she could still hear the cheering. Enara held onto the wooden cat in her hand and took a shaky breath.

"The king awaits you on the balcony," a guard said.

She turned to Trissa, who took her bags. "I will meet you later. You will be okay," she promised, rubbing her cheek lightly. Enara nodded and turned towards the black castle. The dark stone gave a foreboding look, despite the sun shining through the windows. The rain had quieted and left little puddles around the courtyard. Several servants bowed to her before carrying on their way, and she squeezed the cat before stepping inside.

The entryway was neat and orderly. A plush, deep red carpet greeted her as she stepped inside, and a servant took her coat and disappeared through a serving door on the right. A large staircase stood before her that split off in two directions at the top. A chandelier of diamonds twinkled above her, and she heard the soft footfalls of someone come from the stairs. She looked up at the staircase and saw a figure dressed in all black standing to the right. Their face was hidden by a silk veil, but they lifted a finger at her and motioned for her to come. She hesitated for a moment, a crawling fear running up her spine. When the figure did not move, she started up the stairs scrupulously, keeping her head low, before stopping in front of them.

They said nothing as they turned and led her through the castle halls. More banners were strewn about the dark stone walls, along with heads of boar and elk. She walked quickly to keep up with the veiled figure, and after going up a tight twist of stairs, they stopped outside a wooden door.

They continued to be silent, simply standing beside the door. Enara looked towards it, and with a small sigh, turned the doorknob. The door swiftly opened after taking one last look at the figure outside the room. The room was small, just big enough to fit a table for four comfortably and the stone walls were bare. The wooden floors creaked slightly under her weight. A man stood near the balcony doors, scanning the outside. Enara took a breath and raised her voice.

"I am Queen Enara of House GoldThorn."

"I know who you are, Lady GoldThorn," the man said, turning towards her.

Her eyes widened at the face who greeted her. "You—you're that lord from the ball," she stuttered. She recognized his honey-colored eyes and dark hair. He asked her to dance at Rose's coronation ball. She could still remember his charming, woody scent. She knew something was different about him. But now, more questions bubbled in her mind.

"Yes, I am sorry for the deception. I am Lord Aldrian Silvand," he said with a small smile—nearly genuine.

"Why did you lie to me?" she asked, her knuckles whitening from their grip on the cat. That seemed like the only question she could grasp onto.

"You would not have trusted me had I told you who I was," he answered. A shot of pain ran up her arm, and she grimaced. He stepped closer to her and took the wooden cat from her hand, setting it on the table. She did not flinch at his touch but eyed him warily.

"How did you get in? Why were you there?"

He rubbed her aching hand with his own. "Malum sent me there to see your sister for myself. He wanted me to… see if what you said was true. That she was unfit to rule Ignis; I will say you were right in calling for us."

"All the luck that got me," Enara whispered.

Lord Aldrian gave a small laugh. "I did not bring you all the way simply to scare you, my lady. I wanted you to see the 'Dark Kingdom' for what it truly is," he told her as he ushered her towards the balcony. She looked at him quizzically. "This is the true Dark Kingdom. The city of Reverand." He opened the doors to the balcony, and they stepped out into the sunlight. The sun streamed through the castle yard, where thousands of people gathered to look at her. She looked down to see the same faces looking up at her with admiration and delight.

"This is the true kingdom. Our kingdom," he said and waved towards the crowd. Enara looked from him to the masses, her mind spinning. When his words processed in her mind, she felt her heart drop into her stomach.

"You... don't mean—"

"We are betrothed, yes. This is your kingdom, and soon, all of them will be yours. Once we are one," Aldrian told her.

Enara looked at him horrified. Behind his pleasant eyes, she saw chains, chains that would wrap around her. Her hand burned and she gripped it.

She knew she had no way to say no. At this point, she did not deserve even the chance to. She made her bed. Now, she must lie in it.

She looked back out at the kingdom and gave her best look of content through her wavering lips.

For even if she was loved, she was still a prisoner in a kingdom of hate.

44 NADAHI

The kindling crackled lightly against the burning logs of the fire the group had made. They happily told stories and laughed, throwing their mead around.

"No, no, Torgir, you've got it all wrong! It was Skidi that threw the goat, not me!" Erling laughed.

"Is that so? And here I thought you were the only one with the beard that could rival a giant's ball sack," Hakon replied. The group burst into rapturous laughter as Nadahi turned her gaze towards the small outcast. Rose sat by herself at another small fire, her gaze focused on the burning logs.

"Erling couldn't even carry a keg, let alone a goat. Have you seen his arms? My mother could lift more than him," Torgir toted.

"Your mother's dead, Torgir."

"Exactly." A mead was thrown, a face hit, and the laughter continued. Nadahi stood from her perch and weaved through the group, setting herself down in front of the *Runa*.

Rose's face was scrunched in focus, her eyes not even looking up to acknowledge her new companion. Nadahi noticed every crease in her forehead, every flicker of magic behind her eyes. The mage would finger the ruby around her neck when she would concentrate. Nadahi was surprised to see it give off a faint glow.

"You are not very practiced at magic, are you?" she asked in the Common Tongue with a hint of tease.

Rose flushed and sighed, dropping her fingers from the ruby. "I've never been good at it. Trissa and my mentor helped me somewhat, but they were no mages. My mother was the only one who could have taught me," she answered, her eyes darkening when she mentioned her mother.

Nadahi shifted herself, pulling her cloak around her arms, and smiled at the freckled girl. "You forget my father. He and the mother healer will help you with your magic after we return from the ruins. Have no worries," she said.

Rose looked up at her. "Is he a mage?" she asked.

A hearty laugh was the reply she got. "Not at all. He is just skilled in the craft. Our family has passed on knowledge of witchcraft for generations. If the Mother shows you the way, then my father can take it from there," she said with a bright smile.

"Your father was ready to behead me not a day ago," Rose argued.

Nadahi's smile faltered. "Yes, and that was a mistake on his part. But now we know *Runa*, what you are and how important you are."

Rose caught her gaze and held it for a moment. She couldn't find the proper wording to respond, so instead, she simply cleared her throat. "It seems my importance may be misplaced if I cannot wield my magic properly."

Nadahi looked down at the sword strapped to her waist. "Perhaps I can train you in combat instead. I may not always be there to protect you."

Rose's eyes widened. "I've never even held a sword before—"

"Now is as good a time as any to learn. Come," she said, standing up.

"Right now? Isn't it a bit dark out?"

"You don't need to see to hold a sword, Rose."

Rose begrudgingly stood up, following the huntress further away from the camp. Nadahi pulled her sword from its rest and flipped it over, pointing the handle at the mage. Rose carefully took hold of it, and when Nadahi let go, its tip plunged into the snow.

"I-it's very heavy!" Rose exclaimed. The sword was nearly as tall as her.

Nadahi laughed. "Perhaps we should get one to fit your size." She went behind Rose and placed a hand over hers, helping her lift the sword. "Here." she pulled her other hand around, her hands fulling covering Rose's small ones, feeling the soft heat she gave off. "Think of the sword as an extension of your arm. It moves with you." she swung it slightly, forcing Rose to move with it.

"A very large extension of my arm," Rose said, earning a chuckle.

"Perhaps so. Now, keep it up." Nadahi released her hands, and Rose visibly struggled to hold it steady. Nadahi walked around her, lifting the sword slightly with a hand. "Always aim for the weaker points of a man. Between the ribs or under the arm. Aim where there is less fur or armor. You may be small, but that means you will be harder to hit." Nadahi took the sword from Rose and did a test swing, showing her the stance she used.

Rose groaned and rubbed her arms. "This will be the death of—"

A screech tore through the area, making the hairs on the back of Nadahi's neck stand on end. She quickly flung herself onto Rose, sending them both barreling to the ground. A demon dove above, barely missing them with its black talons.

"Forsaken! Claim your arms!" Nadahi yelled. She quickly got up, forcing Rose with her, and drew her sword. The demon flew high into the sky, disappearing into the night.

The other four ran up to them, swords and shields drawn.

"Protect the *Runa*!" Liv ordered. They circled around Rose, shields side by side. Nadahi scanned the dark area, the chilling wind biting against her nose and cheeks.

"To the east!" Erling yelled.

He raised his shield, and the demon appeared out of the shadows, slamming into him and knocking him back into Rose. She grabbed onto his shoulders, steadying him as the demon ascended back into the sky.

"Where is its master?" Torgir asked.

"Keep your eyes out!" Nadahi ordered and heard a *thunk* and turned as Hakon brought his shield up, an arrow piercing the wood.

"To the south!" Liv yelled. A man clad in black leather jumped from the shadows, slamming into her. She brought her shield up, bashing him in the face, then slashed her sword up. He dodged the blow and grabbed onto a leather strap of her chest, flinging her to the ground.

"Liv!" Nadahi yelled. She turned to the man as the other three moved around to protect Rose. The man swung his two swords down, and Nadahi blocked them then sliced out with her own. He parried the blow and swung around again. Nadahi kicked her foot out and hit him in the stomach. He fell to a knee, and Nadahi sliced her sword through his throat.

Another screech and Torgir grabbed Rose, flinging her onto the ground as the demon slammed into his shield. Its talons closed around the shield as its beady red eyes tore through him. Its beak snapped at his face, and Erling swung at the demon and sliced through its wing as it screamed. It turned its gaze towards him and lashed out too quickly for him to raise his shield. It sliced him across the face and sent him tumbling to the ground. Hakon's shield bashed it, and it lifted into the air but couldn't get altitude with its injured wing.

"Come here, you bastard!" he yelled. Hakon and Torgir turned to the bleeding demon as it screeched at them. Flinging itself down towards the two, they brought their shields up in unison, slamming into the demon.

"Now!"

The two pushed their shields against the demon and knocked it back. They brought their swords around, stabbing clean through the neck. With one last screech of pain, its head split off its body and landed on the snow, talons still twitching.

Nadahi watched as another Forsaken loomed over Rose, the dark markings on his face twisted with pleasure. He swung his sword but was struck with an ax in his shoulder. He cried out, and Nadahi jumped up, slamming her foot into his back with a yell. He fell to the ground away from her as Nadahi rolled and pulled Rose up. She twirled her sword around.

"Is that all the Cursed God can send? Some lowly slaves?" she mocked in their language.

"Your *Runa* cannot save you, filthy insect," he replied, spitting blood at her.

She smiled. "Then this insect will crush you under her boot." She lunged forward, clashing iron with the man. She ducked under his blade and then bashed him against her shield. He stumbled back, but recovered enough to dodge her attack. He rolled to the side of her, slicing into her thigh. She cried out and slammed her shield down, breaking it against his face.

"Nadahi!" Rose cried.

"I'm fine, Rose!" she replied. She lunged for the man, but with a smile, he disappeared in a blast of smoke. She coughed and waved her hands, trying to push it from her face.

"He is a witch!" she yelled and searched the area, trying to find a trace of the Forsaken. The others were fighting another demon across the way, but there was no other sign of the master.

"Did he flee?" Rose asked.

"Forsaken do not flee," Nadahi answered, the smoke falling from her vision. She continued her search, ignoring the pulsing pain in her leg, forcing her breath to calm.

The wind howled to the north as Nadahi turned and came face to face with a boot. The Forsaken rammed into her, forcing her into the snow. He wrapped his hands around her neck and spoke.

"Your goddess will know hell," he spat. Nadahi fought against his grip as her vision faded in and out, her breaths coming out in jagged puffs. His smile was twisted and bloody as his grip grew tighter. Nadahi cried out, and a blast of light covered her vision.

The grip released, and she gasped as the man was thrown from her person in a ball of flame. He screamed and rolled upon the ground, twisting in unnatural ways. Nadahi forced herself onto her feet and looked behind her at the mage, whose eye glowed an unearthly green.

The Forsaken lunged for her again, and she grabbed her sword, stabbing it through his eye. He slumped against her, and she pulled her sword out, letting him fall to the ground. Rose panted heavily, falling to her knees. Nadahi ran up to her and cupped her face.

"Rose, are you alright?" she asked, and Rose nodded, panting, her eyes returning to her natural green, the ruby on her neck softly pulsing.

"I'm fine. What about you? You're injured," she said.

Nadahi looked at her bleeding thigh. "It is just a flesh wound. It will heal," she smiled.

"Nadahi, over here," Liv called. Their attention was pulled towards Erling, who was lying on the ground, his face covered with blood. Rose pushed herself up and came over to the others. Erling grimaced in pain as Liv wiped his face with a cloth. Three long gashes ran along his face, his right eye just a bloody socket.

"You will not go to *Shor'vaker* today, Erling," Liv said.

He sighed lowly. "And here I was, hoping to beat you."

"You will have many more chances for that." They helped him on to his feet and wrapped his eye. Rose looked at the burned body of the man she had killed, his body contorted in pain.

"The Forsaken...." she muttered to herself. She sat on the blood-covered snow, pulling the furs around herself.

Nadahi turned to her and the dark gaze she held worried her. "Are you alright?" she asked.

"I'm never going to escape it, am I? They will follow wherever I go..." she muttered.

Nadahi bent down, tucking a curl behind her ear. "*Runa*, what do you speak of?"

The small girl finally focused her gaze on the huntress, a steady certainty in her eyes. "I'm going to take back my kingdom or die trying."

45 LAERDYA

Laerdya paced the steps outside of the castle. Her eyes kept wandering to the other side of the stone bridge where the guards stood, ready to escort her. Her mind stepped back to the door, though, afraid to see the shadow of her fiancé waiting for her. The queen promised her safety, but she could not keep her eye out every day. Elmaer would hear of her excursion sooner or later and would face his wrath. Still, for the moment, she was set on leaving the boundaries of the castle.

The door to the castle opened, and her heart jumped in her chest as a figure crossed through the light. She was relieved to see a friendly face, though.

"Nexis!" she cheered. The older elf greeted her with a hug, and they started across the bridge. "You are my escort?"

"I suppose the lady Ravana has taken a liking to me."

"I suppose so, yes," Laerdya smiled. "I will not say I am unhappy, though. It has been a dream to escape this castle." They crossed the bridge, and two guards followed shortly after them. Laerdya could hardly contain her excitement as they passed the guard towers and strolled towards the beginnings of the city.

The sky was brighter than usual with light hues of swirling purples illuminating the buildings above. The city itself was massive, with tall stone structures and statues of the gods lining the bridge. Laerdya had seen only what could be viewed from the windows of the castle, but she knew it would be marvelous to see. When they neared the city, though, it was eerily silent.

"It is nearly midnight. The safest time for you to stroll. If you wish to see any shops, though, the queen has ordered all to keep their doors open for you," Nexis said. Laerdya nodded and scanned the first main street.

The cobblestone seemed to be boundless as the street stretched farther than she could see. The shops that littered the road held soft candlelight inside them, just enough for Laerdya to peek inside. Few cursed elves roamed the shop windows, glancing at the princess with wide eyes. Some whispered to one another, and with one look at the guards, they scuttled away.

It was nearly overwhelming to the princess just how much there was to see and do. Every shop had neat little trinkets or pastries or beautiful gowns. Fireflies danced around light posts and carved benches sat along the side of the roads.

Laerdya eyed a jewelry shop a few stones down and pointed to a delicate chain with a pearl encased in a silver cage. "Nexis, look at that," she breathed. "It's beautiful."

Nexis opened the door to the shop, and she quietly entered, the guards standing in front of the doors.

The shop was small, with only a few glass cases set up with different metal-bound jewels. The twinkle of the bell above the door alerted the shopkeeper to their presence.

"Welcome! My princess, you are a sight to behold!" The stout shopkeeper yelled, scrambling over. He bowed low with his wobbly feet and took her hand. "We have waited to see you for years, my lady. The stories do not do you justice." The little man was shorter than even her, and she couldn't help but giggle.

"Your jewelry here is remarkable. May I try on a few?" she asked.

The man's eyes lit up. "Yes! Yes! Come! You may try any!" He scurried to a case and opened the glass, careful not to hurt the delicate jewels inside. Next, he showed her an immaculate emerald encased in a silver cage. The jewel shimmered in the candlelight and winked a bright green at her. She squealed when she saw it and happily let the shopkeeper place it on her neck.

She tugged on the blessed elf's sleeve to gain his attention away from the other necklaces, and he looked down at her.

"It is beautiful on you, Laerdya," he said with a nod. Her smile grew wider, and the elderly man shuffled in front of her.

"This is for you! It is beautiful!" he exclaimed.

Laerdya fingered the delicate jewels. "I'll take it. How much?" she asked.

The man opened his mouth, but after seeing the guards enter the store, he quickly sputtered out a "Free! For you, anything is free!"

Laerdya's smile faded, but she nodded. "Thank you." Nexis touched her shoulder as she exited the store, the guards slowly strolling behind. She looked down at the necklace and then back up at the elf.

"Nexis, when we return, inform a messenger to bring three-hundred coins to the store," she said lowly.

Nexus smiled softly. "Of course, Laerdya."

As they made their way further down the street, the girl stopped along an alley entrance. She heard a quick tapping of footsteps and a hush of voices.

"We should not go down any alleys, Laerdya. It is not safe," he said. Laerdya made a face and continued, her eyes darting back to the shadow she had seen.

Soon they crossed over a bridge that was built above a glowing river. She watched as vibrant colored fish swam and bobbed up to the surface of the water before disappearing deeper below. The mist that came up was light blue and filled the air in a wondrous haze. She listened to the steady flowing of the water for a moment before speaking.

"Nexis, you promised to speak of my mother. Is now a good time?" she asked.

Nexus glanced down at her. "Of course. What would you like to know?"

Laerdya thought to herself for a moment, trying to come up with all the questions in her mind. "How did they meet?"

"Your father liked to visit this place in his youth. When he first met the queen, he knew little to nothing about the city beyond the portal besides what the stories had told him. When lady Areválla allowed him access after their bonding ceremony, he desired to see more of it—all of it. He never officially told me how he met her, though. I assume at one of the many parties the queen threw."

"Was she nobility?"

"Not exactly. She attended a few of the balls. But she was not among the aristocracy."

Laerdya licked her bottom lip, thinking again. Her head spun with all the questions she wanted to ask; she just didn't know if she had the time. Or possibly she was afraid to know the answer. "Did he truly love her?" she asked.

"Your father was completely infatuated with her," he answered.

She put her hands on the stone railing of the bridge and enjoyed the wind that blew through her hair. "He was married to the queen, though. Why take after a cursed elf?" she asked.

"Sometimes... love can be difficult. You will understand when you are older. He was arranged to the queen through her council and met your mother soon after visiting Nevrak." He paused for a moment before speaking again. *"Rane'abeles* created love out of a strange concoction of emotions that we cannot understand, but sometimes it is for the best."

Laerdya's smile dropped. "And then he died."

Nexis's voice softened. "Yes. The battle was not pleasant. The Dark Kingdom is a force to be feared."

"What is the Dark Kingdom?" she asked. They sat down on a bench overlooking the river as Nexis ran his fingers through his hair.

"A sinister force of darkness and corruption. Lady Ravana would know more than I. She was there when the Dark Knights gained their power."

"And if they break through the portal?" she asked. Nexis sighed lightly.

"Then I suppose a battle would be on our hands. But Avlor is still standing, as far as I know. The portal shall not be broken, and your life is safe," he assured.

Laerdya felt the bruises on her wrist. She was never truly safe. "What happened to my mother?"

Nexis sighed and shifted his robes, folding his hands over his lap. It took him a moment to speak.

"In his maddened wrath... he had killed her."

Laerdya blinked back the crystals that threatened to spill over her eyes and sniffed, adjusting her posture.

"I wish I could remember him. All I see when I close my eyes is his dark face and those black veins."

Nexis put a gentle hand on her shoulder, and she wiped her eyes. "You were young—too young to remember anything but. I do not remember my father either."

Laerdya glanced at him, sniffing. "You don't?"

Nexis shook his head, a soft smile on his lips. "No. When me and Nymvas were just boys, our father had died of a terrible sickness. Our mother raised us as best she could with the help of the community, ensuring our future with an arranged marriage to the queen and a happy home for me—before I blew it up, that is."

Laerdya laughed and hiccupped, causing Nexis to break into laugher as well. When she calmed down, she watched as a group of young elves passed them by, giving them a second look. Her smile fell watching them play. She was never allowed to play with the other children; she didn't have any friends.

"These are your people, Laerdya. Remember that," Nexis said.

"They are not. I am not one of them."

"You are part of them," Nexis assured. "You are also part of the blessed. In your blood runs the bond of both blessed and cursed elves..." he paused for a moment. "If... the blessed queen was ever to decide it, you could lead both races to unity."

Laerdya looked at Nexis, an odd glint in her eye. "The queen would never open the portal to us. We are cursed, remember?"

"Cursed by your skin and location. Nothing else. If you wish to make a world you want to live in, you must take the initiative to do so. Even if you cannot escape here, that does not mean you are trapped. There are a million elves in this city who are ready for the care of a new queen. You must learn to be a part of them."

Laerdya fidgeted with her fingers in her lap. "How do I do that?" she asked.

Nexis put an arm around her. "By learning about the world both above and below. You've read many novels, but how much have you truly experienced of the outside?"

"None," she confessed.

"Then now is the time to make yourself a queen, *luvere,* my child. You are no more a slave as water is to fire. With enough force, you can quench any flame."

Laerdya looked over at the guards standing a polite distance away, then thought back to the slaves held in the castle walls.

"You're right, Nexis. Maybe it is time for change."

The next day, Laerdya stood near her bed, looking down at the soft fabric laid on top of it. She ran a hand through the blue silk of the dress, the same hue as that of the cursed elves themselves. Elmaer had given it to her; a servant had brought it in for her.

She pulled her nightclothes off and gently tugged on the dress. It was beautifully crafted. With swirls of gold trimming the bottom and lighter colored sleeves, it complemented her hair astoundingly. A slave put up her hair while Laerdya's thoughts controlled her mind.

Could she really survive here? Nexis was with her, but so was Elmaer. One wrong move and she could be hung from the ramparts— *no,* she thought. *I am to become queen; I am no slave.* She was Laerdya of the Exalted Forests. And she could be damned if she was to be confined to her room for any longer. He could not hurt her worse than what she had already endured.

After the slaves had done their duty, Laerdya exited her room and made her way down the hallway to the throne room, where she knew the queen awaited her.

When she entered, the queen turned to her with a smile on her face, a skittish Nexis by her side.

"Come, blossom, I have great news to tell you," she purred. Laerdya walked over to her as the queen put a clawed finger on her shoulder. "Now, little blossom. I am hosting a masquerade with the nobility tomorrow evening. You and Nexis shall be attending." Laerdya opened her mouth to speak but closed it. She was never allowed such things before. She was always confined to her room during festivities. Was this her moment to break free?

"My queen... are you sure? I've never attended a party before."

"You are of age now, dear, and you are closer to your bonding ceremony. I must show you off before you are heavy, or else the nobility will think poorly of me," she pouted.

Nexis gave her a sideways look. "No offense, my queen, but I doubt any of the nobility could ever look down upon you."

The queen laughed and perched closer to the blessed elf. "Oh, now don't dote on me. I might have to make use of that mouth indeed."

A fire lit in Nexis' cheeks, and he stammered out a quick reply before fleeing from the room. The queen watched him go.

"Listen and learn, blossom. You can have any man under you. If you only make them think they have control," she said.

Laerdya took to the queen. "You speak ill of your own son?" she asked.

The queen chuckled. "I dare not speak ill of my own child. He is the world to me. But there is nothing wrong with baring your teeth. If you have the bite to go with it." She sashayed away towards the fleeing blessed elf.

"Remember the masquerade, my dear! I shall have the seamstresses call for you this afternoon."

Laerdya was left alone when the doors slammed shut behind the queen. She ran her fingers through her hair and turned to the path to the library—this time to read about balls and dancing.

46 NAVA

Nava pulled a bucket of water from the well and set it down on the ground. She looked up at the blue sky and watched as clouds lazily floated overhead. The morning twitter of the birds filled the farmyard, and the two moons were still barely visible in the rising light.

Nava picked up the bucket and brought it into the farm home as Neve busied herself with breakfast. The young boy tittered in and out of the house as he ran jobs for her in town, stopping only once to say hello to the half-elf. Nava set the bucket on the counter, and the woman gave her a quick thanks before turning back to the pastries on the table.

"What is it?" Nava asked, studying the way she folded the dough with her hands.

"One of my favorite pies. We save enough money from our livestock each year to be able to make this orange pie," she said.

Nava took an orange from the counter and rolled it in her hand. "I've never had orange pie before," she said monotonously. She smelled the sharp citrusy peel and wrinkled her nose.

"We get them imported from the capital. It's a fine day when we can get our hands on one." The woman smiled and wiped her hands on her apron. "You are in for a real treat. Come, come," she motioned and grabbed Nava's shoulder. "Wipe your hands, and then let's get to work."

Nava pulled back slightly. "You want me to bake with you? I've never—"

The woman quickly silenced her with a spoon to the hand. Nava flinched, and the woman grabbed a rag from the counter and put it into her hands. "No excuses. It's about time you learned, girl. You will need to learn to bake if you wish to have a family with him," she sang.

Nava flushed. "I'm not—we aren't together!"

Neve puckered her lips and ignored the girl's remarks, humming to herself. "Put your hands like this on the dough and use your palms to flatten it," she showed, then flipped it over and did it again. She brought the bowl of flour over, and Nava dipped her hands in and patted them dry.

"Try it," Neve motioned, scooting the dough over to her. Nava squinted her eyes and kneaded the dough, and used her palm to flatten, then flip. The woman nodded her head. "Just like that. You don't want to go too long or kneed it too hard, or the dough won't rise well. You must learn just the right amount."

Nava continued as Neve began peeling the orange and cutting the rinds into small strips. The melodic action helped Nava to focus on the bake and nothing else. It had been some time since she simply felt content. In her mind, she was back with her mother, watching her bake tiny berry cakes. The villagers would come over as soon as they smelled the delicious cakes baking and she would hand them out, one by one, till only two remained.

Then, after she was done, she would lead Nava over to a nice field just outside of the village walls and they would sit and watch the sunset through the trees, eating the last of the cakes. Her mother would hum and take Nava into her lap, rocking her back and forth. She would wipe the crumbs from her cheeks and kiss her forehead, all while still humming that melodic tune.

Thinking back to that time put a smile on her face, and she never wanted to stop kneading.

Nava bit into the sweet honey glaze of the orange pie. The small tinge of sourness tickled her tongue, and she giggled. The elder woman gave her a look of approval.

"This is outstanding," Nava exclaimed.

The woman hummed in response and pushed the pie closer to her. "Well, have as much as you like. There is plenty for the boy and me," she said.

Nava swallowed and ran her fingers over the wood of the table. "I must thank you again for saving me," she praised. "I would not have made it without you."

Neve gave a courteous nod and took a bite of the pie before responding. "There is not enough kindness in this world to outmatch the cruelness. Even one life is worth the cost of your own. When that boy came to my door covered in blood and holding a wounded half-breed, I knew that there was still enough hope. It's not common to see someone care so deeply for your kind," she said.

Nava sighed. "Yes. I have been fortunate enough to run into kind folk like you."

The woman sat back in her seat, studying the girl as she poked the pie with her fork. "Were you a slave?"

Nava dropped her fork, eyes widening. The woman raised a hand. "I meant no harm and apologize if I brought up malicious thoughts. That mark is foreign, but I know a cattle brand when I see it."

Nava nodded, her leg bouncing up and down in her seat. "Yes, for a time. I do not wish to relive it."

The woman stood up and patted her shoulder. "You have come this far. You will make it further." She took the pie and set it on the counter, cutting the pieces up and wrapping them in fabric.

"Take this one to the boy. I'm sure even he is lonely," she said and handed Nava the bundle. Nava smiled slightly and graciously took it. "You know," the woman started, "I always could use more hands around the farm. We have spare rooms for the two of you."

Nava's smile widened, and she contemplated it, but she knew she could not stay. What she sought after was more important than keeping warm on a farm. "That is a generous offer. But I believe we both have our reasons for not staying. I hope you understand."

The woman grasped her shoulder. "Of course. You're much too young to stay locked up in here after all. The elf blood in you does not allow leisure," she teased. Nava's smile grew wider, and they stood up. "If you're going to be leaving us, let me make you something to survive off. Meet me at the stables."

Nava nodded and left the house, grasping the warm pie in her hand. She stood near the stables and watched the cattle chew on the grass and goats jump up and down boxes and hay. The cat, Lula, pushed its body up against her leg while purring happily. Nava bent down and scratched its back and ears, earning a head bump in return.

A few minutes later, Neve came over to the stables as Nava was admiring the chestnut beside her. She pointed to the horse.

"She is the fastest one I have here. She belonged to a knight before he was killed in battle."

Nava turned to the woman and saw the bag in her hands. "You are too gracious," she muttered.

Neve set the bag into her arms and placed the pie in as well. "This should last you to the next town." She looked at the horse once more. "She does not belong in the stables. She needs to be outside where she was raised. Have her."

Nava backed up slightly. "What? Are you certain? She could sell for a fortune!" she exclaimed.

The woman petted the mane of the chestnut. "I am certain. Now off you go before the boy drinks himself into another stupor," she laughed.

Nava bit back the tears in her eyes and pulled the woman into her arms. "Thank you," she whispered.

"May the goddess be with you."

Nava pulled away and shouldered the bag. "I will repay you for this," she promised.

The woman knitted her fingers together. "Repay me by making the world kinder."

The horse trotted down the pathway to the village, lulling Nava into a peaceful trance. As the houses started to scroll past her, she caught the weeping of a woman. Her eyes turned to the woman, who was clutching a small boy to her chest, wailing to a guard.

"He is dead! My husband was murdered! Left to die on the road with his companions!" Nava quickly looked away and continued forward. "What will I do without him?" she sobbed.

Nava gripped the reins of the horse and jerked them forwards. The horse picked up, and soon the sobbing woman was from earshot.

Nava's ears rang heavily as blood pumped through her heart. *It was his fault*, she told herself. *The swordsman saved you.* He deserved to die. What happened to that woman and child now was none of her concern.

Nava turned off the main road onto a smaller one and headed towards the tavern. When she entered, she did not see his slumped figure over a table, nor when asking the keeper was he in a room with a woman. She searched across the village for the swordsman and came up empty-handed. She began to wonder if he had left without her. Would he do such a thing? No, he wouldn't get far without a horse anyway. Not that he wouldn't steal one. But he would not leave her.

As she continued down the path of the village, the sounds of pounding metal caught her ears, and she turned her horse down a more worn pathway. She heard the faint sounds of talking as she closed in on a forge. Jared was bent over the forge, his hand grasping a child's as he struggled to hold the hammer upright.

"You've got to work on your forearms. If you can't hold a hammer, you won't be a good apprentice for the blacksmith."

The boy nodded, and Jared released his hand. Nava hopped down from the horse as Jared looked up at her. He wiped the soot from his face and grabbed a rag. "Here to help?" he asked.

Nava shook her head. "You are the blacksmith, not I," she said with a slight smile. Jared turned back to the boy who was trying to pound out the steel of the sword but was having difficulty uncurving it. Jared set the rag down and took the hammer from the boy.

"I've got it. Go and get your master. And bring a bucket of water—make that two. Get your strength up," he ordered.

The boy bounded off as Jared pulled up his sleeves. Nava watched as he easily pounded out the steel of the blade, dipping it into the forge and back again. She could feel the heat from the fire feet away.

"How long have you worked with a forge?" she asked.

"Since I can remember. I always liked forging blades. Was never great at scrollwork, though," he replied.

Nava turned away as her eyes caught the red metal of the blade. "I've already made two. Saw the boy having issues a few days ago and figured I'd help out," he told.

Nava laughed. "You helping out? How much is he paying you?"

"Believe it or not, I'm not a terrible man," he scoffed. Nava chuckled to herself as the blacksmith came up to the forge.

"Ye helping my boy?" he asked.

Jared set the sword into the water bucket. "Yes, sir. He was having trouble lifting the hammer. Might want to put him on bucket duty," he smiled.

The smithy swatted the boy on the back and pushed him towards the woodpile. "See, boy can never trust ya. Go split some wood, and we will see if I can get a man out of ye," he scolded and came up beside

Jared.

"Fine work. You a smith?" he asked.

Jared shook his head. "Just a traveler with a knack for metal, sir."

The smithy swung one of his swords around. "Great balance. Though id of gone cattle hide for the hilt," he critiqued.

"Gotta make do."

The smithy turned to him and flipped the blade, so the handle was pointed towards Jared. "It is yours," he told.

Jared took the blade. "Sure? It would sell very well in the city," he exclaimed.

The man waved him off. "Take it; you made it. And taught the boy how to pound out steel. Though if you're ever lookin' for a job, I'll still be 'ere."

Jared took the blade and thanked him. "I will remember that," he said with a bow. He turned to Nava with sparkling eyes and hopped onto the horse.

"You coming?" he asked. Nava took his hand, and he pulled her up in front of him.

"Safe travels," the smithy waved. Jared whipped the reins, and the horse trotted off.

"You smell of fire and soot," Nava remarked with a wiggle of her nose.

"You insinuating that I need a bath?" he asked.

"I wasn't insinuating anything," she replied, earning a grin.

Soon, the blacksmith was far behind them, and the only landscape was the fields of wheat and flowers. The sun was well into the sky now, and the cicadas had begun their singing.

"How did you get the horse?" Jared asked.

"The farm woman, Neve, let me have it. She is an old warhorse."

"We owe that woman our lives," Jared responded.

"Yes, we do... she also gave us pie for the road."

"Well, why didn't you say anything before!" Jared exclaimed. Once far enough away from the village, the two stopped in a field and sat down. Nava pulled the pie from her bag and handed it over to Jared, who smelled it with a groan.

"Man, I haven't had pie since Olivia made it months ago."

"She was a cook?" Nava asked.

He shook his head. "No, but her mother was, taught her the recipe." He set his sword down beside him as he tore open the cloth, taking a bite from the pie. Nava watched in mild amusement as he devoured the slice. His beard had grown more since she last saw him, and flakes of the crust had settled on it. He looked down at her, and his face fell.

"Sorry about your bow," he muttered.

Nava blinked and laughed. "It's nothing to worry about. My life is more important than my bow. I can always get another."

Jared bounced lightly on his knees as he looked out over the field. "Are... you alright?" he asked after a moment.

Nava rubbed her chest and nodded. "Yes, I've gone through worse," she muttered.

Jared finished the slice and rubbed his thumb over his lips. "You see this scar?" he asked, pointing to his upper arm.

"Yes?" Nava answered questioningly.

Jared pulled off his shirt, and she could see it tracing across his chest. "I got this from fighting with another kid when I was fourteen," he puffed.

"Were you always a troubled child?" she asked, pointing to another one just above his navel.

He laughed. "Nah, this one was over a goat."

Nava held her tongue to stop laughing. "A... goat?" she asked. "You were injured by a goat?"

Jared fell onto his back and shook his head. "No, no, I was injured over an argument *about* a goat," he corrected.

Nava laid down beside him and fiddled with the fabric of her cloak. "Do tell, swordsman," she prodded.

Jared cheekily laughed and started his story. "When I was just a lad, the local shopkeeper had caught a fever and died over the winter—It was one of the worst winters in centuries. A plague had started up in the north over it. It was poor times all around. All his belongings were going to be sold or thrown out, but he also had an old goat that was going to be slaughtered if not sold," Jared started. A leisurely look came across his face.

"My pa had never once had sugared creamed milk before, so I thought that I would buy the goat to give to him. Luckily, I worked up enough *sephim* around the forge and local farms to buy the goat. When I went to get her from the farmer, though, he told me that a lad had already come by to get her."

Nava raised an eyebrow, her suspicion growing as he continued.

"Did you...?"

Jared waved her off. "I'm getting there. So, I learned where this brat lived, and it turns out he lived in Goldtown, the rich part of Ignis. The boy only wanted the goat as a toy thing to kick and prod at. I was furious. With the money still in my pockets, I knocked on the door and bribed the mother for the goat."

"I'm sure that went well," Nava chimed in.

Jared laughed. "As well as expected, when a dirty twelve-year-old orphan comes knocking at your door. She kicked me out, so I had to think of another way. I wasn't letting this little shit take that goat. So, at sunrise the next day, when the boy went into town, I challenged him to a duel to the death."

"Swordsman!" Nava exclaimed, forcing herself up onto her elbow. The laughter in her voice gave away any feeling of madness, and Jared ran a hand through his hair.

"Yep. Right out in the open. A fight to the death using the training swords we were given."

"Training swords? That must have taken a while."

"It did. Neither one of us died from it. We both had a few bumps and bruises before the guards pulled us away from each other. But in the end, I ended up winning, and the boy gave me the goat through snotty tears. Though I got a nasty beating from my pa over getting into a fight with a noble's son." He paused as Nava looked at his scar once more.

"A training sword doesn't give you a scar like that, though," she said.

Jared looked her dead in the eye. "No, but a pissed-off goat will."

Nava broke with laughter, falling to her back. Jared watched as her chest quickly rose and fell, her face creasing from her smile. He rubbed his neck, and the two continued to watch the sky brighten over the fields. Only the sound of laughter ringing in the air.

47 LAERDYA

Laerdya focused on the seamstresses piling around her, trying not to run into one another. The soft fabric was shades of blue and green that scattered about the floor. The neckline rested lightly on her chest. While the maids fitted it to her body, she pulled the sleeves up where they sat on her shoulders. She was more covered than she was used to. The queen must have chosen the dress, not Elmaer. Her hair was curled and put into a spiral down her back. The silver tiara sat lightly on her head, small chains falling down to her shoulders. The emerald necklace sat on her collarbone as the maids flurried around her, puffing the dress and tutting about, covering her bruises with jewelry. The last piece was the silver-lined mask that looked nearly like a butterfly. She heard the servants speaking of the night to come, food being prepped and cleaning furiously.

She heard a knock at the door, and Elmaer entered. He wore a blue suit with green trimming the edges of it. A black cape was draped over his shoulder, and his hair was woven into a braid down his back. He wore a mask of a silver wolf. She gave a half-smile, and he looked her up and down. A frown graced his face when his eyes found the necklace.

"I did not get you that," he tutted.

With a gulp, Laerdya quickly responded. "I—the queen bought it for me," she quickly said.

Elmaer motioned for the servants to leave, which they promptly did. She knew what awaited her and stepped back in anticipation.

He stepped closer to her, and she flinched. "Is that so? I've only been aware of her being in meetings all week," he accused, eyeing her.

"I—she must have made the time. Or perhaps she sent Nexis to buy it for me," she stammered.

He came up close enough that she could feel his hot breath on her face. "I do not like being lied to by my own fiancée," he hissed. He reached for the necklace, but before he could pull it off her, she grabbed his hand. A look of shock spread across his face as Laerdya registered what she had just done. Her rings dug into his palm, and with a shaking voice, she held her own.

"I bought it, my lord. It is mine, and I will keep it," she pushed.

Shock turned to rage as she dodged a slap from him and quickly fled to the vanity. "You dare run from me!?" he growled.

Laerdya stood upright. "I need to finish, Elmaer. Your mother will be displeased if we are late or if my dress is torn," she argued. "Do you wish to face her wrath?"

Elmaer snarled, but stopped short of her. With a shake of his head and a curse, he left the room. Her shaking hands grasped the sides of her vanity as she turned, looking into the mirror. Her flushed face came back without a mark. For that, she smiled.

Laerdya collected herself outside the ballroom. She could hear the orchestra playing inside, as well as the several hundred nobles in attendance. Fiddling with her dress, she glanced to and from, searching for her fiancé. She hadn't seen him since he stormed out of her room a few hours ago. She wondered if he would even show up at all. Part of her was joyed at the thought of it.

Soon enough, though, she heard the prince's footsteps, and he came up to her, his jaw set tight. With his sunken demure, she guessed that he had a talk with the queen, and it did not go in his favor. He glanced at the guards posted around them.

"Stay by my side the entire night, Laerdya. I don't want you causing a scene," he huffed.

Laerdya kept her face neutral. "Of course, my lord," she replied. He held his arm out, and she carefully took it. He nodded to the guards, and they opened the doors to the ballroom. Laerdya's eyes widened at the beauty of the ballroom. Blue balls of light floated in the air as whispers of magic flowed through the crowd. Twinkling stars illuminated the canvased ceiling as couples waltzed around the dance floor. The silver pillars glimmered in the candlelight, and the guests seemed to almost glide across the ground as the violins and flutes shaped the music around them.

The masks ranged from crows to lions and beyond, and the elves themselves draped upon layers of glimmering fabric that swirled and danced along with them. The heavy smell of alcohol and herbs made Laerdya's head spin as the couple passed several groups of elves in compromising positions. Elmaer glared at the slaves, who dared near them with glasses full of sparkling liquid.

There was a buffet of cakes and pastries set up alongside the left wall, along with a lone table of mini pies that called for Laerdya to take one. Eyes started to turn to them, and Elmaer kept a steel grip on her as they inched their way towards the other end of the hall where the queen stood.

She was clothed in a scant amount of black satin. The rest of her was covered in jewels and chains, falling around her hips and breasts. Her face was adorned with a silver raven mask. She broke into a smile when she caught the eye of her son.

"Ah, there you are. I was wondering if you'd come at all. You hate these gatherings," she tutted. Elmaer glared through his mask, and Ravana pulled his arm away from Laerdya.

"What do you think you're doing?" he asked.

"Showing her off, of course. You can't have her all to yourself," she said. She gently led the princess away from the fuming prince and near the dancefloor. The music died down, and all faces turned towards them. Laerdya tried to step back, but the queen tightened her grip on her shoulders.

"Tonight, we celebrate the coming of the season and the debut of your new queen!" she announced. "For a millennium, I have graced your eyes and ears. And as disheartening as it is, I must take my leave of the court. But do not fret. You shall be graced with a new ruler. And one that will continue to have us prosper while those of the outside world kill and maim and starve."

Laerdya could feel the heat rise to her cheeks as whispers caught in her ears.

"Look at her skin. I've never seen anything like it."

"She is magnificent indeed, but will the queen actually step down?"

"A blessed elf of all creatures. What game is Ravana playing now?"

"Now, let the ball commence. We shall remember this night for the rest of our lives," Ravana finished, finally letting go of Laerdya. Clapping filled the room as the music started up again. Elmaer made his way back to Laerdya, but before he could grab her, the queen put a hand on his shoulder.

"Behave yourself. One mark on her tonight, and you shall face my wrath," she glared. Elmaer scoffed and pushed her hand away.

"Be silent, mother, and go entertain your guests." He took Laerdya's hand and escorted her away. With a look back, the queen's gaze turned from her to another person in the room, a feral look crossing her face.

48 NEXIS

Nexis looked out over the crowd of chatting and dancing nobles, attempting to find Laerdya in the mix. He knew he should not worry about her, but the thought of them pouncing on her like wolves made his body tense.

"You look worse than the blossom tonight," a voice said beside him, and he turned to see queen Ravana. She lightly ran a finger along the rim of her glass.

"I assure you I am fine, Lady Ravana. I am simply not used to such... gatherings," Nexis said carefully, pulling his eyes away from the orgy in the corner.

Ravana laughed heartily and took a sip. "I forgot how dull my sister can be. You would think after several millennia, she would have learned something of fun."

"Do these parties not bore you anymore, Your Grace?" Nexis asked, glancing over at her. His eyes scanned down her nearly bare body before quickly looking away, clearing his unbecoming thoughts.

Ravana pursed her lips together. "Seeing new faces every eighty years or so has kept me entertained, I suppose. I've seen a hundred generations of elves pass through these halls, and yet they are all the same," she said.

"And what makes them the same?" he questioned.

"They all think themselves above reproach."

Nexis guarded his thoughts, not wanting to challenge her but wanting to know more. "And you do not think yourself above reproach?" he asked. Her laugh caught him off guard.

"Be careful with your words, Nexis. You might find them failing you," she chided and raised her glass towards him. "Drink."

Nexis eyed the glass warily. He could smell the magic within it.

"Should I ask?"

Her gaze gave him all the answers he needed. He begrudgingly took it, swirling the liquid around in the glass. He took a sip and was immediately hit with a wave of ecstasy and coughed violently, and the queen scoffed.

"You're an enchanter, and yet you cannot take my magic. How unfortunate," she laughed. He gave the glass back to her and kept his gaze away from her.

She leaned into him, pushing her breasts against his robe, and he bit his lip. "Come now, surely you wish to know more. I could show everything you wish to know," she purred in his ear. "Secrets, lies, passion."

Fighting against the magic, he closed his eyes. But all he could hear was the blood rushing through his body and the moaning of the orgy in the corner of the room. *You fool,* he thought. *Drinking from the cursed queen's cup.*

He felt her hand slide down his chest. "It'll take but a moment," she whispered in his ear, and he felt a shiver run down his spine. "Any magic you wish to know can be yours. My magic, my body, if you ask for it."

He clenched his fists, focusing his thoughts on something else. He remembered Via. He remembered her distraught expression when he was dragged away and the way she fell to her knees behind him.

"I'm sorry... Queen Ravana," he started, coughing and breaking free from her enchantment. "But I must decline."

Something changed in her expression when he finally looked at her that he couldn't place. She backed away from him and looked away. "So be it," she said flatly. She spun around and walked off into the crowd, disappearing in the midst of masks. He coughed again and shook himself from his high. The look she gave him burned into his memory. What was it? Anger? Disgust? No. It was something else.

Nexis folded his coat down and started into the crowd to find Laerdya. And stop her from drinking any of the wine.

49 LAERDYA

Laerdya took a bite of a pastry, enjoying the flaky texture melt in her mouth. She went to grab another one when a voice called out to her.

"Are you enjoying the party?" Nexis asked, coming up to her. He wore silver robes and the mask of a dove.

She nodded, and he said, "I see you've been enjoying the cakes, though I'd stay away from the drinks."

She raised an eyebrow at his posture when he said that and turned to the crowd. "It's more than I'm used to," she started. "It's nice seeing fresh faces, though."

Nexis nodded in agreement. "Yes, perhaps this is what we both needed..." he faded off, then he noticed the prince scowling in his direction. He cleared his throat and bent down.

"Might you ask the prince for a dance?" he asked.

Laerdya made a disgruntled face. "Why should I?"

"Well, the nobility is already looking at you. Perhaps if you take the initiative, they shall see you as more than just the wife of the king, but someone who can also take authority," he proposed.

Laerdya put her head down in thought, her lips grazing the pastry. "I suppose..." she sighed.

Nexis gently patted her on the shoulder. "I shall be watching you from here. Nothing shall happen to you. You have my word." He guided her in the prince's direction and watched as she walked off. He bit his lip and looked around at the eyes that followed him. Tonight was going to be long.

"Elmaer?" Laerdya asked, coming up to the prince. He seemed

taken aback by the use of his name and glared at her.

"What? I told you to stay close to me. Why don't you ever listen?" he growled.

Laerdya took a breath. "Would you like to dance?" she asked, ignoring his comment.

He brought his lip up in disgust. "What for? So, these degenerates and charlatans can feast upon us? They're nothing."

Laerdya looked back at Nexis, who gave her an encouraging wave. "You are the king. Shouldn't you demonstrate your prowess?"

"In dance? I could cut down any man in here instead and make my true prowess know."

"Fighting is just like dancing. Let them see your strength in and off the battlefield... let them know the king you are," she paused, observing his expression. He seemed to contemplate her words for a moment before shaking his head.

"Fine, let them feast." He grabbed her hand and led her onto the dance floor. Everyone else quickly dispersed and watched with hawk-like gazes. Laerdya stilled her ragged breath as they began their waltz. She had only a few lessons before the ball with the queen, so she let Elmaer lead. She could feel the gazes, hear the whispers.

"The princess matches the prince quite nicely."

"Did you see him before? He wanted nothing to do with her."

"Well, it seems she talked him into something besides murdering doves."

Laerdya tried her best to ignore the gossip as they glided through the dance. Elmaer kept a vise-like grip on her hand and waist as she matched his pace, hearing exclaims from the crowd. She twirled and dipped and smiled at those around her as the prince only glared and seethed and she received a few waves and polite claps in return. She felt as if she were gliding along the marble floor as the shadows danced along on the ceiling. Aside from the man holding her, she felt as if a part of her did enjoy where she was.

When the dance was done, he quickly led her off the floor and went back to his corner. She felt a small bit of pride in being so close to him and yet being able to come out without a scratch.

The queen sauntered over to her. "You looked lovely out there, blossom. You may yet bloom. Come, I want you to meet some of our guests." She pulled Laerdya towards a couple of cursed elves. They were chatting amongst themselves before they turned at the queen's arrival. It was a man and a woman, both wearing the masks of foxes.

"This is Lord Zeltrith and Lady Arana. They have been at court for nearly three decades now," Ravana said. Laerdya curtsied, nearly flooring the couple.

"Well, isn't she just a darling," Lady Arana cooed.

"Beautiful, I will say. Why did you keep her locked away, Queen Ravana?" Lord Zeltrith asked.

"She is too pale for the outside. Who knows what may happen," Ravana answered, and the couple broke into drunken laughter.

"It will be so nice to see her at more of your soirees. The others in the court will not shut up about how they wish to meet her."

"And now we have the first chance, oh, to see their faces!"

Laerdya gave a strained smile as they touched her hair and face, giggling and gasping.

"Her skin is very warm! Ravana, perhaps you should give her an ice bath. What if she catches a fever?" the lord asked.

The queen laughed. "The blessed run hotter than us. I am surprised they don't burst into flames when they step into the light."

The two laughed again, high pitched and causing her to wince.

"I am out of wine! Oh, the scandal. Where is that damned slave?" the lady muttered, looking around the room, seeming to try and find someone. When she found who she was looking for, she barked loudly at them. "Slave, come here and give me more wine!"

The slave quickly came over and handed her a shaking glass. When it nearly spilled onto her gown, she slapped him hard across the face. "Leave me! You are a disgrace!'

Laerdya flinched as the slave held his cheek and fled the room. Arana turned back to the queen and princess as if nothing had happened and began spouting about how many slaves she had in servitude and the wealth she had accumulated over the years from these gatherings.

Luckily, another song picked up, and the crowd moved onto the dance floor, gathering hands. The queen nudged Laerdya.

"It is a common group dance. Go, enjoy yourself. You've dealt with us long enough," she invited. Laerdya looked at the crowd and smiled to herself. She caught the whispers of the couple behind her.

"Look at her, cute little thing, isn't she?"

"She is graceful; I'll give you that."

"Unlike the prince, she seems to have a personality."

"Why keep her locked in the castle? What's their real game?"

"Perhaps he wanted to keep her to himself."

Ravana cleared her throat loud enough for the couple to hear, and they quickly stammered out an apology and fled. Laerdya quickly looked over her shoulder to the queen, who smiled and took a sip of her drink.

"You may bloom yet."

50 TALIA

Once again, the footsteps of the princess bounced through the trading tunnels, a bag of *sephim* in her hand. She busily made her way through the winding tunnels with practiced precision before coming across the oak doors of the wolf's lair.

She brought her hand up to knock, but before she could, the door swung open, her eyes scanning up to the masked man.

He leaned against the door. "And what brings the fair princess back to my kingdom?" he asked, his voice an animalistic growl.

Talia's answer was thrown on the floor, the gold ringing on the stone.

He looked down at the bag and then back up at the girl. "Now this is interesting."

"You will come with me to the capital," she started. "You are needed, and I will pay."

"Is that so? And does your father know of this little excursion?" he asked. She could hear the smirk in his voice. Talia did not answer. She folded down her dress and put a hand on her hip.

"Will you come with me or not?" she barked.

The man grabbed the door. "I'll take not." He went to close the door, but Talia quickly pushed her hand out, forcing the door back open.

"I will not take no for an answer."

"Why don't you just go through your little portal? Have your guards take you. I have no time to babysit."

"The portal doesn't lead straight to Fira. It's a day's hike, and the roads are not safe. I'm paying you. We're leaving," she ordered.

The man crossed his arms, looking her up and down. "Why me? You have a hundred sell swords at your disposal."

"I've already told you. You're worth more than a hundred sell swords," she paused, turning. "And worse case, I'll sell you to the nearest slavers."

Before he could get another word in, she started back down the tunnels.

"I expect you at the city gates at dawn."

The next morning, Talia rose at sunrise. The waves of the ocean greeted her with their soft thumping against the cliff edge. She quickly dressed before her handmaid could arrive and threw on an old worn cloak and several layers of dresses. She knew the capital would be chillier than it was here, and the coldness of the portal was something she would never get used to.

She had gone through it only twice in her brief life and remembered each time vividly. The first time she was but seven years, going to meet the emperor and empress in Fira. They died only a short time later. The magic of the portal was cool to the touch and thrummed around her skin. When she stepped inside, everything would turn white, and she would be weightless for a moment before the land around her would come back into focus—foreign and unusual. She had asked her father how such magic existed, but he simply shrugged.

Leaving her room, she used the servants' quarters to escape the castle and headed down the streets towards the city gates. Few servants paid her mind as she passed, too focused on their morning duties to realize who she was. She knew Lia would be worried sick after seeing her missing from her room, but she did not want to write a letter in case she warned her father before she could reach the portal. He would find out sooner or later and would face his wrath when she returned, but for now, she set her sights on the gates.

The city was quiet in the morning. Only bakers and servants were awake at this hour, along with the occasional seller. She watched as the windows opened and signs went up. Seagulls flew overhead, chirping as they passed by. The salty wind that blew through the streets made her tongue dry, and she stopped by a fountain for a drink. She sat on the stone slabs surrounding the fountain and watched as beams of sunlight lit the falling water into hues of yellow and orange. She cupped her hands under the falling fire and drank the cool liquid. It ran down her chin and chest, and she smiled to herself.

It had been too long since she swam in the ocean or really enjoyed herself for a day. Her brother's face still kept her up at night. And she feared it would continue to do so for many more. She would often play in the morning tides and pick up seashells and starfish. She would count the crabs that skittered into hiding places and run from jellyfish that threatened to sting her. Her brother would watch from the balcony. He never enjoyed the white sand of the beach. Said it got in too many places and was too hard to clean out of cloth and bedsheets. She never minded, though. The maids would quickly undress her and bathe her before the lord and ladies arrived, and she was never seen with a hair out of place. She prided herself on being able to appear like she was perfect, even with water still sloshing in her ears.

She stood up from the fountain and followed the roads down to the city gates, where several guards greeted her.

"Milady… are you sure about this?" one asked, looking back towards the castle.

"Yes, I am sure. Thank you for coming with me," she said, and curtsied. They quickly bowed and opened the gates for her. A small party waited for her with a carriage, and the horses neighed warily as she neared. She petted the snout of a silver mare and looked back at the gates as the guards spoke to themselves. She knew they were loyal to her, but they would also face the king's wrath when he found out they helped escort her. She would make sure they were paid well.

She kept an eye out for the wolf as she waited. Part of her thought he would not come at all, but she gave him more money than she thought worthwhile. The look the coin master gave her when she asked for the sum made her nearly keel over in laughter. Thankfully, he never asked why she needed such a large amount of *sephim*. Now, if he showed up, that was another thing altogether.

She waited an hour, and the sun was well over the crown of trees. The guards began to grow impatient, and she as well. She sat on the ground outside the walls in the shade and waited in a languor. She nearly fell asleep before a guard gently shook her awake. She opened her eyes to see a hooded figure draped in royal blue standing in front of her. The mask greeted her with a mock bow.

"My lady," he said in his low and unnerving tone.

She stood up and wiped off her dress. "We've been waiting for quite some time."

"I had to pick my most regal wear," he replied. She knew he was mocking her and elected to ignore it. She turned to her guards, who eyed him cautiously.

"Let's be off," she ordered, stepping into the carriage. The wolf followed and sat down opposite her. She gave him a raised brow. "Why are you in here?"

"You paid me to protect you. I cannot do so while outside your carriage."

"Do you think a shadow demon is going to eat me inside here?" she asked with a tilt of her head.

He replied with a tilt of his own. "Maybe I do not wish to walk."

"Velara, help me," she whispered with a rub of her forehead. The wolf only whistled in reply and the door to the carriage shut. She felt the carriage lurch forward and turned her gaze from the wolf towards the skyline where the portal sat ten miles away. She began to think that maybe hiring him would cause her more trouble than it was worth.

51 ENARA

"There are no classes here. We are all one within the eyes of the Serpent," a young maid said while braiding Enara's hair. Enara only briefly heard her name in conversation, *Daealla*, she thought. A young girl with chestnut hair and pale skin. Too thin for her liking, but she never saw her without a smile.

Enara took a drink of her wine. "Is that so?" she asked.

"Yes, we are all one here. We are all happy here. The other kingdoms wish to take our happiness away. That is why the king protects us. The gods as well."

"Gods?" she asked.

"The gods of the mist, my lady. They created this kingdom so we would be free from the ones who would hurt us. The king keeps us safe," she sang. Enara thumbed her glass and looked around the room she was set in. The bed was adorned with silver linens and drapes on the stone walls provided a pleasant atmosphere. A painting of a black dragon sat above her bed, its eyes seeming to follow her across the room. The fireplace crackled softly and illuminated the carpeted floor. The warmth never quite reached the other side of the room, though. She always felt a slight chill.

The same servants cloaked in black had taken her things and placed them in the room without a word. She took the hint that this was to be her room for the time being. Until she was moved to the kings… She ignored the thought and focused back on the tugging of her hair.

"Have you ever been out of the kingdom, Daealla?" she asked.

Daealla looked perplexed when she glanced at her in the mirror. "No, of course not. There is nothing but death outside the kingdom. That's why the gods gave you to us. To help protect us. You saved your kingdom just as the king saved ours," she hummed.

Enara's face fell. "Then you have never experienced snow or climbed the roots of the thousand-year trees. Or seen the people of the sands come in their large boats with stories of dragons?"

"Why would I need those things if I have everything I could ever want right here?" Daealla asked, pulling a thread of yarn through her hair.

Enara sighed softly. "Yes, I suppose you are right," she mumbled. Daealla finished braiding her hair and stepped back.

"I am your servant now until my dying breath. If you need me, please call on me. Your every wish is my command," she said, and curtsied.

Enara looked at the girl, eyeing her body language. She seemed content. She loved her chains. "My every wish?" Enara asked, sitting up in her chair.

Daealla smiled. "Yes, my lady."

"Jump from the balcony."

Daealla's smile did not waver. "If that is what you wish," she complied. She turned from her and started for the balcony, opening the door without a second thought. She walked towards the end of the balcony, and Enara watched as she climbed up onto the parapet. She was going to do it—the mad girl.

Thoughts of her sister's eyes ran through her mind as the young girl started falling forward.

"Wait!" Enara cried, quickly standing. Daealla gained her footing and looked toward the queen. Enara sat back down, her chest heaving. "Stop, get down. I changed my mind," she ordered.

Daealla climbed down from the parapet and walked up toward the queen. Enara looked into the girl's eyes and saw nothing but admiration. Goddess, she hated it here.

"Go get me more wine," Enara ordered. Daealla bowed and grabbed the pitcher from the table, leaving the room. Enara ran a hand along her braid and closed her eyes, wishing she was anywhere but there.

Enara strolled the castle, bobbing and weaving through narrow stairways and winding hallways. Every hall looked the same. The same dark stone, the same candlelit vases and paintings of dragons. She wondered if she got lost if anyone would even find her. She had left before Daealla returned with the wine, the one small moment she had to herself. For days she stayed in her room, barely coming out of it to walk down the main hall or find Trissa.

Most of those nights were spent restless, covered in a blanket, and staring at the ceiling. She thought back to everything she had done to get to this point. Every face that was dead, every mistake she had made. Even the insignificant ones from her childhood were brought forth in her memory. Hitting a cardinal with a book when it took a sweet roll from her plate. Lying to her mother about how she ruined her dress. Blaming Rose for the broken statue in the dining room. Small things that had no impact, and yet her chest still tightened to remember them. Perhaps they helped ease the pain of her worst crimes.

Enara jiggled door handles and peered around corners as she strolled; she was being a bit too curious for her own good. But what did it matter? The worst they could do is slap her on the wrist and send her back to her room. Wouldn't that be a treat?

Enara jiggled another doorknob and found it unlocked. She opened the dark door into a softly lit bedroom. She stepped inside and was met with a warm aroma of flowers.

The room was scarcely decorated with a simple bed covered in bear furs and a bedside table that held a flickering candelabra. A desk sat on the other end of the room with a small chair that didn't meet the size of the desk. It looked like the ones built for her and Rose when they were children. She stepped over to it and ran her fingers down the softwood of the chair. A bowl sat on the desk with a mix of roses and lavender floating in the water. She tapped one of the petals, and it dipped below the surface, only to pop back up again with excitement. She smiled a little and pulled her eyes to beside the bowl where a miniature rocking horse sat.

She picked it up and turned it over in her hand. It was skillfully carved and painted with shades of red and blue. She flipped it onto its back and saw initials engraved into the bottom. *A..S.*

She wondered if this was one of the king's old toys. Though why it was in an abandoned bedroom was beside her. She set the horse down and gently pushed down on the snout, causing it to rock back and forth. She watched it for a time as it happily rocked, its shadow following suit from the candles.

Suddenly, she felt a cold shiver run down her spine, and she turned around to see a shadow in the doorway. She put her hand on the desk to brace herself as the shadow moved into the room. It stopped once it entered, and she realized it was one of the shrouded servants. She corrected her posture and took a breath.

"I did not mean to intrude," she shuddered. The Shroud said nothing, simply turning away and out of the room. She followed, and it led her back to where she came, stopping at the door to her room. She huffed out a quick "sorry" before entering and closing the door behind her. She leaned on the door with a sigh and rubbed her forehead. The Shrouds scared her more than Malum sometimes did. The way they never spoke, even the way they moved, made her feel uneasy.

"Your Grace, are you alright?"

Enara jumped and hit her head on the back of the door. She slouched down with an audible groan before looking up to see Daealla run over to her.

She helped her stand up and sat her down at the table. She rubbed her head.

"I didn't mean to frighten you, Lady Enara," she apologized.

Enara couldn't help but laugh. "Do not worry. You are the least frightening thing I have seen today."

52 THYMAS

The Cathedral of Fira was the largest in Veran, next to those in Rosus. The cathedral had stood since the time of the Elven Crusade, and many came from across the world to bask in its glory. The ceiling was covered in golden carvings of the heavens, and the pillars were wrapped in sculpted vines. A statue of the goddess stood behind the stone pedestal in the middle of the room, and the songs of the choir could be heard from every crevasse. Statues and paintings of Velara were scattered about the sides of the cathedral and were backlit by the stained-glass windows. A sun with five stars surrounding it was molded into the glass: a symbol for the goddess and the Elven pantheon from before the Crusade. As soon as someone stepped inside, it was as if all the air had been taken from their lungs. The old priest in WhiteDrove always told him that you entered during a solar eclipse; you were destined to sit at the goddess's side when your time came.

Thymas knelt in front of the pedestal, hands clasped in front of him. He prayed for the safety of his sister and mother and hoped to end the war soon. His thoughts led him to think of what could happen if the council failed. If not enough soldiers were sent to WhiteDrove, it would be taken, and his family would be enslaved or killed. Anya could not take care of herself, but she could hide. If they took the city, she could easily escape through her tunnels and navigate the wilderness. This he knew. His feelings of worry persisted.

"Dear Goddess above. Bring my people peace and hope. Shed Your tears over the land and bless us with Your heavenly sight. Bring forth Your love for Your children and smite those who would cause You harm. End all war and cease all famine. In all this, I know You to be true. Bring my prayers an answer and keep us safe from harm. To the stars and sky above."

He closed his eyes and waited for a response. He knew she rarely ever did. Only the select of the enchanters had ever heard her voice. Yet, in the back of his mind, he still hoped. Still prayed that she would hear him.

His thoughts were jarred when he heard the soft tapping of feet behind him. He receded from his prayer and turned to face the fabric of satin and hemp. The light pink and red of the dye caught his eyes as they trailed up her body. He was met with a delicate smile once he reached her face. For a moment, he was enraptured by her beauty. The way the fabric sat on her shoulders and her deep amber eyes drew him into almost a trance. If he hadn't known better, he would have thought Velara herself was standing in front of him.

He quickly shook himself out of his daze and stood up, politely bowing. "I apologize, my lady. I did not hear you enter," he said with a small smile.

The woman's mesmerizing eyes turned up towards him. "No apologies necessary. I am the one who has disturbed your prayer. I came to tour your shrines of worship here in the capital," she replied, her accent a bit heavy. Her deep black hair was pulled up and held by an exquisitely designed gold needle. He knew of traders who wore similar dress and manners of speaking, though he had never seen one in person.

"You must be from the Sunset Isles, then. I am Lord Thymas of House Dicesare. It is a pleasure to make your acquaintance, Lady..." he paused and waited for a response which she promptly gave.

"Sara. Priestess of the Temple of Kuraya just off the Silver Coast," she answered. *Her eyes are like stars*, he thought.

Thymas took hold of her hand and brought it up to his mouth, gently running his lips across her skin. The Sunset Isles were just off the east coast and some of the most beautiful places in the known world. They exported most of Veran's *sephim* and silver and had been known for their divergent ways of worship and theatre. Thymas had never personally traveled there but heard the stories from his mother.

"A priestess? What brings you to the capital?" he asked, releasing hold of her hand, and offering her his arm. The lady took his invitation, and they walked the length of the cathedral. He could smell her perfume as she neared him; sweet and floral.

"I have had visions of a strange darkness looming over Veran. The blooming trees have begun to wilt and die. I knew that I must come here to help in any way that I could. The Isles are not known for their armies, but we have some of the best weapons and *sephim* to fund them," she said.

Thymas' smile dropped. "Then your visions are correct, my lady. One of our sister kingdoms was sieged more than a fortnight ago. I am here to speak with the council. Will you be attending?"

Sara shook her head. "No, most will not listen to the words of a priestess. I am no more than a clergyman in the common eye," she sighed.

"Priestesses are highly revered on your Isles, are they not?" he asked.

She nodded. "Yes, our visions and ceremonies help bring peace to our lands. But that is not enough to keep the darkness from spreading. A sickness has broken out across our soils, blighting the ancient forests and darkening the bay waters. We have yet to find a cure."

"I am deeply sorry to hear that, priestess. You must be disheartened to leave your people behind."

The light in her eyes diminished slightly as she sighed. "Yes. I wish I could help them. But I must follow the path that I know is right."

Thymas could almost hear himself talk through her. It pained him to know Veran was not the only place struck by this madness.

"You told me you are in the council?" she asked, changing subjects. "You must be more than just a nobleman then."

"I am the king of Viragrad, my lady. Or soon to be once I find a suitable wife," he said.

Sara's eyes widened slightly, and she backed out of his arm. She quickly bowed, her long, black hair falling around her shoulders like darkness covering the sunset sky. "I apologize, my king. I had no idea!" she stumbled.

His smile returned. "Do not fret on it. It is nice not to be seen as a king for once. Perhaps I will take you as an ambassador to the council. Shall I show you the College of Enchanters? I have yet to see it for myself, but I have heard it is a marvel to look at."

Her face brightened, and she straightened, retaking his arm after a moment's hesitation.

"I would love that, Lord Thymas."

The couple made their way down the streets of the Grand Quarter, where the nobility strolled about in flocks. The looks they gave him did not go unnoticed as they eyed him up and down in their gaudy outfits of goose feathers and gold. The servants that trailed behind them did not meet eye contact as they passed, and Sara leaned slightly into his shoulder.

"I must admit that Fira has… quite the display of wealth," she whispered under her breath. Thymas eyed a woman dressed to the nines in diamonds and pearls, the men close behind. One of them snickered as he passed by.

"It is most definitely something to get used to," he agreed. He wondered if they knew what House he belonged to if they would be as judgmental as now. His clothing was not overly extravagant, even though he was plainer than the people around him. Viragrad was not rich and did not spend time worrying about how shiny the cufflinks were on his coat. The mud on his boots was probably a ghastly sight.

Carriages strolled by as they continued down the streets, whispering to one another. "I had wanted to visit the mainland ever since I was a child. But once they learned of my magical abilities, I was turned over to the temple," Sara said.

"I admit I am not familiar with magic or how one comes to obtain it. How old were you?" he asked.

She looked ahead of her with a tilt of her head. "I believe I was ten. Young enough to be accepted into the temple but a bit old to begin training. I had to learn quickly."

Thymas avoided a puddle of water, and the ringing of the hourly bells drowned out the noises of the streets. He waited for them to stop before speaking. "I can imagine training enchanters is much different here than it is on the Isles."

Sara pursed her lips, seeming to think over something before she spoke. "Yes, you could say that. I am excited to visit the College. I have heard many great things about the magical advisors of the kings."

"Have you heard the story about King Mahin? Once the ruler of WhiteDrove nearly two hundred years ago?" he asked. Sara shook her head and lightly squeezed his arm. "Oh, he was an astounding man. Great in battle. Won many a fight against the Dark Kingdom and fought off an entire armada of pirates alone."

"Alone?" Sara questioned.

Thymas bit back a laugh as he recalled the story. "Before the battle with the pirates, he called upon his Arcane Advisor to create a potion so potent it could blow up an entire army if dropped."

"And did it work?"

"Oh yes, it worked. The madman boarded the ship of the pirate captain, bested him, and then dropped the potion right down at his feet. Both of them perished in the blast, but it took out a dozen ships around him."

"Why did he board the boat? Surely, he could have just thrown it or given it to a raven to carry."

"He wanted his death to be a legend carried for generations. They say before he boarded, he screamed out, 'I may die a young man, but at least I will die with a sword in my hand instead of a hardened cock'."

Sara snorted and covered her mouth. "He does sound like quite a man, I must admit."

Thymas laughed alongside her and ignored the disgruntled looks they earned from passersby. They neared the College, and his eyes trailed up the glimmering white stone tower. It was quite narrow, nearly too tall to see the end, and it sat in the middle of a spacious garden square.

Then entered the garden and passed several initiates cloaked in white. They focused their attention on an iris that glowed a deep purple. They took notes and muttered to themselves.

Thymas was never one to study magic—he didn't have the gift. And Viragrad was so spacious and uninhabited compared to the other kingdoms it was in no genuine need of an enchanter. It was rare that any children from villages in the north had the gift, and he had barely seen it up close. It made the hairs on his arms stand on end and an odd numbing sensation crawl down his spine.

Visitors strolled the garden and pointed to nearly perfectly preserved flowers that opened their petals wide despite the chill in the air. The sunlight felt more potent around the College as well. As if a bubble of heat has been placed around the garden.

"It is quite lovely; I must say," Sara gushed, running her fingers across the petals of a magnolia. "Our magic is used mainly for healing. Only our warriors dabble in the battle or defensive arts."

"Any magic is foreign to me," Thymas told. "It will take some time to get used to."

"It was difficult for me as well," Sara said. "My hands would feel like they were on fire every time I learned to cast a spell."

The couple arrived at the steps of the College, and the blue doors opened for them expectantly. They ascended the many stairs and entered the doors. They shut behind them, seemingly by themselves, and the sound echoed through the room. It was as if they entered another world while looking about. The interior was vast and spanned as far as he could see, with marble pillars and glimmering chandeliers. The walls were blank, but flickering lights danced above them and zoomed down the spacious room. From the outside, it was impossible for the tower to make any sense of how large it was, but he assumed magic did not care for the rules of man.

He watched the priestess's eyes widen as she looked around, and a flicker of light passed by her, flicking her hair. She giggled, and they continued forward.

"I've never seen anything like this before," she breathed.

"Neither have I."

Their feet tapped against the tiled floor, which seemed to shift and move as they walked. Initiates and their masters studied on the floors, walked about the chamber, and otherwise ignored them for their studies. He was somewhat surprised to see no elves among them.

A massive fountain of water stood in the middle of the room. Its water twinkled and sparkled in the lights that dropped from the ceiling. The fountain itself was in the middle of a pool of water, he could only assume was magic lifted the water into the air to cascade back down into the pool. When they moved over to it, he could see his reflection in the water. He saw a halo of blue around his head and heard a chorus of voices in his mind.

"It feels... strange," Sara said, holding her hand out over the water.

"That is the Fountain of Tears," someone said behind them. Both turned to see an older man approach them. His white beard was long and brushed, his hair nearly the same length. His purple robes hung down past his feet, and he shuffled over to the priestess. She pulled her hand back as he neared, and he stopped along the edge.

"Once, after the Great Merging when seven lands became one, *Elu'lathan* covered this entire forest and the hills beyond it. A sprawling city of light that floated in the clouds. Magic is what kept it afloat. The mages, *Avere* as the elves called them, were blessed with such magic. Now we see none of the city that remained but this pool here."

"Since *Elu'lathan*?" Sara asked. "It's been here for thousands of years?"

The old man nodded and ran a hand down his beard. "The ancient elves used this pool as a source for their mana. It was once a thriving lake the size of the Grand Quarter itself. The elves would bathe themselves in the water and come back with years of memories given to them by the last elves who swam. Now it is nothing more than a puddle, but its magic still holds strong."

Thymas stepped beside Sara and stared down into the shallow pool. "Has… anyone gone in it since?" he asked.

The old man took a frightful step back, nearly falling over himself. "No! It is forbidden to touch the tears. It will bring you a thousand years of bad luck."

"Mmmhm," he hummed, looking back at the pool. It didn't seem like it was any different from any body of water you could find outside the city. But he was no enchanter.

"The last one to bathe in the tears was the elven mage Elicia, over a thousand years ago. She used the power of the pool to split the sea and defeat the water serpent of Dethmar. Since then, it has gone untouched."

"It is beautiful," Sara said, with a glint in her eye. Thymas studied the way her lips curled up in a gleeful smile.

The old man nodded. "Yes, yes. Now I must be off for my class, but please feel free to visit the library at your leisure." He stumbled off, and Thymas gave Sara an eyebrow.

"Do you believe anything he just said?"

"You do not?" she asked, her eyes meeting his.

"I do not believe mages exist."

"And why is that?"

"No one has seen any in hundreds of years. They either died off or never existed. What makes a mage so different from an enchanter, anyway?"

Sara turned to the falling water of the fountain. "An enchanter uses magic from books and teachings from their masters to manipulate fire and frost. They can heal wounds and raise the dead for a short time. Those who dabble in the darker magics can even summon malicious beasts from the Otherworld."

She walked around the Pool of Tears, studying the ripples in the water. "But a mage can break the seas. She can tear the sky open and rain fire down upon cities. She can destroy armies and sit on the ashes of kingdoms. They are more powerful than you can imagine."

"That is hard to imagine, I agree," he said.

Sara shook out her shoulders and stepped over to the king. "Anyway. Enough of doom and gloom. Why don't we visit the library, I've heard you can get lost in it for days."

Thymas laughed and took her arm once again. "If that is what you wish, my lady."

Following the guidance of several disgruntled apprentices, the two found their way to the library doors. The large wooden doors stood out against the backdrop of white with small veins of blue magic coursing through the rings.

Before they could even touch the door, it opened it on its own, allowing them inside. He heard Sara gasp and she moved from him and into the room. He watched her go with a smile, his eyes trailing down to the flow of her dress, occasionally showing a hint of her leg.

"Lord Dicesare, come!"

He laughed and followed her into the library, his eyes looking up at the ceiling meters away, hidden by magical clouds and sunlight. Now this… he understood nothing.

Books moved on their own from shelf to shelf and occasionally into the hand of an enchanter. A rumble of thunder was overhead and occasionally sprinkled rain onto an apprentice.

A maze of bookshelves disappeared high towards the ceiling, long ladders sliding back and forth along them. Thousands of books sat on the wooden shelves, some glowing, some just sitting without a binding. Groups of enchanters studied quietly on the ground and groaning chairs, the smell of ink and parchment flowing through the air.

"How could anyone read all of these?" he muttered to Sara, but she did not respond. His eyes scanned the room, going from person to flying book to wisp of clouds… but he couldn't find the priestess. She had disappeared into the maze of books, perhaps never to be found.

With a soft sigh, he resigned himself to the long process of finding her, moseying his way through the library. He occasionally glanced at the enchanters whose heads were stuck in books. He enjoyed reading, but not to such an extent as this. The last time he spent so long in a library was when he was teaching Anya to read and write. She refused to listen to her tutors, preferring to draw her animals. But he had managed to sit her down and teach to her read with the fantastic fairytales of wolf gods and krakens.

He passed a pedestal with several books laying atop it. He paused, running a finger down the binding of one of the large tomes. He curiously flipped it open to see nonsensical scribbles and markings. He flipped another page to actual words on the page.

When an enchanted child is brought into the College, the apprentices are to learn the fundamentals of magic: Conjuration, Divination, and Enchantment. They shall begin with the study of life and science, learning to channel their magic through the pull of the ground and sky. The female apprentices will learn of healing magic and potion making while the male apprentices shall focus on the defensive arts. Within ten years they will take their final trials to become an enchanter, thereafter, training in the Enchanter Court to become vassals for the nobility of the Kingdoms.

Most children manifest their magic between four to eight years of age, and it is crucial to train them as soon as the magic manifests to keep them from causing harm to others. It has been found that female children tend to manifest magic at a higher rate than males though the cause as to why has not been found.

Thymas studied the page and flipped it over. *Is this what Sara did?* He wondered. He assumed the Isles had similar practices. It couldn't have been easy to learn magic, especially if her magic manifested later than most.

If any apprentice or enchanter is found to be studying the school of necromancy, they shall be executed by order of the emperor for treason. Those who dabble in blood magic are an affront to the goddess and a threat to the kingdom and cannot resist the pull of demons.

Executed? That seemed a bit harsh to him, but he could understand why. Maleficarum were necromancers and used blood magic to hurt those around them. But if they were just children… he flipped another page.

It is the enchanter's job to not only teach but learn the ways of the court in their respective kingdom. They shall be tasked with advising the kings and queens of both the advantages and dangers of magic. They shall make tonics and potions, give advice, and be the personal healer to the nobility so long as their magic does not dwindle with age.

If the time comes in great need, an enchanter may be placed with the military and assume the rank of Knight Enchanter, being an enforcer against the Dark Kingdom. Any enchanter conscripted into the military must be approved by the council.

Enchanters could be used for battle? That could mean the emperor will send some with his men for protection of WhiteDrove. He felt his chest tighten. This could be it; this could save his kingdom.

"Thymas?"

He looked away from the tome, seeing Sara standing beside him.

"Oh, I didn't hear you, my lady."

"It's alright." she smiled. "What is it you are reading?"

He looked back down at the book. "The Ways of the Enchanter… not the best read but I think I may know how to save WhiteDrove."

"Oh?"

He smiled wryly. "We may need a few more enchanters."

53 NEXIS

For over a week now, Laerdya escaped the castle at night and went about on her own to the town. Nexis realized her escape early on but allowed the princess her freedom, relying on the guards to keep an eye on her.

The queen had called on him an hour ago while in his laboratory she allowed him to study in. It was the one place he could hide from the prying eyes o0f others and was homely enough that he didn't feel too homesick while busy mixing a new chemical. She had seemed amused when he asked for permission to use the laboratory and gave him free rein of everything—with a promise not to blow the castle apart. That was a slight challenge.

Nexis adjusted his robe and knocked on the doors to the queen's chambers.

"Come in," Ravana responded. He cleared his throat and entered the exquisite room. Purple drapes decorated the walls with golden tassels hanging low. The ceiling was painted to look like the night sky of the mortal world, and magic caused the stars to glow and shimmer. As he walked, the stars shifted, and he could see the moons by the time he stepped into the center.

Her bed was spacious and draped with silver silk, furnished with downy pillows. A simple writing desk was sitting in the corner, along with a vanity and mirror that was a bit out of proportion to what it was sitting on. A shadow moved across the room, dancing away from the flickering blue candlelight. It smiled at him and disappeared into the ceiling.

He found the queen standing on her balcony, delicate flowered jewels hanging around her, her velvet skirt scattered across the floor.

She held a purple shawl around her shoulders and kept a hand on the balcony rail. Her hair glowed pure silver under the evening lights. Her skin shimmered like sapphires, nearly mesmerizing him with each slight movement she made.

It had taken him many a day to get used to the way the cursed elves looked with their dark skin of blue and purple. The queen herself was a beauty among them, he would admit.

She didn't turn towards him, but acknowledged his arrival. "I've assumed you've noticed where our little blossom has been going?" she asked.

Nexis stepped outside and looked out over the city. The wind coursed through his hair and blew through his robes, sending a slight chill down his spine. He could just barely see into the forest beyond.

"I am not ignorant of her ventures. But I am not her guard," he responded.

Ravana chuckled, the lightness of her voice prickling his skin. "No, but she still needs one." She paused, turning slightly to him. The wind ruffled her hair against her shoulders and nearly exposed chest, and she gave him a slight smile. He could not tell if it was sincere or not.

It still surprised him how young she looked. She held no wrinkles or lines, nor did her voice grow cracked or dull. She looked decades younger than him, and he was nearly two hundred. He wondered just how old she was when she was cast to this place.

"She did well at the ball. She will make a good queen," he agreed.

"Perhaps. With more practice and discipline, I believe she will be contented here…" she trailed off, watching the city start to dim. "No one can be truly happy here, even I realize that. But the thought counts, at least. My son will bond with her within the month."

"You don't sound pleased about that," Nexis noted, watching her eyes crease slightly.

"I am overjoyed at the possibility of having a grandchild, blessed elf," she tutted and gave a soft sigh. "I also realize that she is young and has yet to experience this world to its fullest."

"Is that why you allow her to venture out on her own?" he asked.

Her dark eyes slid to him, and her smile turned into a feral grin. "I have not ordered such a thing. She is going to be queen here soon; she may do as she pleases."

"Hmm," he mumbled, eyeing her. He attempted to figure out what she could be thinking, but she wore a clever mask.

"You will prepare her," she said.

"Me?" he asked, raising an eyebrow.

"She trusts you more than me. And my son does not listen to my advice. You shall advise her instead. This is still my city, and for the first time, I am putting it in the hands of a child."

"A child who has the capability to change this world," he retorted.

The queen smiled. "Yes, though for the better has yet to be determined."

54 LAERDYA

Laerdya escaped past the drawn gates of the castle, climbing down into the rut below. She heard the horses neigh above her as she slipped across the water toward the other end. Her shoes sloshed through the thick mud, and she flailed her arms to keep from falling onto her face. She had a dress made that went just above her knees so she would not trip on it. The slaves knew of her escapes but held their tongues when the prince came to find her. For once, they seemed to shield her from his wrath. And for once, she was grateful for the quiet.

She scaled the muddied wall and hoisted her petite frame up the bank towards the city using the grapevines that hung above. Sneaking her way below the bridge, she exited to the left, where the beginnings of the buildings emerged. Her coat snuggled around her waist as she tiptoed her way around the block, going through corridors and open alleys. Those who passed seemed not to notice the lightness of her face hidden under her hood, ignoring her altogether as she slipped by. She watched as a child ran past, waving a torn flag in the air. Two more followed suit, with flags of their own. With the happy screams of the children, she quickly stepped to the side as they chased after them. Laerdya forced herself not to follow as she continued.

Each time she went out, she went further and further into the city, sometimes getting lost for hours before finding her way back to the main square.

She had no idea how immense the city was until she spent hours just in the main housing district, gazing upon the finely decorated exterior patios and windows. Sometimes she would sit just out of sight of the laborers who were heading to work for the day. She listened to their stories of the night before—of children and drinking and sex.

Each one of them had a different story to tell.

Then she found herself outside a tavern. She could hear the music and laughter and smell the tobacco in the air. When she peeked through the windows, she saw topless women and drinking men. Sometimes there were fights, sometimes the entire place roared at a particular jig the guitarist played. No one wore fancy clothing or wore the masks of animals. They all laughed and sang as themselves, letting their joy and sorrow flow freely through the room.

Then, she found herself in a graveyard, looking across the dark, mournful faces cloaked in white. She listened to the Priest of the Five Gods give their sermon as flowers were placed on the grave. Then a fae was summoned to collect the soul and return it to its rest within the forest.

When Laerdya was barely old enough to understand death, her father had explained it in detail. How your soul was transferred to the Otherworld to become one with magic again, and then another soul was born in the mortal realm above. Now that she was in the Otherworld itself, death felt more like a close friend than something to be feared.

Now, her feet took her to the outskirts on the west side of the city, where the Slaves Den and more rundown houses were located. The houses were far less pleasing to the eye here, with haphazardly patched roofs and leaning pillars. Some elves sat on the steps to their front doors, knitting or chatting. Others attended to their small gardens or dragged their children in for bed. Some wore only rags of clothing and shoes that had their toes sticking out.

One woman turned to her as she passed. "It's not safe out a' night, dear. Best gets on your way home!" she called.

Laerdya turned her face away. "I-I will," she stuttered out. The woman gave her an eye and a shake of her head before grabbing up a basket and entering her home.

Her feet stopped as the last of the houses passed, and all that stood were logging stands and an old well. The pail on the end of the rope swayed and smacked against the side of the well as the wind blew by, creating rhythmic drumming. The forest on the other side glowed purple and blue, inviting the girl to play in its depths. Countless died a year going off the pathways carved through it as one wrong move could lead you to a vengeful spirit. She heard a guard tell how one of the patrols chased a thief into the woods and found him the next morning strung up on a tree fifty feet in the air, missing his eyes.

She knew she shouldn't go in; it was not safe for a young girl. Yet something flickered in the forest, calling to her. Laerdya took a hesitant step forward, then another, until she was far into the forest. The rock turned to grass under her feet, and she slipped her shoes off to feel the soil underneath. She giggled as her footprints glowed behind her, illuminating the trail back. She watched as a wisp fluttered above her and zoomed away as she went to touch it. The pulsing lights kept her smile steady as she followed the trail away from safety.

The mushrooms rose high above her, and in their gills hid little fairy like creatures. They poked their heads out at her as she passed, some flying above her. The trees soared to the skies, and bluebirds sang in their canopies. Water trailed down from places she could not see, and when it hit the ground, it floated back up in bubbles. Two-faced monkeys swung from vines and chattered quickly to themselves. She heard the call of bullfrogs in the small glimmering ponds around her.

She pulled her hood down and ran her hands along the trunks of the trees and watched as her handprints left glowing green marks. She felt something shift in the tree, and she looked up to see a face appear. It looked down at her with a snort, and she quickly backed away with a laugh.

How can such a place exist just beyond the darkness? She thought. The forest did not feel harmful or sinister at all. The three-tailed cats that hid in the ferns did not try to attack her or chase her out; they only stared at her with wide yellow eyes.

The wind that blew through the forest was neither cold nor warm but seemed to be guiding hands, gently pulling her toward where they wanted. She felt smaller than she was, less than even a child under the soaring blooms, and as the wind stopped, she did as well. She came to a small grove where a single blooming flower rested in the middle of the twisting grass. She heard it whisper to her as the long grass parted, making a walkway for her.

She walked up to the flower and bent down. It was hues purple and blue, and a pulsing light inside of the closed petals called out to her. Wide eyes followed her hand as her fingertips grazed the soft outside of the flower before quickly pulling away as it bloomed.

Hundreds of little wisps scattered into the forest as Laerdya laughed and fell away. The wisps surrounded her in a spiral of light. Like soft tufts of fur, they sat on her shoulders, bounced on her hair, and kissed her nose. She sneezed and sent several spiraling away from her. She reached out, and a small pink ball of light landed on her palm, barely pulsing and barely the size of a coin. She bopped it on the top, and it spun. She laughed as the others escaped into the air around her and she kept the small one in her hand and raised it to her forehead.

"I wish to be a good queen. And I wish to make my people happy," she prayed. The soft thrum of the wisp faded as it left her hand and soared up into the sky. Hundreds of them scattered to the canopy above her and wished her farewell. Laerdya stood up, tears falling down her rosy cheeks. She felt the wind push against her, and she knew it was time to leave. She followed her footprints back to the city and felt the forest speak her name as she exited, and a pink wisp followed her home.

55 TALIA

The couple sat in silence as the carriage carried them towards the capital city. Talia snuck glances through her veil at the wolf sitting across from her. His amethyst eyes went from the outside to her often. She felt as if he was amused at her. For what, who knew?

"What is so funny?" she asked him.

He cocked his head slightly. "Nothing precisely. I am simply enjoying watching you try to plan out this excursion in your head," he responded.

Her face grew dim. "What do you mean by that, exactly?"

"I meant exactly as I said, my lady. I can see the wheels turning inside your head. Does your father even know you left?"

Talia creased her brow in frustration. "What is that any matter to you?" she quipped.

He turned his attention away from her, seeming to notice something else outside the carriage. "I am simply curious. You brought along nearly half of what a full guard should be. We left earlier in the morning than intended, and no handmaidens were there to help you into the carriage. I am no spy, but I can sense a fleeing girl when I see one."

Talia folded her hands neatly in her lap. "Well, aren't you the astute guard? Anything else you wish to make assumptions about?"

The wolf moved his gaze back to her. "I see you also brought a knife under your skirt. You do not trust me and do not trust your personal guard, either. You are learning," he smiled.

Talia feigned a laugh. "You know me so well by just looking at me. How is that so?"

"I'm a people person."

"Ah, I see," she said, leaning back against the leather of the seat. "Then please tell me what my next move is."

The wolf eyed her with what she could only assume was gaiety. "You will go into the council chamber, think you are in control, and demand that soldiers be brought to WhiteDrove. You will not get your wish, and you will appear weak. Will you go back home and beg for Fathers' forgiveness or plot another way? That, I cannot say."

Talia scoffed. "How shrewd of you, wolf. To know my every plan."

"As I said, I am a people person."

Talia rolled her eyes and played with the fabric of her veil. "You can stop now. Your constant badgering is making me uneasy."

"I did not intend to offend, my lady."

She huffed and crossed her arms, eyeing the wolf who gazed outside the carriage once again. "Is there something spectacular out there that has you so enraptured?" she asked.

"Not particularly spectacular."

"Then something at least curious? Or am I that unpleasant to look at?"

His gaze slid back to her, and she felt her cheeks heat as his jeweled eyes trailed down her body. She shouldn't have asked. "I have already seen most of you, even that face you hide beneath the veil. It is not unpleasant."

"I..." she was at a loss for words. Did he just call her... handsome?

"It would have been a shame to see that thug muddy it up." *There it is*, she thought. She should have known a smart comment would come out of his mouth afterward.

"Good thing I have you to protect me from thugs, isn't it?"

The wolf nodded slowly. "I shall ensure your safety until we reach the city, at the very least."

"How gracious of you. Though I cannot imagine we will run into trouble so close to the walls."

"Again, you are mistaken."

She raised a brow at him. "And why is that?"

"Because two of your men are already dead."

She barely had time to react as the carriage was violently rocked. She put her hand out to steady herself as she heard a cry from outside. Boots thumped against the top of the carriage, and a sword lodged itself inside. Talia crunched down with a cry as the sword was drawn out. She looked out the windows to see the sunlight filter through the trees, but nothing else.

"What is happening?" she asked.

The wolf stayed still, almost bored. "It seems someone wishes to greet you."

She rolled her eyes at him and flinched away as a guard screamed and slammed into the side of the carriage. "Do not just sit there! Do something!" she ordered.

"I am here to protect you, not the soldiers, my lady," he said calmly.

She looked from him to the bloodied window in shocked disbelief. "I paid you to protect me, yes! My guards are being slaughtered, also protecting me! Help them!"

The door violently shook as the killers tried to gain entry. "Come out, lass! We don' bite!" one yelled. Talia felt dread stream through her as the door continued to rattle. The wolf cocked his head slightly, as if listening, and finally moved from his seat. He took his sword from its sheath and, with almost inhuman precision, pushed his sword through the door. Talia heard the gurgling and shouting of the men outside the carriage as the sword was pulled from the door, blood dripping down onto the floor.

"Please keep the window shut," he said, closing the wooden hatch and opening the door. Talia scooted closer as he shut the door and heard the men's muffled shouting at him.

"Give us the girl!" one yelled. "You're the last one alive; it's ten to one."

She heard the wolf chuckle. "I like those odds." She could barely keep up with the sudden gasps and bloodied screams of the bandits and the slicing of swords through flesh. She raised her hand but held herself back from opening the hatch to peer outside. It seemed like only an instant before the door opened again, and the wolf held out a hand.

"It seems we shall have to travel by horse the rest of the way," he said. Talia took his hand, and he gently helped her down the steps. Her stomach fell at the sight of the men dismembered around them. Their bodies were littered along the ground—some without arms, others without heads. The look of terror in their eyes made her feel nauseous.

"By the goddess, what did you do?" she asked in horror.

"Protected the princess. What else?" he asked.

She pulled her hand away from his, the stench of blood wafting to her nose. She pulled her veil to her nose as the wolf cut the horses free from the carriage. After collecting her items, she climbed up onto the horse, refusing to let him help, and they made their way to the capital city. Not a word more being exchanged.

The grey stone walls of the capital came into view from the forest. The walls reached high, and Talia could make out the several guard towers that were spread about it. She internally groaned at her sore backside. She had barely ridden horses while in Rosus. She enjoyed swimming much more. The wolf at her side strode slightly ahead of her as the guards spotted them.

She pulled the official documentation from her bag and handed it to the city guard as they slowed the horses.

"Right this way, milady. The council will begin tomorrow," he informed. The doors opened, and the two were escorted through. Once they were inside the city, servants came up to them. Begrudgingly, she let the wolf help her down from the horse. She handed the reins to the servant and turned towards him.

"To the Imperial Palace, we go then. That wasn't so difficult," he teased. Talia made a face but stayed silent as the servants took the horses to the stables and they started down the main street.

"What, no more guards to escort you?" he asked.

"You've already proven you are far more superior to guards or mere bandits," she answered. "If you run into assassins, though, I shall shudder."

The city was bustling around them with traders handing papers to guards, visitors holding maps, and homeless begging on the sides of the narrow streets. The buildings seemed to stretch for miles; the roads twisting and turning as people zigged and zagged.

The wolf kept a soft grip on Talia's shoulder as they weaved through the crowd. Several people looked in their direction, eyeing the man behind her. Talia continued with grace, and her head held high. Most people moved out of her way, either by recognition or fear of the wolf. The few nobility that were strewn about the quarter did no such thing.

"So, tell me, what is your plan now?" the wolf asked, sidestepping a merchant's cart.

Talia sighed softly. "I will speak with the emperor. If he is just, he will send more soldiers to WhiteDrove."

"And if he is not just? Will you beguile him into doing as you wish?"

Talia paused, looking over at him. "Then I will do what is necessary to save our kingdoms."

The wolf laughed low and guided her forward. "You hold no power in Yalirea. What would you expect to do here? You are a princess of a foreign kingdom, nothing more."

Talia bit her cheek in anger, pushing his hand away from her shoulder. "Then maybe I need to look higher." Her gaze ran up the distant palace walls.

"Perhaps so. If you aim higher, though, you may need more than myself to protect you."

Talia scoffed. "Perhaps another hundred guards, then?"

"Perhaps."

The couple passed into the Grand Quarter, and the giant cathedral gained Talia's gaze. She thought it quite beautiful with its white stone and gleaming stained-glass windows, though not nearly as exquisite as the ones back home. A statue of the goddess stood outside the wooden doors, holding her hands to her heart. Several priests and maidens blessed those entering with purified water and gave blessings to the ailed. A small wedding was being performed in the garden on the far side.

The wolf suddenly grabbed her and pulled her to the side. With a yip, she swirled around and glared at him. "What was that for?" she asked.

The wolf motioned ahead with his chin, and Talia turned. Standing before her were a man and a woman. The man was tall and broad, covered in too many layers to be comfortable. He had short and well-maintained curly hair and a beard; the golden pendant he wore on his coat of an owl gave away his royal blood.

The woman was smaller, with long glossy black hair and silk robes that draped over her with finely crafted patterns and colors. Perhaps she was a priestess.

"Pardon me," the man apologized, earning her attention. "I didn't mean to interfere in your walk."

Talia's eyes widened in recognition. "Lord Dicesare. I did not know you would be attending the council," she said, and curtsied.

He squinted his eyes, seeming to try to place her face to a name. The woman linked to him gave a small smile.

"I am Priestess Sara, my lady..." she began.

Talia folded down her dress and quickly straightened herself. "I am Princess Talia of House Farvell," she greeted.

Thymas' eyes lit up in recognition, and he bowed. "My apologies, princess. I do not believe we've met before."

"It's quite alright. I was just headed to the palace. Is everyone else in attendance already?" she asked.

Thymas nodded. "I believe so, princess. The council doesn't start until tomorrow, though, so I was showing Lady Sara around the capital."

Talia smiled softly at her. "Is that so? Well, I will let you be then, and I hope to speak again."

Thymas bowed again, and the two continued on their way. The wolf bent down to her ear. "It seems you are not the only one hoping to gain the favor of the emperor," he whispered.

Talia waved him away and started back on their path. "That's another voice of reason, then. Let's hope it is enough."

56 OLIVIA

Olivia and Ladrin hid in the shadows of the night, the clouds overcast, and the moons hidden. They watched the guard rotations around the walls of the city, the only sources of light coming from the torches the cultists carried.

"There is an old sewer system that runs through the entire city. But I would not wish anyone to go there," Ladrin said.

"Why? You scared of rats?" she teased.

His face did not move, but his eyes wavered nervously. "The Nightingale Brotherhood own those sewers. No one who goes in has gotten out alive," he shuddered.

Olivia looked towards the sewers. "That is our only option, though, right?" she asked. He nodded solemnly. "Then we have no other choice." She started out of the shadows, and the boy quickly followed, hobbling along and holding his injured leg. She paused as a guard passed the wall ahead, then continued.

"To the left side, under the foliage, should be a grate. We scout it every fifteen minutes. We will have to wait for the next rotation," he whispered. They stayed by the wall, using the shadows cast by the torches to move. "What are you even going to do if we make it?" he asked. "I can't help you."

"I'll find the King and kill him," she said, eyeing the dark figure that passed overhead.

"Are you mad?" he hissed. "The gods will lay their wrath upon us all!"

"Shut up!" she snapped, grabbing onto his face, her nails digging into his cheeks. "You will get us both killed," she whispered. "Now come on."

When they reached the grate, Olivia moved the foliage away to see the dark metal. She paused, looking to her right. She could barely make out a few cultists walking toward them. As soon as they were out of sight, she would move. They backed further against the wall, hiding in the overgrowth, as the cultists came closer. She could sense the boy's fear as he looked back and forth between her and the guards.

It was too fast for Olivia to catch. The boy ran out into the firelight. "Help! She is trying to break into the city!" he yelled.

"You bloody bastard!" Olivia cursed. The cultists turned towards her, and she bolted for the sewers. She grabbed onto the rusted grate and pushed it up. She jumped in, and it shut behind her with a screeching slam and heard the cultists yell as they pushed their way in as well. Olivia sprinted through the sewer, cursing herself for trusting the boy. She should have killed him as soon as they came out of the Mors. She would not make that mistake again.

She turned a corner and bolted down the tunnel, tripping over unseen objects in the pitch dark. The heavy footsteps of the cultists were right behind her and multiplying. She jumped into the horrid water and gagged at the smell, pulling herself up over the other side.

"Stop!" she heard a cultist yell. She reached out to find the wall and followed it to another turn. Her hair stuck to her face as she pushed it away to try and see where she was going. Her fingertips grazed the bumpy brick, and she looked behind to see the torchlight growing brighter.

"Shit," she whispered. She twisted back and slammed her head against metal bars. The force knocked her off her feet and back into the water below. She surfaced and spat, turning back to the flame.

"There!" one yelled. Four men rounded the corner, and she drew her blade.

"You will not take me alive," she hissed. They drew their swords, and one swung at her. She parried the blow and struck him in the back, sending him falling into the water. Another one punched her hard across the face and she yelped and fell back. Quickly getting back up, she brought her sword cleanly through the guard's abdomen and kicked him away as another rounded on her. She blocked a blow but took a slash to the knee. She cried out and fell to her knees.

Olivia was grabbed from both sides, and she screamed. She pushed one back and kicked off another, throwing them all back into the sewage. She scattered up but slipped on the slick sludgy ground and came crashing back down. A sword went through her shoulder as she screamed in pain and rolled over, pulling a knife from her belt and into his thigh. With a curse, he fell, and she held her shoulder as she tried to crawl away.

The three guards left chased after her and heaved her up. They pinned her arms behind her back, and she screamed murder as her shoulder wound tore down her collarbone. The other rounded on her and punched her, snapping her head back. She spit blood and sewage at him.

"We kill the bitch," he ordered. He grabbed her wounded shoulder and dug his thumb into her muscle as she screamed. He forced her still, and he raised the blade to her stomach. She forced herself to stare him down. She would not be a coward in death.

The blade entered her stomach, and she screamed before a knife went through his skull. Blood splattered her face as the man fell to the ground. She was released and fell into the water. She barely had the strength to pull her head up as she watched the guards swing widely at shadows.

"Come out!" one yelled. She pulled herself up out of the water with the rest of her strength and onto the walkway as the guards frantically searched for the invader.

A shadow formed, and an arm grabbed a cultist, twisting his arm around. With a snap, his arm was bent backward, and a knife slid across his throat. He gave a gurgling groan of death as his mate watched in horror.

"Shit! What the fuck!?" he yelled. Suddenly he cried out, and he fell, an arrow lodged in his throat. With a cry, Olivia pushed herself into a kneeling position, watching as the shadows twisted again. A man came up to her, hood covering his face.

"Follow the stars, girl. If you survive long enough to find us, you shall be reborn," he said. He stepped back into the shadows, and the torches faded from her sight as she slumped against the wall.

Follow the stars...

Olivia used the wall as support as she slowly made her way through the sewer. She bandaged her arm using her shirt and held her stomach with her hand, using her other as a guide. She didn't know if the shadowed man was a figment of her mind or not, but so far, she still held onto life. She chose to ignore the hot, wet blood that coated her chest and stomach. If she survived her wounds, she would surely die of infection.

"Follow... the stars... there are no damn stars," she muttered. She felt her hand give way and turned a corner, continuing down. The rats under her feet tripped her time and time again. She felt small enjoyment kicking them.

She wondered why she would want to come to this blasted city in the first place. A need for vengeance? A lust for blood? Or maybe she just wanted to be killed along with her friends, so she did not suffer alone.

This was not the way she wanted to die. In the sewers smelling of shit and piss. She cursed the goddess, cursed the men who put her here, cursed the kingdom for its evil. She fell to her knees and retched blood and bile. Olivia knew she should not have trusted that boy. If she saw him again, she would kill him—If she survived. The amount of blood running down her shoulder left a nice trail for more guards to follow if they wished. Albeit they didn't find her blood-drained corpse lying in shit first.

With a cough, she wiped her mouth and looked over to the side, trying to find the wall again. When her fingers found the stone, they also found a small indent carved into it. She brought her face closer to the wall and traced the indent. It was a star. *The stars...* she got back to her feet and started back at a faster pace.

"Follow the stars.... follow the stars," she muttered. Her fingers found the grooves as she slid along the wall, turning right, then left, then left again. Her feet could barely keep up with her mind as she went from turn to turn. She could feel her body giving out, and she went faster. She just needed to follow where the stars were; she would survive.

Then she saw it, a light in the distance. She felt her knees give way and she collapsed to the stone ground. She vomited again, her vision wobbling, but she pushed herself further. On her hands and knees, she crawled towards the light, and she reach out, watching as it glided across her skin, warming her hand. She looked up at the ceiling, seeing the light filter down through a star-shaped hole.

"The stars..." she mumbled. Then she heard something. It was faint, like a whisper in her ear. She turned and was met with a hooded figure.

"Well done," they said. They grabbed her, and she hissed as they pulled a cover over her head and dragged her away. Only the trail of blood remained as proof of life where she once stood.

The inhuman screaming of the bard echoed through the hall as her wounds were cauterized. Her wrists were bound by leather against a bed, her head still covered. She could see nothing but the light that came through the bag in lined pieces. She heard voices as well, two of them.

"I'm surprised she survived. The wound has yet to clot. The stomach is not nearly as bad; it will not need stitches." It was a woman's voice, lower than most she had heard, but still pitched enough to tell.

"She took on four of the cultists. She's a fighter." A man's voice. Deep and almost growling. Olivia screamed again, and the metal seared against her shoulder. Her flesh popped and sizzled, sealing the wound. She forced herself to stay conscious, focusing on those who had hurt her. The anger she felt, the terror she felt.

"It will leave a scar but heal. You are a lucky girl," the woman said.

Olivia pushed against her braces. "Where am I?" she croaked out.

"We cannot tell you yet. Only if the Old Man allows it."

"You captured me but won't tell me where I am? You have me strapped to a bed with a bag over my head. The least you can do is tell me your names or unbind me and let me kill you," she pushed.

She heard the man laugh. "I like this one."

Olivia heard a door open and felt the woman get up from the bed. "We will be back."

"Wait! Where are you going?" Olivia called. There was no response as the door closed, and Olivia moved her head to the side, hearing for anything useful. She could hear water dripping onto the stone and echoes from tunnels further away. She must still be in the sewers. These people saved her life, more or less, and she was now at their mercy. She knew they killed the cultists and molded the shadows around them. She thought back to the boy's words. The Nightingales owned these sewers. She could assume who these people were—if they were people at all.

The door reopened, and she heard no footsteps before the bed was sat upon again. "We will give you a chance, girl." An unfamiliar voice said, an older man. "You will make a choice here and now. We will take you back into the city and drug you so you shall never remember what transpired here. Or you may take the nightshade and join the guild. I've seen a fire in you that I have not seen in a long while."

Olivia did not speak. Her mind raced. Nightshade? That was a poisonous plant. If they planned on killing her, why not just do it? They would set her free, though, if she chose the other option.

"If you choose the nightshade, you will die but will be reborn as a member of the guild," the older man continued. "You will forget the fear of death and lose your hope of life. But you will find what you seek."

Olivia looked through the black bag at the torchlight. Clenching her hands, she felt the fire grow in her veins for those who deserved to die. She turned toward the voice.

"I choose death."

Burning pain. Blinding pain. Screams of terror and hopeless breaths. That's what her body felt. She could take the iron a thousand times over instead of this. They had force-fed her the plant; it was sweeter than she thought it would be, and the woman had chanted something. Now, as her lungs burned and insides boiled, she screamed and writhed upon the stone floor. They had thrown her into a chamber, her screams echoing along the walls, taunting her. She knew death. She knew fear. Her breaths came shorter and shorter, her life slipping.

She felt sorrow, agony, and torment. Fury towards those who had wronged her. She focused on the anger, hugging her stomach, and screaming. She would survive. She would seek her vengeance. She would be reborn. Her breaths came shorter and shorter, her life slipping. She heard the cackling of an old woman and the flap of a crow's wings. She saw nothing as she took her last breath, and her life was cast from her body.

57 VIA

Hundreds of men stood guard against the thousands that marched against them. Rye stood at the front of the wall of shields, his eyes never leaving the mass of black gaining on them. Via stood near the back, her bow in hand. She knew this battle would not be won. They had arrived back at the camp with mere hours to spare. The men were woken and given their weapons with no food, and no water. They appeared exhausted, battered, and ill-equipped for combat. The look on Garding's face when they arrived and looked upon their haggard forms gave her little hope of morale.

What she hoped was to give enough time for WhiteDrove to strengthen their defenses. The dark army still had maleficarum on their side, as well as Gelum. He himself could slaughter their army. She would have to engage him first. He had won once. She wouldn't allow him to win again.

"Archers!" Rye yelled. The archers notched their arrows as the mass grew closer. Via could feel the tension in the air with the metallic smell of magic. They had no enchanters in their army. They had no defense against the dark magic.

"Draw!" Rye ordered. The archers raised their bows, knuckles turning white under the pressure. Via raised her bow as well, crafted from the elder tree the elven queen sat upon. The only weapon in the army with magical enchantment. She brought the strung arrow up to her lips, the feathers kissing her softly.

"Hold!"

The dark mass grew closer. She could hear the howling of demons and sense the fear rolling off the men around her. She could make out silhouettes against the light morning sky. She could hear Gelum laughing in her mind.

"Your precious kingdom will fall once again, little elf."

Rye kept his hand up, testing the wind against it. He stood firm against the terrors before him. His gold and red armor gleamed against the browns and greys of his soldiers. Via felt the wind in her hair, the smoke in her eyes. She turned her waist slightly, readjusting. Closing her eyes, she sent a prayer to anyone who would listen—a fast end for those who died and a mighty fight for those who still fought.

A screech tore through the sky, and she looked up to see a winged silhouette black out the sun. Its body streaked toward the army, nearing the size of a small house. Via smirked and whipped her bow up, loosing her arrow and sending it straight into the body of the demon. Its shriek of pain sliced against the wind as it slammed into the ground in front of Rye. Its body twitched and convulsed before melting into the ground.

"Loose!" Rye yelled. All at once, hundreds of arrows streaked across the sky toward the dark army. The front cultists screamed in pain as the arrows lodged into their bodies, the cries carrying towards the spymaster. She notched another arrow and let it loose, sending it through the eye of a cultist. His body slumped against the ground as the others continued forward.

A hum of magic filled the air, and Via looked up to see numerous balls of flame speed toward them.

"Shields up!" Rye yelled. The soldiers brought their shields above their heads but did little to prevent the masses of fire from slamming into them. She turned to watch tens of the soldiers burn alive around her. They flailed and screamed and ran for their lives as more soldiers rushed to take their place, pulling the fallen away from the battle. Via grabbed onto a soldier whose torso was engulfed in burns. She dragged him away from the battle, and the healers took hold of him. Rye commanded the army to hold as the screams and shouts grew closer. She turned back and notched another arrow, standing ready. The mass was almost on top of them. She could barely stand upright with the shaking of the ground. She steadied her breath as Rye drew his sword.

"Today we fight, today we stand, and today we hold! For this is our stand against the Dark Kingdom and its terror. Are you with me!?" he yelled. The soldiers around him erupted into war cries as Via brought her bow up.

"May the gods have mercy on your souls," she whispered. She loosed another arrow, and it struck a cultist in the throat, sending him falling back into another soldier. Horns blared through the battleground, and the cultist lunged forward, starting straight toward their army with violent screams.

"For Fira!" Rye yelled. With a crush of metal, the two armies slammed into each other. Via lost sight of the commander as horses reared and fell against the ground. Spears lodged into bodies, and blood flew through the air as she dodged a sword and sent another arrow into the eye of a cultist before jumping back from a fireball. It singed her coat, and she heard a scream of terror as she turned to the side. A demon hound ripped into a soldier beside her and tore out his throat. His bloody gurgles of pain were quickly silenced by its jaws. She smacked her bow into its side, and it jumped from the soldier and lunged for her. She took a dagger from her boot and it slammed into her, bringing her to the ground. With a cry, she plunged the dagger into its throat and tore it across. It howled in anguish and fell to the ground beside her.

She snapped her head up as another cultist swung at her. She rolled out of the way and brought her bow up, putting an arrow through his chest. She blocked another sword with her bow and kicked the cultist back before ducking as flames streaked across the ground.

A flicker of lightning shot across the sky, and the ground trembled against her feet. She could feel Gelum gaining on the army. All around her, soldiers fell in battle, and cultists swarmed them. The demons had jumped over the front lines and were attacking the rear and healers.

Via retreated slightly, dodging blows and loosing more arrows. She was down to two in mere minutes. She rolled to the side as another bolt of fire slammed against the ground and tackled a cultist with a quiver. The cultist fell onto her face as Via sliced her throat and took the arrows, putting them into her own quiver.

"Via!" Rye called. She turned to see him strike down a demon hound, and he ran up to her.

"We are losing ground. We must pull back," he gasped. Via stood at his back, firing across the battlefield as he took the cultists head-on. She ducked as a sword streaked above her, and Rye swung around, slashing him across the chest.

"We have to hold this ground. If we lose the Mors now, there will be no stopping them from getting to WhiteDrove," she breathed. Rye wiped the blood from his face and engaged another cultist, disarming her and sending his sword into her throat. He pushed her body back and stood against Via, both breathing heavily. Men pulled their friends away from the fighting as healers tried to mend the wounds before being killed themselves.

It was chaos. The fires that burned against the ground nearly choked Via. She watched as a winged demon grabbed hold of a soldier and flung him into the air. A demon hound jumped up and latched on, pulling him back down. The body slapped against the ground in a wet mess of entrails.

She could see the rush of cultists gaining ground on their soldiers, slaughtering them. The howls of the demons burned her ears. The two turned and watched as Gelum gained on them, easily slashing his way through their soldiers. The smile on his face enraged the spymaster.

"Go," Via said, grabbing another arrow.

Rye turned to her. "Are you mad? You cannot defeat him on your own," he argued.

"You are the Imperial Commander. Your place is beside your men. Go, sound the retreat."

Rye bit his lip, but nodded. "Stay alive." He turned away and started down the battlefield, yelling for a retreat. Via stared Gelum down as he flung the last soldier away and stopped a few meters ahead of her. His sunken eyes bore into her own, and her thoughts trailed back to that night so long ago—the child in her arms, the screaming of the people around her.

She raised her bow and shot an arrow at him. He caught it in mid-air and tossed it over his shoulder.

"*Tsk*, you should know better by now, little elf," he cackled. He advanced on her, and she threw her bow to the side, taking up a fallen sword. He brought his sword up, and she barely managed to parry the blow before a wave of magic crashed into her, sending her staggering back. She slashed out, and Gelum caught her sword with his own. The ridges along the blade snapped hers in half, and she rolled forward. She used the broken sword to stab him in the thigh. He cried out angrily and twisted, grabbing her hair and flinging her away. She landed hard on her back with a gasp.

Via pulled herself up onto her knees as Gelum pulled the blade from his thigh with an angry curse. Via smiled and wiped the blood from her mouth. He lunged for her, and she rolled out of the way, grabbing her bow and loosing an arrow into his shoulder. With another cry of rage, a black bolt of magic was flung toward her. She barely missed it as it slammed into the ground. Black fire erupted from the impact and singed her coat. She notched another arrow, but Gelum was faster. He ripped the bow from her hands and threw it away, grabbing her by the neck. She choked and fought against his grip as he turned her around and pinned her to his chest. His other hand held her hair as he brought his lips to her pointed ear.

"Look around you, elf. Watch as your soldiers die," he taunted. She watched as the retreating soldiers were mauled by demons and cut down by cultists. Their screams echoed in her ears as Gelum laughed. "This is your legacy. To witness the fall of your kingdoms," he whispered. "To hear children weep and mothers scream. How does it feel to know you failed?"

Via closed her eyes, trying to drown out the screams around her. They couldn't fail. She couldn't fail. Not again. She snapped open her eyes and grabbed a dagger from her belt, stabbing it between the plate mail on his chest. He yelled out in pain, and Via wrenched herself from his grasp. She sprinted away from him as his cursing continued. She pushed a cultist out of the way before screaming in pain as a dagger lodged into her back. She fell to the ground in agony, but forced herself back onto her feet. Gelum grabbed her head and pulled the dagger from her back with a laugh. She screamed and fell back into the dirt. He pushed his boot into her back as her cries were muffled against the ground.

"No more tricks, little elf," he said. She could feel the swirling of magic above her and knew she had lost this battle. She only hoped she gave the commander enough time to escape.

Her vision was wobbly, but she could clearly make out the war cry behind her. She felt Gelum's boot lift off her, and she turned to see Garding swinging his sword at him. Gelum parried the blow and pushed him back. Garding stumbled but managed to keep his footing. His eyes locked onto Vias.

"Go Via. Live to fight another day," he said. Via shook her head, but Garding ignored her, engaging Gelum in a fruitless battle. She searched for her bow and crawled her way over to it and tried to bring it up, but the wound in her back made it impossible to lift high enough. Garding stumbled back, falling to his knees as Gelum stood over him. "Go!" he yelled at her.

Via wanted to run to him, to help him. But she knew she couldn't. She was too badly injured. Instead, she swallowed her pride and fled the field, using her bow as a brace. She didn't turn to see Gelum put his sword through Garding's chest. But she could hear his dying moan. She cursed the gods and cursed herself for losing another friend.

She pushed herself away from the battle, falling over dead soldiers and ducking swords. She could barely process the struggle around her. Most of the soldiers had retreated already. Few still stood waiting to be slaughtered. Her bow gave out under her, and she fell to the bloody ground, groaning at her back. She shakily looked up to see a shadowed figure standing over her. She couldn't move to defend herself. Instead, she allowed the darkness to take hold of her. And then she felt nothing.

58 ENARA

Escorted by guards, Enara made her way up the west tower steps into the Grand Living Quarters. She waved the guards off, and as they stepped away, she entered the bedroom.

The king was sitting at his large desk, quill in hand, seeming to contemplate something by the crease between his brows. His hair, while neatly slicked back, with a loose curl that fell onto his forehead that she focused on. "Aldrian," she announced, stopping at the door.

He looked up, and a small smile crossed his unfortunately handsome face. "Lady Enara, what may I assist you with?"

Enara turned and closed the door. Her chest tightened as she released the knob. "It's about WhiteDrove," she started, eyeing the guard in the back of the room.

Aldrian put down the quill and stood up. "What about it?" he asked, his tone staying neutral.

With a breath, Enara steadied her tone, throwing several letters onto the table. "I heard about the attack on Viragrad. You cannot condemn hundreds to slaughter."

The king tilted his head slightly, looking at the letters, and then back at her. "Didn't you say that you would do what needed to be done for your people to survive?" he asked.

"I want my people fed," she argued. "Not for innocents to be killed."

"Innocents?" he asked, a small smile spreading across his face. She found herself gazing at his smile. "I do not find the army that stands watch mere miles from our border to be innocent."

She opened her mouth to say something, but then closed it and gave a soft sigh. *He has a point…*she thought. *But that does not condone his actions.*

"And WhiteDrove?" she asked. "If you defeat the army, will you still march on the city?"

He turned away from her and picked up a letter, scanning it over for a moment before speaking again. "I have no true quarrel with WhiteDrove. It is Esai that has been the cause of concern."

"Then why attack?"

He dropped the letter onto the table. "Esai has supplied WhiteDrove with the means to attack us. We simply fought to defend our territory—what little is left of it."

"Defend? You call the slaughter in the Mors *defense?*"

"We took the necessary measures to ensure our success in the battle," he stated plainly. "Do you think the queen would actually agree to your terms?"

"How do you know about the letter?" she asked, a cold numbing feeling crawling up her spine. He sighed softly and stepped up to her, tucking a stray hair behind her ear. She could feel his breath on her face, watch the light waver in his honey eyes.

"I have eyes and ears in every city, in every kingdom, Enara. You did well, attempting to protect your people." His voice was sickly sweet, and his finger brushed her ear before he turned away from her and stepped over to the windows. He unlocked the latch to one and opened it to the outside. He looked back at her and held out his hand.

"Come," he ushered. Carefully, she walked over to him and took his hand. He wrapped his other arm around her shoulder, his warmth cutting through the chill in the air. She tried to ignore the proximity.

He positioned her so she could see the city before her. "Look out. What can you see?" he asked. Enara looked down at the courtyard to see several handmaidens laughing while picking berries from the thornbushes. Across the yard, a young man was bringing wood into the side entrance of the castle. A maiden caught his eye, and she waved at him, nearly making him drop the bundle. Enara's face did not lift.

"It is imitation. There can be no happiness here. You know this," she said.

The king rubbed her shoulder, and it sent a shiver down her spine. "Not to them. To them, this is their life. The handmaidens play in the pools by the garden. The smiths forge swords for the soldiers who protect them. Everyone has a job here,it may not be the life some choose, but it is the life they created," he said.

Enara turned towards him. "How can you be so daft? Do you not see the fear in their eyes?" she argued.

"What fear did you see when you allowed Malum to take your city?" he asked her, his eyes darkening. His grip on her shoulder tightened. "Do you see that same fear here?"

"I—" she looked to the ground. "No. I do not."

"Fear comes in many forms. We cannot lie to ourselves to say we know no fear at all. The baker fears a possible burnt loaf, the wife fears her upcoming birth, and the father fears he may not return to his children. But all the same, the fire that fuels the fear is quenched over time once we learn to accept and move forward."

"So, I must accept that my kingdom has fallen because of my actions? That the people here are terrified they may not live another day?" she argued.

Aldrian dropped his hand from her and looked out the window. "Where you see fear, I see only love. We make the best of what we have here. I am no king but a servant of the gods, and you are no queen but a pawn in their game. You will come to love the chains you are given. I take care of my people, and the gods protect us. Your kingdom will find this peace someday, too. And soon, the entire world shall," he exclaimed. "They are not scared of the soldiers within these walls, but of the people who are trying to kill them outside of them."

She looked into his eyes and found no hints of deceit. He truly believed this was the best life he could give his people. He was no more a lord than she was a god. Enara flinched and looked down at her pulsing hand. He took it in his own and kissed it softly. She shivered at the soft touch of his grazing lips.

"I promise you, my lady, you will come to realize the cruelty of this world. And you will know the wrath of the gods that promise to protect you. Keep your wits, my queen. For this is your kingdom now, even if you do not see it." He dropped her hand, and she turned away.

Rubbing her now quelled hand, she closed her eyes. "And if you take WhiteDrove, what then?"

"Then we gain another kingdom to feed and protect. We will use their livestock and grain to feed our people and plow more fields. We will set up trading routes and have a sizable playing field against the capital. We will own most of the western part of the continent."

"And do you think they will not retaliate?" Enara asked, turning back to him. "They will not stand by while you burn another kingdom."

Aldrian stepped over to the table and poured himself a glass of wine and the chill came back into her skin. "War is inevitable. There will be soldiers dying on bloody fields and innocents caught in the middle. But what comes after all the wars that are fought? Peace. That is what we will achieve."

"You think Malum wants peace?" she asked.

The king took a long sip of his wine and sat down at the table. "I cannot claim to know the will of the gods. He will seek power, and we will give it to him. Once he has the power of the continent, who knows if he will be satisfied?"

"Yes, he will go and make a hut in the woods. Foraging for berries and watching the sunrise," she jested.

"Doesn't sound so bad to me."

She snorted without realizing it and quickly composed herself again. "War may be inevitable, but that doesn't mean we cannot try to lessen the bloodshed."

"I agree with you, Enara. But we have fought this war for a thousand years. The people lost in these battles are little more than a speck on the bodies of my people piled high. You cannot know the burden placed on my shoulders."

"Then why continue to fight? Haven't you lost enough?" she argued, walking over to him and placing a hand on his arm.

"Because the moment we stop fighting is the moment we lose all hope," he said, looking at the glass in his hand. "For hundreds of years, all we did was try to make a home where we could be safe. The Elven Crusade did not stop the capital from taking anything they could from us. Even when we offered them sanctuary, they turned their noses up at us. The other kingdoms cut off our supplies and pushed us to the furthest reaches of the Mors. Before the gods showed themselves to us again, we were being slaughtered for an attack on the elven kingdoms we did not commit."

"You mean Velwood?" Enara asked.

The king nodded. "They came in the night, the darkest of nights I remember. Assassins sent by a spymaster. They killed the commander of our army and his wife and children. They would have killed me next if my uncle wouldn't have fought them off. He died protecting me."

Enara looked down, not willing to meet his eyes. What could she say against that?

"That is why I fight." He brought his hand over her own and she felt heat rise to her cheeks. "To ensure that we shall no longer die at the hands of the cruel."

"I see I cannot dissuade you from this then," Enara sighed.

He set his glass down on the table and rubbed his thumb along the top of her hand. "Not of this, I'm afraid. But I do enjoy seeing the fire in your eyes."

Enara stammered out a weak rebuttal before shaking her head and turning away, pulling out of his grip. "We will speak again..." She left the room without another word and broke off into a heavy walk toward her chambers. The heat from her hand was almost as prominent as the heat of her cheeks.

59 VIA

Via's eyes opened into a softly illuminated room. Her head pounded, and she groaned at the pain in her back. She was bare, covered only by a thin sheet, and laid on her stomach on a bed. She listened around her; she could hear the crackling of a fire in a fireplace, the soft footfalls of armored boots outside the room, and could smell the ointment on her back. She also took notice of the small figure gracing her bed.

"I've... never seen an elf here before," the figure whispered.

Via moved slightly, grimacing at the pain it caused her, and looked over at the figure. A girl sat on the edge of the bed, her fingers running softly down the damp cloth coating Via's back. She had light hair and pale white skin that nearly shimmered in the firelight. The soft point to her ears gave Via enough to make an assumption.

"Where am I?" she asked hoarsely, grimacing at her voice.

The girl stopped tracing the bandages. Via took notice of her fingertips—stained black. From ink, most likely. "In WhiteDrove. The commander brought you here. My brother will be back shortly," she said. "I'm Anya Dicesare."

Anya... Via had heard the name before, in a briefing. This must be the half-elf the queen took in some years ago. And if Rye brought her in, that meant he was still alive. "How long have I been unconscious?" she asked.

"A few days. The healers kept arguing about how to heal a cursed blood."

Cursed blood...that was at least a new twist on the name, she thought.

"Anya, where is the commander now?" she asked.

The girl shrugged. "I was told to stay here in case you woke. I washed your clothes. They were bloody."

"Thank you." Via rose slowly from her position, and Anya stood off the bed and grabbed a pile of clothes, setting them beside her.

"I hope these fit. Brother says elves are leaner than humans. Can you run faster too?"

Via laughed and grimaced. "Sometimes."

Anya nodded her head and politely looked away while she dressed, though Via caught her eying her skin.

"You can ask, princess," she allowed.

Anya bit her lip and turned her way. "I've heard the stories. But I've never met an elf. Or a cursed elf—is that your true species?"

Via huffed out another laugh. "Yes. That is what they call my kind."

"That's very mean. You're pretty. I like your skin," she smiled.

Via pulled on her boots with a long exhale of breath and searched the room. "Where is my bow?" she asked.

The girl seemed to contemplate, her large eyes looking above her. "I think... In the armory. I could be wrong. The commander hurried you in here. I never saw where the others went."

Via nodded and started for the door. Anya opened the door for her. "Let me help."

"I'm fine, princess."

"I insist!"

Via sighed and let the girl guide her through the keep. All the while, the girl talked and sang about her wolf gods and her drawings. Via took notice of the stone walls and the frosted windows. Occasionally, a bucket would be placed in the hallway to collect dripping water. The keep was not in the best condition, which meant defense would be harder. But the large, heavy stone exterior would make fires more difficult to spread. The few keepers all gave her large, open-mouth looks as she passed. Elves were not common in Viragrad, and her skin must have been a sight to behold.

She heard their whispers as they passed.

"A demon in the keep?"

"The princess found another odd toy to play with."

"Have you met my brother?"

Via looked down at the young girl bopping along the hallway, her hair bouncing with her frame. "He went to Fira for the council. Is it true the Dark Kingdom will attack us?"

The girl was spirited. Via would give her that.

Via pulled her face into a stoic mask as the two exited the castle and climbed up the wooden ramparts. Anya had stopped talking as more wounded were wheeled through the gates. Via had been to WhiteDrove only a handful of times. It was smaller than she remembered. Good for defending, but easily overrun. The certain walls were wood, not stone. The town itself was merely a village. There was no way to defend it properly. Only one well-placed fireball and the whole thing would burn.

She watched the looks the northern people gave her. Disgust. Astonishment. Fear. She heard their comments about the men being brought in through the gates.

"I told ye. Look at what protection they gave us. Nothin," they said. Via knew one thing about the people of Viragrad—they did not like foreigners. At least she wasn't spat on.

Via spotted the golden hair several yards away and gave a soft farewell to the princess before stepping up beside Rye. He gave a small bow in greeting.

"You're walking. That's good," he said.

Via could hear the tenseness in his voice, his eyes darting back and forth along the plains. The bruises on his face were dark, and a long cut went from his lip to his cheek. "Yes, the healers did well. I take it you saved me?" she asked.

He nodded, then turned to her. "What were you thinking? Taking on Gelum like that. You could have died. Garding—" He broke off, shaking his head.

Via eyes fell to the ground. "I'm sorry. He was a good man."

"He was a great man. And he was slaughtered like the rest of them," he spat, and gripped the pommel of his sword. "Damn them all. We barely managed to escape with two hundred men. They still have thousands."

"There is still Fira. We still have time."

"Maybe a week. They will not get here on time, and the portal isn't large enough to supply the troops we need. WhiteDrove will fall," he sighed.

Via put a hand on his shoulder. "Then we will die fighting."

Rye put his hand on hers with a small smile. "And fight we shall."

A captain came up the stairs and quickly bowed to Rye before speaking. "I am Captain Mulliner, Commander. The queen is ready to meet with you," he said.

Rye nodded at him and looked towards Via. "Let's give her the bad news," he huffed. He pushed past the captain, and she followed him through the small courtyard and back into the keep. She tried to see where the princess had run off to but lost her in the mass of soldiers.

When they climbed the stairs to the queen's room, Rye knocked on the door.

"Come in. I don't have all day," she responded. Via gave a soft chuckle as Rye opened the door. They entered the room with the captain and bowed low. The queen sat near the fireplace, tapping her fingers on the wooden armrest of her chair. A letter was discarded on the floor in front of her.

"Damn girl thinks she can take what she wants. What do you think? One—two hours we hold? Possibly three, if they send us any men at all. Our boys are hunters, but they are not soldiers."

"I have faith that we can still win this battle, Queen Kesanda," Rye told.

She shifted in her seat and brought her hand up to her chin. "Do you see these walls, Commander? They have stood for a hundred years and are made of red oak trees. Pretty, to be sure, but they are rotted and decrypted. A small child can knock half of it down if they are clumsy enough," she retorted. With a slight pause, she added, "How large is their army?"

"Several thousand," Via said.

"And how many men do you have left that can hold a sword?"

"A few hundred," Rye responded.

"And this is why we did not trust Imperials to protect us," the captain spat.

Via looked toward him. "We lost a hundred men protecting Viragrad. Please tell the families of those men that their deaths meant nothing."

The captain pursed his lips, and she turned back to the queen with a smirk.

"How long?" the queen asked.

"A week. Maybe less."

"We have two sizable villages between here and the army," the captain said. We can conscript the men."

"There won't be more than a couple hundred if you count the boys as well," the queen said. "But bring everyone here. We can get the children through the portal at least. The forges outside the city can supply some weapons, but they haven't been used in some time. We can pull water from the thawing ocean to quench the flames. At least the damned keep is made of stone."

"I will send out several parties to gather the villagers," Via told. She bowed again to the queen before making her exit. She counted in her mind the number they would need to stand a chance against the Dark Kingdom. A thousand Imperial soldiers, at least. But she knew better than to think they would get that much. If they sent the civilians through, that meant less time for troops. She knew the politics of the court as well. They would not send that many even if they could. They were on their own.

60 TALIA

Talia sat opposite Lord Dicesare as the council began. On the other side of her sat an elven woman who had not spoken a word since her arrival. Her eyes scanned all of their faces, though, and the contemptuous look she gave told her she wanted nothing to do with them. Talia couldn't blame her; she read of the Elven Crusades. A map of Veran sat on the table with several markers spread about, pinpointing the locations of the armies. She felt the wolf shift behind her as Thymas gave a side-eye to him.

"If I may ask, my lady, where are you from?" he asked, leaning towards the elf. She looked at him but did not respond. He shifted in his seat uncomfortably. "I see you could make it to attendance today, Lady Farvell. It is pleasing to see you again," he said, changing his gaze to her.

"Yes, it is. The herald sent by the king was not properly suited for such a task," she responded.

A slight hint of worry rolled down her chest at the thought of the emperor being displeased with her attendance. The herald was already in the palace by the time she arrived. She had swiftly told him to leave, which he did after quite an argument. Even so, he was the guest here, not her. Even though the servants and gentry did not treat her unwell, she knew they spoke ill of her in secret.

Suddenly the door opened, and the emperor came in with several attendants. The other lords and ladies stood as he entered, and he quickly raised a hand to dismiss them.

Talia sat back down and watched as he sat at the head of the table. Two more people, a man and a woman, sat on the opposite end of the table next to Lord Dicesare wearing garish outfits. It nearly hurt her eyes to look at them as their jewels reflected the candlelight. The woman wore an elaborate headdress that was tall and rounded. Several sheets of fabric draped off it and fell onto her shoulders. The dress she wore nearly took up the entirety of the table, and Thymas shifted to keep the fabric at bay. She cleared her throat and gave a small smile in her direction. Talia returned the smile.

The man was dressed in a white suit with bulging shoulders and a long cape. His hat reminded her of the traders that would come in from the sea, large and floppy. The feather resting on top of it swooped down from the size, and she nearly laughed as he brushed it back with a huff. She could not imagine wearing any of their items once summer came.

The emperor himself was dressed modestly in only a dark tunic and cape embroidered in gold. He was more handsome than she cared to admit, but he looked well beyond his age with the weight of the kingdoms on his shoulders. His hair was cleanly greased back, and his crown sat lightly upon his head. She had only seen him once, when she was a child, during the funeral of the empress. She had died along with their second child in childbirth. It was a great time of mourning throughout the entire continent. His green eyes found her own, and with a small smile, he started the meeting.

"First, let me introduce my Arcane Advisor, Lucius Lancaster," he spoke, pointing his hand at the man at his side. The man was younger than most advisors, probably fresh out of the College. She wondered how he was placed in such a high rank at that age. He was wearing the blue robe commonly donned by enchanters, and his complexion was fair and his hair short. His beard was cleanly shaved, and his dark grey eyes creased happily. He bowed politely, and the emperor turned back to the others.

"This is Duke Percival; he owns much of the Grand Quarter and is a well-trusted advisor."

The duke gave a head nod. "I have been in the family for quite some time. A third cousin of the second emperor of Fira. And I was a good friend to the late Emperor Henri."

"And this is Marquise Josephine." He nodded in the woman's direction, who gave him a smile and a nod.

"I own a portion of the land between Fira and the port of the Sunset Isles. I make sure the kingdom has the supplies it needs."

So important people, Talia thought. Maybe with enough sway to turn the emperor over to her ideas, but it wasn't the full council, this she knew. It may not be enough even if she begged.

Emperor Varen then turned to the others, motioning to the elven woman. "It is good to see an ambassador from Avlor come all this way. I hope your trip was not strenuous, Lady Caeda?"

She gave him a nod, and he took that as a sign to move on. "Unfortunately, the other members of the court shall not be attending. They have elected to return to their territories to prepare."

"What? Does this not affect us all?" Thymas asked.

The emperor sighed softly and knitted his hands together. "I cannot blame them for their fear. Some of the court hold land close to the Mors of Salvia and cannot wait for my word to go to them."

Thymas sat back in his seat with an irate glare.

"Without the approval of the court, can you spare any resources for WhiteDrove?" The woman asked, sitting next to Thymas. The same one who was with him yesterday. Talia tried to remember her name. Sara, was it?

The emperor looked at her and lowered his eyes for a moment. "There is only so much I can do. Commander Rye leads the largest battalion of men closest to the Mors. To send more would take weeks, if not a month. How many men do you have stationed in WhiteDrove now?"

"Maybe a hundred. We can pull more men back, but we are no fortress," Thymas said.

"We have not heard any word from Rye or his forces. If he was successfully able to repel or hold off the Dark Kingdom, we may not need as many men as we think."

"And if they didn't?" Talia asked.

The emperor sighed. "I can send a small force through the portal, but without an accurate estimate of the Dark Kingdom's forces, it is unknown how much it will help."

"Anything will help, Your Excellence," Sara interjected.

"And what of Avlor."

All eyes turned to the elven woman, surprised to hear her speak.

"What of Avlor?" the emperor asked.

"Our orchards are desecrated. Our scouts are dying in more numbers than we can replace, and the undead are beginning to rise near the outskirts of the forest, near the Mors. We fear their numbers will rise."

"Are their maleficarum raising them?" the emperor asked her.

The woman eyed him and shrugged. "Our scouts have not seen any."

"If you can bring us numbers of dead. We may be able to gauge how many maleficarum there are," Lucius commented.

"Is that all? Numbers?"

The emperor unfolded his hands and adjusted his cloak. "We do not have the numbers to fight on two fronts. If WhiteDrove is the key, then we must focus our forces there. If the elven kingdom can send their men to help, we can secure the city and then turn our forces to Avlor. That is how we will defend the kingdom."

"So, we give you everything and leave our people defenseless, is that it?" the elven woman asked, her voice rising.

"That is not why I brought you here, Lady Caeda. I wish both of our kingdoms to prosper. But we need men to fight," the emperor said solemnly.

Caeda scoffed at him, turning her head away. "This is the help humans give. Nothing. When we asked for sanctuary during the Battle of Velwood you refused us. And now you plead for our aid. We fight your wars, win your battles, and you give us villages and undead. We are dying by the dozen while you have your walls to keep you safe. Another Elven Crusade for you!" With the outburst, she quickly stood up and left the room, and Talia looked back to the emperor, who frowned.

"Lucius, could you try to speak with her for me? Tell her we will send aid whenever we can."

The advisor nodded and bowed, leaving the room. "Well, I suppose support of the elves is questionable," Thymas said, running a hand through his hair.

"What of the portal? How many men can go through at a time?" Sara asked, putting a hand on his arm.

The emperor put a finger to his lips. "Not enough. The portals are small, barely large enough for wagons to pass through. We can send men through them, but it will take time."

"Then use the portals. That is why they were built, right?" Talia asked. "If we start immediately, we can surely have enough to hold the keep, at the very least."

"We have no standing army at the moment," the duke spoke up. "At this very moment, all we have are the reserves who will need to be equipped. That, once again, shall take time."

Talia sighed and glanced at the prince, who had a distressed look on his face.

"What of the enchanters you have here? Can't you send some of them through the portal?" Sara asked.

"Our enchanters are not learned in combat. They are mainly healers or alchemists. Very few even have the knowledge of battle spells," the emperor said.

"Then the senior enchanters know how to fight, correct? There are simple spells of barriers and fire that even apprentices learn to cast. Those who cannot fight can focus on wards," Sara said. "Surely they can spare a few for the battle."

Emperor Varen sat back in his seat, drumming his fingers on the table. "Perhaps I can see it done. The College may allow a few veteran enchanters to escort the battalion through the portal, and some healers for the wounded, but they mainly rule themselves. I can do nothing but ask."

"That is all we require, Your Excellence," Sara said with a bow of her head. Talia glanced at her. She was surprisingly well knowledged on magic.

"It seems we can do nothing but send the few men we have and prey to the goddess," the marquise said with a sigh.

The room was quiet for a moment before a knock took them from their thoughts. A messenger entered the room and gave Thymas a letter before leaving. He opened it, and Talia watched his face fall.

"What is it?" Varen asked.

"The Mors have been lost," he started, his voice trembling slightly. "WhiteDrove will be attacked within the week." Sara put a hand on his shoulder, and Talia felt her stomach churn. The lord stood up abruptly. "I'm sorry, Your Grace, but I need as many troops as you can send. We cannot lose two kingdoms to Reverand."

With that, he left the room, and the woman followed, leaving the emperor and Talia alone with the nobles. He stood up and walked to the window, hands clasped behind his back. "I never thought Ignis would fall in a day. And here we are with another kingdom on the brink of collapse."

"Our cities will burn if we do not do something. The rest of the court will see," Duke Percival said with a shake of his head.

"We cannot do anything without the approval of the others. We are lost without them," the marquise argued.

"What of Rosus' army?" Talia asked. "We have enough men to supply WhiteDrove."

"WhiteDrove is hundreds of miles north of even Ignis. There is no way the men can reach there in time," the marquise said.

"They don't have to reach WhiteDrove before the army," she started and stood up, trailing a finger up the map on the table. "We can use our ships, and travel through the Amber Sea up the western coast and through to the port of Driftseerie just north of Stormshold. It won't take more than a few days. We can get behind the dark army. Fight on two fronts."

The emperor turned away from the window and back towards the table. "Do you have enough men?"

Talia pulled the map close to her and put a marker on Rosus. "We have a few hundred on call already. Mostly as navy men to deal with any pirates, but we can have them supplied and ready within a day. We can conscript the other able soldiers and have them ready within a few days. Possibly a thousand that can be ready to march."

"That could be enough," the duke agreed. "It could."

"Will the king send them then?" the marquise asked.

Talia gripped the marker in her hand. "He has said that he will not spare the men to fight in the war."

"Then we are doomed!" the marquise shouted, raising her arms in the air.

"Why? What is his worry?" the emperor asked.

"He believes that if Rosus sends their men north, they will be attacked. But with an imperial edict, you can force him to march."

"That could start a war on its own," the duke exclaimed. "Putting forth such an order is a blatant force of will. They will revolt."

"Not if they know the cost," Talia argued. "The people will know you meant well. We cannot sacrifice WhiteDrove."

The emperor sat back down, rubbing his chin. "I will need to confer with my advisors. Lady Talia, I thank you for your input and your willingness to assist. Please feel free to stay in the capital as long as you wish," he said. Talia knew her time was up, so she stood, curtsied, and stepped out of the room. The wolf followed behind her, and when they were far enough away, he snickered.

"Well, the rose has some thorns, after all. You may earn your chance to seize your father's throne."

"That's not what I want, wolf."

"Is it not? You just stated that you did not care about the fist the emperor would hold to your father at your whisper. I am not judging. I am simply enjoying."

Talia rolled her eyes. "Then keep enjoying. I need some fresh air."

61 LAERDYA

Sneaking out from the confinements of the castle, Laerdya made her way back to the glowing forest. Her feet bounced as she slid between the shadows and past townspeople. Lifting her skirt, she stepped through the muddy pathway of the streets and searched for the lights of the fae to guide her forward. Her cloak concealed her fair skin as several guards ignored her passing by.

She knew the streets well by now and could easily navigate through them without causing much suspicion. Sometimes she would still stop along the way to admire a wedding or look in on a tavern brawl.

Near the edge of the forest, Laerdya heard a crash. She turned towards the noise and found it came from a little bakery down the street. With curiosity, she padded over towards the crashing, the dimly lit road giving little visibility. Another crash and a curse came from the bakery as Laerdya drew near. The door was propped open, and inside, a man rummaged through the shop, knocking things away and placing others into a bag. She neared closer to see the long woven white hair of the man and the deep blue of his skin.

Laerdya dared to near him as he continued speaking to himself and tossing pots. He didn't look like a baker to her, but what did she know? When her foot hit a pot, the man twirled around to face her. He pulled a knife from off his belt, and Laerdya gasped. The man paused, startled by her when Laerdya noticed the blood covering his vest, and she turned to flee.

Running from the shop, he quickly caught up to her, grabbing her by the cloak and tearing it from her shoulders. With a cry, she fell to the ground, crawling on both knees to escape.

"Help me!" she cried, praying that a guard was nearby. The man grabbed her by the leg, pulling her towards him. She screamed and turned, clawing at his face and chest. He easily overcame her and grabbed her flailing arms. He stopped short when he glimpsed her skin, and his face paled.

"Milady. I didn't know," he stammered. She watched as his eyes wavered and as quickly as he had caught her, guards rushed him, yanking him off her and pinning him to the ground.

Laerdya was quickly lifted into the arms of another guard. "Princess, are you alright?" he asked.

Laerdya nodded, still trembling in his grasp, and turned back to the man being pushed into the dirt.

"Take him to the queen. She will want to hear of this," the guard said. The man was heaved onto his feet and bound with chains. The guards set Laerdya down, and they made their way back to the castle.

Laerdya was stripped of her dirty dress and placed in a soft, free-flowing gown. The slaves tended to her wrists, which were slightly bruised, and ointment was applied. She watched as they refused to meet her gaze, and when they left, she made her way to the throne room. She entered the throne room and greeted the queen, who was already sitting atop her throne, her posture rigid.

"My blossom, are you alright?" she asked. For once, Laerdya could hear the worry in her voice.

She smiled politely. "Yes, I am fine. The slaves saw to me and treated my injuries. Thank you," she responded. She sat down next to the queen in her own seat, picking at her nails, and waited for the inevitable.

Her fiancé soon showed up, fuming, and stomped over to his mother. "I want him executed! She is mine!" he yelled; his face was nearly purple with rage. Then turned to Laerdya. "You disobeyed me! I told you not to go out of the castle. I should have you punished just as well!"

Laerdya opened her mouth, but the queen spoke first. "I gave her permission, Elmaer. You shan't keep her locked up here any longer. And for the prisoner, that is not your choice to make," she tutted. Laerdya could see the veins in his forehead throb, but he kept silent, slumping down on the other side of his mother.

"Bring in the prisoner. I wish to speak with him," she told a guard.

They bowed, then left, returning shortly later with the man. He fell to his knees before the queen; his head bowed low. Laerdya could see the bruises on him even through his dark skin. The jailor had not been kind to him.

The queen rested her hands on her lap, tilting her head slightly. "What is your name?" she asked.

The man's head did not raise. "It is Rhangyl, *Aretove*," he said, his voice gruff and low.

"Well, Rhangyl, do you realize you attempted to harm your future queen?" she asked.

His head bowed lower. "Not... at the time, my queen. Not until I had seen her skin," he said. Laerdya could feel the rage coming off Elmaer as he spoke.

"Why did you try to harm Laerdya?"

"I... I was stealing food from the bakery in town, she—the princess caught me, and I acted without knowing my actions, my queen," he confessed. Laerdya bit her lip as he spoke. This was nearly one of the first times she had ever come in contact with one of the city folk. It was not a good impression. She did feel bad for him, but the blood on his vest made her worried.

"Hmm," the queen purred. "Would your family approve of this? Stealing from another family. If you rot in a cell, they will go even more hungry now."

Finally, the man looked up at her, hurt in his eyes that Laerdya knew all too well. "I have no family, my queen. My daughter and wife were killed in a fire a decade ago," he said.

The queen sighed, and after a pause, turned to Laerdya. "Little blossom. What shall we do with him? You are the wounded party in this."

Laerdya looked up quickly, a spasm of anxiety shooting through her. "Me? I don't think—"

The queen shushed her. "You will rule this kingdom someday. You might as well learn now. What shall you do with him?" she asked again, more sternly this time. Laerdya looked at the man, who stared back at her. His eyes changed from sorrowful to a dull acceptance of his fate.

Fidgeting with her hands, she tried to wrap her mind around a punishment. Was the prison too harsh a fate for someone who stole? Or did he kill those around him to have something to eat? He lost everything he cared about. She wasn't sure if his fate even mattered at that point.

She looked over at the guards scattered around the room. She remembered the ones who came to her aid. The ones who had a purpose for her. "You… shall be in my personal guard," she started. "Your punishment for hurting your queen is now to protect your queen," she said, sitting up a bit higher in her chair. Ravana looked taken aback, but quickly laughed.

Rhangyl's posture changed suddenly. He sat up and shook his head slightly. "Princess, are you sure?" he asked.

Laerdya nodded her head. "Yes, Rhangyl, you are now my own protector from this day until your last days," she affirmed.

Elmaer quickly stood up. "I will not allow this!" he blurted out.

The queen hissed a warning at him. "You will sit down now and shut your mouth before I send you to the forgotten forest."

Elmaer turned violet and stormed out of the throne room. Rhangyl was unchained, and he stood up before stepping over to Laerdya. He bowed low. "I humbly thank you for sparing my life, milady. And I will serve you till my dying breath."

Laerdya smiled and stood up, placing a hand on his shoulder. "You will do your late family proud."

He stepped away from her, and the guards escorted him out of the room. She then turned to the queen, who had a twisted grin on her face.

"You chose mercy for those who would destroy you. For this, it is good, but you may not be able to show mercy every time, blossom. Soon there will come a time when you must drench your hands in blood." She stood up and stepped from the throne. "But now is not that time." She swayed out of the throne room, leaving Laerdya to her own thoughts.

62 ENARA

It was a quiet morning. The sun had just begun to rise over the city walls when a knock woke Enara from her slumber. Daealla came in with a smile on her face. Enara sat up and glared at the bright-eyed girl before she was pulled from her bed and into a fitted outerwear gown.

"By Velara girl, what are you doing?" Enara exasperated, swaying from her groggy awakening. Daealla quickly combed through Enara's hair, braiding it down the side.

"The king has prepared a wondrous day for you. He wishes to treat you to a morning out of the town," she spoke.

Enara thought back to their previous fight. How many soldiers had died in that battle? She couldn't help but feel responsible. The losses had to be staggering, if Ignis was any indication. The only thing she could hope for was a quick take of the kingdom. She supposed this was his way of apologizing.

"Where is Trissa?" Enara asked as they exited the castle.

"She told me she had matters to attend to in Ignis. She will be back shortly," Daealla responded.

Enara sighed and continued to follow the girl through the courtyard. She was soon led by guards to a carriage, where both she and two other handmaidens were inside.

"I don't believe we've met," Enara said, sitting opposite of them. The girls both had dark skin and soft brown eyes. They wore riding dresses and sat beside each other in nearly identical fashion. Enara knew they were twins—she couldn't tell the other apart.

"I am Breya, Your Grace," the first one said excitedly.

"And I am Brina," said the second. "The king was worried about you being isolated, so he sent us to come with you."

A small smile rose from Enara's lips. "I appreciate the offer."

The carriage rode off into the main streets of Reverand, never stopping till the gates swung open and they were led outside. Enara felt a sense of relief as they left the city, her breath finally being able to catch up. "Where are we headed?"

"I hope you know to ride a horse, Your Grace; we are going to a ranch not far from here. Most of the king's horses are bred there. They are the best in Veran," Breya said.

Enara looked out the latched window. "I am sure they are."

They arrived at the ranch nearly an hour later, and Brina helped her down, and the other girls got off behind her. The ranch was quaint and quiet, and Enara felt a sense of peace as it reminded her of the ranches back in Ignis. She would often ride to calm herself after a strenuous lecture. Rose was never the best rider, she mainly whined about her backside hurting.

The morning was warm, and the clouds drifted softly by in small wisps. The only thing that could be heard was the melodious singing of birds and frogs. They had to be somewhere far from the Mors; there was no way this beauty could be achieved there.

An elderly man came up to them and bowed low. "The king has requested that our finest horses be released for you today, milady. You may travel through the woods at your leisure. Please follow me." The twins squealed behind Enara as Daealla squeezed her shoulder and pulled up her skirt.

They were brought to the stables as a black mare was being led out of a stall. Enara's eyes widened at the beauty of the horse. It had a small white patch at the base of its snout that she put her hand to. It licked her hand, and she gave a smile. Its mane was soft as silk as she ran her fingers through it.

"I used to have one just like this when I was a girl," she said, thinking back to her riding lessons outside the city. Her mother would read a book while sitting on a blanket basked in sunlight. She remembered the way her hair would glimmer against the yellow glow of the sun. Enara would do tricks to try to get a response, which was either full of worry or slight judgment. She nearly broke an arm trying to stand on the backside of her mare. One of the few times she received full attention from the queen.

"The king told me you liked black mares, so I made sure she was prepared for you, milady," the groom said.

Enara looked at him with a tinge of confusion. "How did you know that? I haven't told him."

"Lady Trissa told me. She said you loved riding horses," he admitted.

Enara sighed happily. "Yes, Ravenspire was my favorite. Thank you, sir, for this gift."

"Do not thank me, Your Grace. This was all the king's doing. May the gods keep him safe," he beamed.

Enara quickly cleared her throat and pulled a stray hair behind her ear. "I… will have to thank him sometime."

A stool was brought up, and Enara climbed onto the horse. Once she was secured, her handmaids climbed onto their horses as well, and they began riding toward the woods. Daealla came next to her, a smile gracing her lips.

"You look like you were born to ride, Your Grace," she said. Enara ran her fingers down the side of the saddle, humming softly. It took just the barest squeeze of her legs for the mare to trot. The occasional happy neigh filled her with joy.

"I always enjoyed riding, but once my mother was killed, I no longer had the time. I had to take care of my sister—" Enara cut off, her words falling off her lips.

Daealla tilted her head slightly. "Why don't you tell me about your sister?" she asked.

Enara stared into the sky, biting her lip. "She was a sweet girl. She was naïve and young and beautiful, but she has—had a heart of gold. She just… didn't understand the way the world works."

"I'm sorry you lost her," Daealla said sadly. They entered the wooded area, and Enara could hear the twins giggling behind her. "Everything happens for a reason, Your Grace. You did the right thing, I'm sure."

Enara looked at the girl beside her. So naïve, just like her sister. "I hope so, Daealla."

Shadows passed overhead as the canopies rose around the group. "Brina, Breya. May I ask how you became handmaids?" Enara asked.

They looked at the queen. "We were brought up as orphans, Your Grace. The king found us and knew our beauty was too unique to be on the streets. He offered us a place within the castle as ladies." Brina smiled at her sister, and Enara shifted in her saddle. The last time she was in the woods was when the very gods she now worshiped had killed her mother. The breeze was cool on her skin, though. The aura was soft instead of hostile. Parts of it seemed lost in a haze. When she looked too far ahead, it was like a veil was cast along it, blurring, and shifting it into focus. She felt something that did not seem normal.

"Brina, look!" Breya pointed. They all looked to a small grove with a waterfall cascading into a pool of glimmering water not far from their position.

"May we visit, milady?" Daealla asked. Enara nodded, and they sidetracked over to the waterfall. Getting off their horses, Enara lifted her skirt to not get her dress dirty as she stepped over puddles. The twins had already run off, pulling off their shoes and digging their feet into the muddy bottom of the pool. Daealla seemed hesitant to enter the water.

Enara walked over to her. "Daealla, is something wrong?" she asked.

Daealla shook her head. "Of course not, milady. I just... never learned to swim."

A small giggle rose from Enara's stomach. "Well, it's never too late to learn. Come on." Enara started pulling off her dress, carefully unlacing and setting her clothing on a rock. She stripped to her undergarments and had Daealla do the same. She pulled her into the water and held her close as they entered the pool. The twins helped keep her afloat, and they slowly got her into the pool until their feet no longer touched the bottom.

The water was warmer than she expected, and the lily pads scattered about danced in the ripples they created.

"A-are you sure about this, milady?" Daealla asked hesitantly.

"Don't be so wussy, Daealla!" Brina laughed. Breya sprayed her with water, in turn hitting Enara. She laughed and took one hand off her maid to splash the girl's back. An all-out battle took place within the pool. Enara felt her spirit lift as she was dunked under the water by her maids and arose again to get a face full of moss. She retaliated with a splash of water as Daealla held onto Enara for dear life. With water and moss flying, the girls barely had time to register the movement beneath their feet.

"Did you feel that!" Daealla yelped.

"It's my foot, dummy," Breya laughed.

"No, I could have sworn—"

"Look!" Brina yelled. All eyes turned towards the edge of the pool where a woman sat on the bank. Enara's breath caught in her throat as she stared at the woman. Lilies were braided into her green hair, scales glimmering against the water that dripped down her cheeks. Her eyes were wide and silted like a serpent.

"Is that a nymph?" Brina whispered.

"It can hear you!" Daealla whispered back.

"Your Grace, we should leave," Breya told. Enara continued to stare at the creature. It slid into the pool and bobbed its head down under the water. It came closer to the girls, who squealed and backed away, all but the queen. Enara stayed where she was as the nymph came up to her, her webbed fingers running through her hair.

"What is it you want?" Enara asked.

The nymph cocked her head to the side with a sweet smile. "A gift for the queen," she whispered, her voice as light as a feather, and tickled her ear. She took Enara's hand and kissed her black veins gently; they seemed to glow a soft purple before fading slightly. Enara brought her hand up to her chest as the woman dipped below the water and then back up.

"Thank you..." she said, confused. The girls quickly grabbed Enara and pulled her from the nymph and back up to shore. Enara kept her gaze on her as they quickly dressed. Daealla brought the horses around, and as Enara climbed onto hers, she heard the nymph's voice in her ears.

"Beware the woman in the shadows."

63 NADAHI

The wind howled as two ravens flew above the small camp. Torgir sharpened his blade as Erling rubbed salve along the claw marks embellishing his face. Hakon gave him a good elbow in the shoulder before the men fell to the ground in a heated tussle.

"Would you two idiots stop before you knock his other eye out?" Liv growled. She received a satchel to the face as a reply.

Over on the other side of the camp, Nadahi led Rose through several combat stances. She took care not to push the little mage too hard. She still worried about her petite frame compared to her much larger one. It perplexed her how her people could be so small and yet so fierce. She could barely imagine the thought of uncovered sunlight and warm winds. She had said there were places that had only sand and felt like walking on the sun. She found it hard to believe her. Rose was still struggling to combat the harsh cold of the north. Nadahi had to cover her in many layers of fur at night to keep the frostbite from claiming her.

And yet, this small girl held the key to her people's survival. The magic in her veins shone as brightly as the winter scape around them. Rose could not control her power, but she would learn to. And the tribes would finally be unified again against the Forsaken.

"Move your left foot forward more," Nadahi told, delicately nudging her foot with her own.

Rose complied and twirled the knife in her hand lazily. "How do you fight in all this fur?" Rose asked.

"You learn young how to carry your weight. Or die as a babe in the frost. The fur is both for warmth and extra protection from a blade. We have none of your metal plates to wear," she said.

Rose shook out her shoulders. "Well, given you're all built like trees, I would expect nothing less," she replied, earning a bit of laughter from the huntress.

"Try to swing your arm up without moving your feet," she taught. Rose did so, and Nadahi pushed her hand down. "Don't let me knock you off balance." She circled Rose, eyeing her stance. It was getting better, but not great. The girl could barely move in her clothing.

Nadahi swung her leg out, slipping under Rose's foot and tripping her. She fell to the ground in an angry fit, snow puffing around her. Nadahi couldn't help but laugh as she could barely get back to her feet.

"Stop laughing. It isn't funny."

"Perhaps we can take a few layers off."

"You wish me to freeze to death!?" she yelled. Nadahi stopped her laughing and looked at Rose who's angry face was mixed with exhaustion.

"What is truly troubling you?" she asked. Rose slumped back down onto the ground, fur nearly completely covering her face.

"I can't help but feel Erling was injured because of me," she mourned, her eyes downcast.

"Why do you think that?"

"Because if I could have used my magic before or learned how to fight, I could have saved his suffering."

Nadahi gave a huffed laugh. "He bears scars that will give him many stories to tell. And he will earn more before this journey is over. It is not as terrible as you may think," she replied. Rose creased her forehead and looked across at the huntress.

"But his eye—"

"He does not care. Now he has something to show the Mother when he enters *Shor'vaker*. He earned those scars by protecting Her daughter from harm and slaying his enemies. All of us bear scars here. And we are all proud of them."

"All of you?"

"Yes, all of us. Hakon bears a scar from his left shoulder blade down to his ass. He got that from fighting a wild boar and protecting careless children of the village. Liv has an abdominal scar due to a difficult labor. Torgir… well, he has many scars. Mainly from drunken fights out in the rain."

Rose laughed. "Yes, I suppose we all do. I just feel like I need to do more. I hate being a bystander."

"Then stop being one," Nadahi shrugged. "Learn how to hold a sword and shield. Learn how to command the flame at will and learn how to have faith in the goddess and yourself."

"That is easier said than done," Rose sighed. "I don't know if I can."

"You can. You killed a man with a simple flick of your wrist last night."

"That was unintentional."

"And yet you still did it. You just need to learn control."

"And how do you expect me to do that?" she asked, with a hint of exasperation in her voice. Nadahi ignored her anger, though.

"There are ways to learn control that our people have taught for generations. You can learn this way." Nadahi pulled Rose back onto her feet and tapped on the ruby around her neck.

"Perhaps you should warm yourself," she suggested.

Rose's eyes widened. "You cannot be serious. I can't produce a flame to save my life."

"And yet you saved mine."

Rose opened her mouth to retort, but quickly shut it. Nadahi looked over at the four around the campfire.

"When I was a child, my father stripped me of my clothing and threw me from the gates. He told me that if I was to be chieftain, I would have to cleanse my soul in the eternal winter. For two days, I stayed outside, hunting with a spear and praying to the Mother Goddess."

"You're lying. No one could survive out here alone. Let alone naked," Rose said.

Nadahi took Rose's knife and sheathed it in her boot. "And yet I did. You must have faith in yourself and in the Mother. You must be cleansed, *Runa*. If you are to lead our people."

Rose stuttered and looked at the camp, then back at the huntress. "You can't make me. I'll freeze to death!" she pleaded.

Nadahi took a step closer. The warmth coming off Rose was nearly hotter than the fire. "Do you trust me?" she asked.

Rose looked away, biting her lip. "I...." she paused, the wind rustling her golden curls. "Yes. I do."

Nadahi gently unclasped the button of Rose's cloak, letting it fall to the snow. She slowly made her way through the layers of fur and leather protecting her soft skin from the harsh colds. Rose stepped from foot to foot as Nadahi continued undressing her. Each layer she revealed left her hands feeling warmer. And Nadahi could not help but trail her eyes down the girl's body when the last of the fur was gone, leaving her in her gown. She looked like a child in stature, yes, but her body did not.

Her breasts were rounded and firm, her nipples peeking out from the cloth from the cold. Her hips were smaller but still held a soft curve. *The Mother is testing me*, Nadahi thought.

Rose was already shivering, covering herself with her hands. Nadahi gathered her clothes and led her to the others.

Liv glanced at the couple as Rose sat down by the fire, her small form curling in on herself.

"The trial? Already? You'll kill the girl," she spoke in their language, shaking her head.

"She needs it. There is no other way."

"Does she need it? Or do you?"

Nadahi gave her a hard glare as the boys finally stopped their tussling and turned to the fire. Nadahi's eyes stayed on Rose as she breathed into her hands. A discomforting guilt ran through her chest. Perhaps this was a mistake. She was not ready. But if she gave the clothes back now, that would be seen as weakness. The *Runa* needed this trial, or the other tribes would not even speak to her. It was a rite of passage, and she knew she could do it. She had seen her kill a man with only her mind. She could take a bit of cold. At least, that is what she told herself.

As the night wore on, the others slept quietly. Nadahi stayed awake, keeping her gaze on Rose. The girl had curled further in on herself, lying on the ground. Her undergown was wet and clung to her skin as she shivered. Her lips were a soft blue, her skin not far off. Her breathing was slowing, and her eyes were closed. Several times Nadahi had to stop herself from coming over and covering her back up. She had to trust the goddess. She would not let her child die tonight.

How had Nadahi felt those nights alone in the wilderness? She was terrified. Terrified of the monsters that roamed the winter, of the Forsaken that killed so many of her tribe. She had no protection but the spear she was given. She had killed a wolf that night and covered herself in the pelts that still adorned her person. She earned her place among the tribe and came back rebirthed from the winter.

But could Rose do the same? A child that seemed forsaken by her mother, who curled in on herself at night. Who hid in combat and still woke screaming, crying another woman's name. Enara. She would not say who it was. She did not ask. The girl who was so frightened of the night that she never strayed far from the confinement of the camp. A girl who could barely hold a sword.

Her guilt got the better of her, and Nadahi stood and walked over to Rose. She bent down and stopped short of touching her, a rush of fear running down her torso. Rose's chest had stopped moving. Nadahi quickly took the *Runa* into her arms. She gripped Rose and brought her cloak around her.

"*Runa!*" she cried. She shook her, to no avail. Her lips were a deep blue, and her eyelashes were still and frozen. Nadahi crawled closer to the fire, nearly letting it touch her.

"Please *Runa*—Rose. Come back. Don't take her," she pleaded. She was wrong. Goddess, she was wrong. She should not have pushed her so far. She thought she was ready, that she could withstand the cold. But it was too much.

She closed her eyes and held Rose close to her chest. She prayed to the goddess to give her warmth. To give her breath.

She heard the howl of a wolf in the air. She rose her head to the side to see a pair of yellow eyes, and in them, she saw a face—a face of a woman that stood in shadows. Nadahi took a breath she didn't know she was holding and looked back down at the girl in her arms. She was still unmoving. The wolf howled again, and Nadahi found herself gripping Rose's cold hand. Another howl and she moved her hand to the flame. It burned her own, and she grimaced, but Rose remained untouched by the heat. It seemed to gather around her like a blanket of orange. It crawled up her arm, and Nadahi quickly released her before her coat caught fire. She let Rose become engulfed by the flames as the wolves' cries filled her ears.

The ruby on her neck pulsed brightly as the fire dissipated into the air, and she gasped for breath. Nadahi crawled to her and pulled her back up into her arms. Rose's skin burned against her own, but she ignored the pain. Green eyes opened to the dark sky as the wolf retreated. A small smile graced her lips.

"I had the oddest dream."

333

"I had the oddest dream."

64 OLIVIA

The sound of laughing woke Olivia from her slumber. With a sudden breath, she rolled over, coughing and gagging. She was bare. The stone was cold on her naked flesh. She looked up to see the faint hints of sunlight through a grate in the ceiling. It was a small circular stone room she was in, the only light coming from the grate. She pressed herself up onto her knees, pushing the hair from her face. She felt... odd. She could feel her heartbeat, but the blood in her veins felt cold. Her breath was chilled, and when she moved, her hands would phase into a dark mist.

Olivia waved her hand across her face and watched as it dissipated, then reappeared. She should have been frightened. Instead, she felt nothing but a dull thrum.

Carefully, she stood up and stepped forward, but her foot turned to smoke, and she fell back down onto the ground. She groaned and rolled over onto her stomach, looking at the sunlight filter through the ceiling and listened to the water drops hitting the floor, occasionally sprinkling her face. Her stomach churned, and she felt she might vomit, but nothing came up when she heaved.

She pushed herself up again and managed to make her way to the wooden door on the other side of the room. Pausing, she put her head to the door, listening to the bickering coming from the other side. She could barely make out the voices, but she thought she recognized a woman's voice. Olivia grabbed the handle, but before she could open the door, it opened on its own.

Olivia jumped back, and a woman entered the room. She looked at Olivia and smiled. Her red eyes glinted in the dim light, as did her ivory hair. She held a pile of black leather in her hands.

"These are for you. I will show you to your quarters when you are dressed," she said and dropped them to the floor. She quietly left the room and closed the door behind her. Olivia carefully bent down and touched the leather, her fingers grazing the smooth hide. She went to grab it, but her hand slid right through in a puff of black. She growled and sat back, rubbing her face. This was not what she was expecting. To be able to just… vanish. It did not feel right. It felt as if her hands turned to air, and her nerves disappeared. Then, as soon as it was gone, they reappeared with feeling. She wanted to feel sadness, grief under her circumstances. But all she felt was crawling anger.

She shot out her hand and grabbed the leather, pulling on the tight pants and vest, and made her way outside the room. The woman stood by the door and motioned for Olivia to follow. The stone was cold against her bare feet as she followed the woman down several dark corridors and past a tavern room. She caught a glimpse of a few others as she passed, all wearing the same clothes as her. The woman stopped at an unmarked door and turned to Olivia. She opened the door and ushered her in.

The room was small. Only a bed, a small cupboard, and a wooden stand fit into it. A mirror was placed on top of the stand.

"This is where you will stay when you are not taking contracts. I assume you know what those are?" she asked.

Olivia nodded. "I've taken a few in my time."

"Good, that will make the transition better." The woman pulled a box from under the bed and set it on top. She opened the latch to unveil two silver swords and a dagger. On the edges of the blades, a language was engraved, but she could not read it. "These are your weapons. You will always have them on you, and you must learn how to handle each one." She took a sword from its sheath and pointed it at Olivia. "You will train with wooden ones until you can handle silver. Then you may join one of the guild members on a mission."

Olivia scoffed. "I know how to use a sword."

"Oh, you know how to phase into a dark room and kill someone in their sleep with it?" she asked. Olivia paused, then shook her head. The woman put the sword back and closed the lid.

"Am I dead?" Olivia asked.

"No," the woman answered, turning back to her. "You are reborn. You are a Nightingale. And you have no home but the one you stand in now."

"Do you have a name?"

"I am called Neph. When you are ready, come to the tavern. The Old Man awaits you there," she said, and with a flicker, was gone. Olivia ran her hands across the smooth leather of her armbands and felt the shift of weight as her hands went through them. She turned to the bed, opening the weapon case, and running a finger across the swords. It almost hurt to touch them, like electricity zapping her. It nearly burned, and when she pulled her hand away, she could see raw flesh on her fingertips. The words on the sword flickered in the candlelight, and she almost heard them whisper to her.

Vel Vahar

She closed the lid and took a breath. She felt as if she almost didn't need to breathe at all and she wondered how long she could go without. Was she even alive anymore?

She turned to the table to peek at what was inside when she stopped at the mirror leaning against the wall. The woman who looked back at her in the reflection was not Olivia. The woman staring back at her had expressionless red eyes and greyed skin. She stepped closer to the mirror, and so did the woman. Olivia ran her fingers through her hair and across her face, and the woman in the mirror did the same. She knelt down, and the realization of her death finally hit her. She had chosen a fate worse than death, she imagined. She was no longer human. No longer the girl she grew up as. She no longer needed to be the Olivia she once knew. She had no one left who knew her as that Olivia. She had a new life and was reborn as a Nightingale.

She took the dagger from its sheath in the case and pulled it up to her face. With precise cuts, locks of brown hair fell to the ground as she stripped herself of the woman who died. She stopped when it was just above her chin. It danced around her face, and red eyes gleamed in approval. She scooped up the fallen pieces of hair and put them on the table in front of the mirror. With surprise, she watched as they burnt away into ash. A formal introduction to her new life, she supposed.

After putting the dagger away, she made her way down the tunnel to the tavern. The flickering of the torches hurt her eyes as she stepped past them and into the shadows they cast along the wall. It was colder than she remembered, and the heat from the torches never seemed to reach her skin. She could hear voices coming from further down the hallway and followed them to the tavern. When she entered, all eyes locked on hers.

There were twelve people tucked into chairs and dark corners of the room. Only the bartender paid her no attention, focusing on cleaning the tankards.

"She arrives," Neph said, leaning back against her chair. "Welcome to our little family."

"She's skinny, don't you think?" A man said across the room, leaning on a wooden pillar. His red eyes were visible through the soft light of the room, and his dark hair was pulled back from them. He ran a hand down the sword he held with an analytical eye. "She couldn't even hold a sword."

"And you are too big to fit into a shadow cast by an elephant, Cronis," Neph snorted.

He stood, broad and imposing, and walked over to her. "Is that so? Why don't you say that again in my ear," he growled. Olivia raised a brow as Neph stood up, kicking her chair back and looking him in the eyes. "I said you're a fat ass."

He brought his sword up, but before he could strike her, a booming voice echoed through the tavern.

"Enough!" the voice yelled, silencing the bickering couple. Olivia turned to the farthest corner of the room, where an older man emerged from the shadows between two torches. His form was large and wide, but his shoulders held a weight that made him bend as he made his way over to the group. He wore a black cloak with a dagger sewn into the back of it. His beard was short and white, the same as his hair. A scar ran down the right of his face that covered his closed eye. The other one was not red but dull gold. He walked with a cane in his hand that was a dark metal and *tinged* against the ground with every step. The grip was shaped into two crows' heads that looked out on either side of the cane. The red jewels in their eyes flickered in the torchlight.

"A new member joins in a century, and all you children do is bicker. At least get her a drink," he told. His voice was raspy but still held a commanding tone.

"Sorry, Old Man. I meant no offense," Cronis apologized, walking over to the bar.

"Of course you meant an offense. Next time, take action instead of whimpering like a mut trapped in a cage," he spat. Neph snorted out a laugh as the old man sat down at a table with a grunt. He motioned for Olivia to sit opposite of him. She complied, and a tankard was brought over for her.

"You are not from these lands, are you, girl?" he asked. Olivia shook her head. The old man sat back in his chair and eyed her warily. "Where are you from?"

"Does it matter?" she snapped.

The old man smirked at her. "I see what emotion you died holding, heh," he laughed. "No. It doesn't matter." He looked around the tavern as the others resumed their activities, and Olivia took a swig of the ale she was given. It was bitter and made her mouth twitch.

"Anything you drink or eat will be like shards of glass in your mouth now. One of the downsides to our curse," the man stated.

Olivia grimaced and put the cup down. "Curse?" she asked.

The man nodded and tapped his cane on the ground. "Yes. We were forged from the first dark prince of Reverand. We were his shadow, his eyes, and ears across Veran. One of the only times the Dark Kingdom still retained some power on this blasted continent. It wasn't until he was assassinated that we turned to the depths of the city. There are other guilds that patrol the higher grounds, but they are nothing but puppets of the new kings. They are many, and we are few. But from the shadows, we see all that transpires from this kingdom to Fira."

"And your contracts?"

"Anyone can pray to us if they wish. Many come to the grand cathedral to summon us, but few ever receive the privilege of our contract. Our names alone bring enough fear to Veran to out pay any price."

"What contracts *do* you take?" she asked.

"Heh, only the ones worth our while. And we kill none other than those contracted, or those who threaten our own."

"Are there more of us?"

The old man looked around at the faces in the room, "Yes, a few are out fulfilling their jobs now. But our numbers have dwindled over the centuries. Neph!"

Neph came as summoned and stood at attention in front of the table. The old man pointed at Olivia and turned his head towards the assassin.

"You will train her well. She knows much, but still too little to take a contract."

Neph nodded, and Olivia stood up at her call. "Come, we will begin." Neph started out of the tavern, and Olivia followed before getting stopped by the Old Man.

"I see many futures in your girl. Some that may lead to contentment. Many will lead to sorrow."

Olivia did not look back at him as she followed Neph out of the tavern.

65 TRISSA

The city was worse than before, Trissa felt. Ignis was not the prosperous city it once was in the hands of Queen Elena. It seemed as if a shadow had crossed over the entire city, painting it in a bleak gray. Even though the sky was clear, and the sun streamed through windows, it did not light the people's faces or bloom the violets growing along the road. Homes were still being rebuilt, and vultures circled overhead. She ignored the presence of the cultists to the best of her ability as she navigated the streets she once knew so well.

She was granted leave by the king of Reverand himself when she asked. And she knew Enara would protest if she went, so she did not tell her. Oh, Enara. The little girl who sat in a library reading books all day and studied in classes without a single grievance spoken. The little girl with a smile that rarely showed but filled Trissa's heart.

She couldn't say what her daughter had become now. She killed her own sister, capsized her kingdom into the maddening waters below, and was now forced into marriage to the dark king himself. She honestly didn't know how they would survive this or if Enara was even still the little girl who would curl up in her lap after a vicious thunderstorm while her mother was away. She hoped a part of that little girl was still there.

Trissa entered the central part of the castle after showing her papers to the guards. They let her pass with simple nods of their heads, and she could have sworn one of them was barely thirteen. As she passed through the halls, she noticed people hauling rocks and cleaning the carpet, wearing chains around their necks. Slaves. It made Trissa want to vomit. In all her years, she had never seen such cruelty as this.

She clutched the letter in her hand that had brought her back here in the first place. It was a simple letter, with barely a couple of sentences written on it in scratchy ink.

Come back to where mothers weep. The queen's blood runs heavy.

The signature belonged to the Arcane Advisor, Enchanter Dravis. Trissa knew he was badly injured in the fighting; she was surprised he had survived for so long. Now he sat in one of the rooms of the infirmary, giving his last breath, surrounded by cultists and slaves.

Trissa descended the east stairs towards the servant's quarters and passed room after room of dying and injured. Some were nobles; some were cultists that she assumed had been caught in revolts of a back alleyway. The healers tended to all of them without judgment, though. She recognized one of the healers as a young girl with hopes of moving to Fira and becoming a doctor when she was old enough. The worn look in her eyes and the blood on her dress made Trissa think she had given up those hopes.

She stepped past one more room before finding the one the enchanter was in. A girl was sitting on his bed, rubbing a damp cloth over a nasty gash on his chest. The wound was nearly black, as if he had been burned, and oozed a putrid green liquid. Trissa knocked on the door, and the woman turned to her. The enchanter opened his eyes and shakily raised a hand at her.

"L... leave me," he whispered. The woman nodded and stood up, placing the rag into a bowl on the bedside table. She gave a small curtsey to Trissa before leaving the room. Trissa closed the door behind her and stepped over to the bed.

Being closer to him, she could see the wound glowing a very faint red. "I... ran out of pre-made elixirs. Anyone... who can make more was killed," he sighed, coughing heavily.

Trissa sat on the bed, and he groaned, adjusting. "I can send a letter to Enara. See if any of the maleficarum in the Dark Kingdom can make you a potion," she said, doubtingly. The wound was festering.

He shook his head slowly. "I won't... last that long, I'm afraid." He coughed again, and she could see puss rise from the darkened skin. "I... needed you to come here... to warn you."

"About what? Your letter did not say," she pushed.

He closed his eyes and took a ragged breath. "I did... everything in my power to protect the princesses from Malum's grip," he started, "But the queen. I could not prepare enough for her. There was nothing we could do."

"What do you mean, Dravis? Prepare for what?"

"She cannot control it… no one can. What she has. What she is. I tried to tell Elena, but she wouldn't listen."

"Dravis, you make little sense. Tell me what is happening!" Trissa pleaded. "Let me protect her."

He shook his head, sweat beading around his eyes. "Go to my quarters. I… I have everything there. It will tell you." His breathing came rapidly, and Trissa came closer to his side.

"Dravis? Dravis tells me what is going to happen. What about Enara!"

"The moons will fall… the rivers will rise. And the serpent awakens. Find her. Find the elf," he mumbled.

"Elf? What elf?"

"My chambers… go to my chambers. You can save us." He coughed violently, and Trissa stood up from the bed. As his breathing grew more and more labored, she fled the room, calling for the nurse. "You will know what must be done," he whispered.

Trissa calmed her increasing heartbeat and took off toward the servant's quarters. She followed the stretching hallways to the enchanter's room and opened the door. Elixir bottles were strewn about, and the smell of burning metal pierced her nose. Papers were thrown about the room, and she bent down to gather them up in her arms. She placed them on the bed and sorted through them. Potion recipes, spells, scribbled notes on Rose's progress. Nothing about Enara. Why? Why Enara? Why was she so important?

She went through drawers and piles of scrolls, finding nothing worth noting. For hours, it seemed she was searching. She felt hidden latches or secret places in the room, combing through diaries and clothes. She turned to the bed with a sigh, looking at the mess she had created. Why couldn't he just tell her? He still had enough breath. Maybe she could go back and demand he say what was happening. Albeit he was probably dead by now.

She took a pillow off the bed and fluffed it, attempting to find a string of peace in the familiar movement. She looked down at the tan bedding and the misplaced mattresses. *Mattresses…*

She quickly turned over the bed, tossing the mattresses onto the floor and flinging pillows away. She pulled the covers off and found a single scroll lying at the base of the bed. She went to her knees and took the scroll, feeling the parchment in her hand. Her hands shook, and she unraveled the scroll, reading the contents within it.

Her heart fell into her stomach as her eyes scanned the page. The words never seemed to end as she read them over and over again. She wanted to cry or hit something or maybe just sit there. He hid this from the world. She couldn't do it. She wouldn't.

Enara would never see this scroll.

She stuffed it in her pocket and stood up. She wiped the tears from her face and composed herself. The scroll was wrong. It had to be. She would make sure of it.

She fled the castle with a steel resolve, the scroll still in her pocket. As she rode in the carriage back to the Dark Kingdom, she prayed to the goddess to give her strength. And to watch over her daughter.

66 JARED

The horse trotted down the old dirt path, lulling the elven girl into a soft slumber, her head resting on the swordsman's chest. Jared kept his gaze fixed forward as the entrance of a village appeared. Jared slowed the horse to a walk as they approached. The settlement was walled off with a wooden fence that was around ten feet tall and hastily constructed. The only thing he could see over it were the two guards standing atop the gate. Their shimmering skin and leather armor pointed them out as elves. The first he had ever met.

"State your purpose," one demanded. Nava stirred awake and mumbled something under her breath before looking up at the guards.

"Just passing through," Jared replied.

"Go around then. No humans allowed."

Jared creased his brow as Nava shifted in the saddle. "Elves. They don't like humans in their villages," she said sleepily.

Jared sighed. "Look, just let us pass, and we'll be on our merry way."

The guards turned their bows to them. "Turn your horse around, or we will be forced to remove you," they growled.

Jared put a hand through his hair. "Damned elves," he cursed.

Nava slid off the saddle and walked towards the gates. "When was your last raid?" she started, "Two-three days ago? You've got to be low on stock. We promise you our swords if you let us pass through."

Jared looked at her quizzingly as the guards turned to each other.

"And what could you do to help us?" Two humans?" they argued.

Nava pulled her hood off. "If it comes to it, you may give me to them. Half-elves are expensive in these parts," she bartered with a cold laugh. The two turned to one another again, and after a moment of frantic talking, the gates opened.

Jared came behind Nava, and she led the horse through the gates.

"You just sold yourself off to a bunch of elves? What kind of negotiation is that?" he mumbled.

Nava looked up at him. "They're scared. It's not uncommon for raiding parties to demand half-elves as payment," she explained. Jared's eyes gazed around at the collapsed houses around them. Several elves helped pull valuables from the fallen buildings as others stood on rooftops, attempting to patch holes. The two stopped and tied their horse up, Nava untying the saddle.

"They just give up their kids to some filth to keep them happy? Why don't they just go back to their city?" Jared asked.

Nava set the saddle down and fixed her hood. "Their city burned down thousands of years ago. And Avlor hasn't the room to accommodate a million elves. Supposing they would even take them. So, they make do with what they can. We have always been targeted by humans." She turned to look at the villagers who were helping wounded rangers into a healer's tent.

"Bloody wrong if you ask me," Jared started, "Preying on those who have done nothin' wrong."

"That's the way the world works. You must live with it," she shrugged.

Jared threw on his bag and shook his head. "You grew up in a place like this?" he asked.

Nava made a sour face and nodded. "Yes. A settlement, not a day's ride from here. It's not there any longer."

Jared bit his tongue and turned when footsteps approached them. An elven woman came up to them with soft chestnut hair and eyes. She wore a silver circlet on her head and had on a thin green dress. She folded her hands together.

"I am matriarch Avira. I was told we had visitors. I was not expecting a human and a half-blood, though," she tutted.

"We are just passing through; once we rest, we will be on our way," Nava said.

The woman eyed her and shook her head. "No. You will rest here for a night and offer us the protection you promised. It is only adequate you do this." Her smile didn't reach her eyes.

Jared looked at Nava. "Well?"

Nava sighed and dropped the saddle to the ground. "So be it."

Jared leisurely made his way around the small walled-off village. The elves who passed him by looked at him with fright, urging the others along quickly. He guessed that any human measured up the same in their eyes. Not that he could blame them.

It was odd seeing a full-blooded elf. They were lithe people, with long hair and skin so pale they seemed to radiate light themselves. Their skin shimmered in the sunlight, and their large eyes reflected like an animal in the shadows. *They are nothing like Nava*, he thought. With her dark hair and soft, brown eyes, the only indication she was part elven at all was her ears with the delicate point. Sometimes, if he caught her at the right moment, her skin would give off the faintest shimmer. He could not find these people attractive; they reminded him too much of the malevolent creatures that roamed the forests. Nava though...*Stop*, he thought.

His eyes caught a reflection of light and he winced and blinked, looking over at the source. An elven merchant had a stall up, bottles and cups laying atop it. He moseyed over to the stall as the merchant was busy with something behind him. He looked at the bottles, attempting to read the writing on them. He knew the smell, though, the sweet smell of alcohol.

The elven man turned and jumped when he spotted Jared. Jared pointed to a bottle. "How much?"

The man cocked his head and eyed the bottle he was pointing to.

"You speak Common, right?" he asked. The elven man nodded. "Then how much for a bottle?"

"...What do you have?" he asked, his accent heavy. It was Jared's turn to be perplexed.

"What do you mean? I have some *sephim* still, but I don' know if I have enough."

The elven man shook his head. "We do not take coin. We trade."

Well shit, Jared thought. He scrounged around in his bag, looking over the items. He pulled a loaf of bread, still uneaten, out and unwrapped it. "Will this work?"

The elven man took the bread and broke it, smelling it. He gave a satisfactory nod and gave him a small bottle of the alcohol. *Eh... close enough*, he thought. He thanked the elf and started on his way, popping the cork.

"Now time to find the half-elf," he hummed.

Jared found Nava sitting along the riverbank on the outskirts of the town. Her eyes were trained ahead, her fingers playing with the grass below her. She turned at his approach, but kept her eyes forward.

"Man, this elven stuff knocks ye' off your ass," Jared started, falling to his knees before taking a swig of his bottle, feeling his chest grow warm.

"The elven brews are made with herbs and roots many mundane would not think to use," Nava responded. The two sat in quiet contentment for a moment, listening to the rhythmic bubbling of the river and the chattering of birds. He grabbed a rounded rock and threw it into the stream. It skipped twice before plopping in.

"I'm guessing you never stayed around your village much," Jared started. "You seem much happier in the forest."

A fraction of a smile rose on her lips. "Yes. I never enjoyed working in the village. I stayed with the hunters when I was a child. Then once I became of age, I hunted on my own." She paused for a moment, looking into the sky. Her gaze followed a starling that flew overheard and into a nearby tree.

"I would bring back bigger game than many of the hunters. Deer, boar, elk. I wanted to prove to them that I was capable of handling myself."

"Did your parents not like that?" Jared asked, taking another swig.

Nava brought her knees to her chest. "My father was a human. He traded goods with our village. When my mother told him she was heavy, he left. It was disgraceful to bare a half-blood. My mother raised me on her own until she died. She never wanted me out in the forest. I think..." Nava paused, seeming to lose herself in her thoughts. "... I think she was scared I would meet a human, too."

Jared let the bottle swing from his fingertips while he looked at the minnows swimming through the water. A smirk rose. "Well, looks like she lost that bet, huh? I'm the worst type of human you could meet," he drunkenly laughed.

Nava shook her head. "You are far from the worst. Trust my judgment on that."

Jared's smirk dropped, and he held out the bottle to her. "I don't like sharing, but..."

Nava put her hand up. "No, I am fine, Swordsman."

Jared shrugged his head and gulped the rest down. "Still calling me that, huh?"

"Until you earn your name, yes."

Jared chortled. "Earn my name? I think I've well earned that. I saved your little ass many times," he teased.

Nava elbowed him. "Earning your name is not easily done. In my culture, we all earn our names."

Jared raised an eyebrow. "And how did you earn yours?"

Nava stood up and shook herself off. "My name is Nava, the huntress." She turned and fled into the forest as Jared watched. With another shrug, he threw the bottle into the river and lay on his back with a heavy sigh. As he watched the clouds, his mind drifted away from him and to thoughts of his missing part.

It had been weeks, and he had yet to hear of Olivia. Surely, she would have passed by one of these villages, but none had seen a young bard. He feared the worst and hoped for the best. The Dark Kingdom would not take what he cherished most. They almost took Nava, and they might have taken Olivia.

Jared looked back into the forest, searching for a green cloak. He wondered to himself. He was fit enough to travel alone now; his wounds were healed. If he left tonight, he could reach Fira in a week's time. He would not stop to rest until he needed to. But the voice in the back of his head stopped him. The woman in the forest needed him as much as he needed her. He couldn't leave her when she had done too much to help him. Olivia would wait for him. He knew she would.

67 THYMAS

Thymas sat on the bed in the room granted to him by the emperor. The room was spacious, with two plush couches and a tea table on the right side of the room. The bed was massive, with white pillows and a golden-trimmed comforter. He thought he could fit nearly the entire court on the bed if he tried, and the space made him uneasy. He could hear footsteps outside, and the setting rays of the sun made him yawn. He pulled his tunic and undershirt off and threw them on the couch. Sitting back down, he put his head in his hands and ran through his hair with a sigh.

He wanted to return home immediately. But without knowledge of how many men the emperor would give, he would leave with nothing but hope and guesses. He would have to wait. And waiting was not something he was good at. With less than a week until the battle, there was no way an army could march to WhiteDrove. The only thing that could be done was a small force through the portal, and that would not be enough. WhiteDrove would fall. He would need to get the townspeople to safety and get them through the portal, but that would mean less time for troops to enter.

He felt less like a king now than ever before. He could do nothing to protect his people and yet they still wished to put a crown on his head. *Damn it all,* he cursed.

He heard a faint knock on the door, and he pulled his hands from his hair. "You may enter," he allowed, putting his arms on his knees. Lada Sara opened the door and gently shut it behind her. He felt his neck heat and quickly realized he was undressed. He stood up and grabbed his shirt, throwing it on.

"My lady, I was not expecting you—I apologize for my immodesty."

She gave him a small smile and a bow. "No, it's all right. I am the one who has come knocking on your door. Though it must not look well in the eyes of the court for a priestess to visit a prince at night…" she paused and looked back towards the door, seeming to contemplate if she should have even come. And he hated to admit he didn't want her to leave.

"Who cares about the court? All they do is gossip anyways," he said with a laugh and looked over at her. Her dark hair glowed like fire in the dimming light, and her eyes reflected the brightening stars. He couldn't help himself; she was beautiful.

"I… came to see how you were doing. You were very distressed after you read the letter." She slowly stepped further into the room, and he sat back down on the bed.

"I left my mother and sister to come here to ask for aid from the emperor. Now I know that I will not receive the aid I had hoped for," he said. She came over to the bed and sat down beside him. She was far enough away that there was space between them, but if he wanted to, he could extend his hand and touch hers.

"You fear for them?" she asked.

"Of course, I do. I am to be king, and yet I cannot save my kingdom. It is maddening."

"The fact that you are here is proof enough that you will be a good king. You are trying to protect your kingdom. And you will fight alongside your men. Most cannot say the same," she told.

He gave a small laugh and put his head down, staring at the carpeted floor. "You have more faith in me than I of myself, Lady Sara."

"I can see it in your aura."

"My aura?" Thymas asked, turning his head to her.

"Yes. Magic is not just a conjuration or manifestation. It is alive and breathing, like the plants in the garden or the squirrels in the trees. It courses through each of us from our first breath of life to our last, even if we cannot wield it ourselves. Each of us carries an aura if you know how to see it. Yours is blue."

"Is that good?"

Sara laughed, a light laugh, like the twinkling of bells. "Yes. Blue means serenity. It means a calm sunny day in summer, but it can also be dark and stormy, like a thunderous night. It can be protective or destroy without warning. But it always comes back to its proper hue."

"And what is yours?" he asked with a smile.

"I do not know. I cannot see my own aura as much as I wish I could."

"That seems unfair," Thymas said. "Being able to read others without truly knowing yourself."

"I think that, in a way, none of us knows who we truly are until we are put into the position to find out."

Thymas face fell slightly. "And if that time comes sooner than you wish?"

"Then you face it with will and strength." She moved her hand closer to his own, and he desperately wanted to reach out and hold it, but he restrained himself. "Do you know when you will leave?"

"As soon as I know how many men the emperor will send," he answered with a sigh.

"I wish to go with you."

Thymas put his head up, looking toward her. A rolling ball of fear traveled up his throat. "It is not safe for you. You should stay here in the capital."

"I am a healer. I cannot do my part if I am away from the men who need me the most," she pushed. The look in her eyes made him melt. He knew he could not say no to her. He wanted her to stay with him tonight. Tomorrow. Through the battle.

"I cannot change your mind, can I?" he asked.

She smiled and shook her head. "No, you cannot."

"Then I suppose I am at your mercy." He moved his hand only slightly, his fingers reaching out to touch her own. His eyes did not move, but he felt her fingers entwine with his own, warm and strong.

How could this woman appear and cause such a change in him in only a matter of a day? She saw into him, stirring up his every emotion, and her heat melted the chill from his bones. The goddess had to have sent her to him. He prayed, and she responded. That was the only logical answer. She was a blessing, an omen of fortune that he would be mindless to ignore.

He looked over at her, and she looked down at their hands. He wanted to move closer, use his fingers to explore every covered inch of her. To run through her hair, to feel her neck, to touch her lips. But before he could do anything brash, another knock came at the door, and he stood up.

"It appears I am popular tonight," he laughed softly, pulling his hand from hers. He opened the door, and a messenger awaited on the other side. His face immediately fell when he bowed to the prince.

"The emperor gives his utmost apology, Your Grace. But he can only spare two hundred men and eleven enchanters to enter the portal, along with some carts of weapons."

Thymas nearly keeled over then and there. "Two hundred? That is all he can spare?" he asked harshly.

The messenger bowed again. "Without the full support of the council, the emperor's hands are tied, Your Grace. You will receive two hundred of the best-trained soldiers of the Imperial army. And the enchanters are senior and masters in the defensive arts."

Thymas took a long breath. "Fine, thank you."

The servant bowed once again and fled the chambers. Thymas closed the door and leaned on it, groaning. "We already have the best they can offer being slaughtered on their way to WhiteDrove. What good will two hundred more do?" he asked angrily.

Sara stood up and walked over to him, gently placing a hand on his shoulder. "Two hundred men is still more than none. We will take this with gratitude and protect WhiteDrove to the best of our ability. We can win."

He looked down into her eyes and sighed. "You are right. We will depart in the morning." He opened the door for her and noticed her hesitation to step out. Perhaps she did feel the same way as he.

She bit her lip and looked at him to the door. "I... hope you have a good night's sleep, Lord Dicesare."

"And you as well," he whispered. She bowed her head and stepped from the room. With one last glance in his direction, she fled, and he was left alone in the shadows of the night that now crept through the windows.

68 OLIVIA

The wooden sword smacked against Olivia's face as she fell hard against the floor. The pounding of her skull was only drummed out by the heavy gasps of air coming from her mouth.

"Again, Olivia," Neph said, circling around her. Olivia pushed herself up onto her feet and took hold of her sword. Moving it between her hands, she watched as Neph snaked around her.

"Use the sword as not just an extension of your arm, but as a tool. Use it as an advantage. Phase without dropping the sword," she ordered. Olivia gripped the sword and focused, letting herself fall into darkness. She watched her hands bled black as she lost grip of the sword. It fell to the ground, and Neph kicked it away.

"If you cannot learn to phase with your weapon, you will be killed. Do not rely on this to help you. Without shadows, you will burn." Neph lunged, her sword cracking against the ground as Olivia dodged. Neph phased, disappearing into the darkness of the training room. Olivia scanned the room and slowly inched towards her sword.

A boot caught her foot, and she tumbled to the ground. She barely dodged the sword again and grabbed hold of her own. Neph grabbed Olivia by the hair, pulling her down with a cry.

"No one will show you mercy. Phase!" she yelled. She brought her foot down as Olivia tried to move the shadows to her will. Unable, she received a boot to the abdomen, pushing the air from her. Neph dropped her and let Olivia catch her breath. "You are not focused."

"You are constantly hitting me. Of course, I am not focused!" she yelled.

Neph let her sword dangle at her fingertips. "Anger."

"What?"

"Anger. That is the emotion you died holding onto," she said.

Olivia got to her knees, putting her hands on them with a breath. "What does that mean?"

"When we take the poison and are reborn, the last emotion you hold on to is often the one you feel the strongest. You lash out without ration. You held much hatred in your heart when you chose the shadows."

Olivia looked down at the ground, watching the way the shadows twisted against the firelight. "There are many names I wish to erase from my memory. Faces that I want to see covered in blood."

"Do not let it consume you. The emotions we feel can be worse than the blight. It can tear through you like a parasite and never let go until all of you is consumed. You will only hurt yourself if you do not learn control."

"That is why you are teaching me, right? To learn how to kill?"

"We take contracts. We do not take the life of those without. It is against the code," Neph answered, twirling her sword.

"Then what is the point of having these abilities if we are bound by how to use them?" Oliva asked, finally pulling herself onto her feet.

"They are a curse as much as a gift. The gods decide who is worthy of life and death. The contracts are given to us to fulfill the wishes of the gods."

"And when those contracts run out?"

Neph gave her a twisted smile and stepped past her. "We are done for today," she said, ignoring the last question.

"Again, I want to go again," Olivia pushed.

"If you still wish to train, meditate next to your bed. Learn to phase yourself, then work on your sword. Once you can master the shadows, you will be ready to take the contract," she said. "It will take time. But you will learn to master your emotions and the shadows at once."

The women stepped from the training room and down the tunnel. Olivia searched Neph's face, trying to put a number to her appearance. "How long did it take you?"

"A while. I do not remember how many years."

"How long have you been a Nightingale?"

Neph gave her a side-eye as she turned a corner. "Fourteen, possibly fifteen years. You begin to lose count after a while."

"Do you age?"

"Yes. Slowly. No one has lived long enough to know for sure how long our life span is. The Old Man is centuries old at this point."

Olivia turned her gaze to the ground. She could outlive any human, maybe outlive an elf. She could overturn dynasties and live to see new ones rise. It was hard to determine her feelings on the matter. If she had any.

"We are here," Neph said, unlocking a wooden door with a silver key. She held the door open for Olivia and closed it behind them. The room was small and circular. Words were carved into the walls in a language foreign to her.

"What is this place?" she asked.

Neph stepped in front of her and into the middle of the room, where a small light shone down from above. "This is our place of meditation. Every full moon, this room will be fully lit. It will be your next trial once you learn to phase. If you find the shadows within the cracks of light, you will be able to take your first contract."

"And the writing on the walls?"

"It is a prophecy we have carried through this guild for generations."

Olivia walked towards the rounded walls and slid her hand down the carved letters. "What does it say?"

"The dark prince will cast light unto shadow," Neph read.

Olivia turned towards her. "Dark prince?"

Neph shrugged. "Some say King Aldrian will be the one to defeat the Dark Knights. I do not believe it."

"Why?"

"Because behind him lies the viper. And no sane man would take a step closer to it without fear of getting bit."

"Do we fear the viper as well?" Olivia asked.

Neph smirked and lifted her head. "A bird of prey has no fear for the viper which it feasts on."

Olivia shared the smile and nodded. "Then perhaps it's time to cut off its head."

69 ENARA

A knock came at the chamber door to Enara's room in the early morning hours. Daealla had just helped Enara dress before the knock came. Biscuits and jam still sat uneaten on the table beside them as she finished braiding her hair.

"Come in," Enara invited. She was surprised to see the king stroll into the room and, with a polite bow, stood at a fair distance away. Enara gave him a cursory glance before looking out at the shining sun through the windows.

She had not seen him since after the argument about WhiteDrove. She wondered if he still held resentment towards her for it. When he did not make a move to enter further into her private space, she waved Daealla away.

"Could you give us a minute, Daealla?" Enara asked. The maid smiled and curtsied before leaving the room, shutting the door behind her. Once she was gone, the king finally stepped over to the table and poured a glass of wine.

"I am happy you enjoy her company," he said fondly.

"Yes, she and the rest of the girls have been nothing but kind to me," she replied.

"And the mare? Do you enjoy her as well?"

"Yes," she agreed. "You have spoiled me."

He gave a small laugh. "I can stop if you wish?"

"I never said I didn't enjoy it," she smiled. From the soft smile to the way he lazily drank his wine, she inferred he did not, in fact, hold a grudge against her. That alleviated some of her anxiety.

"Good," he started, "I thought today you would like to tour the city with me?"

She felt her stomach constrict at the thought of being out in the city. She knew none of it. Heard the stories…but she also remembered the way the people looked at her when she arrived. Unbridled joy. If only Trissa were here to help her through.

"You don't have to say yes, Lady GoldThorn—"

"No, no," she interrupted, "I'll go—I would love to go."

She stood up, and he set the wineglass down, taking her arm in his. She felt her cheeks flush at his touch and cleared her throat. *Cage your thoughts, Enara,* she told herself. *Even if he is to be your husband, he is not to be trusted.*

They made their way down the castle steps towards the main entrance, and she caught a glimpse of the Shrouds hidden in the dark corners of the vestibule. She wanted to bring it up to Aldrian but couldn't find the words to speak.

The guards opened the castle doors for them, and they stepped out into the sunlight. She blinked to adjust her eyes, and they strolled the path toward the town. The buildings were not as composed as the ones in Ignis; she could tell that some of even the finer ones were built from recycled wood and clay. Some needed repairs and the people walking atop the roofs tried their best to patch the holes.

"Due to our location, we do not have many resources at our disposal. The Mors around us do not provide stable enough wood to keep the houses steady for more than a few years. But we make do," he told her.

"That is a shame," Enara frowned. No one should have to worry about their houses collapsing in on themselves.

"With Auratus' support, though, we can begin logging the forests around the city and rebuilding what is needed. With your permission, of course," he said with a squeeze of her hand. She opened her mouth but closed it again after seeing more of the buildings in need of repair.

"I don't see why not. However, I would prefer it if we did not stray too far toward the villages along the Golden Hills. If we begin cutting down the trees, it will scare away the game; they need to trade and eat."

Aldrian nodded his head in agreement. "A wise sentiment, my lady. We can begin here soon. Both of our kingdoms can flourish under our order. All of Veran will see our unity and strength to rebuild."

Enara gazed down at the road as they walked, thinking back to how many houses needed to be rebuilt and salvaged from the attack. "You will divert some of the timber to Ignis, of course," she pushed.

He did not waver from her tone. "Of course. You are the queen of my kingdom, as I am the king of yours. I will not let one suffer while the other prospers."

Damn him... she thought. He was good at making himself seem righteous. Maybe he was.

As they passed through the streets, several people ran up to them and were stopped by cultists and pushed back. Others simply dropped to their knees in reverence. She smiled unsteadily at them. She was used to the decorum the people had around her. But the way they simply worshipped the ground she stepped on made her uncomfortable. She was not a god. She was just a woman who made a few bad choices.

The king took her around the main square of the market, where vendors sold food and clothes. She came over to a stall selling wine. He saw her and dropped to his knees.

"Your Grace! You grace us with your presence. I have heard much of your beauty!" he cheered.

"Thank you, sir. May I see your collection of wine?" she asked politely. He quickly stood up and turned to his cart of casks.

"Yes, yes! Let's see here. We have the sweet reds of Rosus...soft white of the winter grapes...oh!" He pulled a cask from the top and set it on the ground. He gleamed up at them as he opened it and poured three glasses.

"This is the green wine of the Dracon. Famous for its fire-like taste. In the Common Tongue, it is called the Green Flame." He handed them the cups, taking a drink himself first—to prove it was not poisoned—she guessed. She swirled the green liquid in her cup and smelled it. It smelled nearly like paprika and chili. The king nudged her, and she smiled. Together they drank, and fire filled her mouth. She coughed and dropped the cup, waving her hand in front of her face. Her tongue and throat burned as it went down, and the king laughed at her.

"I suppose it is not for everyone."

"How can anyone drink that?" she coughed.

"The Dracon apparently. The dragon people are quite the race."

"If they can drink that with a straight face, I shudder at their composure," she laughed.

Aldrian turned to the wine merchant. "I will take the cask. Thank you."

She slapped his arm, and he pulled her away as a servant took the cask back to the castle. They began strolling along the street again, and she gladly took a glass of water from a servant.

"Despite what the other kingdoms think, we are not savages," Aldrian said, pointing to an artisan painting a portrait of the castle. Two young children surrounded him, watching in awe. "They even know how to smile."

Enara responded with an eye roll as they circled around the square. She stopped by a few booths that offered her anything she would like. They had hand-painted shells, wood-carved animals, and magnificent accessories. She denied many of the items except for a silver brooch. It was a simple yet delicate floral design. It had a small rose quartz stone in the center of the flower. She thought Trissa might enjoy it when she returned.

"Down that street leads to one of the main cathedrals of the city," Aldrian said.

"Can we visit it?" she asked.

His grip on her tightened. "I wish to soon. Unfortunately, there are guilds that reside there that do not welcome us. We are attempting to… negotiate with them. I want you to be able to see it."

"Oh," Enara sighed. "I hope I will get the chance to."

He pulled her away from the street up a pathway towards a large garden. When they entered it, they passed under a beautifully carved hedge, and she doted on all the sculptures. Some looked like people, others like animals. Some were so abstract she couldn't figure out what they were.

"I don't think I've ever seen hedges this way," she said, amazed. Aldrian stood prouder at her statement.

"Every year, we have a contest of artists to see who can sculpt the perfect hedge. It can be quite amusing." They passed a hedge of a woman and a child, a deer, and a massive dragon.

"My parents created these gardens before they fled. It's one of the last pieces I have of them," he said with a long sigh.

Enara looked at him and his saddened expression. "Why did they leave?" she asked.

"They wanted nothing more to do with the Dark Kingdom or the Knights. So, they took my younger brother and fled, leaving me to rule."

"They left you. Why?"

He shrugged his shoulders with a sigh. "I suppose they thought a member of the family line could still save this kingdom. Or they simply didn't care enough."

"That is cruel. What happened to them? Do you know?"

He looked away from her and at the gardener shearing the bushes beside them. "Last I heard, they were all killed, and their bodies burned. I am the last of my line."

"I am sorry to hear that," she said sadly. She felt pity for him. The look in his eye was the same one that stared at her in the mirror. They were both the last of their Houses.

They passed a beautifully sculpted hedge, and she paused, staring at it. It was of a woman. She looked down at her with a soft expression. Her hair hung down her face, and her dress was draped around her legs. Her hands were folded on her lap. It reminded her of her mother.

"It is a sculpture of you," Aldrian said. "I asked our best artists to make a hedge of you straight from how I described you the first time we met. I hope you enjoy it."

Enara stared into the face. She could see the high cheekbones and the soft look in her eyes. "Yes, it is indeed beautiful," she breathed. She turned her gaze back to him and his smile. He motioned forwards.

"I have set up a table in the center of the garden for our lunch today. I overheard the cooks speaking of sweet cakes. Shall we go see?"

Enara laughed. "Only if they have jam."

The two sat at a glass table in the middle of the garden. It held plates of small cakes and a cheese spread along with some wine. The king pulled out her seat for her, and she gratefully sat down. He sat opposite of her and plucked a cube of cheese from the board and into his mouth. A servant poured a glass of wine for her, and she thanked him before he disappeared behind a shrub.

"Have you enjoyed the city so far?" he asked.

Enara took a sip of her wine and nodded. "Yes, it will need some repairs, but I am sure we can get up looking fine within a few years. Ignis, though..."

"Will look better than it has been. I am sure. Once the fires are put out, and the homes are rebuilt, it will once again become a market for trade and goods," he said.

Enara eyed him. "Who will trade with us?"

"Once we take the ports, we will have access to the seas and countries beyond it. We won't need to rely on Fira for gold or supplies."

"Rosus is the only port aside from Fira with a steady flow of commerce. Not WhiteDrove," she argued.

"We are looking into it, Enara. Your kingdom will not fall under while I am alive," he assured, taking a drink of his wine.

Enara took a cake from the stand and set it on her plate. "Shall I ask what you mean by that?"

"Not until the final steps are in place. It's all hearsay at the moment."

"That does not calm my nerves."

The king laughed and ran a hand through his hair. "You think too much about the future and not enough about the present. Right now, both our kingdoms are well taken care of."

"How can I take you at your word? I have not seen Ignis in weeks to know how it is faring," she argued, fingering the cake.

"Your nanny—Trissa—she traveled back to Ignis, did she not? You can ask her how the city fairs when she returns," he shrugged.

Enara bit into the cake and took a sip of wine to wash it down. "I wish she would have told me she was leaving."

"I think she did not want you to worry about her while she was away."

"Did she ask you permission to leave?" she asked.

"She did. And I gave her permission and an armed escort."

Enara sat back in her seat and ran the rim of the glass across her lips. "An armed escort?"

"Yes."

"So she will be alright?"

"I assure you."

Enara took a breath and nodded her head. "All right. But I will count the days till she returns."

"You care for her deeply, and she, you. How close are you to her?" he asked and grabbed a pitcher of water, pouring himself a small glass.

"She was practically my mother whenever Mother was away. Or perhaps more. She was constantly with Rose—both of them were. But when the thunder would get too loud, or I would get overwhelmed, she was there to comfort me. And then when my mother died...she was all I had left to fill that void."

Aldrian nodded, taking a sip of his water and setting it back down on the table. "I heard of Queen Elena before she passed. Bright woman. Held many secrets to her chest."

"And how do you know that? Did Malum tell you?" she asked.

He looked at her and then towards the sky. "When I lost my mother, I felt as if the whole world collapsed around me. I had no one to care for me but my uncle, who set me atop the throne and pleaded to the gods to keep me safe. Every day I still mourn their deaths, but I realize that all things happen for a reason. Whether that be destiny pushing us to our fates or the will of the gods, I cannot say."

"You believe destiny wanted your family to die?" she asked.

"I believe that there was a purpose for their flight and a reason for their deaths. I cannot see it yet, but the gods have put me in a position to take back what was stolen from us. And I plan to use that opportunity to the best of my ability, as the same for you."

"To bring peace to the six kingdoms?" she asked.

"Yes," he smiled. "To bring peace to us all."

70 JARED

The half-elf exited the forest with two rabbits and a squirrel strung over her shoulder. She caught the eye of the swordsman, who gave a curt wave and stumbled up onto his feet before her. "Please tell me you are not still drunk."

He held up his hand in dismissal. "Only a little; I'll be fine."

Nava shook her head and handed him the animals before setting off toward the village.

"You think they will trade us anything good?" he asked.

"Perhaps some leather or medicine. Are your wounds healed?"

Jared pulled up his shirt showing the nice scar left there by the Knight. With a proud drunken smile, he said, "Hey, now we might match."

"No."

"Milady, you wound me."

"Stop talking."

The banter continued through the village as the couple traded their meat for supplies and helped clean up the streets as they went. Jared helped pick up some rubble and set it onto piles. Nava helped corral children back into school while the walls were being repaired. They ended up getting a small number of herbs for medicine and bandages, along with some jerky and arrows. They rested for the evening in the tavern, and Nava counted their trade out quietly while Jared focused on sobriety.

"Only a week to Fira. Never thought I could miss the stench of the city," he said with a sigh.

"Cities never impressed me. Too many people."

"Guess it can seem like that to someone who grew up with this," he shrugged.

Nava looked up from her counting, and Jared bit his tongue before sliding his thumb down his tea mug. "Shit's gross. Nothin' like the tea in Ignis."

"Your tea is called ale," Nava responded, earning a chuckle from the swordsman.

"Yes. Guess yer right."

Jared looked up at the tavern door as it opened to see the matriarch step in. She searched the room before landing on the couple. Jared pulled himself up to a proper position as she stopped at their table. Her face was grim.

"Can I help you?" he asked.

The matriarch set a letter on the table in front of them. Nava picked it up and skimmed through the writing, her face turning pale.

"What's wrong?" Jared asked.

"They will come again tonight. You promised you would help. Keep your promise," the matriarch said. She turned from the table and left the tavern as Nava still held on to the letter. She was holding the paper so tightly that her knuckles turned white. He had never seen her so shaken, her eyes never leaving the letter.

"Nava, C'mon," he guided, gently pulling her fingers from the paper. She dropped it onto the table and stood up violently.

"I need a moment," she whispered and fled the tavern. Jared stood to follow her but stopped short. He picked up the crinkled letter to read it himself.

You have till nightfall to gift us twenty bushels of grain and two carts full of game. If you do not provide this, we will burn your village to the ground.

Charming people, Jared thought. The letter itself was nothing extraordinary. The thing that did catch his eye, however, was the stamp of a coiled serpent at the bottom. The same one that was seared into the flesh of the half-elf he rode with.

The village was eerily quiet; the only noise came from the flickering flames of torches on the protective walls of the village. Jared stood beside two guards atop the walls, Nava standing further to the left of him. Even in the dark, he could see the trembling of her fingers on the string of her bow. There were few protectors of the village. The rest had been killed or hauled off by the bandits. Jared did not favor their odds tonight.

Part of him felt as if he was back in the forge, watching the bandits murder his father and set fire to their home. That would not happen again.

The sounds of horses filled the air as three men rode up to the gates of the village. From the weapons on their backs to their matted hair and worn horses, they had to be the bandits. The one in the middle spoke first, with a long scar running up his cheek.

"You received my kind letter," he started. "Now do us a favor and bring it here."

"Not going to happen," Jared responded.

The scarred man looked at him with a dirty glare. "Did I ask for your fuckin' mouth?" he yelled. "Bring me the supplies now!"

Jared felt a guard shift beside him and gave him a kick in the shin before turning his attention back towards the men. "Leave now. I won't ask again."

The scarred man laughed and spat on the ground. "Hidin' behind a human now, eh? Do you think he can save ya? I'm going to enjoy cutting that tongue of yours out, little boy. Let's go."

The horses turned away and started back out of view, and Jared let out a breath he didn't realize he was holding.

"That can't be it," Nava whispered.

"Maybe they were just pussies after all," Jared laughed. "Now let's get—"

An arrow lodged in the face of the guard beside him, spitting blood over his shoulder and dropping to the ground below them.

"Cover!" Jared yelled, falling to his knees as another arrow lodged into the wall below. Nava fell to the ground and notched an arrow.

"You jinxed it, didn't you?" she asked. Jared gave a shrug, and she straightened herself, aiming and loosing an arrow. Jared heard the meaty thud as it found its target.

"We still have the high ground," Jared said, looking to the other guards around them.

"We don't have a clear line of sight. They will pick us off."

"Then let's not give them a chance," Jared said. He jumped from the wall and ran towards the gate.

"What do you think you're doing?' Nava called.

"Something stupid!" Jared replied. Elves fled into their homes as a fire arrow lodged in a building near him, setting it ablaze. He stopped at the gate and hauled the bar off, kicking the door open. Nava landed beside him.

"You're going to get us all killed!" she hissed.

"Eh, we will see."

He pulled his sword and waited, feeling the hoofbeats grow nearer. Nava raised her bow, pulling the string back.

"Let's do this, you shits," Jared growled. Barely out of the firelight, Nava caught movement and loosed an arrow, sending it into the rider. He gasped and fell to the ground while the horse bucked and ran past. Another elven guard fell to the ground dead as more arrows caught fire around them. Two horses raced towards them as Nava sent another arrow. A rider swung at Jared, who jumped out of the way. He slashed the leg of the horse, and it squealed and fell to the ground. The bandit sprung up and unsheathed his sword—the same one who called him out at the gates.

"You think you're special, boy?" he asked.

"And I'm the one who likes to talk?' Jared retorted. The man snarled and lunged at Jared, who side-stepped and swung his sword. The bandit parried his shot and whipped around. Jared brought his sword up to block and twisted it to the left. He grazed the bandit's hand, and he stumbled back before coming around again for another blow.

Nava took off in a separate direction as he dodged another strike. Jared parried a blow from the scarred man and slashed him across the shin with a spin. The man cried in anger and stumbled back.

"You think this will end with me? I'll make sure this village burns to the fuckin' ground!" he yelled.

"It won't be tonight, bud," Jared responded and lunged toward the man. His wounded shin made him slower to parry blows, and Jared managed to grab his shirt and throw him to the ground. The man spat dirt from his mouth and glared at the swordsman.

"Bloody bastard."

"Shut up already," Jared groaned, slicing into the man's chest. His gargled cursing was swiftly stopped, and Jared sighed before moving further into the village, readying his word for more blood.

71 NAVA

Nava loosed another arrow into the bandits drawing near. The fire in her lungs burned against the smoke. She turned towards Jared but could do nothing to help for fear of hurting him instead. She barely missed an arrow to her side and watched as another guard fell to the men. Villagers ran past screaming as bandits grabbed them and slit their throats, hauling some off from the village. Some of the men grabbed girls, flinging them to the ground and ripping off their dresses, laughing. She heard the scream of the matriarch and ran towards the sound.

The matriarch howled in pain as a bandit swung her to the ground.

"This is what you get, bitch!" he yelled. Nava skidded to a halt and fired an arrow. It sliced his cheek, and he turned towards Nava, fire in his eyes. "I'll deal with you later," he growled at the matriarch.

He sprinted towards Nava, who quickly pulled another arrow from her quiver. Before she could shoot it, he brought his sword down, slicing it into her hand. She cried out and dropped her bow. He swung again, and the tip ripped her shirt and cloak. She fell to the ground and rolled, dodging another blow. She reached for her bow and flipped around, parrying the sword with the thick wood. She ripped the sword still lodged in her bow from his hands and brought her leg up, kicking him in the groin. He screamed and fell to a knee, and Nava stood up, pulling a knife from her boot.

Nava rolled her sore shoulder, and the bandit's eyes lit up. "You... you were Havan's girl, weren't you?" he laughed.

Nava froze, the brand burning against her skin. The bandit spit at her feet. "You're still his. You will always be his little girl. You can't run from us."

Nava's face contorted, and she brought her hand down hard across his face. "You know nothing," she snarled.

The man laughed, wiping the blood from his nose. "Then kill me, you cunt," he spat. "Or are you weak, like your pathetic mother?"

Burning anger blew through Nava's veins as she grabbed the man's head and dug her dagger into his neck. She hated the feeling of enjoyment watching his body spasm against her hand. She only pulled away when her hand slipped from the blood-coated handle. She watched his body slump to the ground and turned away from the stunned matriarch, finding some place away from the smoke.

She sat down at the river, holding her bloody hand, and watched as elves pulled buckets of water for the fires. She heard the muddy footsteps of the swordsman come up beside her.

He touched her hand, and she flinched and pulled back. "I'm sorry—are you alright?" he asked. Nava turned her gaze from him, shaking her head. "Do...you want to talk about it?"

She didn't respond, and he sighed. She didn't want to look at him, didn't want to look at anyone. The bandit's laughter still rang in her ears.

He pulled a handkerchief from his pocket and gently took her hand again. She didn't resist as he pulled it over to his lap to wipe it off. Her fingers shook as he gently wiped away the blood, rubbing his fingers along her own. Most of the blood wasn't hers, he would come to realize. He wrapped her hand in the handkerchief, and it slowed its shaking.

"I'm sorry," she whispered. Her hair fell around her face, and she sniffed.

"Don't be. We saved them. That's all that matters," he replied. She sniffed again and nodded. The swordsman clasped his hand around her own, his warmth spreading up her arm. She let herself lean against him, hearing his rhythmic breathing.

Beyond the pain felt that night, a veil of comfort found its way around them. They said nothing else as the moons rose in the night sky.

72 LAERDYA

Laerdya neared the bakery she had once visited; three guards were close behind her. One of the guards, Rhangyl, froze when they neared. She turned to him, to his newly polished armor and braided hair with a playful smile.

"I'll be back. Stay put," she ordered.

"Princess, are you sure?" Rhangyl asked, eyeing her. She could see his uneasiness in the way he clasped his hand around the hilt of his sword.

"Yes, I am sure. I'll be but a moment." She turned and bounced into the bakery. When she entered, a woman popped up from behind a doorway.

"I'll be with ye soon as I can!" she shouted. Laerdya patiently waited, running her fingers across the countertops and spying on the sweet little pastries on top of them. She hated to admit that she enjoyed the sweet treats made for her in the castle. The queen had scorned her before on her sweet tooth. Told her she would grow fat if she ate too many.

Soon the woman came from behind the door and wiped her hands on her apron. "How may I—oh princess!" she exclaimed, quickly bowing low. "I did not know of your arrival today."

Laerdya gave a blithe laugh, then pulled a purse from her belt. "I heard your shop was robbed of its belongings a few nights ago. I wish to give you this as compensation," she said, setting it on the counter.

The woman looked shocked. "I-milady, I cannot accept this. It was not you who broke into my shop," she stammered.

"But someone now under my service. Please, let me help," she insisted.

The woman looked at the purse and bit her lip. "Well, I suppose I cannot deny an offer from our future queen," she said and took the purse gratefully. She set it aside and grabbed a large bowl from under the counter. Laerdya perked up and toed over to her.

"What are you baking?" she asked. The woman glanced over at the princess, a knowing smirk running across her face.

"I was going to finish the pie for my daughter's wedding tomorrow. It is nearly done. I am simply garnishing it."

Laerdya rubbed her hands together. "May I help? I've never baked before."

"Of course, princess. Here, you may help me add the fruit." She went into the back and returned with a bowl of different fruits. "Cut these up for me, and then we will decorate the pie," she hummed, handing Laerdya a small knife.

Precariously, Laerdya cut the fruit into small sections, and the shopkeeper brought the pie out. It was small but beautifully baked. Laerdya handed her pieces of the fruit as she carefully decorated the pie. With delicate fingers, the pie was covered in swirls of fruit and garnished with a sweet dressing. Laerdya was amazed at the decorum of the pie, bouncing slightly on her heels.

"There, hopefully, my daughter shall appreciate this. I spent four nights on it," the shopkeeper smiled to herself.

Laerdya spoke carefully. "Would you bake the pie for my wedding with the prince? I will make sure you are paid well," she asked.

The woman was silent for a moment, only staring down at the pie, then back at Laerdya. "Milady? Are you sure?" she asked.

Laerdya nodded. "Yes, I will give you any ingredients you may require."

The shopkeeper nodded and bowed again. "It would be an honor to bake for you, milady," she said gleefully.

Laerdya cocked her head slightly. "And perhaps I could take a few goods back to the castle with me...?" she hinted.

The shopkeeper laughed and said, "I'm sure we can work something out."

Laerdya bounced through the castle, small tea cake in hand. She had spent hours with the baker as she taught her how to mix and knead and prep the stone ovens. In the end, she created two small but edible little cakes. She had topped them with whipped cream and a small cherry. The baker was very pleased with her work and even invited her back to bake whenever she wanted. She would go every day if she had the chance.

She carried one cake towards the queen's chambers and knocked softly. Rhangyl stopped behind her, and she put her ear to the door.

"Do you hear anyone?" she asked.

"I do not believe so, princess," he responded. She puffed out her cheeks and jiggled the doorknob, finding it unlocked.

"I'm sure she won't mind me leaving it in her room then," she sang. He stayed outside the door and watched as she entered and placed the cake delicately on top of the vanity in her room. She heard a whispered laugh come from the ceiling, and she smiled back.

"There we go. Now time to find Elmaer." She padded off to her own room, and he followed behind. "I am not sure if he likes cherries, he never said. But he did treat me well at the ball; perhaps he will be in a better mood today as well," she hummed. She kept the cake steady in her hands as she bounced through the halls and towards the room they shared. She knocked on the door and heard a disgruntled reply.

"What is it?" the prince asked.

"It's just me," she said and toed open the door. Rhangyl stayed outside of the room as she entered and found Elmaer sitting on his bed, angrily looking at a scroll.

"I will never understand these damned slaves. We give them bedding, and we give them food. And they are still not happy," he fussed.

Laerdya paused and bounced on her toes. "What do they ask for?"

"More living quarters—*better* living quarters. It's ridiculous. They are *slaves;* they can make no demands of me."

"Of course not..." Laerdya paused. "It couldn't hurt, though. They do a lot around the castle. Without them, this city would not be half as nice."

"Don't speak as if they are our equals!" he snapped. "They are slaves and are to be treated as such. You should have enslaved that damned elf when you had the chance. Now you *mingle* with them."

"Elmaer, I made you something," she exclaimed, diverting away from their current conversation. She held the cake out to him, and he looked down at it.

"What is it?"

"It is… a cake that I made… for you," she said with a pep.

"You made that in the kitchens?"

"No… I went into the city."

"Without my permission?"

She paused and pulled the cake closer to her. "The queen said I can go as I please."

"She is not who you obey. You obey me." He stood up quickly, and she stepped back.

"You can just say no if you don't want it. I'm sorry," she said.

He grabbed the cake from her hands and threw it to the floor, where it splattered into a pile of red. "I don't want your damned poison cake," he snarled. He stepped over to her, and she backed further away.

"Your dress is muddied and you reek of their filth. You are no better than those peasants. You disobey me at every turn you take. It is unacceptable."

"I—I am sorry, Elmaer, I only wanted—"

"To what? To make me into one of them? To skip away into town with swindlers and eat their mud cakes? I am a king, not a pleb. You will not go out of this castle again without my permission."

"I—" Laerdya looked down at the ruined cake and back up at his fuming gaze. "I want to explore. You can't keep me trapped in here like a dog!" she argued.

He looked almost stupefied at her speaking back to him. His face turned violet, and he raised his hand.

"You dare raise your voice to me!?" he yelled. "You little bitch." He swung his hand down, and she flinched and closed her eyes. She held her breath, but felt nothing hit her. Instead, she heard a strong voice.

"It would be unwise to lay a hand on the princess."

She opened her eyes to see Rhangyl holding onto Elmaer's extended hand. His vice-like grip on him made Elmaer twitch. His face turned from shock to rage. "How dare you touch me, filth! I will have your head!"

Rhangyl released his hand and stepped in front of Laerdya, straightening himself to his full height. "I am the princess' guard; it is my sworn duty to protect her from harm. That includes you."

Elmaer scoffed and tried to sidestep him, but he only blocked his path. She could almost hear the steam coming from his ears.

"Mother will hear of this, so help me," he hissed. He stormed from the room, and Rhangyl stepped to the side.

"Are you alright, princess?" he asked.

Laerdya nodded sadly and sat on her knees, looking at the ruined cake on the ground. "I'm fine. But perhaps it's time to retire to bed." She took the cherry from the floor and carried it out with her in the palm of her hand. It dyed her hand red as she rolled it between her fingers. The juice streamed from her hand and onto the floor, leaving a trail of crimson where she walked.

73 ENARA

Enara heard the creaking of doors and the tapping of footsteps outside the study as she sat back in her chair, gazing out the window. A book lay open in front of her, 'The Finesse of Finance'. One that bored her more than the maps she had memorized that hung on the walls. Her fingers traced her hand that had begun to sting as she kept a steady gaze on the residents outside.

The study gave an exposed view of the garden below and a perfect scene of her mother and sister. She watched as her mother combed through Rose's unruly hair as she protested. When she closed her eyes, she could hear her mother humming as she stroked. She could almost feel the wind on her skin or the scent of the white roses scattering the garden.

Then the scent turned copper, and she opened to eyes to see the sky turn dark shades of black. Enara quickly rose from her seat, forcing herself onto the windowsill. Her mother took no notice of the growing darkness, nor the figure that emerged from it.

Enara slammed her hands against the glass, screaming for her mother's attention as the figure neared. Her screams were deafened by the crackling of thunder as the dark figure unsheathed its sword.

"Mother, please!" she screamed. The figure plunged its sword through her mother's heart and into Rose's head, sending blood splattering their pretty white dresses. The white roses turned red as Enara wept above. The figure turned its gaze toward her and raised an outstretched hand.

"Do val mor."

Enara screamed as her hand caught fire and her flesh burned to black. Lightning crashed into the widow and sent her flying back and—

"Enara!"

Enara bolted from her bed and into the arms of Trissa. She gripped her firmly, burying her head in her chest. Trissa softly stroked her head, cooing. "It was just a dream, Enara. You are safe."

After a moment, Enara pulled away and composed herself. Wiping her eyes with the palm of her hands.

"I'm sorry, when did you get back—did you need something?" she asked.

Trissa stood up off the bed and grabbed a silver tray from the bedside table, bringing it over to the queen. She set it down in front of her and grabbed a pitcher of milk, pouring a cup and handing it to shaking hands. "There is news of Ignis. A raven came early this morning from Sir Alran. All kingdoms have refused trade. No matter the cost. The economy will not last long without aid."

Enara sighed and pinched the bridge of her nose. "How long?"

"With the cultists now in the city, a few thousand at least, it had decreased the time we believe we once had. A couple of months at most before the stores are depleted."

Enara stood from the bed and took a sip of her milk. "Barely time to even bring food into Ignis. The fields are just being plowed for next season. We will need to ration. And the cultists..."

"They are taking what they please. They have no one to oppose them."

"Then I will oppose them!" Enara yelled. She stepped over to the window with a huff, watching the rain drizzle on the glass.

"I am still the queen of Auratus and will not let this continue. I will speak with Aldrian at noon."

Trissa stepped over to the fuming girl. "You can only do as much as you can, Enara. You must remember we are still guests here. Without the support of the king, you cannot protect Ignis."

"Are you saying that I should submit and let my people suffer?"

"No. I am telling you to be careful. I know you are strong-willed and determined. But we must watch what we say and do as we are told. Or else more than Ignis may suffer the consequences."

Enara sighed and rubbed her hand. A headache formed in her temple. "All right. I'll be careful. I promise."

"Good," Trissa responded. "Now let's get you dressed."

The queen's footsteps bounced from one stone wall to the next as she made her way to the king's chambers. She was still unused to the eerie quiet of the halls and rooms around the castle. The servants seemed to disappear as quickly as they appeared. She hadn't even spoken to one. They would come in, bow, and leave without a word. She missed hearing the latest gossip about the stable keep or how cook Merantha had created a new recipe from red berries and sweet corn. This place was anomalous. No matter how close she stuck to the fire in her room, she always had a chill down her spine. Trissa seemed to be the only thing to keep her mind calm. Even her maids did little to stave off the effects of the darkened sky.

Enara stopped in front of the chamber doors, hesitating from knocking, hearing voices inside. She could make out King Aldrian, but the other voice...

"She is within the white frost."

"I thought you killed her?"

"It did not take. Sovrum will take care of the matter. She will no longer be a threat."

"You say that as if the northlanders have not invaded before. They will rally around her."

"That matters not. You have your queen. Keep with your promise."

Enara flinched from the door as it opened in front of her. Malum and the king stood together, and both looked toward her.

Malum had a twisted smile on his face. He gave an elongated bow before disappearing into black mist.

Enara took a breath to steady herself before entering the room. With a huffed sigh, the king sat at his desk. "What is it you need, Lady GoldThorn?" he asked while rubbing his forehead.

"What was he talking about? What northlanders?" she asked.

The king sat up in his chair and grabbed a scroll from the desk. "Issues have arisen in the lands north of Veran. We believe that they may gear for an attack."

"If you take WhiteDrove, that will be your problem," Enara said, a bit snarkier then she would have liked.

"Yes," he snapped, "It will then be my problem. But don't worry for now. It's merely rumored. What did you come here for?"

Enara sat down in front of the desk. "Ignis needs more support. Grain, cloth, meat. The cultists have hoarded everything for themselves."

"What do you think I can do about that?"

"You are the king. Either send aid or remove the cultists from the kingdom," she argued.

The king set the scroll down. "If I remove my troops, Ignis will be retaken by the emperor, and you will lose everything else you have."

Enara paused, staring into his hardened eyes, challenging him. "You did this in the first place, and my people are suffering. You have enough resources."

"I did not start this," Aldrian said, leaning over the desk. "You did by calling on us."

"That—"

"Is the truth, and you know it. You sold your kingdom away and now bargain for it back, but what you fail to realize is I have no control over who Malum chooses to rule or how many people suffer because of it. You made your choice, Lady GoldThorn. Now deal with the consequences."

Enara sat back in her chair, and the two were silent for a time. The kind man who strolled around the city with her had receded with the sunlight outside, and now a new man sat opposite of her. She picked at her nails while the king read through a scroll. The thunder outside shook the castle walls, and the king looked toward her.

"I will do what I can, Enara. I promise," he sighed. "Malum is not giving me many options at the moment, and there are many more issues than just Ignis to worry about."

"Like what?" she asked.

He tossed the scroll onto the table. "None that you can help with, Enara."

"I cannot help if you do not tell me."

She finally saw a smile give way, and he sighed. "If you would like to deal with taxes, please be my guest," he motioned and threw the scroll at her. She caught it as the rain began to patter the sides of the windows.

"How many hours did I spend looking at scrolls like these, pretending I knew what I was doing?" she reminisced.

"As much as me, I am sure. Spending day and night sitting in a stifling study drawing dicks on the paperwork given to me by my tutors."

Enara snorted, and he smiled wider. She quickly cleared her throat. "These taxes are heavy. Why?" she asked, scanning the paper.

"We do not receive supplies or help from any other kingdom. We tax to keep the walls standing and people fed. With Ignis' help, we may be able to lower them."

"Then what you are saying is that is in mutual interest to help both kingdoms...?"

"Yes, Lady Enara. It is. But I cannot move men from the city. I may be able to pull some back from the surrounding villages in the Golden Hills, but I can do no more."

"I suppose it is a start," she sighed, looking out at the window. Thunder crashed again, and she saw lightning light up the sky.

"I never enjoyed the rain," she pondered. "It always made my mood sour."

"That is because you cannot enjoy it to its true potential. I used to run amuck with my brother in the rain. Jumping into puddles and mud. Come back wetter than a dog. My parents would make the servants carry us to the bath."

Enara shook her head. "A future queen is not supposed to engage in such trivialities. She is to stay inside and not get her gown muddied."

"Is there anyone to say you cannot do it now? Miss future queen?" he asked.

She raised a brow at him and glanced outside. "Are you offering to jump into puddles with me, King Aldrain?"

He looked at his scrolls on the table. "Perhaps taxes can wait for a moment." He stood up and offered her his hand. She feverishly took his hand, and they fled the room with mischievous grins.

74 ROSE

The temple was only a few days away at this point. The wind was a bit more manageable now that Rose had completed her trial. She couldn't say that she understood what had happened, but she felt... different. She stole a glance at Nadahi, who had a melancholy look on her face. Erling made a comment to her in their native tongue, and she hissed out a response before catching eyes with Rose. She turned her frown slightly upward before looking away.

"You can feel it, can't you?" Erling said, Rose barely being able to understand them.

"Of course, I can feel it. Who couldn't?" Nadahi replied.

"The *Runa* doesn't seem to notice."

"She has yet to understand the power. She does not know our lands to see the signs."

But Rose did notice; the signs were everywhere—the signs of chaos. The darkness seeped into their bones and made their horses twitch nervously. The usually grey skies now held a darker hue among them. The Ruins of Astira were once holy grounds, but the Forsaken had corrupted most of the lands around it. Now not only did the black tribe scavenge the area, but demons far greater. The amount of bloodshed upon the snow there caused the Mother herself to weep.

Rose's horse whined, and she kicked it forward.

"It is getting worse, Nadahi. We might have to travel the rest on foot," Liv said.

"The snow is too deep for the *Runa*."

"Then carry her. The horses will go no further."

"Fine, we will stop here and take the rest on foot."

"On foot? Is that wise?" Rose asked. The group pulled their horses to a stop, and Nadahi helped Rose down.

"It's the only way. We must travel to the ruins on foot. We will help you if need be."

"I—no. I'll be fine."

Liv and Hakon heaved the supplies onto their backs and patted the horses away. Rose watched with displeasure as they galloped into the white haze. The snow nearly came up to her knees. It would be a long, arduous trek from here.

"Come, it's only another day," Nadahi told her. Rose turned her back against the departing mounts and followed the hunters through the sogging snow. They seemed to be able to keep a steady pace, their long legs being able to quickly clear the snow. Rose was starting to grow agitated with their grace and agility. They had been born and raised in this wilderness. They were large and tall and proud people, and yet here they were, carrying Rose around like a little woven doll.

"How... do you say hello in your language?" Rose puffed out, pulling her leg up above the snow.

"*Celuf,* why?" Nadahi asked.

"Just curious. I don't enjoy not being able to fully understand the language. If I can't walk like you, maybe I can at least converse with the others."

"I can teach you if you wish, Rose," Nadahi said with a small smile.

"That would be lovely, yes."

Erling said something, and then Hakon replied and laughed. Liv shook her head with a sigh and Rose raised a brow. "What are they talking about now?" she asked.

Nadahi scrunched her face. "Perhaps we should start with the basics."

Mountains had begun to surround the party as they grew closer to the ruins. Rose could barely see the top of them through the snowstorm and wondered what things might be watching them through the white veil. Her legs were exhausted from the strain of pulling them through the snow, but she refused to tell the others for a break. She would be fine, even if she could no longer feel her toes. Though she hated seeing how easily they scaled the mountains, or spoke to one another, or rode their horses. They said she wasn't an outsider but she felt like one.

Nadahi stopped suddenly and put a hand up, forcing the others to stop as well. Liv turned behind her, surveying the area. Two crows cawed above them, and Rose heard a horn blare seconds before the group had armed their shields and forced her between them.

"Forsaken?" Hakon asked.

Nadahi narrowed her eyes, backing up to the rest of the ground, ax in hand. "Shields raised to the east. Watch the mountain passes," she ordered. The group did as told, keeping Rose squished between them. They moved as one being; Nadahi never taking her eyes off the mountain. Their deliberate dance around their shields made Rose dizzy as they continued on the path.

She heard another horn, and the group stopped. "West, they've surrounded us," Liv said.

Nadahi was visibly tense as she drew her shield up. They were in no position to fight off an attack on the low ground. Another horn sounded, and she caught a glimpse of green. "*Fe ose tei*!" she called in her tongue.

A cloaked figure appeared through the snow, bow in hand. Rose peeked through the gap in her guards and saw the figure stop a few meters from the ground. Nadahi lowered her shield but kept a grip on her ax.

She asked something else in her language and the figure pulled his hood down, and Rose saw green markings adorning his face. His hair was short, and his beard was braided. He had a bear pelt draped over his back, and his leather vest was tinted green. The man looked toward the others, and they squeezed Rose tighter between them, hiding her from view.

"He is from the Tribe of Bear," Liv whispered to Rose.

Nadahi and the man bickered back and forth in their tongue, and Rose watched as Nadahi became more disgruntled. The man raised his hand, and more tribesmen appeared around them, bows drawn.

He took a step closer to the ground, and Nadahi followed suit. Rose pulled Liv's furs from her face to peek outside the circle. Even without understanding them, she could sense the tension in the air. They were not Forsaken, but they weren't on friendly terms either.

"I am warning you, *jo ra*, back away now," Nadahi growled.

Rose glanced at the tribesmen surrounding them. At least a couple dozen compared to their six.

The man laughed and balled his hand into a fist. "*Os ruust.*"

Nadahi brought her shield up quickly, the others following suit, and Hakon pushed Rose to a crouch. She heard the arrows slam into their shields, and Liv grunted as one lodged into her boot.

"Space now!" Nadahi yelled, backing up to join the rest of the group. She grabbed Rose's shoulder and forced her up.

"You stay behind us at all costs, you hear me?" she ordered. Rose nodded, and they brought their shields up again to block another barrage of arrows. She heard a horn bellow and a cry of men as they jumped from the passes to surround them. They came barreling towards them as Nadahi barked out orders.

"Hold!"

The leader of Bear gave a pleasing smile and threw his bow to the ground, unsheathing a sword instead. The group held steady as the men drew nearer. When they were mere feet away, Nadahi yelled again. "Bash!"

The group brought their shields out, slamming into the men around them. With powerful swings, they chopped heads and arms off, slicing into fur and bone. The guttural sounds of death shook Rose's stomach. Liv twirled on a man and sliced into his throat, sending a stream of blood across her face. The others were bashing and dodging, taking knives to the arms and torso. Nadahi threw a woman from her and blocked an ax with her shield before bashing him across the face.

Rose threw herself to the ground to dodge an arrow, and a tribesman swung down on her. She scampered out of the way before Erling slammed his ax into his head. He kicked the man away before countering another blow. Rose backpedaled to a set of several large snow-covered boulders. She was still no good in a fight. She didn't think she ever would be, and her magic seemed to have a mind of its own.

"*Ophae tei?*" someone said behind her. Rose turned to see the main tribesman smile down at her. "A youngling? Is that what they were hiding, a child?"

Rose could only make out a few words he said as she quickly looked around for any sort of weapon. He grabbed her by her coat and brought his face close. He looked her up and down before his smile dropped. He pushed her, and she hit the boulder hard before falling to the ground.

"You are no youngling. Who are you?" he asked in a heavily accented voice.

She rubbed her head and looked up at him. "I'm no one," she spoke.

The man's lips drew up in a snarl. "Liar. Have they thought of involving the Lowlanders in their petty war?"

"N-no I—"

"Get away from her!" Nadahi yelled. She was between them in an instant, swinging her ax toward the tribesman. He parried the blow and jumped back a few paces.

"Now you fraternize with Lowlanders. You are treasonous and pathetic."

"You know nothing, Bear."

"Then who is she?" They exchanged more blows, Nadahi being able to just barely parry and dodge.

"She is of no importance to you."

"If you are willing to die for her, then I would say that is enough." He swung down, clipping Nadahi's hand and forcing her to drop her ax. She bashed him with her shield and lunged for her weapon. The man was quicker, though, and kicked her hard in the stomach. Before she could recover, he grabbed her ax and tossed it away.

"Wolf. You should have known you could not win this battle," he said and circled her, tapping his sword on his leg. "How shall I kill you? Or maybe I should string you up for your father. He would enjoy that."

Nadahi pulled herself to her knees and stared him down, spitting on his shoe. The man laughed and grabbed her hair, pulling her head back, and set his sword along her throat.

"Stop!" Rose cried. They both looked toward her, and Rose held out her hand. "I'm the *Runa!* Please, just let her go!"

He kept the sword at her throat. "You lie."

Rose closed her eyes and focused on her hand, forming a small ball of fire in her palm. The ruby on her neck pulsed, and the flame grew larger. She could feel the mountains around her shake and groan as sweat beaded around her forehead. Piles of snow came crashing down around them and slammed into the tribesman, burying them alive. Their screams were muffled through the dense patches of white.

The man released Nadahi and stood straight, eyes wide. "By the Mother," he whispered. Rose clenched her fist, extinguishing the flame.

"Leave her alone, Bear," Nadahi called, standing upright.

He turned to her. "Why would you hide this from us, Wolf-heart?

Did you think she would save you?" he accused.

"She isn't your concern."

"This is no longer about you, Wolf-heart. You brought a *Runa* here, and you didn't inform the other tribes. That is treason." He pointed his sword at her accusingly, and he turned back to Rose, a dark look crossing his face. He walked past her and blew a horn, ceasing the fighting. Everyone turned to him, and he brought his hand up, pointing to Rose.

"The Mother has gifted us today with a child of her womb. By the will of herself alone, we shall allow safe passage to the Ruins of Astira." All eyes looked at Rose, and she backed into her fur. The remaining tribesmen dropped their weapons and fell to their knees, bowing low to her. Nadahi came behind Rose and put a hand on her shoulder.

"This is not over, Wolf-heart," the man said. "You will not keep her from the rest of us." He took his men, and they fled the mountain pass, leaving the group to heal and rest.

"Are you alright?" she asked Nadahi.

"I am in your debt once again, Rose. It will be you who decides my time to enter *Shor'vaker*, it seems."

Rose did not smile. "Then I will try my best to keep that from ever happening."

The group mended their wounds and prepared for the rest of the journey. Rose attempted to ignore the bodies that were trapped in the fallen mounds of snow. How many had she killed? The face of the man she burned alive was engraved in her memory. She did not enjoy killing. It made her want to cry and scream. She wasn't ready for this. She was a terrible ruler, a terrible Runa. She was just a little girl who shirked her duties to play in mud puddles with her friends.

Rose took a long breath. *Enough whining Rose*, she thought, imagining her sister scolding her like she always did. *Get up and do something about it.*

Rose looked at the cloudy sky, watching the flakes of snow melt on her cheeks. *It's time to be a grown woman and take back your kingdom.*

75 TALIA

Talia dressed in her finest dress that evening at the emperor's request. While it was not a style of the Empire, it was a modest aqua blue gown that accentuated her waist and was laced with black pearls. The emperor had invited her to dine with him, and that put a bounce in her step. If anything, it kept her mind away from the sorrow of the near battle. The wolf sat outside her door as the maids finished tying her corset and brushing out her hair. Applying the littlest amount of rogue to her lips, she set out of the room and towards the main wing. The wolf walked behind her slowly, humming a tune she didn't recognize.

"You seem to be in a fine mood this evening," Talia said. The wolf said nothing in reply, simply continuing his song. It wasn't until they passed another hall towards the dining chamber that he spoke again.

"How long have these walls stood?" he asked. "A thousand years, more? And how many emperors sat on their asses staring at the Dark Kingdom with a glass of brandy in their hand."

"Is there a question in that?" Talia asked.

"All nobility are alike. They fear their enemies but do nothing to stop them because they think nothing will happen to them. They have one goal in life. To become rich and fat and die happily on the backs of others."

"Is that what you think of me?" she asked, stopping, and turning towards him.

"You, my lady, have yet to gain enough weight."

Talia rolled her eyes. "You are quite cynical; do you know that?"

"Living in a sewer for years can do that to a man."

"Didn't you choose to live there?"

He cocked his head at her. "I cannot be feared if I live in a cottage in the woods."

"No, but you would be much more appealing."

His mask hid his expression, but she could tell he was pleased. She turned her back to him and continued towards the dining room. She enjoyed seeing all the gowns and outfits the nobility wore around the palace, even if they were gaudy. She must seem very underdressed by their standards, and the way they scrutinized her did not help her feel welcome.

"Is this emperor all you could have hoped for, princess?" The wolf asked after a short pause.

"He has done nothing to warrant any disfavor by me, if that is what you are asking."

"Is it?"

She hated his rhetorical questions. The thought of simply telling him to leave her service crossed her mind, but she snuffed it down after remembering what happened on her way here. She thought back to her conversation with the emperor, and his unwillingness to go against his advisors and send as many men as was needed. He needed to take a stance; he was the emperor, and he didn't need their approval for anything. He just needed power.

They made their way to the dining chambers and knocked politely before entering.

"Your Excellence, Lady Talia Farvell arrives," the servant announced. She curtsied, and he motioned for her to sit.

"Your dress looks lovely on you, Lady Farvell," he complimented.

She smiled brightly at him. "Thank you, Your Majesty. I have some of the best tailors in Veran to service me. Though I cannot compare to the finery here." She sat beside a young boy as the wolf hid scant in the corner.

"This is my son Marrin," Emperor Varen said. She looked at him with a smile, and he nervously looked away.

"I apologize. It's been a while since he has had to interact with anyone outside the palace."

"I take no offense, Your Majesty," she reassured.

Soon the food was brought in on shining plates, and she thanked the staff.

"This looks delicious, Your Majesty. Thank you for inviting me here," she said, taking up a fork.

"It would be rude to let the princess of Yalirea eat in her room. You are welcome anytime," he replied. She blushed slightly and noticed the prince look from her to his father. The stuffed duck on her plate reminded her of the meals back home, but the garnish was slightly different from what she was used to.

The emperor noticed her attention to her plate and, with a small laugh, said, "They are herbs from Avlor, a delicacy there, I am told. The queen sent some with her ambassador as a peace offering."

A small tingle graced her throat, and she wiped her mouth with a napkin. "At least they were kind enough to make sure we do not go hungry."

"It tastes like dirt," the prince said.

"And yet you will still pretend to enjoy it if the elves or other visitors are around," Varen said sternly. The boy quickly took another bite, and he relaxed in his chair.

"I hope you know I did everything I could to help WhiteDrove, my lady. And I will do what is necessary to protect Rosus as well."

Talia swallowed before answering him. "I believe you, Emperor. I can only wish for as few deaths as possible and a battle won."

"Will they kill the king of WhiteDrove if they win?" Marrin asked.

Varen looked down at him and nodded. "Yes. They will. The Dark Kingdom does not know of mercy. We can show none back if we are to win this war." The prince set his fork on the table with a look of despondency.

"But if we win," Talia said, leaning over to the boy, "We will have saved thousands of lives. And that is worth any cost. Don't you think?"

The prince nodded slightly, and she sat back up.

"If I may ask, my lady," Marrin started quietly. "Who is the man?"

Talia turned to the wolf, who stood leaning in the corner. He gave a half-wave with his hand as the other guards eyed him.

"That... is my guard. Like your father, I have my own protection."

"Only one man?"

"I could kill a hundred if I wanted," the wolf responded. The emperor raised a brow, and Talia sighed.

"Ignore him. He enjoys his fantasies of heroism," she said, turning back to the table.

"I believe him," Marrin said.

"Good," the wolf replied.

"If you don't mind me asking as well," Varen started, "Why did you come here when your father already sent an ambassador?"

Talia froze, tapping her fork against her napkin. She could almost feel the wolf's enjoyment behind her. "I wanted to see the beauty of the capital myself," she smiled. "My father would have disapproved, so I came on my own time."

Varen looked at her guard, then back at her. "Then I am glad you chose to come here, my lady. It is a shame we are at war, so you cannot truly enjoy the palace and the city. But if you have any wanting to explore, please feel free to come to me."

The prince gave another look towards the two and then at the wolf, who made a gagging face. He smiled and cut another piece of his duck.

"I cannot imagine that ruling a kingdom, much less a continent, could be unchallenging, especially after the loss of your wife," Talia started, feeling his gaze on her. "You must have high fortitude indeed."

The emperor gave a soft sigh. "I cannot say it has not been hard, Lady Talia. Luckily, I had the court to help prepare me since childhood to one day take the throne. The loss of Helene was devastating, but the court has helped me through the darkest of my days. We may disagree on some terms, but I believe the Empire is strong with their support."

Talia took a bite of her duck. She could sense he was exaggerating to some degree. "I cannot help but hear a bit of distaste in your speech. Is there something the matter?" she asked.

He put his fork down and wiped his mouth with his napkin, and placed it back on his lap. "There has been some discourse with the quarters recently. I believe it is due to the rumors of war and the fear of the people. We have had many refugees come through the city gates in the past few weeks. Many of them elven. The quarter is already crowded, so we have placed them in the Lower Quarter and are currently looking at options for work. Some of the nobility… are tense with our arrangements."

Talia felt the wolf shift behind her. "That is unfortunate. But I am sure you can make peace with your people. They will listen to you. You may just need a stronger hand."

Marrin finished his meal and made a face at the vegetables, sitting back in his seat. "Why do the elves have to complain so much?" he asked. "Lady Sumati says they want to take more of the city for themselves and leave the common people homeless."

She saw Varen stiffen and tap his fingers on the table. "It is always wise to hear from more than one source what the latest gossip is. And not from one party, either. We are settling several communities within her jurisdiction, so she is musing her complaints. She will come to understand."

"A wise statement, Your Eminence," Talia beamed. "We should strive to help everyone who comes through our gates. If you are to ever become emperor, they will be *your* people to protect."

"I guess," Marrin shrugged.

Once they finished eating, several servants came in and cleared the table. The emperor cleared his throat and stood. "I must retire to my study and fill out some reports tonight. I do wish you a good night, Lady Talia," he bowed. Marrin followed after him, and she stood up herself.

"Everything you could ever want," the wolf laughed. She ignored him and fled the room to her chambers. She said what she could. Now to see how well she could fit into the predatory gazes of the court.

The wind outside the palace was colder than what she was used to. She sat on the balcony to her room, leaning against the stone railing. She listened to the birds chirp in the trees and chase one another through their courting rituals of spring. A pair of robins landed on the balcony beside her and played their songs before bopping around her and then flying off. She heard the wolf stride onto the balcony and lean against the door. She did not turn to face him.

"What is death like?" she asked.

"What an odd question."

"I worry about the people of WhiteDrove. About the men that will die and mothers that will grieve. Do you feel anything as they set you on the pyre, or does your life flash before your eyes before you pass to the Otherworld?"

"Don't you believe in your goddess?" the wolf probed. "Shouldn't your priests know the answers to that?"

"They do. But it does not give me the comfort I should wish," she said with a sigh. She brought the shawl she wore further up her shoulders and watched the city around her go on. "I sit here in hopes that my voice made a difference for the people, and yet I am not there to see it for myself. To know their safety."

"I do not believe you know how to carry a sword, princess."

She rolled her eyes at him. "*I know that.* I just want to do more."

"There is little more you can do but wait for the nobility to get off their asses and help the kingdoms around them. If they ever do. I'm interested to see how you fare with them. Will you stand up to their pomp and priss, or will they eat you up like a chicken pie?"

She turned to him and rested her back on the rail. "How do you know about the nobility here, wolf? Sewer rats tend to not know what the lions are up to."

"I've seen my share of court in the years I have lived. I used to protect some of them for a time. Not worth the money."

"Am I worth the money yet?"

He cocked his head at her and was silent for a time. "Not yet. I'll wait until something interesting happens to make my grand judgment."

"You might get that wish someday," she said, her face turning sour. "If they win WhiteDrove, they might as well come here next."

"You have little faith in your countrymen."

"I have faith. I just don't know if it is enough."

"I think there is something to say that you even worry for their safety. Many in this city do not."

"They should. We cannot sit idle while the kingdoms around us burn." She looked inside her room, where several dresses were laid out on the bed for her to scrutinize. All the newest fashion in the capital, and all way too puffy.

"I know that gleam in your eye," the wolf noted.

Talia stepped from the balcony and into her room, looking at the dresses. "Perhaps it is time to show the court who I am. And what I can accomplish here." She ran a hand down the ruffled skirt of one of the dresses.

"A new march for you then?" the wolf asked.

Talia smiled at him. "Perhaps. A push is sometimes needed to get us where we need to be. Here, it seems, a shove might be required."

76 OLIVIA

Olivia held her wooden swords as Neph circled her in the training room. The woman's blood eyes showed little emotion as she twirled her own silver sword.

"Try and phase to me," she ordered. Olivia took a breath and focused on the woman. She listened to her faint breathing, the pattering of water along the wall, and the scuttle of rats underneath them.

She darted towards Neph in a mass of shadow but lost grip of the swords. They clattered to the ground as Olivia caught herself from tripping over Neph. She stumbled and put her foot out to steady herself, a cold chill running down her spine. With a side-eye, Neph pointed to the swords.

"You forgot those," she said monotone. Olivia sighed and walked back to pick them up. Neph cracked half a smile as she circled Olivia again.

"You are focusing too much on the shadows. You try to find each one on a bright and sunny day. You must not think, only let them absorb you and need to think of them as an extension of you, not as a tool."

"How often must you tell me that?" she asked.

"Enough for you to listen."

Olivia moved back into stance, and Neph lunged for her. She managed to parry the blow, but her feet were swept out from under her. She landed hard on the ground and lost hold of her weapons.

"Phase!" Neph yelled, swinging her sword down. Olivia brought her hands up, and the blade sliced into her arm. She cried out in anger, and Neph raised her sword again.

"If you die here, you die a coward! Phase you bastard girl!" she yelled.

Olivia seethed as she brought the blade down again. She felt the shadows tug at her body, calling her to them. She answered the call and vanished into them. Neph's blade cracked against the wooden floor, and she felt herself shift under her, using her own shadow as a pathway. She forced herself to materialize behind her and fell to her knees with a gasp.

"You did it. Terribly, but it's done." Neph said. Olivia winced at the long cut running down her arm. With a sigh, Neph turned around and grabbed Olivia's injured arm. "You rely too heavily on your emotions. They will not help you," she scolded. "These blades can kill demons just as well as they can kill us. You can hurt yourself and others if you are not ready to train with them. Now, get your swords and clean up. Meet me back in the tavern once you are ready."

Olivia picked up her training swords with a grimace and placed them back in her room. She washed out her wound and touched the still burning flesh. Neph had told her that the swords could harm them as much as they did the corrupted or cursed. Were they truly any different? Her red eyes were that of the beast that killed men. Her longing for the dark and craving for blood tied her to them.

After wrapping the wound, Olivia walked back to the tavern where Neph and a man sat. They looked up as she entered, and the man looked at her arm.

"You don't go easy on her, do ya?" he asked.

"If I didn't, she would already be dead," she replied. Olivia sat down and recognized the man as Cronis.

"Well," Cronis said, "You like our cozy little hovel, milady?"

Olivia scrunched her face at him. "It's better than sleeping in the Mors."

"Ha! You've got that right," he laughed. "I'm assuming Neph never told you about me?"

"I assume you have a history. Given your outburst the other day," Olivia replied.

"We were inseparable, her and I," he started. "Fifty years back, we got a contract to kill a foreign ambassador from Drovelak, the capital city of the Dracon. Took us four weeks to find him—"

"—And another six to recover from our injuries," Neph added.

"Yeah yeah, Dracon are hard bastards to kill with their weapons. But we did. Sent that horned beast straight to the Otherworld."

"How many times will you tell that story?" Neph asked.

"As many times as it takes to get you back into bed with me," he replied with a sly grin.

"Then please proceed to tell the entire kingdom."

Olivia snorted, and Cronis frowned. "How many years have we been married?"

"Too many."

"You're married?" Olivia asked with a raise of her eyebrow.

Neph ran her fingers over the wooden table. "We died together and were reborn together. Basically, marriage without the ridiculous dress and priest in attendance."

"Now that I would love to see!" Cronis laughed.

"You are not getting me in a dress. Ever."

"Fine, fine, be that way. I'm getting an Ale," he said and stood up, pushing his chair back. As he walked away, Olivia popped a question she had been meaning to ask.

"How often do you get contracts? I received a shipment every few weeks. But I was a lone mercenary. Only joined a company when I needed the extra hands."

"It depends. During wartime? Hundreds in a week. When it is somewhat peaceful, it can go down to only a few dozen in a month."

"And how many do you take?"

"There are less than twenty of us left. We only take what contracts are worth our time, and only a few ever are. There is one that I will take here soon. You will come with me."

Olivia's eyes lit up. "You trust me with this?"

"Of course not. You cannot even carry your sword. You will be backup in case anything goes amiss. That is all."

Olivia's face fell, but she nodded. "I will do whatever it takes."

"Good, maybe you will not get yourself killed. Many do not make it past the first trial."

"The first trial as in just sitting there and watching you kill someone?"

"Yes. This kingdom is a dangerous place. If anyone is caught wearing our brand or armor, we are killed on sight. The new king does not like our presence in his city."

Oliva sat back in her chair. "I thought you served the dark kings?"

"He cannot control us like he can the other guilds. We have fought to keep our place here, and he knows we are no mere bandits.

Sometimes he will send a brigade our way to see what numbers we still have and test the waters. But he has yet to turn his full gaze on us."

"Is that a good thing or a bad thing?"

"Depends on who you ask."

Cronis came back with three ales and set them down on the table. Olivia grabbed one and swirled it around. "I can't stand the taste of this stuff."

"Neither can we. But that is the price we pay for glory. To death!" she cheered. They clanked their tankards together with bitter laughter.

"May she grace us all with her warm embrace."

77 THYMAS

The once small village of WhiteDrove now held people from every region of Viragrad inside the walls of the courtyard. The soldiers that positioned themselves along the wooden walls looked drained and defeated already. The large pile of fallen soldiers still smoked outside. Thymas took Sara by the arm and led her through the garden. They passed more wounded, as well as blacksmiths and townspeople, boarding up their houses and building defenses for the keep.

"I wish I could have seen this before," Sara said sadly.

He gave a half-laugh. "Unfortunately, it is not much better beforehand."

They made their way inside the keep, and several servants ran to attend him, taking his cloak and bowing to the lady. The maids scuttled off, whispering to themselves.

"I must find my mother. She should be in her study," he said. Sara took in the scenery of the old keep as they passed through the hallways. It was sturdy but felt past its years. Built for surviving harsh winters and cold summers.

As they passed through the hall leading to the main hall, they heard a soft voice call for the prince. He turned to see Anya running up to him. A smile broke out across his face as he pulled her up into his arms.

"There you are! Are you alright?" he asked.

She giggled, and he set her down. She folded down her dress. "I'm fine. I've never seen this many people before!" she exclaimed.

"I didn't realize you were half-elven," Sara noted.

The princess turned to her with wide eyes. "I'm adopted. Told I was raised by wolves before the queen found me. You're very pretty."

"Anya..." Thymas groaned.

"It's all right," Sara laughed. She bent down to her height and pulled a string of hair from her face.

"You're beautiful as well, princess."

Anya turned back to her brother. "Is she your wife?"

Thymas stuttered out a response, feeling heat rise to his cheeks. He should have known Anya would say something. A ten-year-old had no bounds to the imagination. "No, she is a priestess from the Sunset Isles. She is here to help the wounded."

"Oh," Anya said, disappointed, "Mother will be sad."

"Alright, alright," Thymas pushed. He noticed footsteps and looked up to see a lord from the plains come up toward him. "Why don't you show Sara around the keep while I speak with the people?" He nodded at Sara, and she let the girl lead.

"Take care, my lady," he said.

She smiled at him. "You too, Lord Thymas."

When the girls were gone, he stepped up to Lord Downor, who greeted him with a bow.

"My lord, it is good to see you back."

"How fairs the men?"

"They are beaten and broken," he spat. "The Imperials came to us with their men on wagons and their tails between their ass cheeks. They will do us nothing to help."

"The emperor is sending more men through the portal to help us fight. You have a family, do you not? You should go with them to the capital."

"Capital? Run like a rabbit being hunted by a fox? I think not. You are our king; I will follow to my last breath. As will the rest of these brave bastards who fled their families to fight for this keep."

Thymas put a hand on his shoulder. "You do me proud, Lord Downor. Know that your sacrifice for this kingdom will not go in vain."

The lord put his hand on his arm. "You need not thank me. We will win this battle or die trying. Not one cultist bastard is going to make it into this keep, so help me, goddess." Thymas smiled, and the lord grabbed onto his head, tugging his hair. "You are as brave as your father. He would be proud to call you son. And see you claim your throne as king."

"Let's hope that day comes, my friend."

Thymas scaled the staircase to his mother's room and knocked on the door. When she answered, he opened it. She sat on a chair next to the fireplace, her wine glass empty.

"With all these men here, it's a shock there are any women left to care for the keep. Savages all of them," she muttered.

Thymas closed the door and went to sit beside her. "I can have a word with them if you like."

"Bah," she waved, "That is the least of our worries right now. Tell me that the emperor is sending more men."

"Two hundred through the portal, along with some enchanters. That is all we have time for," he replied.

She shook her head and licked her lips. "Then, at least this battle will be easy. Perhaps they will grant me the dignity of poison instead of beheading."

"Mother..."

"The portal will have to be destroyed if the Dark Kingdom breaks through. You know this, correct?" she asked.

Thymas sat back in his chair. "Is that necessary?"

"If one demon gets through that portal, many more will die. Send the people through, then blast that thing to the Otherworld."

"The amount of magic that would take, we have few enchanters," he argued.

"That blue-skinned girl has a bow meant to disrupt magic, I've heard. Go ask her."

"Are you speaking of a cursed elf?" he asked.

"No, a damned troll. Yes, a cursed elf. She came in half-dead from the previous battle. Ruined my finest bed sheets, too."

"Then I will speak with her. Are... you alright? I will send you through the portal first."

Queen Kesanda laughed at him and tapped her fingers against the table next to her. "I am too old to move from this room. Let alone get flown through some portal. I will stay here."

"Mother, if the Dark Kingdom takes WhiteDrove—"

"Then you will die, and I am too old to bear another son. Send Anya through, and that is it. She can fight for her claim if she wishes. If there is anything left to claim—though doubtful with her half-blood."

"I cannot convince you, can I?" he sighed.

She shook her head and lazily stared at him. "No. Now tell me about this girl I've heard about."

He perked up in his seat. "Lady Sara? How did you—"

"These walls have ears, and so do I. When the prince walks through the portal with a beautiful young girl on his arm, people are bound to talk. In war or not."

Thymas bit his lip. "She is only here to help the injured. She is a priestess from the Sunset Isles. That is all."

The queen humphed and took her empty wineglass, running her finger along the edge. "If you're going to die, a prince might as well ensure an heir."

"Mother!"

78 ROSE

The mountain path stretched as far as the eye could see. Nadahi told her that the temple was just a short way away, but she could barely tell the path from the heavy snow. White flakes drifted down from the sky and Rose rubbed her nose.

She had spent the day learning their language and attempting to speak it back—albeit terribly. Now, the sun had set beyond the pointed mountains, leaving a cloudless, starry night sky. The wind was brisk, but not unbearable, as she wrapped her coat tighter around herself. She was still amazed that the trial that Nadahi had put her through worked, and the winter was less harsh on her skin.

Suddenly, something caught her attention, and she paused, listening. It was the sound of falling water, clear and fresh. She tapped Nadahi on the shoulder and the huntress looked down at her. "Do you hear that?" she asked.

The huntress gazed away from her, listening. "Yes. It is water."

"Oh, bless the Mother!" Erling cheered. "I haven't had a bath in weeks!"

"We can tell," Hakon huffed, and the others laughed.

Nadahi turned back to Rose. "If there is a spring up ahead, we can rest for the night. The temple is still a ways away."

The group continued, the sound of the falling water getting louder and louder until they came upon a small pool snuggled in a small rock crevasse. The water trailed down from a hole in the mountain and fell into the glimmering pool.

Rose bent down and touched the water. It was frigid, and she quickly pulled her hand away. "I do not feel like losing my toes today," she said, shaking her head.

Erling wrapped an arm around her shoulder and squeezed her to his chest. She squeaked as her cheek squished against his rough leather tunic, his beard tickling her nose. "Ah, no worries. We have a firestarter right here!" he proclaimed.

Rose made a face and Nadahi wrenched his hand from her and pulled her back. "She is not a toy, Erling," she scolded.

He shrugged. "Sure is good at producing that fire, though. Make this pool into a nice hot spring."

The others quickly looked at Rose, and she backed up. "Uh… I can try?" she said, rubbing her hands, her chest squeezing slightly. "Though knowing my luck, I will evaporate the whole pool."

"If you are worried, *Runa*, you needn't try. We can rest and continue on tomorrow," Nadahi said and smiled, looking down at her.

Rose blushed and turned her face away. "N-no. I want to try. It would be nice to bathe."

Erling nodded vigorously and Torgir chuffed, as Rose carefully made her way back over to the pool. She watched the water ripple as it fell from the rocks and kneeled, putting her hand into the water. Her fingers froze nearly instantly, and she winced, forcing herself not to pull back.

You can do this Rose… she told herself, closing her eyes. *Just like Dravis said, focus your energy.*

She sighed and focused on her hand, willing it to warm. Her fingers slowly regained feeling, and she felt sweat bead around her brows. She wiggled her fingers, and she felt them heat. Then, she heard the pool begin to bubble and felt steam rise to her face. She opened her eyes and found her vision clouded.

"Ahahah! Finally!" Erling cheered.

Rose pulled her hand out and stood up, feeling the heat come off the pool of water. "Good job, *Runa*," Liv said, lowering her head.

"Thank you… I'm honestly surprised I was able to do that."

"You dropped a mountain on top of us and you are amazed at being able to heat a pool?" Hakon asked, raising a brow.

Rose shrugged. "Heat of the moment, I suppose."

"Quit your yapping and get in!" Erling cheered, stripping and throwing his clothes to the side. Rose gasped and covered her eyes as the others laughed. She heard a splash and flinched when water splashed onto her shoes.

"Agh! Erling, there is no need to soak our clothes!" Liv scolded. Rose peeked between her fingers to see Erling happily submerge himself in the water then come back up, throwing off the bandages on his eye.

"It's wonderful! The goddess has blessed us this day!"

"I see no point in standing around. Enjoy the pool. It may be the last bath we shall take in a while." Nadahi said.

Rose lifted her hands from her face. "You're all going in at once?"

Nadahi turned to her, a small smile gracing her pale lips. "We have little running water in *Rolheim*. It is brought into the tribe bath house and heated with wood there for everyone to use. If you wish to bathe alone, we will respect your wishes, *Runa*."

The others nodded, and Rose bit her lip. She supposed nudity was not seen as illicit here in the winter wilderness. She was used to seeing the barest of people from the taverns and parties... but this felt different. Though she supposed Nadahi had already seen most of her during her trial. The thought of it brought heat to her face.

"I... I'll bathe with you," she said after a moment. Erling cheered, and Nadahi threw a rock at him.

The group began undressing, whispering to themselves in their language, and she attempted to understand them. She could only make out a few words here and there, and they seemed to speak of the journey, and their fatigue. She didn't blame them; It seemed all they had done was run and fight. She had seen more battles these past few weeks than in her entire life.

She slowly undressed herself, taking time to unlace her coat and shirt. She kept glancing at the rest of the group as they undressed and entered the water. They all laughed and talked among themselves while washing their hair or running under the waterfall. The steam from the spring helped hide their bodies in the water and Rose looked away, pulling off her shirt and throwing it to the side.

She thought back to her friends, who would often bicker and fight, throwing each other around with mud and water. She missed being dragged into their fights, coming back to the castle stinking of a farm. She felt her eyes sting and pushed the thought away.

A chill ran down her spine as the wind nipped at her skin as she pulled off her underdress and shoes. Carefully, she unwound the bandages on her chest, looking at the scars that now rested there from the demon. The wound itself was healed, but she knew she would carry the marks forever.

She thought back to what Nadahi had told her. *"All of us bear scars here. And we are all proud of them."* She traced her hand along the marks and took a breath. She had no need to be self-conscious about them. If they all bore scars too, perhaps that meant she was closer to them, and the Mother Goddess.

She looked back over at the group, but they paid her no mind. She stepped over to the pool, the melting snow cold against her feet, and Nadahi looked over at her. She felt herself blush and cover as much of herself as she could with her hands as she quickly tried to enter the water but slipped on the muddy bank. Nadahi quickly moved and grabbed her shoulders, making sure she fell into the water and not on the solid ground.

She went under the water for a moment before breaching the surface, coughing and spitting. She pushed the hair from her face as Torgir and Erling broke into laughter. "Good fall." Erling nodded and Rose glared at him.

"Leave her alone, you sods. Go back to washing that rat tail on your face," Nadahi teased.

Rose felt the huntress's hand still on her shoulder and she looked to her side. Her dark hair was glued to her forehead and ears, spreading out across the water. Rose noticed two small bells braided into her hair that tinkled softly when she moved her head. The paint on her face was lighter than before, most likely rubbing off with the water, and she trailed her eyes down to her large shoulders and down further to—

No! Rose thought, shaking her head.

"Do you need help washing?" Nadahi asked suddenly, and Rose brought her eyes to the huntresses.

"Uh, no, I am fine," she spoke.

The huntress released her shoulder and ran her fingers through her long hair. "Alright. If you need help with your wound, do not hesitate to ask, *Runa*."

Rose did nothing but nod and swam over to the farthest corner of the pool, slowly cleaning herself. She started with her hair, dunking under the surface and back up again, raking her fingers through the knots. The water was hot and therapeutic, releasing the tension in her muscles and calming her breath. She heard the three men bickering again and looked over at them.

Hakon was the largest of the group, with a strong, broad chest and scars that ran down his torso and arm. Erling and Torgir were nearly fully submerged in the pool, arguing. She tried to make out what they were saying when they went under the water for minutes at a time. *A competition*, she thought.

Liv was sitting on the bank, braiding her hair. She hummed to herself, and Rose took notice of the long scar that ran from her stomach down past the hair of her crotch. Nadahi said that she had gotten that scar during childbirth.

Then her eyes turned to Nadahi, who stood under the falling water, her arms above her head. She watched the water stream through her hair and down her stomach. Her eyes were closed, but her mouth was moving. Rose could not hear what she was saying, but she assumed she was praying. The blue of the paint across her nose dripped down her cheeks and neck, down through the valley of her breasts and navel.

Rose found it hard to look away from the huntress as she continued to clean herself. *I shouldn't be looking*, she told herself. But she couldn't help it. The woman was like a goddess incarnate.

Nadahi opened her eyes and locked onto Rose, who quickly blushed a deep red and turned around. *Stupid!* she thought. Then she felt the water shift behind her and felt the hair on her back lift.

"Let me help with your hair, *Runa*. If you do not mind." Nadahi's voice was in her ear, her breath hot on her neck.

"I-I don't mind," Rose flushed. Nadahi scooped up her hair, moving her fingers across her shoulders to collect all the strands. She was whispering something again as she ran her hands through her hair. Rose could not make it out. She tried to ignore how close their bodies were to each other. If she took one step backward, she could touch the huntress' bare skin. She felt herself grow hot thinking about it and shook her head.

Nadahi laughed lightly. "You'll pull your hair if you keep doing that, *Runa*."

"Sorry…" Rose apologized. She closed her eyes and took a breath, focusing on the steaming water.

From the sounds of the conversing group to the water gently falling down onto them, to the feeling of Nadahi behind her, she knew one thing. That if she had the choice, she would never leave the pool.

79 SARA

Anya bopped around the keep, showing the priestess every little nook and cranny it had to offer. She stopped at a hanging drape on the wall; a snow-white owl was sewn into it.

"That is our House heraldry," Anya said, pointing to the owl. "I like the owl. It's pretty."

"Yes, it is," Sara agreed. Anya smiled and continued on her way, soon entering the small garden snuggled into the far reaches of the keep. Sara had not had a chance to actually enjoy the splendor of the garden; Thymas had hurried her inside.

"This is my favorite spot," Anya said, pointing towards a small stone-carved bench sitting on one of the trails.

"Why is that?" Sara asked.

"Because I can see the portal."

Sara glanced at the portal that sat in the middle of the garden, ten feet high and carved from marble. The middle of it swirled with pink and blue magic and happily pulsed at her. She stepped over to it and put her hand up, feeling soft heat rise from it. The thrumming of magic whispered in her ears and wrapped around her feet.

"What are you doing?" Anya asked.

Sara pulled her hand away. "I am sensing the magic within the portal. Sometimes if you listen quietly, you can hear it whisper to you." She bent down and gently took Anya's hand, pulling her towards the portal. "Do you feel it?" she asked.

Anya closed her eyes and pursed her lips. She wiggled her fingers, trying to feel the magic around them. "I..." she started. Sara pushed her closer to the portal, her hand almost touching the swirling mass. "Barely," she admitted. She opened her eyes with an exasperated sigh.

"That's alright," Sara said. "Do you know how the portals came to be?"

Anya shook her head, and Sara led her over to the bench. They sat down, and Sara folded her hands in her lap. "After the great war of kingdoms and fall of *Elu'lathan*, came the birth of the Six Kingdoms of Veran. The kings and queens of the kingdoms were still afraid of the might of the Dark Kingdom and searched for a way to keep the other kingdoms safe from such a far reach. The last of the mages of the Temple of Kildan spoke to the spirits, explored the forests, and prayed to the goddess for an answer. And it came in the form of a wish. With that wish, the kingdoms came together, and through an abundance of magic and potions, the skies opened wide and welcomed the mages. The mages used the magic of the skies and bound it to the doorways they had built. These doorways are the closest we can reach the heavens and come with both a blessing and a burden."

"Why is it a burden?" Anya asked, still staring at the portal.

"Because we are not the only beings who can access the power of the portals. Wherever we walk, darkness may follow."

The wind rustled the shrubs around them, and Sara pulled her coat tighter around herself.

"Will the Dark Knights take WhiteDrove?"

Sara looked down at the girl beside her, her face now solemn. "No. I don't think they will."

"Thymas will protect us. He always has," Anya smiled. "He would never let anything happen to us."

"I believe you, Anya. He seems like a kind man."

"He likes you. I like you too. Are you going to stay?"

Sara blushed slightly, adjusting her skirt. "I don't know. I want to stay and help after the battle. But I fear I may burden you more than I could ever help."

"What do you mean?" the princess asked.

Sara sighed and stood up. "Why don't you show me some of your drawings? I've heard little of your gods. Perhaps you can teach me?" she asked.

Anya's face lit up. "Yes! Fang and Shade! Let me show you!" She bounded through the garden and out the door. Sara looked back at the portal with a frown before turning away and following the child.

After quite the afternoon of playing and talking about wolves and gods, she found herself among the healers and herbalists that had set up in tents around the courtyard. She entered a tent to see several women laying sheets on cots, setting down saws and knives, and mixing elixirs. The looks on their faces were grim, and she heard a man's screams come from the other tent. One older woman looked at her and handed her a basket full of green vials.

"It's to help the pain if they get wounded. We don't have enough to drag men over to the tents. Maybe they can do it themselves. If you could hand these out, we would be grateful."

Sara bowed slightly. "Of course, I will." She left the tent and started towards a group of soldiers sitting around and drinking. Although they laughed and conversed, she could see if it did not reach their eyes. She stepped over to them and softly entered into their conversation.

"Here, these are for if you are injured and cannot find aid. Please take this and come to the tents where we can help you." She handed out the vials, and they thanked her.

"Do you know what they are saying?" one asked, his face dirty and pale.

"They say they 'ave even more demons now. That they can get into your head, make you kill your own brothers like what happened to Faden. He just got this look in his eye when he saw his mate killed by cultists. Fell right on 'is own sword. That ain't gonna happen, right, healer?" The rest turned to her, and she looked away from their gazes.

"No. Demons cannot do that. I promise. We will win this battle."

"You don't hear what they say up on those walls. They say they can hear the screeching from up there. I don't want to take watch," another one said. She handed out the last vial and walked away with a heavy heart. These were just boys. Farmers and miners, and anglers. They were terrified. And who could blame them?

She could help, she knew. But she was also terrified. Terrified of what may happen once the battle ensued and what would happen afterward.

She made her way slowly through the camp, gifting the vials to wary soldiers until she came upon the king-to-be. He was dressed in only a tunic and pants; sweat beaded heavily off his face and chest. He trained with a sword, slashing a straw dummy over and over. From the look on his face, he was thinking not about the dummy, but about something else. He didn't notice her approach as she grabbed a vial from the basket. She held it in her hand and looked back up at him.

She didn't want to give him one. Giving him one meant that there was a chance he could be wounded or killed.

"Lord Dicesare?" she asked loudly. He seemed to come out of his mind and looked over at her. His breathing came heavy, and he wiped his forehead with his hand.

"Lady Sara. I am sorry, I did not hear you come near." He stepped over to her, and she took a breath and held out the vial to him.

"Its… medicine to dull the pain in case you are wounded… and we cannot get to you," she said.

He looked down at the green liquid swirling inside the vial and gently clasped his hand over hers. "I am grateful," he thanked. He pulled the vial from her grasp and placed it in his pocket. He set his sword and took a rag to wipe his face.

"Will you be fighting with the men?" she asked.

He nodded and put the rag over his shoulder. "I am a king, and this is my kingdom. I will not let it fall while I hide in the keep or in the capital. If my kingdom is to fall, I will fall with it."

She felt her heart grow heavy at his words. But she knew she could not dissuade him. This was his home. And he cared more for it than many others cared for their children.

"What about your mother and sister?"

"Anya should be going through the portal as soon as the rest of the men arrive. My mother is stubborn. She will not go through either."

"Will Anya be alright?"

He gave half a laugh and looked out past the walls. "She is known for getting herself into trouble. And out of it. I believe she will be fine. Though I worry the court may smother her in their dresses."

Sara laughed and repositioned the basket onto her hip. "Please try to be safe, Thymas," she softly pleaded.

He gently ran a hand down her arm. "I will try, my lady."

80 JARED

The walls of the giant city came into view. Jared reigned his horse up to Nava as she stared at guards atop the walls.

"To be honest, I never thought I would actually see these walls," Nava said.

Jared raised a brow. "And why is that?"

"When I was lying on that table... my only thought was that I would never reclaim what was mine. Never see the shine of the palace," she admitted.

Jared sighed softly. "Well, you're alive now."

"Yes, I am."

As the crowds condensed, the couple unmounted and led their horses through the commoner gates of the city. The guard's presence was hefty, and the lines were long. They checked bags and carriages and pushed some people away.

"Why are they being so forceful?" Nava asked.

"Most likely because of the Dark Kingdom's presence in Ignis."

"Do you think they could attack here?"

"I don't know."

It took several hours for them to pass the gates, and they paid little mind to them or their belongings. As the crowds dispersed along the streets, Jared found a stable and, with more *sephim* than he wanted to part with, left their mares to the keeper.

Hearing the chatter, the calling and the children running around reminded Jared of Ignis. In Ignis, you couldn't step a meter without seeing a stall lined with goods and women sewing dresses. Here was a bit busier. More fancy gowns lined the streets, and servants ran after diplomats. Criers held out papers to read, and someone pushed a herd of sheep across the street.

"Do you know where she could be?" Nava asked, pulling Jared from his thoughts.

"What—no. I don't."

"Then perhaps we should part ways here and meet back up later."

Jared opened his mouth but didn't say anything. He barely knew the layout of Fira. He could check the Beggars' Quarter for taverns where Olivia could be. But he was truly at a loss. To be honest, he didn't expect to get this far either.

"Yes. Let's meet up in the city center. There is a lake there, I heard."

Nava nodded and shifted her bow. "Alright. I will see you then." With a small nod, she brought up her hood and disappeared into the crowd. Jared felt a chill creep up his spine as he turned and started down one of the roads. It felt odd not having her by his side. It had been a grueling month, and it would have been longer without the horses, but something about it had a place in his memory. A small bubble of contentment.

After a few questions and some bribery, Jared managed to find the Beggar's Quarter and several taverns scattered about. Beggars in and of itself wasn't as terrible as the poorer districts in Ignis, but the homeless still begged for coin, and the wood along the rooftops still dripped water. Children ran around in rags and played in puddles. Jared sidestepped a cart stuck in the mud with a bickering couple outside of it and entered a tavern called the *Wayman's ale*. It was cozy enough. Most of the patrons were still out about the town since the sun had yet to set. The few in the tavern were casually talking or sleeping on the floor. He greeted the stout man tending the bar.

"'Scuse me. You see a woman come in here from Ignis?" he asked.

The bartender gave him a look and picked up a tankard, setting it in front of him. "Drink first?"

"The woman—"

"Drink."

Jared sighed and threw a *sephim* onto the table. The man took it and poured him an ale. "So, a woman from Ignis, ye said?"

Jared took a drink and nodded. "Yes. Long dark curly hair. Dressed like a bard or tavern maid. Might have said where she was coming from."

The bartender thought for a second, wiping a tankard down with a rag. "Lots of gals come through 'ere every day. But can't say none said they were from Ignis. No one had been from there."

Jared sighed and rubbed his eyes, downing the rest of the ale. A headache had already started to throb in his temple, and he sighed. He stood abruptly and waved the man off before leaving the tavern and crawling to the next.

81 NAVA

The distant sound of thunder and creaking of store signs led Nava further into the city. At each cloth or jewelry stall, she stopped, looking for the item she had longed for. The muddy steps of townspeople and the clucking of chickens kept the streets alive with noise. She even dared to go into the elite stores and was pushed out quickly by the salespeople.

She did well to cover herself, nearly no one paid any mind to the half-elf as she searched, and as the day wore on, she grew more desperate. Fira was large. It would take days to find what she was looking for—if she ever found it. It was the only thing she wanted, the only thing she *needed*.

"You look lost, lass. Is there something I can help you with?" A man asked. She turned to him. He sold children's toys from his stall. Small, handcrafted horses and dolls. She came up to him with soft steps.

"I am looking for a locket. One that might have been taken from a raid on a village. Do you know of anyone who sells odds and ends?" she asked.

The man stroked his beard. "You can try over on Beggars Corner, just a few blocks down the road 'ere. They tend to sell stolen goods. But be careful. Pretty girls tend to get sold there too," he warned. She thanked him and went on her way, passing several streets before entering the alleyway. Several people stood in the shadows, all with a glint in their eyes that made her anxious. She passed by the homeless and sick as they coughed and begged for change. She made her way over to a man who looked at her under his worn hat.

"What is a pretty doll like you doing down here? Looking for work?" he asked.

She shook her head. "I am looking for a locket. One that has an elven woman's portrait on the inside. It is gold. Have you seen it?"

The man looked around at the other people in the alley. "Can't say I have. No one around here keeps gold for very long. Probably long melted down for another button on the emperor's trousers. But you could ask the wise man."

"Wise man?"

"It's said he can get you anything you want. Women? Slaves? A noble's son? Anything is up for grabs if you pay the price."

She looked at him warily. "And what is that price?"

His smirk reached far past his nose, nearly crawling into his eyes. "Just a piece of you. Not a large part. A taste. Then some more later." The look in his eye made her skin crawl, and she backed away.

"I…I think I am okay." She started back down the alleyway.

"Don't you want to see your mother again, little huntress?" he asked. She stopped in her tracks. His voice was sour in her ear, and the rest of the city folk seemed to disappear into the shadows. She turned her head to look back at him, and his eyes gleamed in the dying light.

"I can show you. I can show you the way to the wise man. Only a *sephim* for me." He extended his hand, and the bones seemed to reach past his skin, pulling it taut against the muscle.

"No. I'll find it on my own," she stammered. She quickly fled the alleyway, and the sun began to shine upon her again. She didn't dare go back to where she came. Instead, she headed towards the Beggars Quarter as the rain began to come down. The pitter-patter of the water droplets hitting the ground reminded her of the village. Staring out at the forest, watching the trees sway against the wind.

Just one more place. Someone must have it, she thought.

It was stolen by someone during the raid that destroyed her village. They had to have sold it; it would be no use to them except for gold. She passed a small antique shop and paused at the window. It held ceramic pieces and priceless porcelain. Some jewelry was scattered about, none looking that fancy to her. But it was worth a shot. She entered the small shop and was met with a short woman who was mending a leather purse on a haphazardously built wooden table. She looked up from her position and adjusted her glasses.

"Can I do something for you, miss?" she asked in a squeaky voice. Nava glanced over at the various items strewn around the shop. Rusty bikes, some worn parchment, and the entire place smelled of an old shoe.

"I am looking for an elven locket. Gold. Might have a picture of a woman inside of it."

The woman scratched her head and hopped from her perch. She disappeared behind the counter, and Nava could hear her ruffling through containers. She saw a pair of hands come up and slam an old box onto the counter. Nava neared and peered at the box, and the hands disappeared again. She ran a finger along the dusty outside and wiped her hand on her pants. The woman appeared again with a small box and hopped onto a stool to open them.

"I deal with some elven artifacts or goods. I even have a sample of the God Text, mmm," she hummed. "Now a locket..." She pulled the top off the box, and Nava sneezed at the dust. She set the top aside and pushed them towards the half-elf.

There were necklaces, bracelets, and a few small keychains inside the box. She scrounged for something else, but found nothing she was looking for. She turned to the smaller box and opened the lid. Inside sat three lockets, all rusted. Nava's heart picked up slightly as she took out the lockets and placed them on the counter. One was much too large to be the one she was looking for, and the other was silver. The last one was gold with just a hint of rust on the edges. She took the locket in her hand and opened the clasp.

Her heart sank.

Nothing.

She set the locket back on the counter with a sigh.

"I'm sorry, lass. I hope you can find what you are looking for," the shopkeeper said with a small smile. Nava pulled her hood further towards her face and gave a farewell.

The rain was now heavy on her shoulders as she stepped outside the shop. She started back down the street, dodging people running from the rain. She was knocked away by a group of children, and she turned a corner and slammed into a noble lady. She fell to the ground, and a guard grabbed onto the lady to keep her from falling as well.

"How dare you!" the woman cried. "Now my dress is ruined!"

Nava looked up to see a mud smear run down the skirt of her dress and stood up, ignoring her now-drenched pants.

"My apologies—"

"You damn street rats. You never learn, do you!"

"I said I was sorry—" she cut Nava off again.

"Guard, deal with her!" she screeched. The guard stepped in front of the lady and grabbed Nava by the shirt, punching her hard across the face. She fell to the ground again, and he kicked her in the stomach. She groaned, and the noble lady sidestepped her.

"Good riddance, filth," she spat. The guard left with her, and Nava pulled herself up, feeling the bruise under her eye already beginning to swell. Her stomach pulsed painfully, and she forced herself to stand straight. She guessed that was the end of it then.

She sat down on the roadside, feeling the rainfall against her cloak. She closed her eyes and imagined being back there.

She heard her mother humming softly, sitting on the steps of their small cottage. The other elves passed by, looking at the half-breed child. Her mother paid them no mind. She twisted strands of hair together to make a perfect braid down Nava's back. She still remembered the tune. She felt her mother's hands gently pick her up and bring her back inside.

She could remember being curled in her mother's arms in their bed. And she remembered when she gave Nava the locket. They went together to the local painter and had a portrait done of both of them. The last time her mother smiled.

A carriage rolled by and knocked Nava from her memories. The rain began to grow more consistent, and she stood up. Perhaps it was time to meet with the swordsman. If he would be there. If he found his Olivia, then he would leave her. They would be together again, and he would no longer have need of her assistance. And why should she be upset with that? If one of them had found what they came for, then that was enough. She could find her way back, possibly return to that village with the farm. They would treat her well there.

She looked down the street toward the gates of the city as the thunder came again.

Just wait and see, she told herself. She turned away and started towards the lake, a small glimmer of hope that he would be there waiting for her.

82 JARED

Three taverns later, and with no luck finding the bard, Jared sat on the edge of the road, bottle in hand. The rain and falling daylight seemed to mock him. He went through every direct town to Fira, and no one had heard from Olivia. And he had searched every dusty tavern in Fira and still no trace of her. He didn't want to admit what he knew was true.

He took a long drink from his bottle and lay against the rough stone. The cold on his back clashed with the warmth in his face and stomach. He had barely survived that night. He could still feel the heat on his skin from the burning buildings around him.

Rose was probably dead. The Dark Kingdom came hard and fast. The first place they would have hit was the castle. Both his friends were gone, and here he was. A drunkard bastard with nothing else left. The rain came heavier, and Jared pulled himself up and started towards the center of town, following the promise to a half-elf.

She was better off without him as well. He wondered if he should even meet her. They both went their separate ways. They were done. He needed nothing else from her.

And yet his feet kept moving, and his mouth kept drinking. The streets became deserted as the rain fell hard, and he stumbled and tripped over forgotten carts and toys. A group of children ran past, and he ignored them, nearly hitting one in the head with his bottle. He took a long swig and stumbled, falling to his knees. The world swayed around him, and he closed his eyes. The pain did not stop like he hoped it would. Instead, it festered inside him like bile, waiting to be thrown up.

His eyes caught the shimmer of a skirt, and he looked up. Dark locks caught his gaze as a woman passed him by, holding up the hood of her coat to keep herself dry.

"Olivia...?" he asked. The woman's silhouette faded into the blurry distance, and he pushed himself up onto his feet. "O-olivia wait!" he called.

He stumbled but caught himself, dropping the bottle and hearing it break against the stone street. He chased her shadow as she weaved around puddles and disappeared into a building. His drunken mind kept himself locked in pace with her, negating any arguments about trespassing.

He stumbled into the building, catching himself on the thick wooden doors. The world spun, and he leaned against the door, his breathing labored and quick. He shut his eyes tightly, trying to find his place. When he reopened them, the world wobbled and shifted suddenly, and he fell to the ground.

He landed on the cold marble floor and took a sudden breath as it seeped through his sopping shirt. "Olivia," he whispered. His voice echoed around the room, bouncing off the windows, and he grimaced.

He rolled over, putting his face to the floor and taking a deep breath. The cold was soothing against his hot face, and he moved his arms under him, pushing himself up. Jared kept his eyes on the ground as he crawled. If he could just find her, he would be safe. He would be happy.

He crawled, watching his red knuckles shift with every movement from his hands. He heard a tap of shoes to his right, and he looked over but saw nothing. He kept crawling.

When it seemed the room was endless, his hands hit something hard. He lifted his hand, feeling shaped stone. He moved his hands up, through layers of the stone like a skirt. He took a breath and looked up.

A woman looked down at him, her marble eyes gleaming in the firelight. She held her hands over her heart, her veil falling around her face.

The room was silent except for the pattering of the rain on the windows, and the puff of the candelabras on the table beside him. He stared at the woman in front of him. Olivia was gone, disappearing into the night and leaving nothing but a statue of a woman in front of him. A goddess he barely prayed to.

"What do you want from me?" he whispered, sitting back on his heels. The woman did not answer; her eyes stayed locked on his own.

He felt as if he were about to break. It wasn't fair. None of it was fair. Why did the goddess let him live and not the others? He was no one special. No one but a drunken man with no name and no family. All he wanted was to see her face again. To feel the warmth of her skin, the feel of her hair. He began to wonder who he was talking about.

His mind was foggy and dazed. He wanted her, he did. He missed her smell, the way she laughed. He buried his head in his knees and took a long and shaky breath. His stomach churned, and he fought back the bile in his throat. The alcohol didn't help. Not anymore.

"Tell me please," he cried, digging his nails into the palm of his hands. "Tell me what you want from me."

He lifted his head angrily. "Tell me!"

His voice echoed through the room, bouncing from pillar to pillar, through his ears, and down his spine. Still, the woman did not answer. He gripped his hair and screamed.

Thunder crashed outside, loud and roaring, and he jumped, looking above him as the windows rattled. The woman was illuminated in the lightning, an arch of light like wings at her back. He watched as the candles flickered and the doors swung wide, slamming against the walls. He looked behind him and saw a shadow in the doorway.

He stood up shakily, and the shadow stepped away into the street. His breathing was calming, and he looked back at the woman. Her gaze was now upcast, towards the ceiling.

He took a long breath and turned away, following the shadow back out into the street. The shadow faded into the dying light of the roadway and he stumbled his way through the town, his mind trailing from the woman to the thoughts of a promise he had yet to keep.

Eventually, he found the lake in the middle of the city and fell to the grass below him, letting the rain pierce his hot skin. Thunder crashed against the sky, and he watched the water ripple and spin. He closed his eyes and rested his face on her knees, taking long, deep breaths.

It felt like hours until he felt a presence sit beside him. He didn't bother to open his eyes to see who had invaded his stupor. Did you find it?" he asked.

"No," she responded. Her voice was soft and light. Like a feather had landed on his shoulder and tickled his ear. A heavy weight pushed down on his chest at her reply, and he sat up, running his fingers through his hair.

"That is disappointing."

"Did you?"

Jared opened his eyes and felt them sting with the water running down his face. "No."

There was a pause.

"I'm sorry."

Jared looked at her, at her bruised eye, matted hair, and pale lips. He wanted to laugh. She looked worse than him. Instead, he bit his lip and choked out a sob.

"She's gone. I couldn't save her—I should have—" Another sob wracked his body, and he felt her hands go around his shoulders. She pulled him into her chest and ran her fingers through his hair. She smelled like lavender.

"Shhh, it's alright. It is not your fault, Jared."

He laughed between his shaken sobs and brought his hand around her back. "You said my name."

"Yes... I suppose I did."

"Thank you."

They held each other tighter as the rain came down, and the moons pulled themselves from the clouds to mirror the pool around them. Jared set his eyes on the water and slowed his breathing.

"Will you stay with me?" he asked.

"Always," she responded.

83 ROSE

The temple was in sight now. Rose could feel the thrum of magic through the ground. Her ruby pulsed lightly around her neck and warmed her skin against the cold. The snow had lessened considerably as they coursed through the mountains. She could now walk without being impeded by three feet of wet obstacles. It was a heavenly sight to see the cave entrance.

"The door is over here," Nadahi said, leading the party over to a large stone entryway. The door had carvings of animals etched into it, along with runes and markings Rose could not identify. On the four corners of the door, one animal stood. A bear, a stag, a wolf, and a fox. In the middle of the door was a small slot, barely bigger than a thumb. Nadahi ran her hand down the door, whispering something to herself.

"This door hasn't been opened in thousands of years. There used to be an honor guard that kept watch over the ruins, but the corruption forced us to retreat."

"Do you know how to open the door?" Rose asked.

Nadahi shook her head. "I was hoping you would be able to."

Liv gently led Rose to the door, which stood well over two meters high. She pulled her glove off and traced the runes along the stone.

"What does it say?" she asked.

Nadahi wiped snow from the side of the door with her ax, mouthing the words. "Only the stone who casts the first light shall be welcomed into the Mother's heart," Nadahi translated.

Rose scrunched her brow and stepped back from the door. "Stone who casts the first light...?" she questioned. She gazed out across the mountain tops, and Erling sauntered up to the door.

"Why don't we just try and break through?" he asked.

"Do you want to be smited by the Mother?" Hakon retorted.

Erling paused, then shrugged. "Think she'll still let me into *Shor'vaker?*"

"With that mouth of yours, I hope not," Liv laughed.

"What stone could this be referring to?" Nadahi asked.

"There are none in the legends I remember," Hakon said. "And we have no such stone to try."

"Then we cannot enter," Liv sighed.

"Well, we cannot give up yet," Rose said and fingered her necklace. *Wait!*

Rose ran up to the door, pulling snow from the thumbprint hole in the door.

"It's my necklace. It's the stone," she said. Pulling her necklace off, she placed the ruby in the slot on the door. The door began to shudder as the ruby lit up a bright red light. The light traveled through the markings in the door, illuminating the animals as it passed through.

"Well, would you look at that," Torgir laughed.

The door slid open with a shudder, revealing a dark hallway behind it. The whispers of magic called out the *Runa,* like a longlost song. The party peered inside before Rose pulled the stone from its holder and strung it around her neck.

"I suppose we go inside now," Erling muttered, tapping his fingers on his shield. Rose took a tentative step forward, feeling the stone ground beneath her. Even just placing her body inside the cave made the temperature swell.

Nadahi went after Rose, keeping close to her. "Be careful. We cannot know if the corruption has spread ins—"

Nadahi was knocked back, slamming into Liv and sending them skidding back into the snow. Rose spun around as they pulled themselves up.

"What in the Mother's name was that?" Hakon asked.

Erling took a small step forward, holding out his ax. It hit an unseen barrier, and he slid it down. Energy seemed to ripple from his ax, and it made a drumming noise as he ran it along the barrier.

Rose walked back to the group and put her hand out, but found no resistance. "I don't understand?"

"It seems the goddess only wishes her child to enter," Nadahi said, a frown marking her lips.

"What? By myself?" Rose exclaimed, a ball of panic welling up inside of her.

Nadahi stepped as close as she could to Rose and cupped her hands in her own. "This is your next trial, Rose. Trust in yourself. We will be here when you return," she said with a small smile.

Rose blushed and nodded. "All right. But please don't leave me here."

"I promise you we will stay here. Go, *Runa.*"

Rose dropped her hands and turned around, taking a deep breath. She re-entered the cave hallway and watched as the door closed behind her, casting her in darkness. Whispers filled her ears, the shadows wrapping themselves further around her. She grabbed her necklace and shakily held her hand out. With a soft prayer to Velara, a small ball of flame rose in her palm. More than what she could conjure mere weeks ago. It was enough.

The flame bounced off the stone walls as she continued through the hallways. The walls and ceilings showed carvings of battles, none of which she could remember from her studies. They all showed those of the Northlanders engaged in battle with a giant, four-headed serpent. The first carving revealed them battling the serpent, blades, and bows held high. The next, they had all fallen in battle, the serpent's wings covering the battlefield. Then a figure held up one hand to block out the power of the serpent; in their other hand was a glowing sword. The last, a figure stood on top of the fallen creature, the rest of the people bowing to them.

The runes cast against the ground lit up as she walked past. The whispers only grew louder around her.

After what seemed like hours, she found an opening in the hallways. She stepped down into what looked like a small spring. The area was the size of a small room, and moss had made a home along the walls. A trickle of water coming from a crack in the ceiling fed the spring. The light cast along the water made the entire room appear blue in hue.

Rose dropped her flame and stepped across the rocks to the spring, stopping just from setting foot inside. The whispers grew silent as small balls of light faded in and out of the water. She looked down to see her own reflection wave along the ripples of the pool.

"Come, my child."

Rose looked around her, searching for the voice. It was in Nadahi's tongue, but she understood it.

"Long have I waited."

Rose looked back down into the water and gasped. It wasn't her who looked back at her, but her mother's face. She smiled softly at her child. It was as if she called to her from the water, inviting her in.

"It is time."

Rose stood up and pulled off her furs, her legs feeling as if they were lead. She threw the fabric aside and pulled off her boots before stepping into the pool. The water felt warm, warmer than the room itself. It called to her, pulling her deeper.

"Come."

Rose walked until she was neck-deep in the water, her heartbeat steadier than it should have been. The water felt denser now, sogging her clothing. She looked at the ceiling; the light blinding her eyes. With a deep breath, she pulled herself down under the water. She felt hands grasping at her, pulling her further under. She felt the ruby burn against her clothing. She felt her lungs shake.

And as if she was no longer in the water at all, she opened her eyes. In front of her, a large tree stood, its bark shining every color of the sky. Crows nested in the thick and twisting branches and cawed loudly at her.

"Where am I?" Rose asked.

"You are here. You are everywhere."

Rose took a step toward the tree, and it seemed to grow larger with every step she took.

"I weep for my children."

Spirits danced around Rose, barely touching her, pushing her further toward the tree. A flash of silver caught her eyes, and she looked to the side to see a white wolf walking beside her. Its purple eyes looked into her own.

"Only four remain. Only together can you end Maganth's tyranny."

"Maganth, who is Maganth?"

"My Love. My life. My death. His children roam my chest. Slaughter my own. Four remain."

Rose reached the branches of the tree and watched as fae played among the leaves. The crow's cawing was louder than before, and their red eyes pierced through her.

"What do you want of me? How can I stop the Forsaken?"

"Four for four. A life for life. Claim my children, and the prince shall awaken."

"How? I am stuck here in this winter. Please, help me!" she cried.

A crow flew down to Rose, tapping against the glowing ground before her.

"One stands before me now. One lies in exile. One runs from darkness. And one gleams in the light. Maganth is held in shackles."

The crow flew away, and Rose bent down, wiping the dirt from where it stood. Her fingertips hit soft leather, and she pulled a tome from its place. It was large; the rigged pages stained yellow from the fate of time. She held it in her lap and ran her fingers down the binding.

"When four of the damned meet the fate of man, the final seal will be released unto the world."

"What?" Rose asked, looking up at the tree. "What does that mean?"

"Claim the four. Break the shackles. And set my children free."

The light of the tree faded, and her lungs constricted in her chest. She gasped and held the book to her chest, and she fell from the ground into an endless void. She clawed and fought for air, swimming against the darkness.

She surfaced from the water of the pool and threw the book onto the shore, hacking up the water in her lungs. The spring was quiet. Only the sound of falling water remained. She lay there for a time, catching her breath, before dressing and starting back down the path, watching the stone carvings flicker against the light. She could still hear the whispers in her ear.

Cast light unto shadow.

The doors opened for her, and Rose found the group camped outside, huddled over the fire, eyes trained ahead. When Nadahi saw Rose, she jumped from her position and wrapped her in a tight embrace.

"*Runa,* you're alive," she gasped.

Rose blew hair from her face before responding. "Yes, I'm back. Is everything alright?" she asked.

Liv stood up from the campfire. "You've been gone five days, *Runa.*"

"What?" Rose exclaimed, pulling away from the huntress. "It didn't seem that long."

"Magic is mysterious. Time flows differently with it. Did you find what you were searching for?" Nadahi asked.

"Yes." She showed the tome to the group with a shaky breath, who all stared at it in disbelief. "I know what we must do."

"What is it?"

Rose took a breath.

"We must kill the Dark Knights and unleash death upon the world."

84 THYMAS

Thymas woke with a start—the keep shook underneath him, and he heard a thunderous *boom* echo through the room. He quickly dressed and took his sword as screaming filled the halls. As he stepped from his room, guards ran past him.

"Defend the keep! Defend the people!" they yelled. *No*, he thought. *It's too soon.*

Thymas rushed past the guards, bumping into them and pushing them away as he ran up the stairs to his sister's room. Shoving open the door, he dragged her from her bed. "Anya, get up, now!" he ordered.

She groggily looked up at him. "Thymas? What's going on?" she asked. He quickly pulled her coat over her shoulders and pulled her out of the room. The walls shook again due to another blast, causing bricks to come loose and shatter against the ground. Paintings fell from the walls as he moved her under his arm to shield her from the debris as it cleared.

A guard ran up to them hastily. "Your Graces, are you alright?" he asked.

Thymas pushed Anya towards him. "Take her to the portal with the others, see she is safe." The guard nodded and grabbed her arm.

"Thymas, no! Please!" she pleaded.

"I love you, Anya, be safe," he said. He turned away and ignored her cries of protest and raced down the hallway towards his mother's room. Another blast shook the keep, and he fell to his knees, covering his head as a wall toppled in front of him. The bricks shattered as they hit the ground and he coughed from the dust and mold that invaded his nostrils.

When he looked out the hole in the wall, he could see smoke on the horizon. He saw men scurry up the ramparts and heard them shouting orders. He forced himself back onto his feet and climbed over the debris to his mother's room.

He entered her room, but she was already up, looking out the window.

"I can see the darkness even from here," she muttered. "I pray our men are enough."

"Please, mother, go through the portal," he pleaded. "The battle is upon us. I do not want to see you fall."

She shook her head. "I will stay and barricade the door. Go, boy, you have a kingdom to protect."

Thymas cursed and turned, heading back out the door. "Thymas."

He turned, and he saw her eyes waver. "I lost two of my children already. I do not wish to lose another."

He smiled slightly. "Then I give you my word; I will not fall today." He closed the door behind him. The floor under him rocked and shook, and he nearly lost his balance as the sky pulsed black. He heard the wooden barricade go down on the other side and ordered soldiers to stand outside her room.

"The rest of the men with me!" he ordered. The soldiers followed him from the keep and into the courtyard, where screaming women and children ran towards the portal, desperate to escape. The chaos below frightened even him as more fighters lined the walls and buckets of water were set up beside the wooden gate. Squires ran amok, handing out arrows and carrying armfuls of wood. He heard the Imperial commander barking out orders atop the walls.

He knew they had little chance of victory, but if he could only give enough time for Anya to escape, maybe they could retake WhiteDrove someday. Knowing that there may yet be an heir to survive gave him a false glimmer of hope. *Be safe, Anya,* he thought.

"Thymas!" he heard Sara yell. He looked towards the medical tents set up beside the keep and saw her run up to him.

"Stay away from the battle, Sara; we can handle this," he said. Her hands wrapped around his own and he saw her dark, beautiful eyes waver. He took in her face, her eyes, her mouth like it was the last time he may see her. If he were to fall, perhaps she could survive as well. He could not bear the thought of seeing her lying dead on the field.

Her solemn face gave away her emotions. "If it comes to it," she started, "I want you to know that I never lied to you."

Before he could respond, she kissed him hard on the mouth. He was surprised for only a moment before his own mouth opened for hers, and he pulled her close to his chest. Her tongue tasted of berries and sweet cream. Her hair smelled of spring. It was only days, and yet it felt as if he had loved her for a lifetime. But to love something so strongly meant he had to protect it. She moaned softly as he forced himself to let her go.

"Sara." He whispered her name like a song. "Please be careful. Go through the portal if you must… I cannot bear to lose you."

She touched his face, her hand warming his chilled cheek, then she turned away and fled back to the tents. Thymas turned back to the walls and gripped the pommel of his sword, praying for victory.

85 VIA

Via watched over the horizon at the massing army that awaited her. Hearing the sounds of the boots hitting the ground made her back ache painfully. The last battle was lost. They could not lose this one. She gripped her bow in her hand and notched an arrow. The army was less than a mile away from her reach. She could hear the townspeople running and screaming behind her as they fled. The portal would stay open as long as it could. But she knew she would have to close it if they stormed the keep. It was the only way to keep Fira safe.

Commander Rye stood beside her; his eyes set on the horizon. The sun had barely risen over the landscape, but her eyes allowed her to see the growing mass even in the darkness.

"I am with you, Via," Rye told her.

She shook the nerves from her body and smiled sadly at him. "And I am with you."

She watched as a priest walked the walls, an incense brazier dangling from her hand. The smell of myrrh wafted through her nose and she felt her fingertips tingle.

"Goddess Velara, bathe us in Your holy grace. Cleanse our sinful hearts and guide us to the heavenly plains to be by Your side. Bless the men who fight in Your name and purge those who shall cause them harm. To the stars and sky above."

The men around her, Rye included, bowed their heads and whispered their prayers as her eyes stayed locked onto the dark army. She doubted their goddess could save them now.

Eyeing the battlefield, she searched for Gelum but could not find him in the mass of bodies. He was her target. If she could defeat him, victory was assured.

The few enchanters in their army stood behind the walls, hands raised, creating a soft shield of light in front of them. Even she knew the barrier would not hold for long. She felt the wood beneath her tremble as black lines shot into the sky, covering the rising sun. They grew larger, and Via made out the flying demons. They spun in the air and unfurled their wings, screeching for blood. Via raised her bow and followed the path the demons had taken to their master. Taking a breath, she loosed her arrow and sent it flying towards the maleficarum who summoned them. Several of the demons exploded into a black fog as her arrow hit, but the others dove down, talons at the ready.

"Notch!" Rye yelled. The archers drew their bows as she did. She aimed towards one of the winged beasts and waited.

"Draw!"

The beasts were directly above them now, ready to strike.

"Loose!" Dozens of arrows pierced the sky as they hit the demons and cultists alike. Several of the demons fell to the ground in black twitching masses, but others survived and ripped through the barrier, tearing men from the walls, sending them tumbling down. Via shot an arrow at a demon that had taken hold of a soldier and carried him into the air. She pierced its head, and it screeched and dropped the man, combusting. The man fell to the ground with a cry, and she saw the priestess and another soldier grab him and flee. She turned back to the army and sent another arrow at the commander's orders. A host of demons and cultists fell to the arrows, but more stood to take their place.

Via heard it before she could see it. "Duck!" she screamed. She pulled Rye down as a fireball slammed into the barrier, shattering it and causing molten rock to fall on top of them. They stood as another ball hit the courtyard. Demon hounds jumped from the army and ran towards the walls, mouths dripping in their black tar.

"Ready the spikes!" Rye yelled. Men began hoisting up giant spiked balls of blessed iron and set them down where they stood. Rye brought his hand up as the demon hounds grew closer. She notched another arrow and whispered a prayer to *Ethena'ethal*.

"Hold..." he ordered. The men lifted the balls onto the walls and waited for their drop. The demons howled and snarled, and they jumped and latched onto the wooden walls with their claws. She watched them climb nearly to the top before Rye spoke again.

"Drop!" he yelled. The men threw the spikes from the walls as they slammed into the demons and crushed their heads and backs. They howled in pain, and Via loosed another arrow in the eye of a demon. A few managed to scale the walls and pounced on the men. Ripping into their throats and arms. The man beside her was thrown from the wall and screamed as a demon ripped his arm off. She felt his hot sticky blood splatter her face. She quickly turned and put an arrow into its back. It fell to the ground, and the healers pulled the man from it. She turned back to the Plains to see another burst of flame hit the keep.

"Hold steady!" Rye commanded. The army was nearly on top of them now. As the archers continued the arrow barrage, she picked off the maleficarum and watched for Gelum's return. He still had yet to show his face, but she knew he was there. And he was waiting for her.

86 THYMAS

Thymas watched the chaos unfold atop the walls as he grabbed a wounded man and took him to the healers. He heard someone scream behind him and watched a wolf-like demon hound rip into an enchanter's neck. He swung his sword and slashed it across the face. It screeched and jumped back. It circled him, and he kept his eyes locked on its bloodshot, bulging ones. It snapped and snarled at him, taunting him.

"Well, come on then!" He yelled. It lunged, and he blocked with this sword as it slammed into him. He pushed it off and stab it through the back. It cried out, and he jumped on top of it as it bucked and kicked. He drove his sword through its neck and twisted. Its head rolled away from his twitching body and evaporated under him. He stood up and wiped his face, giving a soft prayer to the dead soldier. He heard the commander call out as another fireball slammed into the keep, sending embers flying. A healer's clothes caught fire as she scrambled to escape. He grabbed a bucket of water and poured it on her as she cried.

"Go! Now!" he yelled.

Sara came over and grabbed the lady and pulled her to safety. Ash fell from the sky like snow as the fires exploded around them, scattering the men and drowning out the cries. More demons poured from the walls and sky as he met with the other soldiers. Some were lying on the ground screaming in pain, holding their arms and legs. One of them was holding his right hand, which had been torn completely off, bits of bone and tendon laying in his lap. Thymas bent down and pulled the green vial from his pocket, pouring it into his mouth. His screams ceased nearly instantly, but his eyes were still wide with terror.

"My king, get back!'" Lord Downor called, coming up beside him. His face was smeared with soot and his leg was wounded. He took Thymas by the arm. "You must get back!"

"I am not leaving," Thymas argued. "This is my city, my kingdom. I will not leave my people to defend themselves."

"You are the heir to your House, the only son. You cannot throw your life away," the lord argued.

"I am not. I will be no heir if I have no House left to defend," he argued.

They both ducked when another fireball soared across the sky, hitting a house beyond the keep. "Go!" Thymas yelled. "Get the people to safety through the portal."

"I am not leaving you, my liege," Lord Downor said, shaking his head. Then, both looked towards the walls as an ear piercing wail cut through the sound of the battle. A demon seemingly larger than the sun shadowed the keep, its wails making his ears ring.

"What in the bloody hells?" Lord Downor questioned. They were both knocked off their feet as a giant burst of green fire shot through the gate of the keep, exploding the wood and sending splinters flying. The men atop the gate screamed and batted at their burning skin, falling from the walls. The ball of flame died out near Thymas, and he watched as the dark army cheered in glory and charged the keep.

Thymas stood up as the demons screamed above. He took his sword and gripped it tight. "For our home! For WhiteDrove!" he yelled, rallying the men. The soldiers cried with him and rushed the gates. "For victory!"

87 VIA

Via knew as soon as the shadowed beast covered the sun that Gelum would arrive. The beast dipped low and dove for the keep. It slammed into the ground in a mass of black that blew anyone in the vicinity away. The ground grew dark and withered, and men choked and collapsed in sickness, tearing at their bloodied eyes. Gelum appeared in the mists, and Via jumped from the walls.

"Leave now! Move!" she yelled, sprinting past soldiers and wounded coming in from outside the gates. Via grabbed a sword from a fallen guard and, with a yell, swung it towards the Knight. He blocked it with his own and laughed.

"The elf returns. How many times do I need to carve my blade into your back?" he sneered.

"You will not leave here alive, beast," she spat. He laughed again and swung his sword, crashing into her own and shattering it. She dropped the sword and quickly loosed an arrow at him. It pierced his shoulder with a *thunk*, and he roared.

"Bitch!" He lunged for her and grabbed her by the coat, flinging her into a stack of wood. She hit it with a cry, and Rye slammed into the Knight, pushing him back. He sliced his sword through his arm, and the Knight stumbled.

"Argh!" he yelled. He backhanded Rye away and lifted his hand. A green ball of magic formed, and he launched it at Rye, who brought his shield up in time to block it. He was thrown onto his back, and with a groan, rolled back up. Via pulled herself up and grabbed her bow. She watched as the men were being overrun by the cultists and retreating away from the gates. Demons poured from atop the walls, and she turned her focus back to Gelum.

"Run Via! Get to the portal! Close the portal!" Rye cried.

Gelum turned to her, and she loosed her last arrow. He grabbed it and snapped it in half. "Not again, bird," he sneered.

Rye bolted up again, and they clashed swords. "Via go now!" he ordered. She watched as he exchanged blows with the Dark Knight, and Via cursed and turned from the commander, sprinting through the courtyard towards the garden. She grabbed a quiver from a dead soldier and jumped over the bodies of the townspeople. She fought off demons and cultists alike, earning a stab to the shoulder and arms. She dodged another sword and shot an arrow into a cultist's chest. She continued through the yard, ignoring the other people dying around her.

She entered the garden and saw those still trying to get through, fighting off demons that ripped their way inside. Via raised her bow and killed a demon atop a mother and child. As another towns person tried to enter the portal, she heard the screeches of more demons approaching. She notched an arrow and pointed it at the portal. She bit her lip at the people fleeing, screaming, begging for their lives. A woman pushed her son through the portal, and a demon ripped into her leg.

"I'm sorry," she whispered. She snapped her hand back, and the arrow flew to the portal and lodged into the magic of the center. An explosion of magic blew Via back as the portal collapsed in on itself and trapped them all within the walls of the burning keep. She pulled herself up and dodged another demon's talons. As she fought them off, she pleaded to herself for a quick end.

88 THYMAS

"Retreat!" Thymas yelled, pulling his men back from the gates of the city. He watched as hordes of demons climbed the walls and openings and cultists slaughtered their way through the gates. He pulled a sword from an enchanter and grabbed a soldier, dragging him away from the advancing army. He dragged him to an aperture of the keep, and the courtyard filled with the sounds of metal and shouting. The remaining townspeople picked up swords and shields and fought with the rest of the guards for their lives. Thymas ducked down from a winged demon and heard a cry as the commander was thrown by a knight in black armor. He landed hard on the ground and wiped his bloodied face. Thymas forced himself to go near and spotted the healer's tent in flames. His breath caught in his throat as he thought of the priestess trapped within the blaze.

"Sara!" he yelled. "Where are you!?" He pushed his way past the fighting men in the battle as he was shoved and beaten down by cultists. He pushed his sword through a chest, dodged a ball of flame, and parried another sword. His breath was labored. The world seemed to turn and slow around him.

He barely felt the blade lodge into his back as a maleficarum cackled behind him. He fell to his knees and groaned. He watched as the commander was lifted by the throat by the Knight. He could not make out what he was saying, but the commander spit in its face.

As the world stilled, the air crackled around him. He looked upward, his vision obscured, as the sky took on tones of blue and purple. He heard the maleficarum behind him scream in pain as thunder crashed against the sky. Lighting came down from the heavens and struck her, and Thymas was blown onto his stomach. He watched as a bolt of lightning slammed into the Dark Knight and he dropped the commander. Thymas covered his head as all around them, cultists and demons were struck drown. The impact of the lightning charred the ground black and caused it to break and snap, shooting up into the sky. His ears rung painfully and he cried out as dirt sprayed on top of him. The Dark Knight swiveled around in anger, blocking another lightning bolt with a barrier of green magic.

Thymas pushed himself back up on his knees to see a woman appear from the smoke and ash. "*At al ve vestras!*" she yelled. Giant black hands burst from the ground and wrapped around the Knight's body.

Thymas couldn't believe his sight when Sara stepped from the smoke, her eyes alight with blue magic. Her entire body shimmered and shook as she stared down at the Knight. He almost thought she was a spirit.

"MAGE!" Gelum screamed.

"You have harmed this world for too long," she spoke, her voice like thunder itself.

"We will hunt you down!" the Knight replied.

"Then let them." She raised her hands, and the sky itself opened around the keep. The spinning, glowing vortex crackled and spit lightning down onto her body, and she threw her hands down. The lightning slammed into the Knight, enveloping him and bouncing off his armor. He screamed and fought against the hands holding him down.

With one last cry, a ball of green flame shot into the air and exploded, raining down on the courtyard. The only thing that stood where the Knight once did was ash and a sword. A cloud of black smoke launched across the sky and away from the keep as the remaining cultists charged in anger and sorrow.

Sara dropped to her knees, and he forced himself up and ran to her. He grabbed onto her shoulders as she collapsed against him.

"I'm sorry," she whispered. The bells of chaos rang again as the cultists screamed in rage and blood. He looked down at her flowing hair and dark eyes, closed in exhaustion. The remaining men formed a circle around the two with swords and shields drawn.

"Protect the king!" he heard Lord Downor yell. He and Captain Mulliner held the circle in front of him. The army slammed into them, and Thymas looked up into the brightening sky through the shadow of swords and shields. The crackle of thunder subsided, and in the hordes of men screaming, he heard a horn blow.

Everyone looked up towards the gates where the cultists still poured in. The ground began to shake again, and he could hear the thunderous beat of horseshoes.

"Is that...?"

"It's blue banners. It is Rosus!" a soldier yelled from atop the wall. Thymas felt his heart lift as the men surrounding him pulled him and the priestess up and towards the healer's tents. As the tent flaps were pulled, he could see the massive army of Yalirea engage the cultists, and it was the end.

The silence that was set forth across the fallen keep was less despondent than he thought, but the wounded still cried, and women wailed over their fallen husbands. The army of men Rosus had given helped pile bodies and clear wreckage off stranded soldiers. His bandaged back stung as he made his way through the rubble of his home. He found the priestess sitting over the darkened spot where the Dark Knight had once stood. The sword still lay forgotten and rusting.

"You are a mage?" he questioned.

She sadly inclined her head, not meeting his gaze. "And now the entire Dark Kingdom knows. They will never stop hunting me." Thymas turned his gaze away from her and at the dead and wounded in the field and on the walls.

The spymaster stepped up beside him and looked toward Sara. "That would have been nice sooner," she said coldly. Sara ignored her and stood up, wiping off her skirt. Via bent down and rubbed the ashes of the Knight between her fingers. "May your soul be judged."

The commander came near her, wounded but alive. "Thank the goddess you're alive," he sighed.

"You are the one who took on Gelum," she replied.

"I've never felt power like that, seen power like that before," he said, looking towards the mage.

"That is the power of a mage. And one who can control her power at that. We may win this war yet."

Sara helped patch Thymas' wounds, and he put his elbows on his knees. Her fingers never stayed on his skin too long, and she refused to make eye contact. Perhaps she thought he hated her, for not telling him who she was. He could never hate her, though. No matter if the entire world was against them.

The wind that whipped through the castle smelled of charred corpses and wood. "We will set up pyres later this evening," he heard Rye say. "We will need a full estimate of the dead and wounded as soon as possible." The spymaster picked up her bow and left the courtyard as a man came through the main gates on horseback.

The man reached them and dismounted the horse, walking up to the commander. "I am captain Nicholas. I led the army here in WhiteDrove's defense," he said.

Thymas looked up to see him salute Rye. "I will send my sincere gratitude to the king," he said.

He turned towards Thymas. "It was the emperor who sent us, not the king."

"Then I will thank the emperor." Thymas stood up and walked past the commander. "We have dead to burn."

The night was heavy as over a hundred lay upon the pyres. Soldiers, women, children. Thymas stood beside his mother, Sara stood off with the other healers. The wind danced around the bodies of the dead, and torches were lit. One was handed to Thymas, who took it with a hardened expression.

"Tonight, we mourn our dead," he started. "We burn our brothers and sisters who gave their lives to defend their home. But this was a battle won. Now, one less Dark Knight can prey upon the weak, and we know of hope. We know that these 'gods' can be defeated, and we know that together we can vanquish the Dark Kingdom and bring peace to Veran."

Thymas started forwards with the others. He stopped at a pyre and looked down into the face of a young boy, no older than Anya, gripping a painted toy soldier in his small hands. He thought back to his sister, who made it through the portal before it collapsed. How many children didn't make it through, and the cultists who held no remorse. The Dark Kingdom would be defeated, he promised. He set the torch on the pyre and backed away as the flames rose to cover the child. He looked over at Sara, who stared at the ground. A tear ran down her cheek as the other pyres were lit, and the sky was illuminated once again.

89 LAERDYA

The seamstresses poured around the elven princess as they took measurements and held fabric up to her chest, inspecting the quality and flow. The queen sat in the back of the room, silently watching, a small grin on her face. As the ladies continued their work, Laerdya turned to the queen.

"*Aretove*, may I ask a favor?" she asked hesitantly.

A seamstress took a jute of fabric from her chest and over to the queen, who ran her hand through it. "What is it, blossom?" She waved the fabric away, not to her liking, and looked towards the girl.

With a fiddle of her hands, she asked, "I would like the wedding feast to be in the town square. For everyone to attend."

Ravana narrowed her eyes as another seamstress offered up a different fabric. The queen stood, took the fabric, and walked over to the girl.

"That's a very dangerous situation to put yourself in, blossom," she said, holding the fabric up to her body. It was turquoise satin that sparkled a soft hue of blue in the light. "Why do you want this so?"

Laerdya felt the fabric as she spoke. "I wish to have the people's graces as well. I'm to be their queen. I wish to make them happy."

The queen tutted and pulled away. She gave the fabric to a seamstress. "Make a dress from this and a veil to match. Sapphires are to be sewn into the dress and crown," she ordered. Returning to the girl, she helped her step down from the stool. "This kingdom was mine for thousands of years and will still be mine after you are dead. If you truly believe you can make a difference with my people and my son, I do invite you to try, though not everyone shall change their heart."

Laerdya paused, then nodded. "I know. But if I can help only a few, then it was enough."

They sat at a table stacked with cheese and grapes, and Laerdya popped one into her mouth. The queen sat opposite her and watched her eat. "I feel like there is something else on your mind, blossom," she pushed.

Laerdya fiddled with the stem of the grape and twirled it between her fingers. "What do you know about the Dark Kingdom?"

Ravana sat back in her seat with a soft sigh. "I know much about how it was created. But unfortunately, I do not know as much about what it is like now."

"I read about... the knights? The protectors of *Elu'lathan*?"

"Templars," she corrected.

"Templars?"

"Yes," Ravana ran her eyes around the blue-hued room and tapped her nails against the glass table. "That is what their titles were when they were still the *noble* knights we created them to be."

"And that changed?"

"As does with magic. You cannot contain that much power in your veins without it exploding in time. Without being a mage, at the very least. Why do you ask?"

"Nexis told me why he came, to get wards against the Dark Kingdom. He seemed worried."

"He does show much disconcertment, doesn't he? Doesn't fit him at all," she tutted and grabbed a grape, popping it from the stem and into her mouth.

"Do you think they could attack Avlor? Or here?" she asked.

Ravana glanced at the girl still twirling the stem in her hand. "Possibly."

"Does that not frighten you?"

Ravana turned fully to the princess and set her elbows on the table. "If the time comes when my sister is finally dethroned and thrown into the Otherworld, I will not celebrate but prepare for what happens next. They will come here, I imagine, and try to take this city from your hands."

"Why?"

"They have an infatuation with me. Well, mages in general. But I'm better than any that may still be out there in the mundane world."

"If they do come?" Her expression grew more worried as they talked, and Ravana popped another grape into her mouth.

"Then it will be up to you to defend this city and the people you so much adore. Are you prepared for such a thing?"

Laerdya looked down at her lap. "No—I don't know. Elmaer would probably know."

Ravana snorted. "My son has the backbone of a hen. He will crawl into the lowest part of the castle and hide like a coward." Laerdya held back a smile and took a piece of cheddar. "It will be up to you to save the people."

"Then I hope that day does not come."

"Wouldn't you want to see the sun again, blossom? You talked about it much."

"Not at the cost of elven lives."

Ravana raised a brow and cocked her head. "Then you are more considerate than I."

Laerdya strolled the castle before finding the door to the laboratory. She could hear bubbling and muttering coming from within. She knocked but got no reply from the inhabitant. She knocked again and heard a crash and more muttering. Finally, she decided to open the door and enter before quickly ducking out of the way as a fiery explosion shook the ceiling. Small stones and dust fell on top of her, and she coughed, standing upright.

"By the gods, Laerdya!" Nexis exclaimed. He ran up to her and dusted her off.

"Are you trying to blow the castle apart?" she asked.

He wiped her face and patted her head. "No, you just came at an unfortunate time," he replied. He scurried back over to a long table full of elixir bottles, odd twisting glass tubes, and herbs and plants she did not recognize. The room itself was smaller, but he somehow stuffed small carts full of supplies into it with some walking room left over. Papers scattered the floor and laid on top of beakers. Notes were scribbled onto them in barely legible handwriting.

"What are you making?" she asked, padding over to the table.

"Attempting to make an herbal remedy for the blight you have here. The nasty thing rips through your skin and organs in weeks."

Laerdya made a face as he sprinkled a blue herb into a bowl and crushed it with a pestle. "Do you enjoy alchemy?"

"Yes, and I thank the queen for allowing me this room inside the castle. I was cast out of Avlor for exploding one too many trees a few years back." Laerdya raised a brow and stepped slightly to the side as he poured the crushed herbs into a jar of clear, bubbling liquid. "I don't know nearly any of these plants. Ravana had them sent to me for study from the forest."

"You're playing with things you don't even know?"

"That is how science works. You don't know anything until you test it."

"So, you will be blowing the castle apart, then."

He shook the jar and set it down, bending down to the table's height to see it go from clear to a bright red. He scribbled down notes on the journal on the table with a pleased hum.

"Poisons, medicine, tonics, and fireworks. All things that the earth gave to us. That *Ethena'ethal* created."

"I don't think I've ever seen you so happy," Laerdya laughed.

He quickly ran over to a cart sitting along the far wall and picked up a blue flower sprouting purple berries. "Here, try one!" he pushed, setting a berry in her palm.

She gave it a critical glance. "Are you sure...?"

"It is fine; I've been feeding it to the mice for weeks."

She sniffed it, and it smelled off, almost dusty. She popped it into her mouth and found it increasingly chewy. "It doesn't dissolve!" he noted happily. She continued to chew and popped a bubble in her mouth.

"It's definitely interesting. What is it called?"

"I call it bubble berries. Though it's a work in progress."

"I feel as if you could use this to build houses."

"As I said. Work in progress."

She persisted in chewing on the gummy berry and looked over the shoulder of the elf as he mixed more tonics and took notes.

"Maybe you could make something for my wedding?" she asked.

He stopped in his tracks, head snapping up. "Wedding...Wed...Oh! I completely forgot," he mused. "I can try to make something. And *not* burn the city down." He gave her a wink and several more berries to snack on later. She left him to his happy experiments and started on her way back to her room.

90 ROSE

The campfire was the only source of light for Rose as she scrolled through the passages in the tome. It was entirely handwritten, some passages more hastily inscribed than others. It was mostly all in a foreign language, one long lost to the world of man, but there were a couple of passages written in an older version of Common she could read. Most of it was accounts of the fall of *Elu'lathan*, the ancient city of elves. Rose had heard the stories from her mother, but nothing concrete. This felt as if she was actually there. One text, in particular, called out to her. There was no author for it, but the story pulled her in.

Athelas has fallen. I still hear the screams of my sister from the castle walls. The main gates have given way to the templars and they will soon be upon us. Even our best warriors cannot stand up to their might. Every hour, more of our brothers and sisters fall to the wrath of demons. The city around us crumbles under their chaos. We wanted peace, hope of a better future for our two races. But what have we created in our vanity? A vision of ourselves too corrupt to see the darkness we spread—a version of our power that holds nothing but chaos. We wanted power, control, immortality. And here we pay the price as our protectors slaughter us to gain what they already have.

I am tasked with going through the portal. Empress Elathana waits with the last of the mages in a despite bid of fate while I carry out my duty. I believe in the magic even If I do not practice it myself, but this magic... It is wrong. This magic should not exist. The amount of blood that has been shed for this spell still burns my eyes to see. But the queen says it is the only way, and as her last supporter, it is my duty to carry out her wish.

The chaos around us will never give way unless I go through the portal and find her again, gifting her this small bundle I carry in my arms. It is the only way. She wants me to stay, not come back through the portal, but my loyalty can only go so far. She is my friend, my queen, but I cannot abandon my kin. I do not want to see another kingdom burn to the ground, and I will pay the price to live to see peace.

The last of the elves shelter in the Temple of Kildan, praying for the gods to awaken and help save them. We all pray for the sealing spell to work. Even if the cost is great.

This is my last entry for years to come. All I hope is that our children's children shall know peace.

Rose fingered the text across the page, nearly hearing the battle in the letter. Was the fall anything like what happened in Ignis? The city had fallen in mere hours. *Elu'lathan* must haven't been much longer. Rose turned the page to see a spell smeared onto the backside of it. She recognized a few words from it. Her mother had cast it when she fought Malum all those years back. It wasn't word for word, though.

What was her mother trying to do? The spell obviously hadn't worked against the Dark Knights. The mages of old had failed.

"I can't believe we are going to awaken Maganth. I mean, piss on us, I guess," Torgir spit.

"If the *Runa* says it must be done, then that is what we will do," Nadahi responded.

"I thought he was just a myth," Liv tutted.

Erling pointed to Rose. "She better learn some more spells if we're going to go poking at him."

Rose looked up from the tome. "Who is Maganth?"

Nadahi looked over to Rose with a dark expression, "He is the cursed god I spoke about. The one the Forsaken wish to awaken."

"And we are going to help awaken him then."

"They wish to bring Him into the world to conquer it. We will have Him killed."

"If he can be killed. We have yet to fight a god," Liv said.

"The Mother has chosen this path for us. We will not stray from it for fear of failure."

"*Shor'vaker* awaits!" Erling yelled cheerfully. Rose looked back down at the tome, reading the spell over again in her mind.

"We can't do it alone. We need allies," Nadahi said.

"The other tribes? They won't help us commit suicide."

"Maybe not," Nadahi said, looking over at Rose. "But the *Runa* can."

"You want me to try to rally the tribes? Bear almost killed us a few days ago," she argued.

"But he didn't. In honor of you. If we are to destroy Maganth, you must lead us to victory."

Rose took a breath and closed the tome. "You all have so much faith in me."

Nadahi rolled out her shoulders and took a swig from her water hide. "Because we have seen your power and your strength."

"And your whining."

"Torgir—"

"It's a good thing!"

Nadahi gave him a whack on the shoulder. "The point is that we are here for you. And we know you have the power to destroy Maganth with training and courage."

"And then I return home," Rose sighed.

"And we shall all be with you."

"It would be nice to see the sea once again," Erling nodded.

"Hopefully your last eye is still there by the time we sail," Hakon chuffed.

"The crows will be my eyes if that time comes."

"Enough," Nadahi said. "We shall return to Rolheim and inform my father. The tribes will be called."

After weeks of travel, *Rolheim* was near, and Rose was happy to be out of the cold and in a nice, warm bed. The weeks they spent out in the cold had officially taken their toll on her. She was lucky she still had all her fingers and toes. She could practically feel the warmth of a hearth and sweet bison stew. It made her mouth water. She was already happy to be on horseback again and not wading through feet of snow, even if it did cause her backside to chafe. And their adventure… Rose didn't know how she felt on it. If someone had told her months ago that she was to be cast out into this frigid land and brought up as a daughter of a goddess she would have laughed in their face. And now she was exactly that, with those around her relying on her power and her strength. Though, she still had much to learn.

Nadahi seemed tense as they neared her home. Rose thought she would be in a better mood now that they had a plan.

"Is something the matter?" Rose asked.

Nadahi took a long breath. "There is something wrong," she said, leading the party. Rose looked out over the horizon but saw nothing extraordinary except the occasional discolored fall of snow.

"What is it?" Rose asked.

Nadahi stopped her horse, sniffing the air. Liv stopped as well, putting her hand out in front of her. She rubbed the darkened snow between her fingers. "It's ash," she said. Rose felt her heart quicken in her chest as Nadahi's face contorted into fury.

"*Rolheim*, it is under attack! Go now!" she yelled. The horses kicked off, and Rose strained against the reins. Nadahi pulled off her glove and put two fingers in her mouth, whistling to the sky. A wolf emerged from the snowy land, chasing after them.

"Go!" she ordered. The wolf howled and darted away, and the ground began to darken. Dropped shields and lost swords scattered the frozen snow. Blood covered the white in blankets, too much to be from a hunt or a small battle. She could smell the smoke before seeing the village. Horns blared in her ears as the sky soon filled with smoky soot.

"To the right!" Hakon yelled.

Rose turned to see a demon wolf sprinting towards them. It leaped into the air and slammed into Liv, sending her flying from her horse. The others stopped, and Rose reared back. The demon latched onto Liv's arm and swung her around like a rope.

"Liv!" Nadahi yelled, jumping from her horse and throwing her ax into its back. The demon dropped Liv and turned to Nadahi with a ferocious growl. It lunged towards her, but Hakon slammed his shield into its face. It yipped and jumped back as the others surrounded it. Rose dismounted and ran over to Liv, pulling her up to a sitting position.

"Come on, you mangy mutt!" Torgir yelled. The demon spun around, choosing its target before lunging towards Erling, who countered with a bash from his shield. The demon lunged again, this time aiming lower and swiping him off his feet. Its teeth bore into his calf as he screamed in rage. Nadahi grabbed onto the demon and ripped it from his leg. She fell on top of it as it snarled and chopped at her. She pulled her ax from its back and sliced it into its neck, decapitating it.

"This isn't the last of them. We must hurry," she said.

Rose helped Liv and Erling mount their horses again and sped towards the settlement.

"Mother Goddess, protect my people," Nadahi prayed. The smoke grew denser as they neared the gates of the village and burned her lungs. Rose could see the flames billowing from the wooden houses. Bodies of Forsaken and the tribe littered the ground before the village, and Rose put her hand to her mouth.

They dismounted, and Nadahi checked the bodies for life as the others continued toward the gates. The doors were left hanging on their hinges; the wall reduced to rubble. She recognized several of the villagers who had brought her gifts.

She stepped closer to the bodies and saw the waving of feathers through the snow. She ran toward them and fell to her knees, uncovering them from the white dust. The headpiece sat forgotten as the mother healer lay half-buried in the snow. Her eyes were closed, a long gash with frozen blood engraved in her neck, and her hand held onto a rune stone.

"No," Rose whispered. She felt tears rise to her eyes as she looked around at the bodies laid discarded and forgotten. The others searched the bodies as well, their faces forlorn, all except the huntress.

"He isn't here..." she muttered.

"Welcome, mage."

Rose looked up, the voice whispering in her ear. Atop the main gates stood a man. His metal armor glowed against the backdrop of smoke as his broadsword hung loose in his hand. In his other hand, he held a rounded object. She knew the Knight, the same one who murdered Valek.

"You have chosen poorly, mage. Now watch as another kingdom is stripped from your hands."

Nadahi ran up to Rose, engraved sword in her hand and shield in hand. She put herself between the Dark Knight and *Runa* and stared him down. The others came around them, shields ready.

Howls and yips started up as Forsaken clambered towards the gates, and demon hounds clawed their way up from the ground. There was no way to win this battle.

"I will take your head for this!" Nadahi yelled. The Dark Knight chuckled and raised the rounded object in his hand out to them.

"Come take it," he snarled. Nadahi went rigid, her entire body

seeming to turn to stone. The smoke faltered, and Rose gasped as the head of the chieftain lay in his grasp. Nadahi screamed and lunged for the Knight, but Liv and Erling pulled her back.

"We must leave!" Liv yelled. The Knight dropped the head, and it tumbled to the ground before the group, landing at their feet. Rose backed away as the Forsaken charged.

The tormented screaming of Nadahi drowned out the battle cries of the Forsaken as they retreated to their horses. She quickly mounted and turned to see the Knight's twisted smile.

"We will meet again, Runa."

Liv flung Nadahi onto a horse, and they raced away from the burning walls. Rose gripped her chest as she watched another city fall to siege. It would follow her wherever she went. It wouldn't stop… not until she ended it. She bit into her lip, tasting blood. *I will end it. I will!*

It wasn't until an hour later that the group stopped to rest. The falling of snow covered their tracks, and Rose felt her lower body strain under the heavy riding.

After the camp was built, Nadahi went out on her own and left the others to tend to their wounds. No one spoke. They simply rubbed salve over their cuts and hung their heads in either rage or sorrow. As the fire crackled against the wood, Liv held her hands to her lips, kissing the rune she grasped. Erling put salve over his eye, and Hakon stared into the distance. Only Torgir stood, pacing the camp, eyes trained downwards. Rose held the small wooden bird the children had carved for her. Its face was stained red, and she ran her thumb over the wings. Children. Little children killed for such cruelty. It had to end. It must end.

She let her kingdom fall due to her ignorance, her lack of will. Nadahi stood there, she wanted to die for her people. Rose could not say the same. She felt her chest squeeze and she dug her nails in the bird. She would be a bystander no longer.

Rose stood, unable to stay any longer, and walked up to Nadahi, who held a wooden necklace in her hand.

"My father gave me this when I passed my trials. He told me that will I become chieftain; I will lead my people to glory." She clenched the necklace in her fist with a growl.

"It wasn't your fault," Rose said.

Nadahi shook her head. "I should have fought. I should have died with them."

"And leave me?" Rose said. She looked over at her, her expression sorrowful, and Rose gently took hold of her hand. "We can take back your village. I promise. We still have the other tribes."

Nadahi opened her hand. "If they are still standing."

"I know they are. And your father died in battle fighting a man who thinks himself a god. If that does not guide him into *Shor'vaker*, nothing will."

Nadahi smiled slightly. "I suppose I am the chieftain now. A tribe of six." She put the necklace back on and took out a small blue vial from her pouch.

"When a child passes their trials, they are marked by the tribe. You have fought beside us and mourned with us. You bear the braids of unity and magic of the Mother. If you wish to take the markings, you will be accepted into our tribe." She opened the vial, sticking her finger in and pulling out blue paint. She waited for Rose to respond, who bit her lip. She looked up at her face, scanning the markings that adorned her, studying the way her lips parted. After a second, she nodded.

"As the new... Chieftain of the Tribe of Wolf, I mark you as a member of our family. May the Mother bless you with her wisdom and courage and welcome you into *Shor'vaker* at your final breath."

Rose took a steady breath as Nadahi ran a thumb across her nose and cheeks, then down her lips. She paused at her chin, looking down into her eyes. Rose's eyes did not waver from her own. The way the huntress looked at her... It was not like a newly marked child. It was a woman's gaze, and she felt herself grow hot as her face grew near. Nadahi bent down and gently touched her lips to Rose's, smearing the paint that tasted of blueberries.

Her lips were rough compared to Rose's. Soft to calloused. But she was warmer than any hearth, softer than any fur, brighter than any sun. Nadahi gripped Rose in her arms, careful not to hurt her. She was small and fragile, yet when Nadahi held her, she felt as if she were an unbreakable stone. The woman who had protected her, held her, guided her through the frozen landscape, asking nothing in return. She felt her ruby pulse against her hot skin and she knew the goddess guided them together for a reason.

Nadahi pulled away, and Rose took a breath, her hands still grasping her coat. She brought a hand to Rose's cheek.

"I will protect you with my life, my *Runa*. Until the spirits of frost call me home, I will be by your side. I will move the mountains, cross the Frozen Sea, and build you a throne of gold to sit upon. It's time to take back our homelands. Are you with me, Rose?"

Rose smiled and gripped the ruby on her neck. "Yes, I am ready."

91 OLIVIA

Olivia sat in the ritual chamber, focusing on the shadows that danced across the inscribed walls. The falling sunlight pooled around the door from the small circular holes in the ceiling. She sat in the middle of the room in a patch of sunlight with her wooden swords in hand.

Her skin felt like it was boiling under the light as she closed her eyes and felt for the shadows around her. When the clouds would pass over the sun or a shadow crawled its way over to where she sat, she would try to merge into the connected pathways and appear on the other side of the room. One thing she learned was that it was impossible to phase without a branch of darkness to guide her away.

A clear day was the most dangerous for contracts. Most had to be taken at night, and even then, the light reflected from the moons could cause complications as well.

She crawled on the walls and raced around the scattered fragments of dusk. She reappeared on the other side of the room and heaved a sigh when she saw the forgotten swords laying where she sat. It still took the energy from her to phase. She still couldn't hold her swords. Wooden or metal. It infuriated her.

She heard the door open and turned to see Neph lean against the door.

"You will be accompanying me on a mission tonight," she said.

"What mission?"

"You will find out. It is not a contract."

Olivia sighed in frustrated disappointment, but nodded her head. Neph looked around the dimming room, setting her eyes on the swords in the middle.

"You are doing better than many others before you. Be proud of what you have achieved in this time."

"It is not enough."

"It will never be enough for *you*." Neph stepped from her perch and turned from the room.

"Be prepared. It will be a long night."

That night, Neph guided Olivia through an expanse of new tunnel systems and hallways for the mission. Neph entered a side hallway, and when they reached the end, she pulled a lever that opened into catacombs.

"This leads straight into the cathedral where prayers are heard and contracts are taken," Neph said. Olivia followed her, and the door closed behind them. It was pitch black in the catacombs, and the piercing smell of decay filled the air. Olivia found it difficult to adjust her eyes to the darkness, and she tripped over a skull. She heard Neph laugh.

"You'll grow used to it. Take this as another part of your training."

Olivia pulled herself up and continued to follow Neph, barely able to see her outline. She resorted to closing her eyes, focusing on the sound she heard. Neph's footsteps, the sounds of dripping water, the eerie squeaking of rats. As they walked, she became lighter, and her footsteps because softer. The darkness became welcoming to her, and she could feel her body giving in. It was almost in an instant that they appeared at the entrance to the cathedral. Olivia came back to her senses, feeling her feet touch the ground, and Neph ran her hand down her arm. Neph pulled another lever, and the ceiling opened from a statue. They climbed the stone steps and entered the cathedral. It was quiet in the night as the statue pulled itself back into place in the middle of the room, and Olivia scanned her surroundings. It was strangely beautiful. The pillars were silver, and the marbled floor swirls of blue. The statue was that of a cloaked figure with four arms, each holding a chalice. What she could only assume was wine rested in one of the cups; the other three were empty. The shadows of the room shifted, and she took notice of a draped hunchbacked man on the far right of the pews. He scuttled away, and Neph motioned towards him with her head.

"That is the caretaker. He is the one who listens to the prayers and sends us the contracts," she said.

"Sounds like a pleasant job."

"It is not."

They left the cathedral, and the heavy rainy wind forced Olivia to take a breath. The cloud-covered sky blocked the light of the moons and kept the city shrouded in a dark haze. The torches on the side of the cathedral flickered and blinked in the rain.

"Where are we going?" she asked.

"We are heading to another guild to pick up a contract," she answered.

"We take contracts for other guilds?"

"Sometimes, if the contract turns out to be beyond their skill range."

Olivia followed her through the rainy town where few were outside. They passed a man in rags who did not notice them, only stared with empty eyes towards the thundering sky. A woman was crouched down, eating a rat that squealed and cried. Her teeth ripped through its skin as blood trailed down her hands and face and met with the puddles on the ground. Neph stuck to the shadows of the decrepit buildings as Olivia focused her attention on leaping between the light. Neph did it with such ease it was as if she teleported from shadow to shadow. Olivia had more difficulty finding the trails and hands that reached out to connect the spots of black. She felt as if she were air each time she shifted from one corner to the next and felt overly heavy when she came into the light. It was freeing to not be seen or heard, to be there, but not noticed. The light made her feel nauseous and exposed.

They passed several streets with condemned buildings and broken carts before turning down an alleyway. They stopped at an unassuming wooden door at the end.

"Stay here. I will only be a moment. The guild of Zelonoth can be averse to strangers."

Olivia held back a laugh at the name.

"What is so funny?" Neph asked.

"I killed a few of their men when they went after my friend," she said.

"Then the contract should have gone to us." She entered the building, and Olivia leaned against the wall beside the door. The stone of the old shops was covered in moss and tiny newts that scampered up the sides. The small white flowers that bloomed in the cracks of the street were the only attractive thing to be seen.

She closed her eyes and listened to the rain pattering against the houses, the dripping of drainage pipes, and the moans of someone down the street. Olivia focused on the moans, where they came from, *what* they came from. It sounded like a woman from the pitch and an injured one at that. She opened her eyes and sunk into the shadows. She crawled along the walls and streets, searching for the noise. She soon found a woman curled in on herself on her knees. Her ragged sobbing and violent shaking made her seem almost bestial. Her clothes were in ribbons, and her wet hair was entangled against her head. Olivia came out of the shadows and approached the woman, who seemed not to notice her.

"Are you ill?" she asked. The woman shot up, her eyes black, dark throbbing veins twisting her face. She screamed and lunged at Olivia, slamming into her. Olivia fell to the ground and grabbed the woman's chest as she bit and clawed at her. Her mouth foamed as she screamed incoherently, spitting over her face and chest. Olivia pushed her off and quickly receded into the shadows. The woman twirled around and sniffed the air, making quick clicking noises. Olivia pressed further into the shadows, her heart racing. The woman then twirled around, bounding towards her, and screamed again, pulling her from the dark and throwing her into the wall.

"Shit!" Olivia yelled. She grabbed a knife from her belt and dodged the woman. She stabbed her in the back, and she howled in rage, throwing herself back and hitting Olivia in the face. She stumbled back, and the woman lunged again, completely ignoring the wound. Olivia grabbed her neck as she bit and clawed and plunged her knife straight through her chin up into her mouth. The woman gagged and spurted black blood onto her face as she fell limp against her. Olivia spat the blood from her mouth and rolled the woman's corpse away from her. She laid on the ground and wiped her mouth with a ragged breath.

"I wasn't sure if you could kill it," Neph said, coming out of the shadows herself. Olivia sheathed the knife and sat up, putting her hands on her knees.

"What was that thing?"

"A cursed one. They roam most parts of Reverend. The cultists keep them at bay near the castle."

Olivia stood up and rolled the goopy blood between her fingers. "I have never seen something like that before."

"It's what happens when the dark magics corrupt a person. It is what happened to the cursed king of Velwood. Come, we have the contract."

Olivia followed Neph from the alleyway, and she glanced back at the woman lying in the street, hoping that would never be her fate.

92 NEXIS

The grand hall was decorated with silver silk and gleaming balls of fire overhead. The court was standing, chatting quietly, decorated to the highest degree, awaiting the queen to be. Nexus stood beside Ravana, who looked nearly skittish as she played with her hands, though her face did not show it.

With a small smile, he whispered, "Do you remember your bonding ceremony, *Aretove?*"

Ravana glanced at him and back at the altar set up atop the staircase. "It was nearly two thousand years ago, Nexis. Of course, I remember it. Though I can say I felt the same as the little blossom that day." She paused, looking around. "And I recollect having much brighter skin."

Nexis chuckled softly before the choir sang. All voices hushed as the doors opened, and the prince stepped out, starting down the aisle. He wore deep blue robes trimmed with silver; his cape held by sapphire encrusted pendants. His hair was braided down his right shoulder as he walked sturdy but loud down the aisle. He reached the stairs and scaled them before coming to rest in front of the officiant. He glanced at his mother, who cocked her head at him.

"He will be no wise king, but perhaps one who will keep the people alive for a thousand years longer," Ravana said, clasping her hands together.

"I hope they both shall reign prosperously and maybe even change it for the better with their children," Nexis added. The queen gave a tuff as a reply.

"Let the people watch as her majesty approaches," the officiant said. All eyes turned back to the door as it opened once more. There Laerdya stood, a veil over her face, her dress flowing around her. As she walked carefully down the aisle, her dress shimmered shades of blue, the sapphires reflecting the lights of the room. She stood smaller than everyone else around her, but walked with a passion. The train behind her flowed as if it were water as she walked. Her hair was intricately braided and adorned with jewels on top of her head. Her back was bare but painted golden swirls branched out from her spine.

When she reached the steps, Elmaer took her hand, helping her up. When she reached the top, she faced him. Elmaer lifted the veil from her face, bringing it over her head. Her eyes shimmered with blue dust, her lips a plump pink.

"Let us be here today to witness the bonding and crowning of our queen and king," the officiant boomed across the grand hall. Both turned to him as he pulled a cloth from his pouch. "With this cloth, shall we bind the souls of Princess Laerdya of Avlor and Prince Elmaer of Nevrak to the destiny of the five gods." Slowly, he folded the cloth around their hands and put his hand atop theirs. "With this seal, shall their souls be bound to one another, and to *Rane'abeles* till death shall claim them." He unfolded the cloth, and they turned to one another.

Elmaer grasped Laerdya's hand forcefully. "With this marriage, you shall be mine for all of time. You shall bear my children and be by my side as the kingdom prospers under my rule," he spoke. Nexis could feel the tension come off Laerdya as she took a breath.

"With this marriage, I shall keep our kingdom safe from those who would harm it and rule beside you to bring prosperity and joy. May our children know happiness within these walls," she responded. They leaned in as Elmaer kissed her harshly, only pulling away after Laerdya had stopped. A young boy brought over a pillow holding two crowns atop it. The couple turned back to the officiant as he grasped the first crown, silver and sculpted as if it were tree branches woven together. The officiant raised the crown above his head as Elmaer bent down.

"This crown now shall lie atop the head of the new King Elmaer. Forever shall he reign."

"Forever shall he reign," the crowd chanted back. The crown was placed atop his head, and he turned to the crowd. The officiant grasped the smaller silver crown as Laerdya bent down.

"This crown now shall lie atop the head of the new Queen Laerdya. Forever shall she reign." The crowd once again chanted back as the crown was placed atop the new queen's head, and she turned. She took Elmaer's elbow as the crowd clapped.

"Forever shall they reign!" the crowd cheered. The couple stepped from the altar and made their way through the doors. Nexis glanced at the queen, who seemed to be lost in thought.

"Are you alright, *Aretove*?" he asked.

Ravana turned to him. "I am no longer queen, Nexis. Please call me Ravana," she said. Nexis was at a loss for words as she turned from him and started down the aisle as the court bowed to her. He followed soon after, and the rest dispersed, ready for the feast to commence.

93 LAERDYA

The town square was alight with lights and revelry. As the carriage took Elmaer and Laerdya into the square, Elmaer made an aggravated face. "Look at them all. If they decided to kill us all, they could easily do it."

"Why would they do that?" Laerdya asked.

"Why not? They don't think."

"I believe that they think that they love their new king... and queen," she said. Elmaer snorted as they crossed the bridge, and the people jumped up to see the new couple. Children ran alongside the carriage with sparklers and popping rocks. The lively music had already filled the streets as they passed, and she waved at the oncoming crowds. They all cheered and clapped, and lights shot into the sky and exploded, sending fae spinning into the air. Laerdya smiled and cheered as the carriage came to a stop.

Rhangyl opened the carriage door for Laerdya, and she stepped out into the crowd. They walked side by side as Rhangyl stayed mere steps behind her with the rest of the royal guard. She noticed Ravana and Nexis sitting together on a dais for the royal family just a few paces ahead. As the couple was escorted up the dais themselves, they were seated as the performers began to dance and spit fire. Nexis leaned over to Laerdya as the songs picked up with the dancers.

"I must admit, this is much different from the parties I am used to."

"I didn't realize you had been to many parties," she responded.

He gave her a sly grin. "I'm not as dull as you may think." Ravana tapped him on the knee, and his attention was drawn away from her. A performer came up to the edge of the dais.

"To King Elmaer and Queen Laerdya," he bowed. As he straightened, a hundred doves flew into the sky, and with an explosion of magic, they turned into a flaming dragon that soared above the square. Laerdya gasped in delight as it circled the dais and the townspeople ducked for cover before the dragon flew high into the sky and exploded into purple and blue streams of flame. Elmaer looked ready to burst himself as the applause gained volume. She ignored him, though, instead focusing on the people around her enjoying the party.

Laerdya clapped along with the others as an immaculate pie was brought out and set down on a large table. The woman from the bakeshop bowed to her.

"*Aretove,* for granting us this audience, please accept this pie as our thanks to you." She motioned for her and held out a knife. Laerdya stood up and looked towards Elmaer, but he wanted nothing to do with it. She shrugged and stepped from the dais. The knife was given to her, and she was led over to cut into it. She heard Elmaer angrily hiss at his mother. "Why are they paying attention to her?"

"Maybe because they like her. Have you tried saying hello to anyone this past decade?" Ravana responded.

Laerdya happily slid the knife into the pie and cut out a large slice. The townspeople clapped as berries and wildflowers flowed out from the inside of the pie and sprinkled the ground. She graciously took a piece and went back to the dais. The king was handed a piece next, which he ruefully took. Then the queen mother, then Nexis.

"This is delicious. I'm surprised you chose well, blossom," Ravana told her. Laerdya could not contain her smile while eating, and the festivities continued.

The common folk took each other's hands and formed a circle as a song began. When Laerdya finished her pie, she stepped down from the dais and entered the circle as they twirled and weaved and danced. She ducked under arms and was swept up into spins and kicking feet.

From dancing to sculpting to flower weaving, the night carried on. Elmaer mostly stayed on the dais as Laerdya engaged in several of the activities. She tossed balls, danced with the children, and even talked several of the nobility into joining in, which Ravana had apparently found amusing.

"If I could get you to weave a flower crown, I would sell my soul to the Dark Knights now," Laerdya overheard Nexis say to Ravana.

"If I were to weave a flower crown, my entire reputation would go down the drain. Is that what you wish?"

"Have you need of a reputation now that your son sits on the throne?" he retorted. She gave him a knowing look and peered at the rows of flowers lined on a table where children snatched them up.

"I only enjoy the glowing violets."

Hours into the party, when the vortex in the sky had grown dim, most of the nobility stood on the outskirts of the square, conversing to themselves, with the exception of the few the queen had dragged into her dances. They watched the common folk sing and play and celebrate as if they were of higher status themselves. A preposterous sentiment to them. In the middle of the square, though, Laerdya grew drowsy, with a full belly and a bit too much to drink. She swayed on her feet and brought her hand up to her warm face.

"I wish this night would never end," she muttered to herself, fixing the crown on her head.

"It is." She heard Elmaer come up behind her and place a hand on her shoulder. She felt herself go stiff and her eyes fluttered about, trying to find Rhangyl. Elmaer's grasp tightened. "It is time to retire, Laerdya."

She knew what that meant. It meant her time of enjoyment would come to an end... and their bond would be consummated. She was too tipsy to fight against his grip as he led her to the carriage. The few townsfolk left bowed low to her as they passed, whispering words of encouragement and reverence. Her eyes stayed ahead of her as she was pushed into the carriage, only turning slightly to see Nexis. He gave a frown as Elmaer sat down beside her and yelled for the carriage to move.

She picked at her nails as they made their way to the Bone Castle; her gaze never wavering to him. "Stop doing that," he scolded, grabbing her hand and forcing it into her lap. She thought back to the night, to the fun and the games, and the joy she felt. She said nothing to him as he pulled her from the carriage and up the steps and into the castle.

She watched the shadows twist along the ceiling, following them to their room. The smiling faces were now frowning. She felt herself frown with them.

They passed a slave on the way, and Elmaer barked at her. "No one is to disturb us." The slave bowed, and Laerdya could not stop herself from shaking. *You are a queen,* she told herself. *Nothing can harm you.*

Elmaer opened the door to their room and pushed her inside. She nearly stumbled and fell before she caught herself, swaying slightly, her mind still fogged from the drinks. The candles created soft, faint light in the room as he closed the door and took hold of her shoulders, moving her over to the bed. As she looked down at the newly made bed, covered in rose petals, she thought to herself. *It is a night like any other,* she thought. But when he moved his hands down her shoulders, grabbing hold of her dress, she felt her lip quiver.

He was not careful nor soft. He aggressively grabbed hold of the back of her corset and ripped it, tossing it to the side. The cloth fell from her chest, and she heard herself whimper. *Do not cry,* she thought. *Do not give him the satisfaction.* She held herself back from covering her bare breasts as he pushed her onto the bed on her stomach. The soft blanket rubbed against her cheek and her vision focused on the red petals in front of her.

You are a queen, she thought again. Elmaer carelessly lifted up her dress, and she dug her hands into the blanket, grinding her teeth together as he entered her. *You are a queen. No one can take that from you.*

She focused on the petals, on the red. Her mind did not process his grip on her, nor on the noises he made. She felt hot tears drip down her face and turn the blanket a darker shade of grey. *You are a queen. No longer shall you feel this way. You are a queen, not a slave,* she thought. *This is the last time. My cage is gone. I shall set myself free.*

She steeled her resolve; the blankets twisting in her grip. She would change this world. None shall know pain like she did. She would be the queen she was destined to be, or she would die trying.

94 OLIVIA

Neph and Olivia sat at a table in the tavern. Neph read over the contract scroll once again.

"It is a noble by the name of Pyrus here in Reverand. He will be headed towards the royal ball at luncheon. That is when we will strike," she said.

"What is the royal ball for?" Olivia asked.

"Supposedly, it is a ball held in the new queen's honor. An engagement party, if you will," Neph said with a shrug.

"Wish we could have one of those!" she heard Cronis yell. Neph ignored him and set the scroll to the side.

"You will be back up if I need it. But I doubt I will. This will be a packed event. People will be in the streets in the light of the day. There will be guards who will kill you on sight if you are seen. You are not ready for this, but I want you to see it. Understood?" she asked. Olivia nodded. "Good, prepare yourself, then meet me at the cathedral steps in the morning."

Later that day, Olivia sat on the floor of her room; a small candle set in front of her. It flickered as she focused on the shadows it cast along the walls and floor, its reflection bouncing off the mirror on the nightstand. She felt the shadows pull her under the bed, then up the walls. She turned to vapor and crawled on the ceiling, still able to see the candle. Smell the smoke. She focused on the paths of flickering light and navigated around the room, dodging bursts of color and flashes of heat. She landed on her bed with a sigh, and the candle burned low. She took a long breath and felt her heartbeat slow. It was a good feeling, being free from the shackles of the mundane world, being able to step where others could not and race across the city in mere moments.

She sat up and pulled the wooden box from under her bed. She set it on top of the sheets and opened it, running a hand down the silver swords. It still stung to touch them, but she didn't mind the pain. It was a consistent reminder of her fate.

She took a sword from its place and stood up, twirling it in her hand. It was heavy in her grip and felt like cutting through concrete when she slashed down. Even the light mocked her from under the door. It did not approve of her, not yet. She went to slice up, and it dropped from her hand with a clatter. She sighed and bent down, picking it back up. It was infuriating, still not being good enough to take a contract herself. She couldn't even hold a sword properly. But she was making progress, and she supposed that was all that mattered.

Olivia met Neph in the morning at the cathedral, and she could hear the mass of people outside the doors, clambering to get a look at the new queen.

"I honestly didn't think there were this many people in Reverand," Olivia noted as she stepped outside the doors. The sunlight hit her eyes, and she blinked uncomfortably. The streets were packed with women and children as they marched their way toward the castle. They seemed in cheer, but their eyes disturbed Olivia. Nearly empty through all the joy.

The two women were dressed as commoners as they walked the streets towards the castle. They moved out of the way of patrolling cultists, and Olivia held herself back from helping the commoners being whipped out of the way.

"Move rats! Keep walking!" they yelled. She watched a young boy get shoved to the ground and kicked as his mother pleaded for them to stop.

"Stay close to me," Neph said, grabbing her arm. Olivia shifted her way through the immense crowd of people and nearly lost sight of Neph several times. When they pulled into a small alcove of a shop, Neph put her hand on her shoulder.

"I need you to stay here. A cart will pass here in ten minutes. If you do not see the window down on the carriage, I need you to get inside," she said. Olivia nodded and Neph disappeared into the building. She stood on her toes to see the crowd and parade pass by. The one thing she didn't miss about Ignis was the scores of pompous nobility that rode around in their frivolous outfits. Thankfully Rose did not mind getting her dresses muddy, her sister on the other hand...

A small girl bumped into her, and she looked down. The girl had bruises up and down her arms and face. She gave a toothless smile and passed along. Olivia wondered what the common life was like in the Dark Kingdom. At least in Ignis, most people still had a roof over their heads. This place seemed full of joyless merriment.

She searched for the shadows cast by buildings and people, looking for pathways to jump through. Her eyes found a cultist, and he squinted before stepping close to her. She quickly looked up, seeing the shadows slowly move towards her as the clouds obfuscated the sun. She stepped into them and crawled up the wall, jumping from building to building and landing on the steps of a house as the sun returned to its full glory.

The people there did not seem to notice her appearance, and she stepped down into the crowd and towards the blocked off street. She shoved a large man away and looked back to see a group of cultists conversing where she vanished from. They pointed into the crowd, and she pulled her hood further up over her head.

She paused next to a family and counted the minutes before the carriages rolled by. Most were worn and disparaged as they passed by and towards the open courtyard gates, but a nicer horse-drawn carriage emerged guarded by several cultists. The white carriage had blue fabric draped over the top, swaying in the wind. The four-headed dragon was painted onto the carriage doors. With the number of guards around it, that had to be the Pyrus.

Olivia searched for the open window and felt a spasm of anxiety when it stayed closed. She looked towards the ground and the shadow cast by the horses and carriage, but there was no connecting path to get her inside—that damned sun. The carriage began to pick up speed, and Olivia took her knife from her belt as she made her way through the crowd and opposite the carriage. She followed its path and monitored the sky. The clouds were shifting towards the sun once again. She just needed a bit more time.

The carriage was nearly to the gates when the clouds covered the sun, and the light vanished from the ground. She surged through the shadows and up the carriage door, slipping inside. She fell into a seat with a harsh thud and pulled her knife up. She paused and sighed when Neph sat opposite her, twirling her knife in her hand. She sat cross-legged and pointed to the dead noble beside her.

"You don't like to wait, do you?" she asked.

Olivia sheathed her knife and crossed her arms. "You didnt put the window down."

"I was getting to it. You are impatient." She kicked the door, and the window dropped open.

"Tada."

"Not funny." Neph grabbed the golden necklace the noble wore and yanked it off his person, weighing it in her hand.

"Would sell for a nice sum, don't you think?" She threw the necklace at Olivia, and she caught it. "Now, I think it is time for us to leave." She disappeared into the shadows, and Olivia followed, chasing her back into the crowd as the sunlight hit the top of the carriage. They appeared in a cluster of unknowing commoners, and Neph glanced at her hand.

"Did you lose it?" she asked.

Olivia looked down at the necklace still in her hand and gave a small smile. "No."

"See, you are learning." The crowd suddenly surged forward, and Olivia got caught in the mass of bodies. She was pulled from Neph and towards the castle walls, where they looked up and cheered.

"Queen, queen!" they cried. Olivia turned and followed the crowd to the castle balcony as the doors opened.

95 ENARA

Daealla finished lacing up Enara's corset and moved her hair back in place with a pleased sigh. "You look lovely, my lady," she exclaimed. Enara looked at herself in the mirror. The silver gown did well to accentuate her face and stood out against her dark hair. The crown on her head was lighter than the weight sitting on her chest. And the sapphire necklace she wore glimmered, unlike her dulled eyes. She could barely glimpse the features given by her mother. Everything seemed to have come from her father, who she barely remembered. Daealla gently touched her shoulder, and Enara waved her off.

"I'm fine. Please, continue," she said.

With a hum, Daealla helped Enara pull on her bracelets and sash before taking a step back. "Perfect. Are you excited, Your Grace?" she asked. Enara gave a small smile and nodded before hearing the door open behind her.

"May I have a moment, Daealla?" Trissa asked. Enara turned towards her as Daealla left the room with a curtsy, and Trissa ran a finger through Enara's hair.

"I must admit, you look radiant this evening."

"I do not feel it."

Trissa's smile faded slightly, and she took Enara's shaking hand, rubbing the darkened veins. "I taught you everything you need to know. Be charming, smile, and never let them know you wish you were somewhere else. What was it that your mother used to say?"

That earned a genuine smile from the queen. "Look at them as if they are chickens with bow ties."

"As yes, chickens with bow ties. I still wonder where she got that phrase," Trissa laughed.

"Oh!" Enara exclaimed. She walked over to her vanity and pulled a box from a drawer, handing it to Trissa. "I got this for you at the market. I thought you might like it."

Trissa opened the box and gasped softly. She pulled the pendant from its pillowed rest and cradled it in her hand. "It's beautiful, Enara, thank you." She let Enara take it from her hand and pin it to her right breast with a small wiggle of excitement. She tapped it and nodded.

"Yes, it looks wonderful on you," she exclaimed. Trissa brought her hand to Enara's cheek and rubbed it softly, careful not to smear the powder.

"Now go on. Show them you are no coward queen."

Enara was gently pushed from the bedroom and through the halls towards the grand ballroom. She could hear the chatter of people echo down the hall as they neared, and when they reached the doors, Trissa gave her hand a squeeze before leaving.

"You'll do fine," she assured. Enara composed herself, flattened down her dress, and took a breath. The guards moved to open the doors when she instructed, and the ballroom sprung to life.

The ballroom was filled with lively people and dark candelabras. The ceiling was painted like the night sky, with silver columns that reached below. Enara walked in with her head held high, and the nobility turned to look at her. The music died down as she was introduced.

"Here she is—my radiant fiancée and light of the kingdom. Lady Enara GoldThorn," Aldrian announced. The ballroom lit up in applause, and Enara nodded politely at the nobles as she took the king's side. He wore a velvety dark coat that matched his hair, and a thin silver chain ran down his right shoulder. She wrapped her arm around his as they made their way toward the center of the room.

"I heard that your maids told you of this party beforehand," he said.

"If you ever expect handmaids to keep secrets, you know nothing of courtly gossip," she replied, earning a smirk from the king.

"Yes," he laughed. "I suppose that is true." The couple made it to the center of the room, where the court stood around them. They looked nearly the same as the ones that she dealt with in Ignis; she just couldn't place names to faces here. The same dress, the same sneering, the same frame of mind. Enara could feel the heat of their gazes on her as the king spoke.

"Within a few months, we shall be joined in union. Two kingdoms become one, and we set our sights higher. No more shall we be confined to the Mors of Veran. Now we travel to its very heart. From the coasts of Rosus to the Frozen Sea, we set our sights. For now, and ever, we shall claim what is ours!"

The ballroom rose in a chorus of cheers as the band played, and Enara's smile faded. Aldrian noticed her hesitation and brought her away from the nobility as they began their dances.

"Here, I have something for you," he said, taking her to a far corner of the room. As they walked, many of the crowd raised their glasses to her or cooed at her dress. It had been many years since she had been looked at so. Ever since her mother's death, Rose had been in the spotlight. The dresses were crafted for her, the people looked towards her, and the gentry praised her name. Enara wasn't proud of her actions. She still mourned greatly. But behind every queen is the person who actually pulled the strings.

"Lady Enara, I believe you know these men?" Aldrian asked, pulling her attention from her thoughts. Enara looked ahead and spotted two familiar faces. Her face lit up.

"Sir Alran, Duke Floric, you are here!" She pulled away from the king and stepped over to her advisors. "It has been too long."

"I am glad to see you well, my lady," Sir Alran said with a polite bow. Duke Floric did the same, and she gripped the hand of the duke.

"What are you doing here? How does Ignis fare?"

The duke gave a look towards the king and, with an unsteady smile, patted Enara's hand. "The king... graciously invited us here to speak on trade agreements with Reverand."

"We will be gladdened to see the two kingdoms prosper," Alran added.

Enara pulled her hand away and turned to the king. "Then I owe you my thanks."

"No thanks are necessary. I want to see both kingdoms thrive under our rule." The advisors bowed once more before politely going separate ways, and Aldrian gained her attention once more.

"The talks will be tomorrow morning; you are free to join them if you wish. Though I'm sure you have better things to do than talk of money and timber."

"Oh, but didn't you know that is my most favorite past time?" she asked. He snorted, and they stopped to watch the dance die out, and the people bow and part ways.

"Perhaps a dance, my lady?" he asked as the orchestra picked up once again. Enara nodded and took his outstretched hand as he led her onto the dance floor. As the song began, he led her through the waltz, and she hated to admit that she missed dancing. She nearly never had the time to or did not feel like entertaining the men who wanted her for the prestige. She remembered standing on top of her mother's shoes when she was younger and led her through dance after dance, ignoring the others and twirling her around and around until she felt dizzy. She missed the feeling of touch, the warmth of the body in front of her.

Enara ignored the other people around her, focusing on the one holding her slightly closer than the dance required. Staring up into the honey eyes of the king, she felt her cheeks flush. His soft smile met her own as he whispered into her ear.

"You are more radiant than any lady here, my queen. You outshine even the brightest of stars."

"You flatter me," she pushed out, dropping her gaze. He lifted his hand and spun her effortlessly. Her dress flowed out around her, and she laughed at the sudden burst of air. He caught her in his arms once more as the song came to a crescendo. The twisting of the music made her feet lighter and her breath steadier. Aldrian squeezed her hand gently, and they twirled across the dance floor, ignoring all else.

She felt as if she were in a play. Watching the main characters have their moment alone. The music would swell, and they would clasp their hands together and think of nothing else but the person in front of them. It was like heaven.

As the music came to a stop, the king dipped her low to the ground, her back arching, bringing his body into hers for a long and hard kiss. She gasped slightly and ran her finger through his hair. He tasted of wine and tart and smelled of myrrh. The partygoers clapped and gossiped as Aldrian pulled her back upright. Enara flushed and tapped the heel of her toe to the floor to ground herself.

"Now it is time to see your people," he whispered. He led her to the balcony and swung open the doors. As she stepped outside, she could see thousands of bodies, all with their hands raised and singing of her praise. Enara grasped the king's hand firmly as he led her to the railing. The crowd roared in delight, and he raised his hand to wave. She did the same and kept a steady smile on her face, even though her hand pulsed painfully.

"Your queen!" Aldrian pronounced. The drumming of the crowd was nearly deafening as Enara reveled in her position of power. Little did she notice the shadowed woman that lingered at the bottom, whose mind filled with cold rage. One word hung in her mind.

Vengeance.

473

The Great Houses of Veran

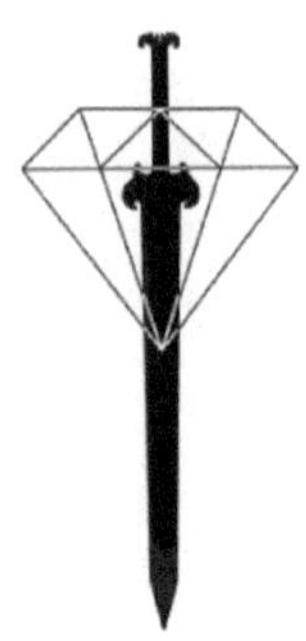

House GoldThorn

House GoldThorn is a relatively new House in Veran— its founding shrouded in mystery. The only known living heir was Queen Elena, who married King Virades in a secret courtship. Both daughters were given their mother's surname.

-JAMES VIRADES, King of Auratus, Lord of Ignis, killed while hunting,

-ELENA GOLDTHORN, Wife of King James and Queen of Auratus, killed during the siege of Ignis,

-ENARA GOLDTHORN, Princess of Auratus, daughter of Queen Elena,

-ROSELLENA GOLDTHORN, Princess of Auratus, daughter of Queen Elena, Runa,

-Advisors and attendants:

-TRISSA, nanny and maid to Enara and Rose,

-LADY VIVIANNA, the lady keeper, killed during the second siege of Ignis,

-SIR ALRAN, the Coin Keeper, charged with currency and exchange,

-DUKE FLORIC, advisor and envoy of the Queen,

-LORD CALIS, Steward of Queen Elena, killed during the second siege of Ignis,

-ENCHANTER DRAVIS, Arcane Advisor to the court,

-Other Notable Characters:
	-Jared, friend of Queen Rose, blacksmith's son, known as the city troublemaker,
	-Olivia, bard and mercenary, friend of Queen Rose, daughter of tavern keeper Kason,

House Dicesare

House Dicesare is an ancient House, spanning since the Elven Crusades. The people of Viragrad have high respect for their rulers, though the rest of the continent think of them as a lesser House.

-NEYMAR DICESARE, King of Viragrad, Lord of WhiteDrove, died from a fever,

-KESANDA DICESARE, Queen of Viragrad, wife of King Neymar, Lady of WhiteDrove,

-THYMAS DICESARE, son of King Neymar, prince of Viragrad,

-ANYA DICESARE, adopted daughter of Queen Kesanda, Half-elf,

-Advisors and lords:

-CAPTAIN MULLINER, Constable of the Crown, tasked with the protection of the city,

-DOWNOR HASHLIN, Lord of Rivercross,

-LYALL ALAYN, Lord of Rillton,

-NALDI, a young page to the queen,

House Farvell

House Farvell came into power a thousand years after the Elven Crusades. The initial royal line of Yalirea had died out, and Keegan Farvell, a lower born lord, took the throne.

-BAREN FARVELL, King of Yalirea, Lord of Rosus,
-ADELINE FARVELL, Queen of Yalirea, Lady of Rosus, died of the plague,
    -VALEK FARVELL, Prince of Yalirea, son of King Baren,
    -TALIA FARVELL, Princess of Yalirea, daughter of King Baren, nicknamed the Princess of Roses,

-Advisors and attendants:
  -SIR LAMBRIN, Royal Secretary to King Baren,
  -ENCHANTER DOUGLEND, Previously Arcane Advisor to King Baren before being exiled from court,

-Other Notable Characters:
  -THE BLACK WOLF, the cocksure elven guard of Princess Talia,
  -TALAHE and ZELUH, noble merchants from the Nishiri Empire, owning most trade through the Amber Sea,

House De'shelven

House De'shelven is perhaps the oldest House on the continent. It has spanned since the Great Merging and survived the fall of Elu'lathan. The royal family has held strong for two thousand years.

-VAREN DE'SHELVEN, Emperor of Veran, Protector of Esai, Lord of Fira, leader of the continent,

-RYE DE'SHELVEN, Commander of the Imperial Army, brother to Emperor Varen, abdicated the throne when the late Emperor Henri passed,

-MARCELLE, Lady of House Castyr, wife of Emperor Varen, died in childbirth,

-MARRIN DE'SHELVEN, Prince of Veran, Prince of Esai, son of Emperor Varen,

-Lords and Attendants:

-DUKE PERCIVAL, oversees the Grand Quarter, advisor to the emperor,

-MARQUISE JOSEPHINE, oversees the port of Fira and surrounding land,

-LUCIUS LANCASTER, Arcane Advisor to Emperor Varen, fresh out of the College,

House Silvand

House Silvand grew to power after the fall of Elu'lathan. When the Dark Knights were banished, those who still followed their doctrine created their own kingdom within the Mors of Salvia. The chosen king and leader, Aydowyn Silvand, pledged to seek revenge against Fira.

-ALDRIAN SILVAND, King of the Dark Kingdom, Lord of Reverand, crowned king after the death of his parents and younger brother,

-MALUM, The King of the Dark Knights, leader of the cursed, vowed to destroy every mage,
   -GELUM, Dark Knight, sent to take WhiteDrove,
   -SEVERUM, Dark Knight, sent after Rose,
   -VERUM, Dark Knight, location currently unknown,

-Attendants:
   -DAEALLA, BRINA, BREYA, lady maids to Queen Enara,

THE BLESSED AND CURSED

-NYMVAS, King of Velwood, protector of Al' Cashan, went mad causing an elven genocide, was slain by Via,

-AREVALLA, Queen of Avlor, protector of Al' Cashan, older than most kingdoms,

-LAERDYA, Princess of Avlor, bastard daughter of King Nymvas, taken to Nevrak as payment for the cursed elves help, married to Prince Elmaer

-CAEDA, young elven huntress, herald of the throne,

-NEXIS, brother of King Nymvas, enchanter and alchemist, known for making explosions, taken prisoner in Nevrak,

-RAVANA, Queen of Nevrak, mage, exiled from the mortal world,

-ELMAER, son of Queen Ravana, Prince of Nevrak, married to Princess Laerdya

-VIA, Spymaster for Queen Ravana, was allowed into the mortal world to help stop the king's madness,

-Advisors and Lords:

-RHANGYL, protector of Princess Laerdya,

-ZELTRITH and ARANA, high nobles in Ravana's court, owns most of the slave population,

OTHER CHARACTERS

-NAVA, half-elf archer, once a slave, companion of Swordsman Jared,
>-NEVE, farmer and landowner, helped Nava and Jared,
>-JACK, farmhand to Neve,

-SARA, Priestess from the Sunset Isles, magic user, companion of Prince Thymas,

-ALRIK WOLF-CALLER, Chieftain of Rolheim, leader of the Tribe of Wolf,
>-NADAHI WOLF-HEART, daughter of Alrik, heir to the Tribe of Wolf, Protector of the Runa,
>>-LIV, healer, teacher,
>>-ERLING, mad but good with an ax,
>>-HAKON, built like a bear, strong and fierce,
>>-TORGIR, the best shield hand in Rolheim,

-MOTHER HEALER, Sage of Rolheim, Bringer of Fortunes, healer and watcher of the spirits,

-NEPH, an assassin in the Nightingale Brotherhood, mentor to Olivia,
-CRONIS, an assassin in the Nightingale Brotherhood, friend to Neph,

NOTABLE GODS

-GODDESS VELARA, the main deity of the Veranese peoples, is said in the Word of Velara scripture that She was once a mortal woman, but sacrificed Herself to the darkness to bring the sun and stars into the sky, creating the mortal world we know,

-THE MOTHER GODDESS, deity of the Northlands, said to have created the earth from Her own body, once married to the False God, and birthed the Runa,

-THE FALSE GOD, once lover of the Mother Goddess, betrayed Her for the darkness and killed Her children, was cast from the mortal world and shackled in the Otherworld,

THE ELVEN PANTHEON

-ETHENA'ETHAL, created the land and sky,

-ZELES, God of the Otherworld, bringing souls of the dead to the Otherworld for judgment, decides which souls will be reincarnated,

-AVLOR'IVES, the Goddess of the Hunt, She gives life to animals, Her name is spoken as a prayer with every kill,

-RANE'ABELES, the mother of the gods, She gifts elves with children, and nurtures the ones who die in birth,

-MAGESENA, from His mind came the whisper of magic, it is He who decides who will receive His gift, and He who decides which children shall be mages,

meet the author

E.R.BROWNING was born in 2000 in Ohio. She studied wildlife and natural science while writing in between classes. Her debut novel, *The Queen of Thorns and Gold,* was her first step into the writing world.

www.ingramcontent.com/pod-product-compliance
Lightning Source LLC
Chambersburg PA
CBHW032103310726
48972CB00001B/80